HEARTSTOPPER

Also by Joy Fielding

Mad River Road

Puppet

Lost

Whispers and Lies

Grand Avenue

The First Time

Missing Pieces

Don't Cry Now

Tell Me No Secrets

See Jane Run

Good Intentions

The Deep End

Life Penalty

The Other Woman

Kiss Mommy Goodbye

Trance

The Transformation

The Best of Friends

HEARTSTOPPER

A NOVEL

JOY FIELDING

ATRIA BOOKS

New York   London   Toronto   Sydney

FIC
Fielding

ATRIA BOOKS
1230 Avenue of the Americas
New York, NY 10020

Library of Congress Cataloging-in-Publication Data

Fielding, Joy.
Heartstopper: a novel / by Joy Fielding.—1st Atria Books hardcover ed. p. cm.
1. Kidnapping—Fiction. 2. Teenage girls—Fiction. 3. Florida—
Fiction. I. Title. II. Title: Heartstopper.
PR9199.3.F518H43 2007
813'.54—dc22   2006050801

ISBN-13: 978-0-7432-9598-7
ISBN-10:   0-7432-9598-6

First Atria Books hardcover edition April 2007

1   3   5   7   9   10   8   6   4   2

ATRIA BOOKS is a trademark of Simon & Schuster, Inc.

Manufactured in the United States of America

"Can You Save Me in the Morning?" (music and lyrics
by Shannon Micol) courtesy of Shannon Micol.
Copyright © 1997 Shannon Micol Seyffert.

For information about special discounts for bulk purchases,
please contact Simon & Schuster Special Sales at
1-800-456-6798 or business@simonandschuster.com.

To Shannon Micol,
whose music inspires me

ACKNOWLEDGMENTS

As always, my thanks to Larry Mirkin and Beverley Slopen for their advice, support, and friendship. Thanks also to my family and friends, and to all the people at the William Morris Agency, as well as Atria Books in the U.S. and Doubleday Canada, for doing so much to make my books a success. Thanks as well to Corinne Assayag for her masterful work on my website, and to all my foreign publishers and translators for their fine job in reproducing my novels.

But most of all I want to take this opportunity to thank Owen Laster, who has been my agent (and friend and stalwart supporter) for more than twenty years. A consummate artist at what he does, a gentle soul, and a true gentleman, he is retiring after forty-five years in the business. While I know he is leaving me in capable hands, I will miss him terribly. He is one of a kind, and I hope I continue to make him proud. Thank you, Owen. I love you and wish you all the best.

HEARTSTOPPER

1

KILLER'S JOURNAL

The girl is waking up.

She stirs, mascara-coated eyelashes fluttering seductively, large blue eyes opening, then closing again, then reopening, staying open longer this time, casually absorbing the unfamiliarity of her surroundings. That she is in a strange place, with no memory of how she got here, will take several seconds to sink in fully. That her life is in danger will hit her all at once, with the sudden force of a giant, renegade wave, knocking her back on the small cot I've so thoughtfully provided, even as she struggles gamely to her feet.

This is my favorite part. Even more than what comes later.

I've never been a huge fan of blood and guts. Those shows you see on TV today, the ones that are so popular, the ones filled with crack forensic experts in skintight pants and push-up bras, they've never held much appeal for me. All those dead bodies—hapless victims dispatched in an increasingly gory variety of exotic ways—lying on cold steel slabs in ultramodern morgues, waiting to be cracked open and invaded by dispassionate, gloved fingers—they just don't do it for me. Even if the bodies weren't so obviously fake—although even the most obvious of rubber torsos look more real than the ubiquitous breast implants held in check by those heroic, push-up bras—it wouldn't turn me on. Violence, per se, has never been my thing. I've always preferred the buildup to an event over the actual event itself.

Just as I've always preferred the flawed, natural contour of real breasts to the perfectly inflated—and perfectly awful—monstrosities so popular today. And not just on TV. You see them everywhere. Even here in the middle of Alligator Alley, in the middle of south-central Florida.

The middle of nowhere.

I think it was Alfred Hitchcock who best summed up the difference between shock and suspense. Shock, he said, is quick, a jolt to the senses that lasts but a second, whereas suspense is more of a slow tease. Rather like the difference between prolonged foreplay and premature ejaculation, I would add, and I like to think old Alfred would chuckle and agree. He always preferred suspense to shock, the payoff being greater, ultimately more fulfilling. I'm with him on this, although, like Hitch, I'm not adverse to the occasional shock along the way. You have to keep things interesting.

As this girl will soon find out.

She's sitting up now, hands forming anxious fists at her sides as she scans her dimly lit surroundings. I can tell by the puzzled look on her pretty face—she's a real heartstopper, as my grandfather used to say—that she's trying to stay calm, to figure things out, to make sense of what's happening, while clinging to the hope this is all a dream. After all, this can't really be happening. She can't actually be sitting on the edge of a tiny cot in what appears to be a room in somebody's basement, if houses in Florida *had* basements, which, of course, most of them don't, Florida being a state built almost entirely on swampland.

The panic won't be long in coming. As soon as she realizes she isn't dreaming, that her situation is real and, in fact, quite dire, that she is trapped in a locked room whose only light comes from a strategically placed lamplight on a ledge high above her head, one she has no way of reaching, even were she to turn the cot on its end and somehow manage to climb up its side. The last girl tried that and fell, crying and clutching her broken wrist, to the dirt floor. That's when she started screaming.

That was fun—for a while.

She's just noticed the door, although unlike the last girl, she makes no move toward it. Instead, she just sits there, chewing on her bottom lip, frightened eyes darting back and forth. She's breathing loudly and visibly, her heart threatening to burst from between large, pendulous breasts—to her credit, at least they're real—like one of those hyperventilating contestants on *The Price Is Right*. Should she choose door number one, door number two, or door number three? Except there is only one door, and should she open it, what will she find? The Lady or the Tiger? Safety or destruction? I feel my lips curl into a smile. In fact, she will find nothing. At least not yet. Not until I'm ready.

She's pushing herself off the cot, curiosity finally forcing one foot in front of the other, propelling her toward the door, even as a gnawing voice whispers in her ear, reminding her it was curiosity that killed the cat. Is she counting on the old wives' tale about cats having nine lives? Does she think a bunch of useless, old wives can save her?

Her trembling hand stretches toward the doorknob. "Hello?" she calls out, softly at first, her voice as wobbly as her fingers, then more forcefully. "Hello? Is anybody there?"

I'm tempted to answer, but I know this isn't a good idea. First of all, it would tip her to the fact I'm watching. Right now, the idea she's being observed has yet to occur to her, and when it does, maybe a minute or two from now, her eyes will begin their frantic, fruitless search of the premises. No matter. She won't be able to see me. The peephole I've carved into the wall is too small and too elevated for her to discover, especially in this meager light. Besides, hearing my voice would not only tip her to my presence and approximate location, it might help her identify me, thereby giving her an unnecessary edge in the battle of wits to come. No, I will present myself soon enough. No point in getting ahead of the game. The timing simply isn't right. And timing, as they say, is everything.

"Hello? Somebody?"

Her voice is growing more urgent, losing its girlish timbre, becoming shrill, almost hostile. That's one of the interesting things

I've noticed about female voices—how quickly they jump from warm to harsh, from soothing to grating, how shameless they are in their eagerness to reveal all, how boldly they hurl their insecurities into the unsuspecting air. The gentle flute is overwhelmed by the raucous bagpipe; the chamber orchestra is trampled by the marching band.

"Hello?" The girl grabs hold of the doorknob, tries pulling the door toward her. It doesn't budge. Quickly, her movements degenerate into a series of ungainly poses, becoming less measured, more frantic. She pulls on the door, then pushes it, then bangs her shoulder against it, repeating the process several more times before finally giving up and bursting into tears. That's the other thing I've learned about women—they always cry. It's the one thing about them that never disappoints, the one thing you can count on.

"Where am I? What's going on here?" The girl bangs her fists against the door in growing frustration. She's angry now, as well as scared. She may not know where she is, but she knows she didn't get here by her own accord. Her mind is rapidly filling with increasingly terrifying images—recent newspaper headlines about missing girls, TV coverage of bodies being pulled from shallow graves, catalog displays of knives and other instruments of torture, film clips of helpless women being raped and strangled, before being dumped into slime-covered swamps. "Help!" she starts screaming. "Somebody help me." But even as her plaintive cries hit the stale air, I suspect she knows such pleas are useless, that nobody can hear her.

Nobody but me.

Her head snaps up; her eyes shoot toward me, like a searchlight, and I jerk away from the wall, almost tripping over my feet as I stagger back. By the time I regroup, regain my breath and equilibrium, she is circling the small room, her eyes darting up and down, this way and that, the palms of her hands pushing against the unpainted, concrete walls, feeling for any signs of weakness. "Where am I? Is anybody out there? Why have you brought me here?" she is crying, as if the correct question will trigger a reassuring response. Finally, she gives up, collapses on the cot, cries some more. When she raises her head again—for the second time, she looks right at me—her large blue eyes are bloated with tears and ringed in unflattering red. Or maybe that's just my imagination at work. A bit of wishful thinking on my part.

She pushes herself back into a sitting position, takes a series of long, deep breaths. Clearly, she is trying to calm herself, while she takes stock of her situation. She glances at what she's wearing—a pale yellow T-shirt that shouts, MOVE, BITCH, in bright lime-green lettering across its stretched front, low-slung jeans pulled tight across her slender hips. The same outfit she was wearing . . . when? Yesterday? Last night? This morning?

How long has she been here?

She runs her fingers through long, strawberry-blond hair, then scratches at her right ankle, before leaning back against the wall. Some madman has kidnapped her and is holding her hostage, she is thinking, perhaps already wondering how she can tell this story to maximum effect after she escapes. Perhaps *People* magazine will come calling. Maybe even Hollywood. Who will they get to play her? The girl from *Spider-Man,* or maybe that other one, the one who's all over the tabloids these days. Lindsay Lohan? Is that her name? Or is it Tara Reid? Cameron Diaz would be good, even though Cameron's more than a decade older than she is. It doesn't really matter. They're all more or less interchangeable. Heartstoppers all.

As am I. A heartstopper of a very different kind.

The girl's face darkens. Once again, reality intrudes. What am I doing here? she is wondering. How did I get here? Why can't I remember?

What she probably remembers is being in school, although I doubt she recalls much, if anything, of what was being taught. Too busy staring out the window. Too busy flirting with the Neanderthals in the back row. Too busy giving the teacher a hard time. Too ready with the smart remark, the sarcastic comment, the unasked-for opinion. No doubt she recalls the bell sounding at the end of the day, releasing her from her twelfth-grade prison. She likely remembers rushing into the school yard, and bumming a cigarette from whoever is closest at hand. She might remember snatching a Coke from a classmate's hand, and guzzling it down without thank-you or apology. Several cigarettes and snarky comments later, she may even remember heading for home. I watch her watching herself as she turns the corner onto her quiet street; I catch the tilt in her head as she hears the soft wind whisper her name.

Someone is calling her.

The girl leans forward on the cot, lips parting. The memory is there; she has only to access it. It plays with her senses, goading her, like the bottom line of an eye chart, the letters right there in front of her, but blurred, so that she can't quite make them out, no matter how hard she strains. It lies on the tip of her tongue, like some exotic spice she can taste but not identify. It wafts by her nose, trailing faint wisps of tantalizing smells, and swirls around the inside of her mouth, like an expensive red wine. If only she could give voice to it. If only she could remember.

What she does remember is stopping and looking around, listening again for the sound of her name in the warm breeze, then slowly approaching a row of overgrown bushes at the edge of a neighbor's untended front lawn. The bushes beckon her, their leaves rustling, as if in welcome.

And then nothing.

The girl's shoulders slump in defeat. She has no memory of what happened next. The bushes block her vision, refuse her entry. She must have lost consciousness. Perhaps she was drugged; maybe she was hit on the head. What difference does it make? What matters isn't what happened before, but what happens next. It's not important how she got here, I feel her decide. What's important is how she's going to get out.

I try not to laugh. Let her entertain the illusion, however fragile, however unfounded, that she has a chance at escape. Let her plot and plan and strategize and resolve. After all, that's part of the fun.

I'm getting hungry. Probably she is also, although she's too scared to realize it at the moment. In another hour or two, it'll hit her. The human appetite is an amazing thing. It's pretty insistent, no matter what the circumstances. I remember when my uncle Al died. It happened a long time ago, and my memory, like the girl's, is kind of hazy. I'm not even sure what killed him, to be honest. Cancer or a heart attack. Pretty run-of-the-mill stuff, whatever it was. We were never really all that close, so I can't say I was terribly affected by his death. But I do remember my aunt crying and carrying on, and her friends offering their condolences, telling her in one breath what a great man my uncle was, how sorry they were at his passing, and in the next breath, complimenting her on the wonderful pastries she'd prepared, saying "Could we please have the recipe?" and "You have to eat something. It's important to keep up your strength. Al would want that." And soon she was eating, and soon after that, laughing. Such is the power of pastry.

I don't have any pastry for this girl, although in a couple of hours, after I've grabbed something to eat myself, I may bring her back a sandwich. I haven't decided yet. Certainly a good host would provide for guests. But then, no one ever said I was a good host. No five stars for me.

Still, the accommodations aren't all that bad, considering. I haven't buried her in an underground coffin or thrown her into some snake-and-rat-infested hole. She hasn't been stuffed into some airless closet or chained to a stake atop a nest of fire ants. Her arms haven't been bound behind her back; there's no gag in her mouth; her legs are free to traverse the room. If it's a little warmer than she might like, she can take comfort in that it's April and not July, that it's unseasonably cool for this time of year, and that it's evening and not the middle of the afternoon. Given my druthers, I too would opt for air-conditioning, as would any sane individual, but one takes what one can get, and in this case, what I could get was this: a dilapidated old house at the edge of a long-neglected field in the middle of Alligator Alley, in the middle of south-central Florida.

The middle of nowhere.

Sometimes being stuck in the middle of nowhere can be a blessing in disguise, although I know at least two girls who would disagree.

I discovered this house about five years ago. The people who built it had long since abandoned it, and termites, mold, and dry rot had pretty much taken over. Far as I can tell, no one's made any attempt to claim the land or tear this old place down. It costs money to demolish things, after all, even more to erect something in its place, and I seriously doubt that anything worth growing would grow here, so what would be the point? Anyway, I stumbled upon it by accident one morning when I was out, walking around, trying to clear my head. I'd been having some problems on the home front, and it seemed like everything was closing in on me, so I decided the best thing to do was just remove myself from the situation altogether. I've always been like that—a bit of a loner. Don't like confrontations; don't like to share my feelings all that much. Not that anyone was ever much interested in my feelings.

Anyway, that's the proverbial water under the bridge. No point brooding about it now, or living in the past. Live for today—that's my motto. Or die for it. As the case may be.

Die for today.

I like the sound of that.

Okay, so it's five years ago, and I'm out walking. It's hot. Summer, I think, so really humid. And the mosquitoes are buzzing around my head, starting to get on my nerves, and I come across this ugly, old field. Half-swamp really. Probably more than a few snakes and alligators hiding in the tall grass, but I've never been one who's afraid of reptiles. In fact, I think they're pretty awesome, and I've found that if you respect their space, they'll usually respect yours. Even so, I'm careful when I come here. I have a trail pretty well etched out, and I try to keep to it, especially at night. Of course, I have my gun, and a couple of sharp knives, should anything unexpected happen.

You always have to guard against the unexpected.

Somebody should have told that to this girl.

The main part of the house isn't much—a couple of small rooms, empty, of course. I had to supply the cot, which was kind of tricky, although I won't get into any of those details now. Suffice to say, I managed it all by myself, which is the way I usually do things. There's a tiny kitchen, but the appliances have been ripped out, and there's no running water in the taps. The same is true of the bathroom and its filthy toilet, its once-white seat cracked right down the middle. Wouldn't want to sit on that thing, that's for sure.

I've thoughtfully provided the girl with a plastic bucket, should she need to relieve herself. It sits in a corner to the left of the door. She kicked at it earlier, when she was flailing around, so right now it's lying on its side at the other end of the room. Maybe she doesn't realize yet what it's for.

The first girl chose to ignore it altogether. She simply lifted up her skirt and squatted right there on the floor. Not that she had to hike her skirt very far. It was so ridiculously short, it could have passed for a belt, which I guess was the look she was going for— strictly Hooker City. Of course, she wasn't wearing panties, which was pretty disgusting. Some might say she was no better than an animal, although not me. No way I'd say that. Why? Because it disrespects the animals. To say that girl was a pig is to slander the pig. Which, of course, is why I chose her. I knew no one would miss her. I knew no one would mourn her. I knew no one would come looking for her.

She was only eighteen, but already she had that knowing look in her eyes that made her seem much older. Her lips had frozen into a cynical pout, more sneer than smile, even when she was laughing, and the veins on the insides of her skinny arms were bruised with the piercing of old needles. Her hair was a frizzy cliché of platinum curls and black roots, and when she opened her mouth to speak, you could almost taste the cigarettes on her breath.

Her name was Candy—she even had a bracelet with candies for charms—and I guess you could say she was my test case. I'm the kind of person who doesn't like doing anything halfway—it has to be perfect—and once I knew what I had to do, I realized I'd have to plan everything carefully. Unlike so many people you read about, I have no desire to be caught. Once this project is over, I plan to retire and live peacefully—if not always happily—ever after. So, it was important that I get things right.

Hence, Candy.

I met her at a Burger King. She was hanging around outside, and I offered to buy her a burger, an offer she accepted readily. We talked, although she didn't have a lot to say, and she clammed up altogether when my questions got too personal. That's okay. I understand that. I'm not too fond of personal questions myself.

But I did find out some key facts: she'd run away from home at fourteen and had been living on the streets ever since. She'd met some guy; he'd gotten her hooked on drugs, and the drugs had, in turn, gotten her hooked on hooking. After a while, the guy split, and she was on her own again. She'd spent much of the last year moving from place to place, occasionally waking up in a strange hospital room or holding cell. One place was pretty much the same as the next, she said.

I wonder if that's how she felt when she woke up here, in the underground room of this forgotten, old house.

Did I neglect to mention this room is underground? Shame on me—it's what makes the place so special, the "pièce de résistance," if you will.

I said before that, for the most part, houses in Florida don't have basements. That's because they're built on what is essentially quicksand, and you could wake up one morning to find yourself up to your eyeballs in muck. Entire homes have been swallowed up, and I'm not just talking about the older, less substantial ones. There's a brand-new subdivision going up not far from here, built almost entirely—and ill-advisedly, in my humble opinion, not that anybody has asked for my opinion—on landfill, and one day, one of the houses just up and disappeared. The builders didn't have to look very far to find it, of course. They were standing on top of it. Serves them right. You can only go so far challenging nature.

If I were going to build a house today, I'd hire the guy who designed this one. True, it's seen better days, but whoever constructed it was a genius. He created a whole warren of little rooms underneath the main floor, rooms he probably used for storage.

I have something quite different in mind.

Candy didn't think much of the place when she realized it wasn't the kind of holding cell she was used to. Once I finally showed myself, and the seriousness of her predicament became clear, she tried all the tricks in her arsenal, said if sex was the goal, there was no way she was doing anything with me on that dirty old cot. She'd do whatever perverted things I wanted, only not here. The idea of sex with this person was so repugnant I was tempted to kill her on the spot, but the game was far from over. I still had some surprises up my sleeve.

Ultimately I killed her with a single bullet to the head. Then I dumped her body in a swamp a few miles away. If anybody finds it, and I doubt they will—it's been four months after all—there'll be nothing left to link her to me, no way of determining exactly when she died, at what precise moment her heart stopped beating. Even had she been found immediately, all in one piece, I know enough about DNA, courtesy of all those surgically enhanced forensic experts on TV, to ensure I've left no clues.

Just as Candy left no mourners.

But this girl, this heartstopper with the big blue eyes and large, natural breasts, will be different.

Not only will a lot of people be out looking for her—they may even be looking for her now—she'll be more of a challenge all around. Candy was a trifle dim-witted to be much fun. This girl is stronger, both mentally and physically, so I'll have to up my game, as they say—move quicker, think faster, strike harder.

She's looking this way again, as if she knows I'm here, as if she can hear the scribbling of my pen. So I'll sign off for now, go grab something to eat. I'll come back later, initiate phase two of my plan.

Maybe I'll keep the girl alive till morning. Maybe not. Risk management after all. It doesn't pay to get too cocky.

Stay tuned, as they say. I'll be back.

chapter two

"Okay, everybody. Get out your journals."

Sandy Crosbie leaned back against the front of her desk at the head of the twelfth-grade classroom and watched her twenty-three students—it should have been twenty-five, but both Peter Arlington and Liana Martin were absent—reluctantly separate their journals from the rest of their books and plop them down on their desks with varying degrees of disinterest and dismay. Bored, glazed eyes rolled slowly back toward her. Bodies slumped dispassionately in their seats. Denim-covered legs stretched lazily across the floor. Pencils absently tapped out an overlapping series of unrecognizable tunes. Everybody, including Sandy Crosbie, clearly wished to be somewhere else.

And why not? Who in their right minds wanted to be cooped up inside a stuffy portable when they could be outside cavorting in the sun? (Would any of her twenty-three students—twenty-five if you included the absent Peter Arlington and Liana Martin—even know what *cavorting* meant? And was cavorting exactly what rumored sweethearts Peter Arlington and Liana Martin were doing in their absence?) Sandy's gaze floated above the five rows of reluctant scholars toward the portable's long expanse of side windows. Outside, it was a beautiful April day, although much cooler than was usual for this time of year. At least that's what everyone kept telling her. "You should have been here last April," they kept saying. "This is a good ten degrees colder than normal." But Sandy didn't mind the cooler temperatures. In fact, she actually preferred them. It reminded her of upstate New York, where she'd been born and raised. Everyone—especially Ian— had always complained about the brutal Rochester winters, but Sandy was one of those rare creatures who'd genuinely enjoyed the snow and often frigid temperatures. She liked bundling up. It made her feel safe.

What the hell was she doing in Torrance, where the average annual temperature was a humid eighty-five degrees?

Last summer's move to Florida hadn't been her idea. It had been Ian's. He'd spent the better part of two years promoting the move from big northern city to small southern town. "It'll be good for my practice, for our kids, for our marriage," he'd promised, cajoled, and ultimately badgered. "I've made some inquiries, and you won't have any trouble finding a teaching position. Come on. Where's your sense of adventure? At least give it a try. Two years tops. I swear if you're not happy, we won't stay."

At least that's what he said. What he meant was: I've fallen madly in love with this woman I met on an Internet chat line, and I'm determined to sell my practice, uproot you and the kids, and move to this little town in Florida to continue the affair in person. If it doesn't work out, then we can leave.

Which he had. Exactly seven weeks ago today, Sandy calculated silently, her eyes focusing on a poster promoting literacy at the back of the class, in a concerted effort to keep from bursting into tears. While she doubted this was his first affair—her suspicions had been aroused, although never proven, several times over the years—the news that he was leaving her came as a total surprise. She'd actually considered the reason he was so eager to leave Rochester might have been to get away from a dalliance gone stale. It had never occurred to her he might be running toward a fresh one.

So she'd watched in shocked silence as he'd packed his old suitcase and his new doctor's bag, the one she'd given him as a gift when he'd opened his new office, and moved into a spacious, one-bedroom apartment on the other side of town, which just happened to be around the corner from the home of Kerri Franklin, Barbie clone and Internet paramour extraordinaire. The only thing that had prevented him from actually moving in with the big-lipped, bigger-haired divorcée was that her mother had already beaten him to it, settling in comfortably after the collapse of Kerri's third marriage, and showing not the slightest inclination of moving out again.

Since local gossip held that it was Rose Cruikshank's money that was responsible for the recent—some might even say alarming—increase in the size of Kerri's bosom, Kerri was naturally reluctant to kick her mother out in the cold. This April being, after all, ten degrees cooler than usual.

There was also the matter of Kerri's daughter, Delilah. Sandy glanced toward the first seat of the third row, where, in another of life's annoying little ironies, the unfortunately named teenager had landed front and center in Sandy's first-period English class. She currently sat chewing nervously on the end of her black, ballpoint pen, and looking toward the floor, obviously hoping she wasn't about to be called on to read her latest entry aloud.

Because Torrance had a population of barely four thousand people—according to the sign on the outskirts of town, its official total was 4,160—and most of those people lived in what locals referred to as the suburbs, and what Sandy called the swamps, there was only one high school in town. Torrance High was host to almost four hundred teenagers, and the teacher turnover rate was almost as high as the daily student absentee rate, hence Sandy's ease at finding a job. The school itself, a sprawling one-story structure, was an attractive, if unimaginative, mix of modern and traditional, wood and stone. It was originally built to hold a maximum of three hundred students, but a sudden explosion in the number of young people in the area had resulted in the recent addition of four portable classrooms at the back of the parking lot. Being the new girl on the block, Sandy had been assigned the last of these mini-prisons, and it was here she taught English literature and composition to the largely disinterested sons and daughters of the good citizens of Torrance. Included among them was Kerri Franklin's daughter, Delilah.

The name Delilah was unfortunate because, unlike the notorious biblical siren, Kerri Franklin's eighteen-year-old daughter, while pretty enough, was what once might have been described, euphemistically, as big-boned. When Sandy was feeling generous, she concluded that Delilah likely resembled her father, Kerri's first husband, who had disappeared from her life when the child was two; when she wasn't feeling quite so generous, she decided Delilah no doubt looked exactly like her mother had before plastic surgery had turned her into small-town Florida's answer to Pamela Anderson. When Sandy was feeling downright peckish, she liked to imagine Kerri Franklin's multiple surgeries collapsing all at once—the tiny button nose popping and falling from her face, the cheek and breast implants leaking, then imploding, the giant lips deflating, the wrinkle-free forehead shriveling, the miles of Botox in her system turning malignant and unleashing their toxins, causing Kerri's skin to flake, discolor, and turn scabrous.

Sandy sighed, louder than she'd intended. The wayward sigh caught the attention of Greg Watt, a muscle-bound troublemaker she'd moved from the back of the class to the front in her latest effort to retain at least a semblance of control over her restless brood. Greg—tall and vacuously good-looking, with closely cropped blond hair and small, dark eyes—was staring at her as if he were about to pounce. If he were an animal, Sandy thought, he'd be a pit bull.

And she'd be the poor little toy poodle he was about to tear limb from limb, she thought, tucking her curly, chin-length, brown hair behind her right ear, and feeling vulnerable, although she wasn't sure why.

"Something wrong, Mrs. Crosbie?" he asked.

"Everything's fine, Greg," she said.

"Glad to hear it, Mrs. Crosbie."

Was it her imagination or had he placed undue inflection on the *Mrs.* part of Mrs. Crosbie? Certainly it was no secret in Torrance that her husband had just left her after almost twenty years of marriage. Nor was it a secret whom he'd left her for. In fact, Sandy had quickly learned that there were few secrets in a town the size of Torrance. It hadn't taken much longer to realize that, in spite of this, everybody seemed to have one.

"Okay. Who wants to read their latest journal entry?" Sandy asked, bracing herself for the rush of silence she knew would follow. "Any volunteers?" Why am I not surprised? she continued under her breath when eager hands failed to push their way into the air. She looked up and down the first two rows, finally settling on Victor Drummond, in the second-to-last seat of the second row. The boy was dressed completely in black, his naturally tanned face covered by a layer of white powder. Pale blue eyes were outlined in black; the natural pout of his lips was exaggerated by bright, Marilyn Manson–red lipstick. "Victor," Sandy said with all the cheeriness she could muster. "How about you?"

"You sure you can handle it?" Victor asked with a smirk. He glanced toward the similarly outfitted diva in the seat beside him. The girl, whose name was Nancy, and whose thinly plucked left eyebrow was pierced with three small safety pins, stuck out her tongue.

Sandy winced. She couldn't bear the sight of the metal stud jutting out from the middle of Nancy's tongue. It looked too painful. And didn't the girl worry about infection? Didn't her parents? Sandy suppressed a second sigh. She considered herself lucky that neither of her children had seen fit to disfigure themselves with stray piercings or tattoos. At least so far.

"I'll risk it," she told Victor. "I'm sure you have some very interesting observations to share with the class." If he was thinking about shooting up the school, she might as well have some advance warning, she reasoned as she walked around her desk, then sank into her chair, waiting, and wondering when this whole Goth fad was finally going to run its course. Hadn't it been around long enough? Certainly she'd seen enough of it in Rochester, and while she recognized it was largely a rebellion of style over substance, it troubled her nonetheless. Still, she couldn't help but like Victor, in spite of his ghoulish getup. Unlike most of her students, he possessed an active and fertile imagination, and his compositions, filled with often bizarre and exotic imagery, could usually be relied on to be, if not as provocative as he might have wished, at least moderately interesting.

"You want me to stand up?" Victor hovered several inches above his seat.

"Not necessary."

Immediately he lowered his skinny backside into his chair. He paused, cleared his throat, then paused again. "'It's a full moon,'" he began, reading without expression or inflection. "'I'm lying here in bed, listening for the howling of the wolves.'"

"There aren't any wolves in Florida, dipshit," Joey Balfour called

out from the back of the class. Joey was the nineteen-year-old cap-
tain of the football team, who was repeating his senior year. He was
a strutting stereotype—big, brawny, and brainless—and altogether
way too proud of it.

The rest of the class laughed. A paper airplane flew across the
room.

"Dipshit," Victor repeated quietly, but with just enough venom
to recapture the class's attention. "I was talking metaphorically."

Joey laughed, lifting large hands in front of his wide face, as if
trying to shield himself. "Whoa. I didn't understand. He was talking met-a-phor-i-cally."

"That's a pretty big word for such a scrawny little guy," Greg
Watt said, his smile curdling, his voice growing dark.

"Does somebody want to tell the class what it means?" Sandy
interjected, hoping to ward off an actual confrontation. She'd
taught a whole lesson on metaphors earlier in the year. It would be
nice to find out if anybody had actually been paying attention.

Delilah raised her hand.

Wouldn't you know it? Sandy thought. Not only did she have to
have this oversize reminder of her husband's betrayal staring her in
the face first thing every morning, but now the misguided young
woman actually felt the need to contribute. Didn't she know that
every time she opened her mouth, it was like a dagger to Sandy's
heart? Talk about metaphors, she thought, shaking her head and
dislodging the hair she'd just tucked behind her ear, realizing, technically, it was a simile. "Go ahead, Dee," she said.

"*Dee?*" Greg repeated incredulously. "*Dee?!* Hey, if you're gonna
give her a nickname, how about Deli? Yeah, that's better. God
knows she could eat everything in one."

Once again, the class erupted in laughter. But unlike Victor,
Delilah had no quick comeback, no clever retort.

"That's enough," Sandy warned.

"Tell that to the Deli," Joey Balfour shouted from the back of the
room. A fresh wave of laughter swept through the class.

"Or how about Big D?" Greg continued. "You know, like the
song—"

"I said, that's enough."

Delilah lowered her head, creating an unfortunate double chin. Sandy felt immediately guilty. The poor girl had enough problems without being saddled with a nickname that was worse than the real thing. What had she done? It wasn't the teenager's fault that her mother had seduced Sandy's husband during an intimate online chat. It wasn't her fault that Ian had grown restless and dissatisfied being the proverbial small fish in a big pond, that he'd yearned to be a bigger fish in a smaller pond.

Make that the biggest fish, Sandy amended. The smallest pond.

Make that frog, she amended further. Make that quagmire.

"Okay. No more of that. Unless you all want to stay late after class." Immediately the room fell silent. No need for clever retorts when you had power. "Delilah," Sandy encouraged.

"That's all right. I like *Dee*," Delilah said in the soft, little-girl voice that never failed to surprise Sandy. The voice seemed years— not to mention pounds—removed from the person speaking.

"Okay, then . . . Dee. Tell us what a metaphor is."

"It's a symbol," Delilah began. "A comparison. Like when you use a word or phrase that normally means one thing to mean something else."

"What the hell is she talking about?" Greg asked.

"It means Victor wasn't actually lying in bed listening for wolves howling," Brian Hensen answered without looking up from his desk. Brian was the sickly son of the school nurse, and his complexion was as pale naturally as Victor's was after half a jar of powder.

"Then what does he mean, smart-ass?"

"He's listening for things that go bump in the night," Brian answered matter-of-factly. "For danger." He raised his eyes to Sandy's. "For death."

"Wow," said Victor.

"Cool," said Greg.

Then, for several seconds, no one said anything. "Thank you, Brian," Sandy managed to whisper, fighting the urge to give both Victor and Brian a huge hug. Maybe she was contributing something after all. Maybe her months here hadn't been a complete and utter waste of time, as she'd lamented on more than one occasion. Maybe somebody was actually learning something. "Victor, please continue reading your journal."

Again Victor cleared his throat, then paused several seconds for dramatic effect. "'Of course I know there aren't any wolves in Florida,'" he read, an audible sneer in his voice as he glanced toward Joey. "'But that doesn't stop me from imagining them gathering outside my room. Will they be there later? I wonder. Will they be waiting for me, as I sneak from my warm bed into the cool darkness of the night? Will they follow me into the forest as I shed my skin, like the thin snake that slithers across my bare toes in the moonlight?'"

"What forest, dipshit?"

"Joey . . . ," Sandy warned.

"Don't tell me. It's another metaphor."

"'I find a quiet piece of damp earth,'" Victor continued without prompting. "'I take the kitchen knife from my belt. I run the serrated edge of the blade along the inside of my arm, watch as blood bubbles to the surface of my skin, like lava from a volcano. I lower my lips, taste my sins, drink my unclean desires.'"

"You're a nut bar," Joey pronounced.

This time, despite the literary merits of what she'd just heard, Sandy was inclined to agree with Joey's assessment. "Okay, Victor. I think we've heard enough. Much as I admire the skill with which you're able to express your fantasies, this was supposed to be an exercise in recording what you actually did last night."

Victor's response was to extend his left arm and roll up the sleeve of his black shirt, revealing a long, jagged line that traveled up the underside of his flesh.

"Cool," said Nancy.

"Holy crap," said Greg.

"I think you better have the nurse take a look at that," Sandy said, closing her eyes to the sight.

Victor laughed. "What for? I'm fine."

"I'm not so sure," Sandy countered. "Please, go see Mrs. Hensen.

Now." She made a mental note to call Victor's parents at the end of the day, alert them to their son's nocturnal activities. Was it possible she'd be telling them something they didn't already know?

Mind your own business, she could hear Ian scold. He'd always said she got too caught up in the lives of her students. *Worry about your own life,* he'd said.

Except at the time he'd said it, she hadn't realized she had anything to worry about.

"Crazy faggot," Greg muttered as Victor opened the door of the portable classroom and vaulted over the three steps to the pavement.

"Okay, Greg," Sandy said, jumping to her feet and almost knocking over her chair. "That's quite enough of that." She returned to her former position at the front of the desk. "And since you seem so eager to speak, let's hear what you wrote."

"Uh, it's kind of personal, Mrs. Crosbie. Wouldn't want to embarrass you."

"That's all right. I'm not easily embarrassed."

Greg looked slyly in Delilah's direction. "I guess not."

The rest of the class, except for Delilah, joined in, although there were a few gasps from some of the girls. "Can I see your journal please, Greg?" Sandy's tone indicated this was not a request.

Reluctantly, Greg handed it over. Sandy opened the notebook, her eyes scanning the collection of mostly blank, lined pages. She flipped to the last page and was surprised to find it covered with a series of amazingly good, cartoonlike sketches of instantly recognizable people. There was Lenny Fromm, the so-laid-back-he-was-almost-supine principal of Torrance High, pictured with his blond comb-over almost completely covering his sleepy features; Avery Peterson, the science teacher, who, at thirty-eight, was the same age as Sandy, but who looked much older since he was almost completely bald, and who was portrayed in these drawings as an enormous bowling ball perched atop a pair of tiny, spiderlike legs; and Gordon Lipsman, the drama teacher, represented here by a square, boxlike head containing a large, bulbous nose, and a pair of vaguely crossed eyes.

Sandy was both flattered and appalled to find herself included in the group. She recognized herself immediately in the unruly curls of the caricature's hair, the exaggerated point of her chin, the pronounced mole that nestled above her full upper lip. The sticklike torso was covered in a long, shapeless dress, and thin arms waved bony fingers high above her head. Is that how they see me? she wondered, scanning the curious faces of her students. A skinny, frazzled harridan?

Is that how Ian saw me?

Her eyes drifted toward the page beside it, where the frazzled harridan was fighting with an Amazon whose gigantic breasts, flowing blond hair, and high-heeled shoes clearly identified her as Kerri Franklin. In the background was a monstrous-sized girl, tears leaping from bulging eyes as she attempted to stuff an entire chicken into her gaping mouth. A second sketch showed the triumphant Amazon holding a man with an enormous erection above her flowing blond mane, her high heels digging into the shapeless form of the prone harridan at her feet, as the monstrous-sized girl reached for another chicken, this one alive and squawking.

Sandy closed the notebook, returned it to Greg without comment. Her heart was beating wildly. But it was important to appear calm, she was thinking, even as she felt a scream rising in her throat. "Tanya," she said, suppressing both the scream and the threat of tears as she turned her attention to one of the prettiest girls at Torrance High. "Could we hear from you, please?" Sandy forced a smile onto her lips, gratified by how unruffled she'd managed to sound.

Tanya McGovern rose in her seat. Along with Ginger Perchak, who sat two seats over and to the left, and the absent Liana Martin, who normally sat directly behind her, the three girls formed the most popular clique in school. The boys fought for their attention. The other girls emulated their hairstyles, clothes, and attitudes. Even Sandy's normally sensible seventeen-year-old daughter, Megan, had recently fallen under their spell. At home it was always, Tanya this, and Ginger that. Sandy shuddered, wondering how long it would be before Megan requested a MOVE, BITCH T-shirt, like the one Liana had been wearing yesterday. Where are the parents? she wondered, as she had wondered earlier.

"I'm afraid I didn't exactly get around to writing in my diary, Mrs. Crosbie."

Sandy nodded, acknowledging defeat. "Okay, Tanya. You can sit down."

The girl quickly complied.

"All right. It looks as if you've all got a busy night ahead of you," Sandy told them. "In addition to writing two journal entries—and handing them in at the start of tomorrow's class—there'll be a test on the first chapter of *Cry, the Beloved Country*. Anyone who is absent or who fails to complete the assignment will receive a zero."

A cascade of groans rumbled toward Sandy's desk. "What if we're sick?" someone whined from the back of the room.

"Don't be."

"What if we get a note from Dr. Crosbie?" Joey Balfour asked. Once again, several gasps punctuated the laughter that followed.

Mercifully, the bell sounded. Immediately the students jumped to their feet, began fleeing the room. Sandy remained where she was, praying her feet would support her until everyone was gone. "Tanya," she managed to spit out as the girl was hurrying by.

"Yes, Mrs. Crosbie?"

"Maybe you could tell Liana about tomorrow's assignment?"

"Sure thing, Mrs. Crosbie."

"And, Greg," Sandy added, catching him at the door. "Could I talk to you a minute, please?"

Greg backed away from the door, slowly retraced his steps.

"Catch you later, buddy," Joey Balfour said on his way out. He winked at Sandy. "Be gentle."

"I'm sorry about those drawings," Greg began. "Obviously I didn't mean for you to see them."

"Then you might consider leaving them at home next time you come to class."

"Yes, ma'am."

"You might also consider applying to art college after you graduate," Sandy continued, as Greg's eyes shot to hers. "You have talent. Real talent. It should be developed."

"We're a family of truck farmers, Mrs. Crosbie," Greg said, blushing at the compliment, then brushing it aside. "I don't think my father would take too kindly to a son who draws cartoons for a living."

"Well . . . something to think about anyway."

"We're not exactly big thinkers," Greg said with a wink. He started back toward the door.

"Greg . . . ?"

Again he stopped, swiveled around on the worn heels of his brown leather boots.

"Go easy on Delilah, would you?"

A sly grin skewered Greg's generically handsome face. The door to the portable opened, and Greg Watt disappeared in a flash of morning sun.

chapter three

Deputy Sheriff John Weber sat behind the massive oak desk in his small office and leaned back in his uncomfortable, hunter-green leather chair. The chair was uncomfortable for two reasons. First, the delicate, Italian design, selected by his wife after perhaps one too many glasses of wine at lunch, was incompatible with his expansive, American frame. (He stood six feet five inches and weighed more than two hundred pounds, and while he used to boast it was two hundred pounds of pure muscle, that was three years and thirty pounds ago.) Second, despite the old building's spanking new air-conditioning system, which kept the temperature of his office hovering around freezing, the leather somehow always managed to stick to his back. Every time he shifted position, the leather would rip away from his shirt like a Band-Aid, leaving creases in the once crisp, beige cotton. As a result, John always looked vaguely unkempt. His wife, Pauline, complained that people no doubt attributed his slovenly appearance to her poor ironing skills. "They'll think I just lie in bed all day, drinking and watching TV," she once whined, a lament that might have been funny had it not been perilously close to the truth. As far as John Weber could tell, lying in bed, drinking and watching TV, was exactly what his wife of nearly sixteen years did with her days.

John stared out the long window that occupied the west wall of his office and wondered how long he could put off going home. Almost everybody else had already left. Only a skeletal staff remained, since nothing much ever happened in Torrance after dark, other than the occasional traffic accident or an impromptu outbreak of fisticuffs. It was almost six o'clock now, and if he stuck around another hour or so, there was a good chance that the frustrations of the day would be offset by a glorious sunset. And John loved the sunset. Not just because the spray of brilliant oranges, pinks, and yellows spattered across the turquoise blue of the sky was so achingly beautiful it made his heart sing, but because the whole process was so wondrously tidy. Having spent most of the last twenty years cleaning up other people's messes, forty-five-year-old John Weber had developed a profound appreciation for all things neat.

Of course, if he stayed in his office until after the sun had set, he'd have to contend with Pauline's familiar rant that he was never home, that he was always working, and didn't he want to be with her? Didn't he want to spend time with their daughter?

The answer to the first question was easy: no, he didn't want to be with her. The answer to the second question was also no, although not so easy. Much as John Weber hated to admit it, he didn't care much for either his wife or his only child. And while it was somewhat acceptable to dislike the woman you'd married because you were too inebriated and careless to appreciate the consequences of not wearing a condom, it was another matter entirely to dislike your own flesh and blood. Their daughter, Amber, named for the color of the wine they'd been drinking the night she was conceived, was now sixteen and already hovered close to six feet tall. She might have been a formidable presence had she not been so damn skinny, and not just normal, everyday skinny, but bones-jutting-out-from-every-angle, so-skeletal-it-made-you-nervous-just-to-look-at-her skinny. As a result, he tried not to look at her. Lately, he avoided even glancing her way, doing so only when it was unavoidable, and then trying his best not to cringe, although one time he couldn't help himself, and she'd caught the look of horror in his eyes and run crying from the room. That was months ago, and he still felt guilty.

The whole thing was his fault after all.

He'd been arguing with Pauline because she'd forgotten to call the plumber about the leak in the faucet of the bathroom sink, and the damn dripping was keeping him awake half the night, and she'd promised she'd do it first thing that morning, and of course she hadn't, which meant he'd have to endure another night of Chinese water torture, and then he'd have to call the plumber himself tomorrow, when he was supposed to be working, and he was still irritated—hell, he was irritated now, almost eight months later—when he saw Amber in the kitchen helping herself to the last of the peach pie in the fridge—the piece he'd been saving for himself—and he'd made some stupid comment about how if she wasn't careful, she'd end up like Kerri Franklin's daughter— talk about the pot calling the kettle black—and next thing he knew, the pie was in the garbage and Amber was dropping pounds as if they were flies, and now she was maybe 125 pounds—six feet tall and 125 pounds!—and it was all his fault. He was a lousy parent. A terrible husband and a worse father. So how could he go home when every time he walked through the front door of their messy bungalow, he was greeted by his own failings and swiftly wrapped in the open arms of despair?

He'd tried talking to Pauline about their daughter, but she'd brushed aside his concerns. *"Pas de problème,"* she'd sniffed in her annoying habit of throwing French phrases into their conversations. It was the style to be superskinny these days. She rhymed off a bunch of television actresses he'd never heard of, then pointed to the covers of half a dozen fashion magazines that lay across the bed, like squares on a quilt. All boasted pictures of shapeless young women, their monstrous-sized heads overwhelming their sticklike bodies. Whatever happened to tits and ass? he'd wondered.

Of course, if tits and ass was what you were looking for, there was always Kerri Franklin.

John shook his head, trying not to picture the voluptuous woman writhing beneath him, trying not to hear his name escaping those obscenely lush lips. Their affair, wedged in between husbands number two and three, had lasted only a few months, although it had enjoyed a brief resurgence after the departure of husband number three. That was after the surgery on her eyes but before the latest round of implants, and definitely before Ian Crosbie had arrived on the scene. John wondered if there'd be another heated reunion once the good doctor came to his senses and went back to his wife. He wondered what it felt like to have silicone breasts and collagen-enhanced lips. He wondered why women did such terrible things to themselves, why they were so willing, even eager, to turn themselves into living cartoons.

Skeletons and cartoons, John was thinking as the phone rang. He reached across his desk and picked up the receiver. "Weber," he announced instead of hello.

"Good," his wife said. "You're still there."

John smiled. Finally, he was thinking. Something they could agree on. "What's up?"

"I was wondering what you felt like for dinner."

John felt instantly guilty—for thinking ill of his wife, for his affair with Kerri Franklin, for dredging up excuses not to go home. "I don't know. Maybe—"

"I thought you could pick up something from McDonald's. They've been showing these commercials for McChicken sandwiches all afternoon, and it's really put me in the mood."

John rubbed at the bridge of his nose, scratched at his receding hairline, and let out a deep breath. "I'm not sure what time I'll be getting home," he began, grateful when he saw a late-model, white Cadillac pull into the parking lot, and Howard and Judy Martin emerge, a look of grim determination on their faces. Clearly something was wrong. Just as clearly, he would have to stay and find out what it was. "Looks like I might be tied up here for a while—"

The line went dead in his hands.

"Thank you for being so understanding," John continued, waving the Martins inside his office. "Howard . . . Judy," he said, rising to his feet and motioning toward the two brown, high-back chairs in front of his desk. "Is there a problem?" It was a stupid question, he realized, sitting back down, and noting the stiffness of Howard's posture, the anxious twisting of the tissue in Judy Martin's manicured fingers, the look of fear in their matching blue eyes. They'd been the best-looking kids in high school, and twice been crowned prom king and queen, an honor that had yet to be repeated. Judy had gone on to win a host of local beauty pageants—Miss Broward County, Miss Citrus Fruit, second runner-up to Miss Florida— before marrying Howard, and her brown, upswept hair always looked as if it were awaiting its tiara. But even with too much makeup—John tried to remember if he'd ever seen her without it—she was a beautiful woman.

Howard, tall, trim, and still boyishly handsome, grabbed his wife's hand and held tight to her trembling fingers. "It's Liana. She's missing."

"Missing? For how long?"

"Since yesterday."

"Yesterday?"

"Apparently, she didn't come home from school."

"Apparently?" John repeated, thinking he must have misunderstood. Howard and Judy Martin were involved, concerned parents. If one of their children hadn't come home from school the previous afternoon, why had they waited until now to pay him a visit?

"We were in Tampa," Judy explained softly, as if reading his mind. "Howard had some business there, and Meredith was competing in this junior pageant. We thought we could combine . . ." Her voice drifted off. She stared out the window behind John's head.

"We called home last night," Howard continued, "but the boys never said a thing about Liana not being there. Apparently they assumed she was with her boyfriend, and they didn't want to get her in trouble."

"We got back around two o'clock this afternoon," Judy said. "We assumed everyone was in school. But when Liana wasn't home by five o'clock, I started to get worried. I asked the boys if their sister had told them she'd be late, and that's when they confessed she hadn't come home yesterday. I called Peter right away. He said he hadn't seen her either."

"Peter?" John grabbed a pen, began scribbling notes on a pad of white paper. This was starting to sound more serious than he'd first imagined, although he was certain everything would resolve itself favorably in reasonably short order.

"Peter Arlington. He's been her boyfriend for about six months now."

"They fight all the time," Howard added with a shake of his head. "They're always breaking up, getting back together, breaking up again."

"You know how it is with young love," Judy added, the words catching in her throat.

John nodded, although, in truth, he didn't know. He'd never really been in love.

"Peter said the last time he saw Liana was yesterday at school. Apparently they had some kind of disagreement, and they weren't talking to each other, so he didn't call her last night. And then he wasn't feeling well today, so he stayed home from school."

John narrowed his eyes, tried to picture Peter Arlington. The name didn't ring any immediate bells. "You believe him?"

"What do you mean?"

John noted enviously that Howard's hairline was still intact, although he was starting to gray at the temples. He'd grow old gracefully and with dignity, John thought, leaning forward in his seat and feeling the extra pounds around his middle press rudely against the desk. "This Peter kid—do you believe him?"

"I hadn't thought about it," Howard admitted. "I just assumed he was telling the truth."

"Why?" Judy asked. "You think he's lying?"

"I have no idea." John fed Peter Arlington's name into the computer on his desk and was relieved when it came up empty. "He's not in the system, which is good."

"What does that mean?"

"He's never been arrested, never been to jail."

"Oh, no. Liana would never get involved with anyone like that," Judy assured John.

"All right. Let's back up a minute here," John said. "After you called Peter, did you phone anyone else?"

"Of course. I called all of Liana's friends."

"They are . . . ?"

"Tanya McGovern and Ginger Perchak. They're her best friends. I called them first."

John scribbled down the familiar names. Tanya had played one of Amber's sisters in Torrance High's production of *Fiddler on the Roof* last year. Liana Martin had played the other.

"And then I phoned Maggie Mackenzie and Ellen Smythe. I even called Victor Drummond."

"Victor Drummond?" her husband asked. "Why would you call that freak, for God's sake?"

"Well, he and Liana played lovers in *Fiddler on the Roof,* and then she was partnered with him on that science project for Mr. Peterson earlier in the year, and she said he was really nice, that he wasn't weird at all once you got to know him, and I had the feeling that she always kind of liked him—"

"*Liked* him? What are you talking about?"

"—so I thought I'd take a chance."

"She wasn't with him," John stated softly.

Judy shook her head. Her hair didn't move. "No one has seen her since yesterday afternoon. Tanya said she called Liana's cell phone a bunch of times and left a slew of messages, but that Liana never called her back."

"Have you tried her cell?" John asked, although he already knew the answer. Of course they'd tried their daughter's cell.

"The last time we tried it was in the car on the way over here," Howard confirmed. "She's not picking up."

"It's like she's disappeared off the face of the earth." Judy bit her quivering lowering lip. Her eyes filled with tears. The tears teetered precariously on her lower lids.

"Has she ever done anything like this before?"

"Never," Judy said adamantly.

"We're not saying she's perfect," Howard amended. "She's stubborn and headstrong, and she has a mouth on her when she gets mad, but all in all, she's a good kid."

"Can you think of any reason she might have had to run away?"

"Run away?" her mother asked. "From what?"

"Were there any problems at home?"

"What kind of problems?"

John hated when people answered his questions with more of their own. "Was she upset about something? Or angry? Maybe you'd imposed a curfew . . . ," he continued before they could ask for specifics.

"She didn't have a curfew. She wasn't angry or upset. There were no problems."

"Has she been anxious, maybe a little depressed?"

"Anxious? Depressed?" Judy repeated.

"Well, you said she'd had a fight with her boyfriend . . ."

"They were always fighting," Howard said dismissively. "To them, it's foreplay."

"What are you getting at?" Judy asked John, a wrinkle of worry furrowing her otherwise unlined brow. "You think she might have done something to hurt herself?"

"Kids this age are very vulnerable," John said, thinking of Amber. "If she was upset about anything . . ."

"She wasn't," Howard said.

"Would she tell you if she was?"

"She'd tell me," Judy said. Then less assuredly: "I think she'd tell me."

"Is there any chance she might be pregnant?" John asked quietly, hoping the softness of his voice would offset any potential explosion from the other side of the desk. It had been his experience that parents, no matter how open-minded they considered themselves to be, were uncomfortable imagining their children's sex lives.

Howard Martin covered his lips with his hand, cursed under his breath. Even still, the words were clear: "Son of a bitch."

"She was on the pill," Judy volunteered after a pause of several seconds.

"What?" her husband asked.

"She's eighteen," Judy said. Then forcefully: "Liana wasn't anxious. She wasn't depressed. And she wasn't pregnant. She certainly wouldn't have done anything to hurt herself."

"And she wouldn't just take off without telling us."

"Have you checked her computer?" John asked.

"Her computer?"

"You know how much time these kids spend on the Internet. Maybe she met some guy in a chat room." For the second time that afternoon, John found himself thinking about Kerri Franklin. Hadn't she met her Dr. Crosbie in exactly that way? At least, that was the local scuttlebutt. Amber had come home from school one day, breathless with the news that her English teacher's husband had left her for Delilah Franklin's mother, and you'll never believe how they met!

"I didn't think to check her computer," Howard said. "I don't even know her password. Do you?" he asked his wife.

She shook her head. "Maybe the boys know."

Immediately Howard pulled his cell phone out of the pocket of his tan-colored windbreaker. He punched in a series of numbers and waited. "Noah, do you know your sister's password?" he asked without preamble. "Yes, of course, for the computer," he said impatiently. "She won't kill you," Howard assured him. "But *I* might if you don't tell me what it is right now. . . . Okay. Thanks. I take it she hasn't called?" He snapped the tiny phone shut, then returned it to his pocket. "Her password is *Jell-O,* and there's been no word."

"I'll need her e-mail address."

Again Howard looked to his wife to supply it. She did so with a hollow voice that seemed to be coming from another room altogether.

"I'll have one of our guys look into it first thing in the morning."

"Is there anything we can do tonight?"

"Well, it'll be getting dark soon, but I'll have a police cruiser take a look around." John noted a flash of disappointment streak through Judy's eyes. "And I'll snoop around a little myself," he added quickly, trying not to picture the sunset he'd been looking forward to. He understood that most people, especially people in a small town like Torrance, liked to feel they were dealing with the person in charge. In charge of what? he wondered, scratching at his upper lip. When was the last time he'd felt in charge of anything? "Does she have any favorite haunts? Places she likes to go?"

"Merchant Mall," Judy said. "But it'll be closed now."

"And Chester's," Howard added, naming the hamburger-joint-cum-pool-hall that was a popular hangout for many of the area's teens.

"I'll check it out." John had never liked Chester's. It was managed by Cal Hamilton, a former bouncer from South Beach, whose wife was always covered with bruises. "Are any of her things missing?"

"Her clothes are all in her closet," Judy said. "Her CDs, her makeup, everything is where it always is. Except for her school stuff and her purse, which she would have had with her. You don't think something awful's happened to her, do you?" she continued in the same breath, unable any longer to prevent the question that had been circling their heads, like a menacing crow, from swooping into their laps.

How do you answer a question like that? John asked himself. "I don't know," he said, opting for honesty. "I hope not, and certainly there's no evidence to suggest anything bad has happened." Except, of course, that she's been missing for more than twenty-four hours, he thought, but didn't say. Their ashen faces told him they were thinking the same thing.

Still, the reality was that most missing teens turned out to be runaways. They surfaced eventually, not terribly apologetic, some even indignant, and always rather surprised by all the fuss their disappearance had caused. But this didn't seem to be the case here. From everything the Martins had just told him, there was no reason to believe Liana had run away. She was a popular, well-adjusted teenager with lots of friends and few worries. Of course, the parents were often the last to know if there were any real problems, and so he'd have a few officers start interviewing Liana's friends privately, and he'd personally stop in at Chester's before heading home. Pauline wouldn't be pleased. But then, with any luck, she'd be asleep by the time he crept into bed. "Do you have a recent picture of your daughter?" he asked.

Judy reached into her red leather purse. "I have this one. She never liked it. She says it makes her nose look too big, but it's always been one of my favorites because she looks so happy." She removed the small, color photograph from its red leather frame and handed it across the desk.

John smiled at the image of the pretty girl with the long, reddish blond hair. Both mother and daughter were right, he thought. The picture did make Liana's nose look bigger than it was, but her smile was wide and genuine. She did indeed look happy. He hoped she was somewhere smiling right now. He didn't think so, he realized glumly, pocketing the picture. "I'll take this over to Chester's, maybe stop at a few other places, show the picture around, see if anybody's seen her. If she's not back by morning, we'll make up some flyers, post them around town."

"Should we alert the media?" Howard asked.

"That won't be necessary at this time." John almost smiled. There was no real media in Torrance, other than a biweekly newsletter that consisted mainly of local produce prices, advertisements, and obituaries. Most people in the area received either the *Sun-Sentinel* out of Fort Lauderdale or the *Miami Herald*. If Liana still hadn't turned up by the weekend, he'd alert both those papers, as well as the sheriff's departments in each city. If necessary, he'd contact the FBI.

"Do you think she might have been kidnapped?" Judy asked, again reading his mind.

"Well, it's been over twenty-four hours and you haven't received any ransom notes," John told her. "I think you would have by now."

"What if it's not money they're after," Judy continued, speaking more to herself than to the sheriff. "What if some lunatic took my daughter, what if he—"

"Judy, for God's sake," her husband interrupted.

"Let's try to think positive thoughts," John advised, although positive thoughts wouldn't do Liana Martin any good if, in fact, some lunatic *had* grabbed her. He made a mental note to ask everyone he interviewed tonight if they'd noticed any strangers in the area in the last few weeks, and he'd tell his officers to do the same. "In the meantime," he said, coming around the desk, "you go home, and try to stay calm. I'll call you after I've checked around a bit. Here's my cell number. Phone me right away if you think of anything else. Don't worry about what time it is."

"What if she's hurt? What if she's lying on the side of a road somewhere?"

"We'll organize a search party in the morning," John told Judy Martin, knowing that if her daughter was, in fact, lying on the side of the road anywhere in the area, the odds were good she wouldn't be there for long. There was a good reason they called it Alligator Alley.

He ushered Howard and Judy Martin out of his office, promising again to call them as soon as he'd checked things out. "We'll find her," he promised, as another troubling image seized his brain. He recalled another woman who'd sat in his office approximately one month ago, hands twisting in her lap, eyes brimming with tears, as she told essentially the same story. He'd dismissed her concerns—the woman was from nearby Hendry County, and therefore technically not his problem, and she'd admitted her daughter was a habitual runaway and drug addict who often turned tricks to support her habit. He hadn't given the girl's disappearance much thought, but as he watched Liana Martin's distraught parents get into their car and drive off, he couldn't help but wonder if the two disappearances were somehow connected. "You've been watching too much television," he scoffed, trying not to picture his own daughter, Amber, her skinny body lying twisted in a ditch by the side of the road, her neck broken by some lunatic's monstrous hands.

Then he walked purposefully from the room.

chapter four

Torrance wasn't so much a town as a series of isolated streets that had multiplied and merged over the years, a loose conglomeration of farms and orchards and swampland, whose four thousand, mostly white, Christian inhabitants encompassed all socioeconomic levels, from the scandalously rich to the heartbreakingly poor. It was located about an hour's drive west of Fort Lauderdale, just past the junction between Highway 27 and that strip of I-75 known as Alligator Alley. Its small downtown core consisted of several banks, a post office, a pharmacy, a few restaurants, a store that sold hunting and fishing equipment, a pawnshop, a women's clothing store, an insurance agency, and a legal firm whose slogan, hand-painted across the front window in frosted silver letters, promised its all-purpose legal team—a father, his son, and their much put-upon assistant—were HAPPY TO SERVE, WILLING TO SUE, HOPING TO SETTLE. The rest of the town circled this main drag like a series of expanding ripples. Nearby was the Merchant Mall, with its grocery store, movie theater, tattoo parlor, and clothing stores full of all things denim. Down the way was a McDonald's, an Arby's, and a KFC. There was also Chester's.

Chester's was one of those places common to every small town in America. Located about a quarter of a mile from the main strip, it was relatively unassuming on the outside, its simple wood exterior painted a quiet shade of gray and trimmed in white. Inside it was big and dark and noisy, the noise accentuated by the high, wood-beamed ceilings and dark-stained wooden floors, as well as by the constant clamor coming from the pool tables in the back room. Waitresses in skimpy, pink shorts and provocative, white T-shirts with CHESTER'S stretched in hot-pink letters across their breasts weaved their way from the large, neon-lit bar at the front through the polished wood booths and tables in the middle to the game room at the back, with trays of beer in their hands and frozen smiles on their faces. Chester's, named for its creator, a wily, white-haired septuagenarian who cooked up the best hamburgers in town, was always packed. It seemed everyone in town frequented Chester's, although Chester, himself, had become increasingly reclusive over the years and now preferred to stay holed up in the kitchen, having largely turned over the day-to-day management of his establish-ment to Cal Hamilton. The verdict on Cal Hamilton among the local citizenry was decidedly mixed. Some people—mostly men—found him a swaggering bore; others—mostly women—found him self-confident and sexy. The latter likely hadn't seen the bruises cov-ering his pretty wife's face and arms, although there were always women who were attracted to the so-called bad boys, who failed to recognize them for the often dangerous bullies they were, and who convinced themselves they were different, that they could trans-form the bad boy into a good man.

John Weber pushed his way through the heavy, outside double doors and squinted into the darkness for a familiar face. Torrance was full of all kinds of people. What was one person's idea of heaven was another's idea of hell, which made Torrance just like every other city—big or small—in America. Or the world, for that matter, John Weber thought.

Hell is other people, he remembered his wife telling him once, although he couldn't recall the occasion. He'd made the mistake of repeating this sentiment during a strained conversation with Amber's drama teacher, Gordon Lipsman, at a parent-teacher meet-ing last fall, and the man had nodded his big, condescending head and said he was *très* impressed that the local sheriff could quote Jean-Paul Sartre. The man had then expounded on "the existential-ist doctrine" for the better part of half an hour. Luckily he'd been pulled away by another parent just as John had been weighing the consequences of pulling out his gun and shooting the pompous ass between his disconcertingly crossed eyes.

"Looking for someone, Sheriff, or can I show you to a table?"

John turned toward the familiar voice, his hands making fists at his sides as he absorbed Cal Hamilton's insolently handsome face. It was the kind of face—dark, brooding eyes as hard as pebbles, in sharp contrast to soft, wavy blond hair; a small pug nose; full round cheeks; large, snarling lips covering a mouthful of surprisingly tiny teeth, like niblets of corn—that John Weber always wanted to punch, although the muscles bulging beneath and below the upturned short sleeves of Cal's black T-shirt warned him to keep things nice and friendly. Cal was rumored to have put more than one man in the hospital during his days as a bouncer in a Miami nightclub, although he had no arrest record or outstanding warrants against him. At least none that John had been able to locate. "I was wondering if you'd seen Liana Martin in the last several days," John said.

"Liana Martin?" Cal's eyes narrowed at the mention of the name.

John pulled Liana's picture out of his shirt pocket. He found it interesting that you could actually see the effort it took some people to think. Some, like Cal Hamilton, narrowed their eyes. Others scrinched their brows and pushed their lips into a lemon-sucking pout. Sometimes they tapped the tip of their nose. Sometimes they did all these things, in sequence or all at once. "Apparently, Chester's is one of her favorite haunts."

"Really? Well, let's have a look." Cal took the picture, carried it over to the large bar area, and examined it under the red and gold neon lights. "Oh, sure. I recognize her. She comes in all the time with her friends."

"When was the last time you saw her?"

Cal shook his head. A wave of blond hair fell across his wide forehead. "Weekend, I guess."

"Can you be more specific?"

"Probably Saturday," Cal said, after another narrowing of his eyes. "Why? Is she in some kind of trouble?"

John thought he detected a note of hopeful anticipation in Cal's voice, as if the notion of a young girl in trouble appealed to his baser instincts. He decided to give the man the benefit of the doubt. "Nobody's seen her since yesterday afternoon."

Cal shrugged his indifference. "You know kids," he scoffed, returning the picture to John's waiting palm. "She's probably shacking up with her boyfriend."

"Her boyfriend doesn't know where she is."

Cal lowered his chin and raised his eyes, which John took to indicate skepticism. "Well, I don't think I'd worry too much about her. My guess is she'll be back in a couple of days. Mark my words."

John almost laughed. Did people really say things like *Mark my words* anymore? "I hope you're right."

"You check with her friends?"

An involuntary sigh escaped John's lips. He and several deputies had spent the last two hours talking with most of Liana Martin's friends. The answers to his questions were the same in every house they'd visited. No one had seen the girl since yesterday afternoon. No one had any idea where she might be. Everyone was worried. It wasn't like Liana to take off without telling anyone, they all agreed.

"Why don't you let me treat you to a beer, Sheriff?" Cal was offering now. "You look like you could use a cold one."

John was about to decline the offer, then thought better of it. Cal was right. A nice, cold beer was exactly what he needed, and technically, he was no longer on duty. Officially, his day had ended when he'd left his office, and everything he'd done since then, the driving through the widely scattered residential streets and side roads of Torrance, the interviews with Liana's friends and neighbors, had been on his own time. He'd called home once, but Pauline had refused to pick up the phone—the wonders of caller ID—and when he'd finally reached Amber on her cell, she'd told him her mother was watching a movie on TV and had given strict instructions she was not to be disturbed. He asked his daughter whether she'd had dinner, and she said she wasn't hungry. John decided to order a couple of hamburgers to take home just in case he could persuade Amber to join him, although he knew in his heart it was a lost cause. Hell, that was probably the main reason he'd put on so much weight in the last few years. The less his daughter ate, the more he felt compelled to ingest, as if he were eating for two. The gaunter his daughter's cheeks became, the fuller his got; the flatter her stomach, the rounder his own. If she didn't start eating soon, he was liable to explode. "I'll have a Bud Light," he told Cal. "And give me a couple burgers to go. Make that bacon cheeseburgers," he amended.

"Have a seat." Cal waved toward a recently emptied booth to the left of the bar. "A Bud Light for the sheriff," he instructed a red-haired waitress as she wiggled past. "I'll give your order to Chester."

John tucked Liana's picture back into his shirt pocket as he watched Cal strut toward the kitchen, his thumbs thrust into the side pockets of his black denim jeans. Something about the studied swagger of his hips—as if he knew he was being watched—rubbed John the wrong way. Cal and his wife had moved to Torrance two years ago, which was unusual, to say the least, considering that neither had family in the area, and neither had a job when they arrived. Why would any young couple move to an isolated community like Torrance unless they were running away from something, or hiding from someone? John had briefly considered the possibility they were in the witness protection program, but ultimately decided this was unlikely. People in the witness protection program usually did their best to maintain a low profile. And although Cal's wife, Fiona, was rarely seen out in public, unless glued to her husband's side, Cal, himself, was anything but shy. Indeed, most of the rumors regarding Cal Hamilton's wild past could usually be traced directly back to one source: Cal Hamilton.

Unless, of course, he was lying.

"Hi, there, Sheriff," a voice cooed, as long, bright red fingernails deposited a tall glass of cold beer on the table in front of him. "I understand you've had a rough day."

John immediately pulled the picture of Liana Martin out of his breast pocket, handed it to the waitress with the preternaturally red hair. "Have you seen this girl in here recently?"

The waitress leaned over to get a better look. Her breasts, with their carefully displayed cleavage, brushed against the side of his cheek. He felt an unexpected stirring below his belt and almost knocked over his drink. "Careful with that beer there, honey," the waitress said, and John winced at this easy familiarity from a girl young enough to be his daughter. "Yeah, I've seen her. But not for a few days. Why? Something happen to her?"

"She's missing," John told her, as he'd told her boss just moments before. "Can you do me a favor? Show this picture to the other waitresses, ask if anybody's seen her around lately."

"Sure thing." The waitress took the picture and disappeared into the general throng.

A few minutes later, he saw her showing Liana's photograph to the bartender and watched as the young man shook his head no. "This ain't going to be easy," John muttered into his beer. As promised, the drink was nice and cold. A man of his word, he thought, watching Cal chat up a pretty, young woman standing at the bar. Cal's hand rested provocatively on the woman's substantial derriere, and despite the wedding band on the appropriate finger of her left hand, John noticed the woman made no attempt to brush Cal's hand away. While John had never considered himself a prude and was certainly no poster boy for fidelity, he disliked the casual way Cal Hamilton flaunted his prowess with women. It was one thing to be unfaithful. It was another thing to trumpet your indiscretions, to wave your infidelities in other people's faces.

John took a long sip of his beer. He'd never understood women. His mother had been a study in contradictions, quiet and withdrawn one minute, loud and boisterous the next. Bipolar, they called it today, although when he was growing up, they just called it crazy. Certainly his father had lost patience early on with her erratic mood swings and unpredictable behavior. He buried himself in his work, and when she died of breast cancer in her early forties, everyone said it was a blessing in disguise. But John still missed his mother's wonderful sense of humor and biting wit. His father had remarried within a year of his mother's death, this time to a woman with no sense of humor whatsoever, at least not one that John had ever been able to detect. But she seemed to make his father happy. Another of life's mysteries. John took a prolonged sip of his beer, emptied half the glass. It seemed he didn't understand men very well either. Maybe he was in the wrong line of work.

"Nobody's seen her," the waitress said when she returned to John's table about ten minutes later. "I even asked some of the customers," she added, shaking her head, as if to say, No luck there either.

"Thanks." John finished the last of his beer, returned the tall, empty glass to the waitress's tray. She promptly replaced it with a full one.

"They're on the house," she told him before he could object.

What the hell, he thought. Why not? Two beers simply meant he'd have to sit here a little longer before he got back behind the wheel of his cruiser. He checked his watch. It was already after nine o'clock. He could probably stay and nurse this beer for another half hour at least, and then he'd check in again with the Martins—he'd already dropped over to their house to give them an update after talking to Liana's friends—before heading home. With any luck, Pauline would be asleep. The thought of having to make idle conversation, or worse, of having to make love to his wife, was simply too depressing.

He picked up the second glass of beer, raised it to his lips. When had the thought of making love become depressing? When had sex ceased to be a release and become yet another chore, another burden to bear? It hadn't always been that way. There was a time, and not all that long ago, when just the thought of sex was enough to get him through the day. That he didn't love his wife, had *never* loved her, had never really loved anyone, for that matter, was irrelevant. He'd never been one to confuse sex with love. And for a long time, sex with Pauline had been enough to sustain him. When had it stopped being enough?

He was still relatively young. The waitress tonight had proved he was still capable of being easily, even indiscriminately, aroused. So what was his problem? Why did he find it so difficult to get, let alone sustain, an erection where his wife was concerned?

He knew he couldn't pin all the blame on Pauline. When she'd first sensed his eye wandering and his interest waning, she'd done her best to spice things up. She'd bought some sexy lingerie and sprinkled scented candles around their bed and bath, suggested they try new positions, even hinted he bring his handcuffs into the bedroom. These things worked for a while, and then they didn't.

He doubted Pauline was any happier than he was at what had happened to their sex life, but at least she could pretend. He wished he could fake arousal and orgasm, but it was much more difficult for a man than a woman. Fantasies would take you only so far, and you couldn't bully a limp dick into action. Pauline had it much easier. Hell, all she had to do was lie there.

"Excuse me, Sheriff Weber?"

The cold glass of beer almost slipped through John's fingers.

"I'm sorry. I didn't mean to startle you."

John turned toward the little-girl whisper, saw Kerri Franklin's daughter, Delilah, looking down at him, earnest brown eyes as big as saucers. He twisted around in his seat to see if her mother was behind her. She wasn't. "Delilah," he said, pushing himself to his feet. "How are you?"

"Okay." She stood on her toes, peered through the dark room. "You haven't seen my mother, have you?"

"Your mother? No. Why? Is she here?" John pulled in his stomach, looked toward the back room.

"No. That's the problem. I don't know where she is. She went out late this afternoon to refill a prescription for Grandma Rose's heart medication, and she didn't come home. Grandma Rose is starting to get a little antsy, so I said I'd go look for her. You haven't seen her?" Alarm bells began clanging inside John's head. First the runaway from Hendry County, then Liana Martin, and now Kerri Franklin?

No, he told himself, offering Delilah his most reassuring smile. The runaway from Hendry County was just that—a runaway. As was, in all probability, Liana Martin. As for Kerri Franklin, she had a contentious relationship with her mother at the best of times, and the woman's heart condition had been stable for years. Kerri had probably run into a friend at the drugstore and, not feeling any great urgency to return home, gone for a cup of coffee. Coffee had stretched into dinner, and maybe even a movie. She'd resurface when she was ready. As would Liana Martin and that other girl. What was her name?

Candy, he heard the girl's mother remind him, as she held out the picture of a petite, young woman with haunted, dark eyes. *Actually, her real name is Harlene. Harlene Abbot. But she always hated that name. She called herself Candy. Said it suited her much better than Harlene. And, yes, I know, she's disappeared before, and I know about the drugs and the men, but this time is different, Sheriff Weber. I know it's different.*

Why is it different this time?

Because no matter where she goes or how long she's been away, she always calls me on my birthday. And this time, she didn't. My birthday was the first of March, and I stayed home all day and waited, but she didn't call.

Mrs. Abbot. . . .

Something's happened to her, Sheriff Weber. And nobody wants to help me. . . .

"Sheriff Weber?"

"What? Sorry?" John Weber jumped back into the present tense. Delilah Franklin was looking at him expectantly.

"I heard you've been asking questions about Liana Martin."

"Have you seen her?"

Delilah shook her head. "Not since yesterday. You think something bad's happened to her?"

"I hope not. How well do you know her?"

"Well, we've been in the same class ever since we were kids, but we're not exactly friends. You know how it is. Liana's really popular. And really nice. Not like some of the others. She's always been very nice to me. I like her," Delilah concluded with an emphatic nod of her head.

"Did she ever say anything to you about any problems she might be having at home or with her boyfriend?"

"Oh, she wouldn't tell me anything like that. You'd have to ask Ginger or Tanya about stuff like that."

I already have, he said silently, deciding it was definitely time to go home.

"Sheriff Weber?" Delilah asked again in that incongruous little voice, as her worried eyes made the obvious connection. "You don't think anything's happened to my mother, do you?"

"I think your mother's probably at home right now, worried half to death about you," John told her, downing the remainder of his beer and leaving a tip for the waitress on the table. "Come on. You need a lift home?"

"That'd be great. Thanks. It's a long walk. Especially in the dark." Delilah smiled timidly.

John Weber took her elbow, led her toward the front door.

"Oh," she said, stopping abruptly, turning away and blushing visibly, even in the dark.

"What's wrong?"

"It's Mr. Peterson."

"Mr. Peterson?"

"My science teacher." She pointed with her chin toward a man hunched over in a corner booth. His arm was draped possessively around the shoulders of a girl who looked several decades his junior. The girl looked noticeably upset.

"Who's he with?"

Delilah shook her head. "I've never seen her before, but there are all these rumors."

"What kind of rumors?"

"That he likes younger women," she whispered conspiratorially as they stepped out into the night.

They were almost at Delilah's house when John realized he'd forgotten his burgers. His stomach rumbled its displeasure as he watched Delilah open the front door of her modest two-story home, then turn back, telling him with a shake of her head that her mother had yet to return. "Not a good sign," John said as he pulled the car away from the curb and headed for home.

chapter five

Delilah watched the sheriff's car pull away from the curb with a mixture of gratitude and regret. Gratitude because she hadn't had to walk the fifteen blocks home from Chester's—she was tired enough from the long walk over—and regret because she hated to see the sheriff drive away. She'd always liked Sheriff Weber. Unlike a lot of the people in Torrance, he'd shown her nothing but kindness, and she always enjoyed talking to him. He looked her right in the eye when he asked a question, listened respectfully as she answered, and never told her she'd be such a pretty girl if only she'd lose a few pounds. Probably because he'd packed on more than a few pounds himself since he'd stopped seeing her mother, she thought, closing the front door behind her and wondering where her mother could be.

Officially, she wasn't supposed to know about their affair. Kerri, as her mother preferred Delilah to call her—she said it made her feel younger, although Delilah always suspected it was more because she was embarrassed at having produced so ungainly an offspring—had never directly acknowledged her relationship with the married policeman, although it had been pretty much an open secret around Torrance while it was going on. She'd dropped a few broad hints—something about liking men in uniforms, and not having to worry about speeding tickets for a while—but that was it. Whenever Sheriff Weber had dropped over to the house, Kerri had explained he was there on official business. Delilah never questioned her, even when the kids at school started making none-too-veiled comments about their affair, and even after her grandmother pointedly questioned the logic of throwing away money on cosmetic surgery for her daughter if the stupid girl was going to waste it on a married man. Since Kerri had already decided it was better to look good than feel good, her affair with John Weber had come to an abrupt end. Soon afterward, Kerri had left for Miami to have her already enlarged, "bee-stung" lips "stung" again.

Delilah had lost track of the number of surgical procedures her mother had had over the years. Sometimes, when she couldn't sleep, she made a game of trying to count them—her own, more modern version of counting sheep. Aside from the regular injections of Botox and Restylane, she remembered the nose job, the brow lift, the tummy tuck, the liposuction on her thighs, the several eye jobs, the two breast augmentations—the first time they weren't big enough—and the face-lift. The face-lift was the worst because her mother had come home from the clinic looking as if she'd been run over by a Mack truck. Bruises blackened her eyes and covered virtually every inch of her swollen face, although within a few weeks the swelling had gone down, and the bruises had faded, and Kerri was pretty much back to normal. Whatever normal was, the words *normal* and *Kerri Franklin* in the same sentence being somewhat of an oxymoron. If that was the right word for it. Delilah made a mental note to ask Mrs. Crosbie about it.

Delilah liked Mrs. Crosbie. Not only was she a good teacher and a kind person, she looked the way mothers were supposed to look. The sad truth was that Delilah barely recalled what her mother really looked like. The naturally beautiful young woman proudly holding her new baby in old family photographs was a complete stranger to her.

Delilah enjoyed looking through the old family albums as much as her mother and grandmother despised it. She liked seeing her grandmother sitting imperiously on her folding chair at the beach, as if it were a throne, her fleshy knees up around her chin; she got a kick out of her grandfather clowning around in her grandmother's big straw hat, and Kerri and her two sisters happily riding the ocean waves.

Now her grandfather was dead, as was her mother's oldest sister, Lorraine. Her other sister, Ruthie, had moved to California a decade ago and rarely kept in touch anymore. Which left just the three of them—Delilah, her mother, and her grandmother. The unholy trinity, her mother liked to joke. Where was her mother anyway?

"Kerri, is that you?" her grandmother called from the living room.

"No, Grandma Rose. It's me."

"Oh."

There was no disguising the disappointment in her grandmother's voice, although in truth, her grandmother had never tried to mask her disappointment in her only granddaughter. Delilah entered the cluttered living room. It was hard to say what exactly it was cluttered with. There weren't any books or old newspapers lying around—neither her mother nor her grandmother ever read anything other than fashion magazines—and the room was certainly clean enough. It was just full of *stuff*. Lace doilies were everywhere— on top of the tan sofa, the brown leather chair, the television, the end tables on either side of the sofa. The latest issue of *Vogue* lay beside a small stack of *In Shape* magazines across the glass coffee table in the middle of the room. A glass-doored, mahogany cabinet stood in one corner of the room, next to a grandfather clock that hadn't worked in years. The cabinet was filled with dishes made of Depression glass in translucent pink and green, as well as Grandma Rose's collection of old china figurines. Her grandmother called them antiques; her mother called them garbage. She confided to Delilah she was going to throw everything out—"the whole kit and caboodle," she liked to say—as soon as Grandma Rose passed on.

Kerri always said "passed on" instead of "died." She also said things like "kick the bucket" and "bite the dust," although never in front of Grandma Rose, who considered such irreverent expressions sacrilegious. Delilah knew Kerri put up with her mother's ill temper and demanding ways because she hoped to inherit all her money when she died. Whoops, Delilah thought. Make that "passed on." She might have laughed had Grandma Rose not been sitting there looking as if she'd just stumbled onto a nest of sleeping serpents.

Was that a metaphor? Alliteration? Maybe both. Something else to ask Mrs. Crosbie about.

"How are you doin', Grandma Rose?" Delilah asked now, approaching with caution. Her grandmother sat at the edge of the sofa's middle seat, her swollen feet stuffed into tatty pink slippers that barely touched the floor, her large, masculine hands entwined in her lap. Her hair was colored a deep auburn red, although the gray at her hairline betrayed her need for a touch-up. Her face was round, her features coarse, her brown eyes cold and unforgiving. Weren't grandmothers supposed to be soft and kind? Weren't they supposed to welcome you home with open arms and freshly baked cookies?

"How do you think I'm doing?" came her grandmother's response. "I'm worried sick."

"I'm sure Mom'll be home any minute," Delilah said, although she was sure of no such thing. What was her mother doing anyway? Why hadn't she called? "She hasn't phoned?"

"If she'd phoned, would I be so worried?"

"I guess not." Delilah let out a deep breath and tried not to let her annoyance show. She tried to tell herself her grandmother was snapping at her because she was worried about her daughter, but in truth, snapping was her grandmother's normal way of communicating. No wonder Kerri took every opportunity to be elsewhere. No wonder she was in no hurry to get home. No wonder she spent so much time at her computer when she *was* home, preferring the quiet of Internet chat rooms to the noise of real people. If someone snapped at you online, you could simply snap them off.

"I thought it was her when I heard a car pull up."

"That was Sheriff Weber's car. He gave me a lift home from Chester's."

"Too bad," Rose said. "You could use the exercise."

Delilah forced her lips into a smile as she headed for the kitchen. "Can I get you anything, Grandma? Some Coke or some juice?"

Rose shook her head. "No. And you shouldn't have any either. Do you have any idea how much sugar is contained in one glass of Coke? And they say orange juice is just as bad. Did you know that?"

"I think you've told me that, yes." At least five hundred times, Delilah added silently, stepping into the small kitchen and opening the fridge, stretching for a can of Coke near the back.

"Stick with water," her grandmother advised, as if she were standing right behind her. "They say you should drink at least eight glasses of water a day. Did you know that?"

"That's an awful lot of water," Delilah said, releasing the can's metal tab. A rush of fizzy gas burst into the air, tickling the bottom of Delilah's nose. She raised the can to her lips, took a long, satisfying gulp.

"Foolish girl," Rose muttered, loud enough to be heard.

"You sure you don't want anything? I think there's some ice cream left."

"Lord, no. They say you shouldn't eat anything after seven o'clock."

"Who's they?" Delilah returned to the living room, clutching her can of Coke with grim determination, and plopped herself down on the brown leather chair. It made a great whooshing sound, as if groaning under her weight.

"Everybody says it," Rose said, as if this were answer enough. "It's common knowledge. And be careful with that Coke. If you spill it—"

"I won't spill it."

"—you clean it up," her grandmother continued, as if she hadn't spoken.

The two women sat in silence for several seconds.

"So, how is Sheriff Weber?"

"Fine."

"What was he doing at Chester's?"

"Having a beer."

"I take it his wife wasn't with him?"

Delilah shook her head. "He was there on business."

"Business?" Her grandmother raised one thin eyebrow.

"Liana Martin's missing."

"What?"

"Liana Martin. A girl in my class. She's missing."

"Judy Martin's daughter?"

"I guess."

"Beautiful woman. She was runner-up for Miss America once, you know."

"I don't think it was Miss America—"

"What do you mean, her daughter's missing?" her grandmother interrupted.

"Apparently she didn't come home last night, and nobody's seen her since yesterday afternoon."

It took several seconds for the full impact of that statement to sink in. "What does the sheriff think happened to her?"

"He doesn't know."

"She probably just ran off," Rose said dismissively, although she sounded less than convinced. "Why did you tell me that?" she demanded seconds later. "Can't you see I'm worried enough as it is?"

"Don't worry, Grandma. I'm sure Liana will turn up."

"I'm not worried about *her*, for God's sake. I'm worried about your mother. If there's some maniac out there—"

"Whoa, Grandma Rose. Who said anything about a maniac?"

"I have a bad feeling about this."

"You're starting to scare me."

"What have you got to be scared about? Even a maniac would have more sense than to mess with you."

Tears instantly filled Delilah's eyes. So now she was so repulsive even a maniac wouldn't touch her. She raised the can of Coke to her lips, didn't lower it again until the can was empty. By then her tears were gone. She stood up. "Would you like me to put on the TV, Grandma?"

"No. There's never anything on the damn thing. Maybe you should go out again. Have another look around."

"I'm tired, Grandma. Besides, Mom's probably with Dr. Crosbie."

"No. He has his kids tonight. You don't think she's been in an accident, do you? Your mother's not the best driver in the world, you know."

"I think someone would have phoned." Where *was* her mother? Why *hadn't* she called? "Why don't you get ready for bed, Grandma. It's late and—"

"—and your mother's not home. And a young girl is missing.

And how am I supposed to get any sleep until I know she's safe and sound?"

"You'll make yourself sick," Delilah warned, although she didn't believe it. Her grandmother was a force of nature. She was indestructible. She'd survive Armageddon. Grandma Rose and the cockroaches. Sounded like a good name for a band.

"You can get ready for bed, if you'd like," her grandmother was saying. "You don't have to keep me company."

"I don't want to leave you alone."

"That's all right. I'm used to it."

Delilah rolled her eyes toward the ceiling as she approached the sofa and leaned forward to give her grandmother a kiss on her dry, flaky forehead. Was it her imagination or did her grandmother flinch at her touch? "Sheriff Weber said to call him if Mom wasn't back by midnight," she said as she walked from the room.

"Midnight?" Rose repeated, as if it were a four-letter word. *"Midnight?"*

The angry epithet followed Delilah up the stairs and bounced off the pale pink walls of her bedroom. She sank down on her narrow twin bed, the white-and-pink-flowered comforter billowing up around her wide hips. Pink broadloom covered the floor; pink-and-white-checkered curtains framed the window overlooking the street; a pink lampshade sat atop a delicate white lamp that itself sat atop a white dresser, the dresser hand-painted with pink flowers. It was the ultimate little girl's room, Delilah thought. No cliché had been forgotten or left out. And it didn't matter that its occupant had long ago outgrown the doll-size bed and lost interest in the plush, stuffed animals lining the bookshelves. What mattered was the dream of feminine perfection. What mattered was the ideal.

Except Delilah was as far from the ideal of feminine perfection as a girl could get. Even as a child, she'd fallen short of the room's expectations. While she'd weighed only a puny six pounds at birth and was a pretty average-sized toddler, her weight had begun to climb in the years following her mother's second divorce and had continued its steady ascent, reaching a peak of 163 pounds over the Christmas holidays. While, at five feet five inches tall, this was more than enough to label her as heavy, it was hardly enough to qualify as obese.

She glanced toward the window, her gaze falling to the computer on her desk. Her classmates regularly posted such horrible things about her on their websites. They called her names and made vile, lewd comments about her sexuality. Joey Balfour was the worst. And Greg Watt. To think she'd once thought Greg kind of sweet. One day, when she'd worn a new blouse to class, he'd actually told her she looked nice. That simple statement had kept her afloat for weeks. She'd replayed the compliment endlessly in her head—*You look nice. You look nice. You look nice*—until eventually the words became warped and indistinct, like a CD that's been played too many times. At any rate, those words had long since been replaced by others.

Her mother was always telling her she had such a pretty face, and her mother was right, Delilah decided, pushing herself off her bed and examining her perversely delicate features in the full-length, freestanding mirror standing next to the closet. "All you'd have to lose is thirty pounds," she heard her mother whisper in her ear. "Thirty pounds. *Thirty pounds,*" Delilah repeated in her grandmother's incredulous voice.

But she knew even thirty pounds wouldn't be sufficient to satisfy Grandma Rose. She could swear off Coca-Colas and stop eating after seven o'clock at night, and maybe she'd drop thirty, even forty, pounds, and it still wouldn't be enough where her grandmother was concerned. She thought of the fashion magazines her mother gobbled up as avidly as some people read their Bible, of those skinny girls with sunken eyes and swollen lips who filled the glossy pages. They all looked alike. You couldn't tell one from the other. Was that what her grandmother wanted?

It's what *I* want, Delilah acknowledged sadly. To look like everyone else. To *be* like everyone else. To be invisible. She almost laughed. In a strange way, that's exactly what she was. For all her bulk, nobody really saw her.

If only she had someone she could share things with. A close friend. Or a sister. She'd always longed for a sister, despite the stories her mother used to tell about her own childhood, the constant rivalry with her siblings for their mother's approval, how Grandma Rose was a master at playing one girl off the other. "Be grateful you're an only child," her mother used to say.

Where *was* her mother? She'd left the house around four-thirty to go to the drugstore, and now it was closing in on ten o'clock. Maybe Grandma Rose was right. Maybe there'd been an accident. Maybe she should start calling all the hospitals in the greater area. Maybe she should go back outside, keep looking.

The phone rang.

"Can you get that?" her grandmother called from downstairs.

Delilah raced down the stairs to the kitchen and reached the phone in the middle of its fourth ring, hoping the caller hadn't already hung up. Grandma Rose was in the next room, for God's sake, and she wasn't paralyzed, Delilah was thinking as she lifted the receiver to her ear, prayed to hear her mother's voice. "Hello?"

"Delilah," the voice on the other end said flatly.

Delilah knew who it was immediately. His voice was as intimidating as the rest of him. "Mr. Hamilton," she replied. Had her mother come into Chester's after she'd left? Was she there now? Was there some sort of problem?

"I saw you here earlier," Cal Hamilton was saying, "but you left before I had a chance to talk to you."

"Who is it, Delilah?" Her grandmother appeared in the doorway. "Is it your mother?"

Delilah shook her head. "It's Mr. Hamilton," she whispered. "Is everything all right, Mr. Hamilton? Is my mother—"

"I was hoping you could stop by on Saturday afternoon and keep my wife company for a few hours," he interrupted, as if she hadn't been speaking. "I have to be somewhere, and you know how Fiona hates to be alone."

"Of course," Delilah said, although she knew no such thing. In previous visits to the Hamilton home, Fiona had barely said two words to her. It was like babysitting an infant, she thought, and more than a little creepy. She would have said no, except that Mr. Hamilton insisted on paying her twenty dollars an hour. "He wants me to come over Saturday," she began, hanging up the phone, but her grandmother had already turned her back.

They heard a car pull into the driveway. Delilah closed her eyes, said a silent prayer.

"Hi, everybody," Kerri called as the front door opened. "Anybody home?"

Delilah released a deep sigh of relief. Her mother was home. She was safe. She hadn't been in an accident. No maniac had snatched her. And it didn't matter that she'd been gone for almost six hours, or that she hadn't told anyone where she was or called to say she wouldn't be home for dinner. What mattered was that she was home.

"Where the hell have you been?" Rose bellowed, marching back into the living room. "We've been worried sick."

"Don't be silly," Kerri told her mother, waving bloodred fingernails in the air impatiently. She was wearing tight, red-and-white-checked capri pants and a white halter sweater, her nipples prominent beneath the fine wool. Long, platinum hair fell in loose curls around her shoulders. Red toenails peeked out between the straps of her red sandals. The sandals sported skinny, four-inch heels. "I told you I might be a while." She dangled a large, brown shopping bag from her other hand. "Don't be mad at me. I come bearing gifts."

"Where've you been?" Delilah asked.

"Bloomingdale's," Kerri purred seductively, reaching into the brown bag.

Bloomingdale's? Delilah repeated silently. The nearest Bloomingdale's was in Fort Lauderdale. "You went to Fort Lauderdale?"

"I wanted to get my girl something nice to wear." She pulled a beautiful blue cotton sweater out of the bag and pressed it against her enormous chest.

Delilah thought she'd never seen a sweater so beautiful. "It's gorgeous." She reached for it eagerly, examined the designer label.

"I don't suppose you remembered my heart pills," Rose said.

"Of course I remembered your pills." Kerri ferreted around in her red leather purse for the pills, tossed the small, plastic container at her mother.

"Good thing I didn't need these right away."

"You're welcome," Kerri said.

Delilah checked the size of the jersey, felt a sharp stab of disappointment pierce her heart. "I think this might be too small," she whispered, hating the whine in her voice.

"It's a medium."

"I'm a large."

Her mother smiled. "Well, then, this will give you some incentive to lose a few pounds." She reached for the sweater. "I guess I could wear it in the meantime. So, what's been happening? I miss anything?"

"Liana Martin's disappeared," Delilah told her, watching her mother return the sweater to the shopping bag.

"What do you mean, she disappeared?"

"According to Sheriff Weber, nobody's seen her since yesterday afternoon."

"When were you talking to Sheriff Weber?"

"Tonight. Grandma Rose was worried, so she sent me out to look for you."

"Honestly, Mother," Kerri said. "I told you I might be a while."

"You didn't tell me you were going to Fort Lauderdale."

"It was spur-of-the-moment. Besides, I'm a big girl. I don't have to tell you every little thing."

"I don't like those pants on you," Rose said in response.

"I should call Sheriff Weber," Delilah interjected. "Tell him you're home."

"Why don't you like these pants?"

"They make you look hippy," Rose said.

"They do?"

"I think they look nice," Delilah said, coming to her mother's defense.

"Look who's talking," said Rose.

"So, how is Sheriff Weber these days?" Kerri asked. "Was he worried about me?"

"Worried enough to tell me to call him if you weren't home by midnight. I think he was worried because of Liana."

"Liana?"

"Liana Martin," Delilah reminded her.

"Judy Martin's daughter," Rose added. "Now *that's* a beautiful woman."

"You think so?" Kerri asked. "I always thought she was kind of ordinary. What do you think, sweetie?"

"I think you're prettier," Delilah said.

"Thank you, angel. See, Mom? Delilah thinks I'm prettier than Judy Martin."

"Is that a blemish on your chin?" Rose asked.

"What? Where?" Kerri raced toward the small mirror in the hall. "What are you talking about? I don't see anything."

Delilah shook her head and walked into the kitchen. They'd be at it all night, she was thinking as she picked up the phone and called Sheriff Weber, told him her mother was back, and that she was sorry for any unnecessary worry she might have caused him. "Any news about Liana?" Delilah asked.

"Nothing," he told her.

"Nothing," she repeated, hearing her mother and grandmother bickering in the next room. She listened for several seconds, then she grabbed a spoon from a nearby drawer, pulled a white wicker chair up to the freezer, and ate directly from the container what was left of the ice cream.

6

KILLER'S JOURNAL

Memory's an amazing thing. Our memories shape us, providing a backdrop for our daily lives, a context for our actions, a rationale for our sometimes dubious decisions. Who we are today is inextricably woven through with memories of who we were yesterday, and the days before that—threads in the same complicated tapestry—highlighting episodes from our pasts, spotlighting our latest disappointments and first loves. Or hates. Pull one thread, and watch the whole thing unravel. Who did what to whom, what foods we've developed a taste for, the multiple skills we've mastered or failed at, the movies we've enjoyed, the music we've danced to, what movie stars we admire, what politicians we don't—if we can't remember such seemingly ordinary details, well, then, who are we?

It's our memories that define us. Without them, we have no identity. We have nothing.

Those pathetic old creatures who've outlived their memories and now sit screaming in lonely hospital corridors, scream not with the pain of their deteriorating organs, but rather with the agony of no longer knowing who they are, their ears searching their cries for the sound of a familiar voice. They live in the eternal present, and it's hell on earth.

I never want to get like that. If I ever develop Alzheimer's or some such awful thing, I hope someone will just take a gun to my head and shoot me. I'm sure Liana Martin would be only too happy to oblige. Although sadly, she won't be around to get the chance.

You know how people are always telling you to live for today. I think that's good advice. Remember yesterday, but live for today. Yes, sir, that's my new motto. I should have told that to Liana Martin. Live for today, Liana. Because what's done is done, and you never know what's going to happen next.

Well, no. That's not exactly true. Because I know. I know what's going to happen next.

They also say you should live every day as if it might be your last. More good advice, although I don't think Liana Martin would have appreciated hearing it.

I wonder what memories she conjured up last night. If they were happy or sad. If they were of any comfort to her.

Personally, I have a lot of memories that aren't so pleasant. Like the time I was five years old and almost drowned in a neighbor's pool. It was Robby Warren's birthday and my mother was busy and couldn't go, so my aunt, who was always hanging around, took me over there. I can still see her flirting with Robby Warren's father as she stuffed her face with party sandwiches at the side of the pool. Don't you love party sandwiches? I do. They're solid butter, for God's sake. That's what makes them so tasty.

But anyway, it was real hot and there were tons of kids there, splashing around in the pool, making lots of noise. And the adults were gossiping and drinking, and I don't think it was just lemonade they were drinking either, although my aunt always disputed this. Just as she always disputed my memory of what happened next. She insisted there was no way I could remember the events of that after- noon because I was so young. She said kids that age can't remember things, especially in the kind of detail I can. I stopped trying to con- vince her. She had her truth. I have mine. And she had to live with herself after all.

But she was such a liar. She insisted she was watching me the whole time I was in the water. She claimed she only turned her head for half a second, and when she looked back, I was gone, so she assumed I'd gotten out of the pool and gone inside the house to use the facilities. That's what she always called the bathroom—the facilities. She thought it sounded more genteel. I used to drive her crazy when I'd say, "I'm going to the toilet." I can still see her cringe. Which, of course, is why I said it.

Anyway, she said she went inside the house looking for me. I think she went inside to find Robby Warren's father. But, of course, she said she just ran into him when she was looking for me, like it was my fault she was talking to him, and, yes, maybe she got distracted for a couple of seconds, but no more than that, although others said I was under the water for at least a minute. I don't know. The truth is I don't remember exactly how long I was under that water. I just remember one of the other kids jostling me, and me losing my footing, and then slipping below the surface. I remember the taste of the chlorine in my mouth, the slimy feel of the tepid water as it slid inside my nostrils. I remember my hair lifting away from my scalp and floating around my head, like seaweed. Then nothing.

And suddenly there were voices, and crying, and lots of shouting. And then fists pounding on my chest, and my head being tilted back, my lips being pried open, and someone squeezing my nose and blowing air into my mouth. I remember gagging and spitting water into somebody's lap. And I remember my aunt crying hysterically, carrying on so much, in fact, that there was actually talk of sending *her* to the hospital, then allowing Robby Warren's father to calm her down—he had to take her into the house for a good ten minutes—before she was composed enough to take me home. Then she told my mother how it was all *my* fault I almost drowned, and my mother took *her* side and scolded *me,* shaking me until I was dizzy, screaming that I had to be more careful, not because I'd almost died, but because I'd ruined Robby Warren's birthday party, and we'd probably never be invited back there again. And now what were we going to do in the summer when it got really hot, and there was nowhere to go to cool off?

Actually, the Warren family moved away that summer, and another family moved in, and they were old, and they didn't swim, so they had the pool taken out. Then they paved the whole backyard over, took out all the grass and everything, because old Mr. Jackes said he didn't have the strength to keep picking the weeds out all the time. I volunteered to do it—actually my mother volunteered me to do it—but Mr. Jackes said his wife was allergic to grass anyway, so it was better to just put in pavement. I liked Mr. Jackes. He was big and gruff and usually upset about something. But at least you always knew where you stood with him. There was no pretense. No bullshit. How often can you say that about anybody?

After he died, we went over to pay our respects to Mrs. Jackes. My mother brought a peanut-butter cake she'd bought in the grocery store and was trying to pass off as her own. Didn't matter. As it turned out, Mrs. Jackes was allergic to peanuts as well as grass, and she couldn't eat it, couldn't even have the damn thing in the house. So we took it back home and ate the whole thing all by ourselves. My mother claimed there was no way Mrs. Jackes was allergic to all those things, and that she was just being snooty, thinking she was better than us. We never talked to her again. A few months later, her kids moved her into an old-age home in Hallandale, and eventually a new family bought the house, dug up the backyard, and put in another pool. But they never invited us over.

I never did learn how to swim. Not well anyway. Water always terrified me. Still does. The way it sneaks up on you.

I guess I'm a bit like water, in that respect.

Another unpleasant memory: yearly vacations in Pompano Beach with my mother, grandparents, and of course my aunt. These holidays were always torture for me, largely because of my aunt, who seemed to go out of her way to make my life a living hell. No wonder her husband died before his fortieth birthday. He was probably grateful for whatever it was that killed him. Only way he could get away from that witch was to die.

After that near-drowning incident in my childhood, my aunt had decided it was essential that I learn how to swim. She didn't want to find me floating facedown in the motel pool, she told anyone who would listen—she loved an audience—and she didn't want to have to worry about me being swept into the ocean by some deadly undertow. She just wanted to relax and enjoy her holiday, she repeated ad nauseam. So, almost as soon as we got to the motel, she arranged for this lifeguard I saw her cuddling up to, to coach me. He tried. I'll give him credit for that. And ultimately, he did manage to keep me afloat for more than three seconds at a time, although I never progressed much beyond the dog-paddle stage. He explained that there was no way I could swim properly without putting my head underwater, but I wasn't interested in swimming properly, I told him, and I refused.

This didn't stop my aunt, who never learned when to leave well enough alone. She just couldn't leave me to my own devices. She couldn't understand that someone might actually enjoy reading a book, for example. Or drawing a picture. No, like someone who relentlessly picks at a scab before the sore below has a chance to heal, she was constantly at me, arranging for long boat rides and deep-sea fishing expeditions that always made me sick to my stomach. For someone who claimed she was so terrified of seeing me drown, she made sure I spent an awful lot of time near the water.

One year, she insisted we all take up waterskiing, promising me it was easier than riding a bike, something else I had trouble with. I don't know what lapse in judgment made me believe her, or if I went along with it just to shut her up. Maybe it was that the other kids made it look so easy, so effortless, the way they flew across the water, occasionally letting go of the rope with one hand to wave at those of us watching enviously from the shore, their heads thrown back in exhilaration, but I decided to give it a try. I climbed into the skis, my life jacket tied securely around my chest, and waited for the boat to take off. "Hang on," I can still hear my aunt shouting as I struggled to stand up. Well, I barely managed to rise above a crouch before the speed of the motorboat tore the rope painfully from my hands, and I found myself in the salty water, my fingers scratching wildly at the air as the life jacket pressed painfully against my chin, and the skis shot from my feet to the water's surface. "You big baby," my aunt said, laughing, pulling me onto the deck. She laughed all the way back to the motel.

It was more or less the same thing every year. She never let up. "Where are you, scaredy-cat?" she'd call, searching for me under the wide red and blue umbrellas scattered along the beach. "Come on, chicken liver. It's your turn. Show us what you're made of." It got to the point where I dreaded family vacations even more than a trip to the dentist.

The family outings stopped only when my aunt died.

Boohoo.

I can't get into that now. I don't have time. I've wasted too much time already reminiscing, and I have so much to do. Everything got thrown off schedule, and I have to figure out what to do before it gets too light. Even now, I've only got a small window of opportunity. I can't risk anyone discovering I'm gone. News of Liana Martin's disappearance has swept through Torrance like a snake through grass. Everyone's really spooked.

It'll be even worse once they discover her body.

Did I mention Liana is dead?

Did I mention that my whole schedule got thrown out of whack?

Out of whack—don't you just love that expression?

I'd planned to come back last night, have my fun, finish her off, then bury her in a swamp a few miles away. But you know what they say about best-laid plans. An idiot by the name of Ray Sutter, who'd had a few too many beers, went and drove his car into the ditch at the side of the road right near where I'd buried Candy, and there was a tow truck trying to get it out, and a bunch of people standing around. (This qualifies as entertainment in a town like Torrance.) Good thing nobody noticed me. But then, they never do. Good thing, too, that I did such a good job of burying Candy's body—"If you're going to do something, do it right," my aunt used to say—although nobody was looking much past the old, beat-up, red Chevy that was stuck deep in the muck. I left and came back later, after the tow truck had done its job and everyone had left the scene. I could still hear echoes of Ray Sutter's wife yelling through the darkness, saying *I told you so* over and over. Personally, I'm with her on this one. I think people who drive drunk are a disgrace as well as a danger. I think they should be shot.

At any rate, Candy's grave was undisturbed. She continues to rest in peace. Or should I say pieces? I'm sure the worms and other assorted critters have gotten to her by now.

Anyway, I wasn't able to get back to the house until almost four in the morning. Liana had been sleeping, and she was semidelirious at this point, which took away a bit of the fun. But at first, I think she was actually relieved to see me. Her eyes widened. Her lips formed the tiniest hint of a smile. I wasn't some deformed, slavering monster in dirty, blood-spattered clothes. (Did Liana Martin's parents never read her the fable of the wolf in sheep's clothing? As I recall, it didn't end too well for the sheep.) No, I was neat and I was presentable, and I was speaking softly, trying to get her to calm down, assuring her that if she cooperated with me, we might be able to find a way out of this uncomfortable predicament.

Of course, she hadn't had anything to eat or drink in over thirty-six hours—note to self: remember to keep several bottles of water in the room, in case unexpected delays happen again—and she was weak and really quite desperate, and therefore willing to go along with whatever I suggested, if she thought it would save her life. She still considered this a possibility, the human brain having a seemingly limitless capacity to delude itself. We believe what we want to believe, regardless of the evidence before us, and Liana Martin wanted desperately to believe she was going to escape with her life.

So, I gave her some water and half a sandwich I'd stored in the fridge, and she gobbled it up—remember what I said last time about the wonders of the human appetite?—and we sat and we talked. About all sorts of things. She told me about her parents, how her dad was some big shot with the Bank of America, and her mom was a former beauty queen who'd given up her crown, as it were, when she got married. And how she had two younger brothers, and one younger sister, Meredith, who was only six, and who was already a major pain in the butt because everyone was always telling her how beautiful she was, and their mother was always hauling her all over the state to compete in beauty contests. In fact, her parents had gone to Tampa with her sister for a pageant and might not even know she was missing.

And then she started to cry.

Like I said—girls always cry.

And her eyes were so puffy, you could hardly see them. And they were red because she'd been rubbing them. Which was too bad, because her eyes were probably Liana's best feature. The mascara staining her cheeks didn't help her appearance much either. She looked bruised and bloated, and I hadn't even touched her yet. I asked her why she didn't use waterproof mascara and she just looked at me like I was crazy.

What day was it? she wanted to know. How long had she been here?

I told her it was very early Wednesday morning, that she'd been here since Monday afternoon. I told her that all I wanted was to be alone with her, and that I'd let her go after we spent some "quality time" together. Isn't that what the experts are always talking about—quality time? Tell me things about yourself, I urged, sitting down beside her on the cot, things you've never told anyone else before. She was reluctant at first, but after a while she started opening up. She said she had the same insecurities as everybody else, that she didn't think she was as pretty as her mother or younger sister, that she thought her nose was too big and her thighs were too heavy, and that she was always afraid of not measuring up. Not measuring up to what? I asked, and she shrugged her shoulders, like she didn't even know what she was supposed to measure up to. She talked about her boyfriend, Peter, and said how everybody thought they looked so cute together, but that she really wasn't sure she liked him that much anymore because he wasn't very nice to her. Then she cried some more.

I asked her if she and Peter had sex. She said it was none of my business. I didn't like that, and my displeasure must have registered on my face, because she changed her mind immediately, told me that, yes, of course, they had sex. I asked what sort of things they did together, if she used her mouth. She said sometimes she did, but confessed that Peter never had. I told her that was too bad. A real man would use his mouth, I said.

I asked her if Peter was the first guy she'd had sex with. She shook her head. I asked her about losing her virginity, who it had been with, what it was like, if it had been painful, if she had any regrets.

That's when she started getting really agitated. I could see it in her eyes, the way they kept darting back and forth, as if now that she'd had something to eat and drink and she had a bit of strength back, she was considering making a run for it, although where she thought she could run is anybody's guess. But she answered me anyway. I think she was afraid of what would happen if we stopped talking, so she indulged me. She told me she was thirteen when she lost her virginity, and that yes, it had hurt, although only for a few seconds, and, no, she had no regrets. The boy was the son of their next-door neighbors, and his name was Eric Weir. He was sixteen, and he joined the army right after his high school graduation. He was promptly sent to Afghanistan, where he was killed by a sniper's bullet a week before he was scheduled to come home. I asked her if she ever thought about him. She said no, although she was sorry he was dead. I asked her how many guys she'd slept with. She said four. Then she tried to ask me a few questions, but I wouldn't answer. I told her I was the one asking the questions.

That's when she got mad, started hurling insults at me—I don't remember what they were exactly—I tend to block out some of the more objectionable things people say—and I decided there was nothing to be gained from keeping her alive any longer. I pulled out my gun. That's when she really lost it. God, you could hardly make out a thing she was saying because she was talking so fast. Suddenly, she turned into that other girl, Candy, offering to do whatever I wanted her to. "You want me to use my mouth?" she asked, among other obscenities I won't bother mentioning. That's when I hit her on the side of her face with the end of my gun. The wallop knocked her flat on her back and caused her left cheek to blow up like a balloon. It was amazing how fast that damn thing swelled up. You can't really see it now because the bullet tore off half her head, but trust me, it was impressive.

It may sound strange, especially in light of what happened, but I think Liana was actually starting to like me, at least a little. Although what did I just say about the brain's limitless capacity for self-delusion? So maybe she was just playing along, trying to placate me, trying to get me to see her as a human being, and not as some inanimate object, so that I'd take pity on her and let her go. I read somewhere that if you're ever held hostage, that's what you should try to do, and maybe Liana had read the same article. Apparently it's harder to kill people once you see them as human.

Funny how few people qualify.

Anyway, water under the bridge. Isn't that what they say? Is that a metaphor? At least that one makes sense. It means what's done is done. And Liana is dead and gone. Well, no, not gone, which is precisely the problem. One I have to solve in relatively short order. I have to get back before everybody wakes up. I'm not usually up at this hour of the morning, and people remember small inconsistencies in behavior. I don't want a minor scheduling snafu coming back to haunt me.

So, it's important I get Liana's body into the ground now. I can't risk leaving her here. Even with these cooler temperatures, it won't take long before her body starts to decay. Already, invisible maggots are munching on her torn flesh, and I don't even want to think about what condition she'll be in by the end of the day. So, I'll just wrap her up and carry her to the trunk of my car, find a suitable spot to dump her. MOVE, BITCH, indeed.

I'm sure the powers-that-be will be organizing a search party in just a few more hours. Maybe I'll sign up. Do my civic duty. Maybe I'll even be the one to "discover" her body. Eureka! Over here. I think I found something.

Of course I can't let them find her too quickly. What would be the fun in that? But maybe later in the week. In time to spoil everybody's weekend.

Something to look forward to.

chapter seven

"Tough day?"

Sandy stood in the doorway to Rita Hensen's tiny office, watching as the school nurse finished applying a bandage to the bleeding finger of a ninth-grade student, a girl whom somebody had either accidentally or purposely pushed into a locker earlier in the afternoon. The fourteen-year-old freshman already towered above the forty-three-year-old nurse, who stood barely five feet tall in her platform shoes, and whose open face and ready smile made you want to smile back even when you didn't feel like it. "Tough week," Sandy said, as the young girl climbed down off the examining table and left the room, tossing a barely audible "Thank you" in Rita's direction.

"Like they say—thank God it's Friday." Rita Hensen ushered Sandy inside the closet-sized room and closed the door. "Feel like going out later for a drink?"

"Can't."

"You sure? You look like you could use a good transfusion."

"Speaking of which, did Victor Drummond ever stop by to see you?"

"Count Dracula? No. Was he supposed to?"

Sandy shook her head in dismay. Victor hadn't been back in class since Tuesday, when she'd sent him to see Rita about that gash on his arm. Greg Watt had also been absent the last few days, although Peter Arlington had returned. And of course, Liana Martin was still missing. Which was especially worrisome. From everything Sandy knew about Liana, which admittedly wasn't much—the girl rarely had anything particularly cogent to contribute in class—Liana had never struck her as either bold or adventurous enough to take off on her own without a word to anyone. For all her telegraphed bravado—MOVE, BITCH—Liana had always struck Sandy as a rather conventional, small-town girl. She'd play at being tough and independent for a few years, then morph gradually and gracefully into her mother, marrying young and reproducing future beauty queens with alarming speed and dexterity. If she had dreams of a life outside of Torrance, she wouldn't acknowledge them. They were dreams after all, and dreams had a way of bursting, like bubbles, in the hot, morning sun, then disappearing without a trace.

Like Liana Martin.

Where was she? What had happened to her?

Sheriff Weber had organized a search party, and the whole town, it seemed, had been out looking for her since Wednesday morning without any success. Sandy was thinking of signing up herself this weekend, if Liana still hadn't materialized. Was it possible some lunatic had snatched her? Sandy mulled over the rumors sweeping through the town, then shook her head. More likely, Liana had been seduced by some mysterious Internet suitor, and she was just too embarrassed to come back home. Stranger things have happened, Sandy thought with disgust, picturing her husband with Kerri Franklin.

"What's the matter?" Rita asked.

"Just thinking about Liana Martin," Sandy said. Not quite a lie. Just not the whole truth.

"I sure hope she's all right." Rita stared absently at the eye chart on the far wall.

Sandy wondered how Liana's mother was holding up and tried to imagine what she would do if it were her daughter, Megan, who was missing. She shook the thought away with a deliberate toss of her head. It was simply too awful to contemplate.

"How's Brian been acting in class?" Rita suddenly inquired about her son. "He seem all right to you?"

Although Rita had tried to keep her tone casual, Sandy heard the worry in her voice. "He's fine. We were talking about metaphors the other day, and he was very insightful."

"My son was insightful?"

Sandy nodded. "I think he has quite deep thoughts."

"Oh, God."

"You have a problem with deep thoughts?"

"You want to know what he said to me?" Rita asked by way of an answer.

Sandy wasn't at all sure she wanted to hear what Rita's son had said. "What'd he say?" she asked anyway.

"He hasn't been sleeping well lately. He's been waking up in the middle of the night, wandering around the house, going outside for a cigarette. I've tried to get him to stop smoking, but . . ." Rita shrugged. "Anyway, the other night I confronted him, begged him to tell me what was bothering him, and he said . . ." She paused, released a deep sigh. "He said he didn't think there was enough oxygen in the air."

Sandy might have laughed had it not been for the tears creeping into Rita's big, hazel eyes. "There isn't enough oxygen in the air?"

"He worries about stuff like that," Rita explained, hands lifting helplessly into the air as her gaze drifted back to the eye chart on the far wall. "I just get so scared. Because of his dad. You know."

Sandy knew that Rita's husband, also named Brian, had suffered from depression for many years before finally committing suicide three years ago. Rumor had it that it was the son who'd discovered his father's lifeless body hanging from the shower rod when he returned home from school one day, although Rita had never publicly confirmed this.

"Boys around this age," Rita continued, "you have to be so careful."

Sandy nodded, thinking of her own son. At sixteen, Tim was still the painfully shy boy he'd been for as long as she could remember. Slow to smile, slower to laugh, even slower to make friends, he was the classic outsider: sensitive, introverted, artistic. He preferred classical music to pop, live theater to movies, and books to basketball. Which made him a natural target for boys like Greg Watt and Joey Balfour. Luckily, because he was the teacher's son, and because his sister was as pretty and popular as she was smart and outgoing, the bullies had seen fit to leave him alone.

For now.

"They say that if you can keep them alive until they reach thirty, you've got a chance," Rita said.

"He'll be fine," Sandy told her, in an effort to reassure them both. She stretched for a tissue from the box on the counter and dabbed gently at Rita's eyes.

"Anyway, enough of that. I really think you should come out with me tonight. I have a date, and I'm a little nervous."

"You have a date?"

"A blind one. Ever done that?"

"Just once. When I was fifteen. It was a disaster."

"Then you understand why I'm so nervous, and you'll come with me," Rita said.

"I can't go with you."

"Why not?"

"Because it's *your* date. It would be too weird."

"So I'll call him and ask if he has a friend. . . ."

"No."

"Ah, come on—"

"I remind you I'm a married woman."

"In name only."

"It's only been a few weeks since Ian moved out."

"Seven weeks," Rita corrected.

"Seven, yes." Sandy was beginning to regret stopping by. "Anyway, there's been no talk of divorce. We're not even legally separated."

"What do you mean? You still haven't seen a lawyer?"

"Not yet."

"Well, what's keeping you? I gave you the name of that guy in Miami, the one who handled my cousin's divorce. She said he was excellent."

"When do I have time to go to Miami?"

"Make time."

"I will."

"When?"

"When I have time," Sandy snapped.

"Sorry," Rita apologized. "I think I just crossed a line."

"It's not that I don't appreciate your concern. . . ."

"It's just that you'd like me to mind my own business."

Sandy shrugged. "Ian's coming over tonight to take the kids out to dinner."

"All the more reason for you not to be there."

"I can't." After all, it was possible that Ian's real reason for coming over wasn't just to see the kids. It was possible he wanted to see her as well, that Liana Martin's disappearance had made him realize what a complete idiot he'd been these last few months, and that he now realized how important his family was to him. There was no way he could be happy with his inflatable human doll. He'd been having one of those midlife crises he used to belittle in others. He'd gone temporarily insane. Yes, that was as good a description as any, Sandy decided. But now he'd come back to his senses, and all five of those senses were telling him that you didn't just walk out on a marriage of almost twenty years, you didn't leave the woman you'd married when she was all of nineteen, a woman who'd borne you two children when she was little more than a child herself, while at the same time earning her teaching degree and putting you through medical school. You didn't desert a woman like that. You didn't leave a woman of substance for a woman of silicone.

Except, of course, that's exactly what he'd done.

"So, who arranged this blind date?" Sandy asked, hoping to change the subject.

"I'd rather not say."

"What do you mean, you'd rather not say?"

"You'll get mad."

"Why would I get mad?"

"Because I've already used up all your goodwill."

"Tell me."

"I met him on the Internet."

"Don't tell me that."

"I told you you'd get mad."

"I'm not mad. I'm dumbfounded. I'm speechless."

"Would that it were so."

"How could you agree to go out with a man you met in a chat room? Especially now, when a young girl is missing."

"It wasn't in a chat room. I swear. It was one of those online dating services. I signed up a couple of weeks ago."

"What? Why?"

"Because it's been three years since Brian died. Because I'm lonely. Because I'm forty-three, and five feet no inches tall and weigh a hundred and twenty pounds, and I live in Torrance, where I've already slept with all the eligible men, and even a few who weren't so eligible, and I just thought it would be nice to meet someone who can talk about something other than tractors and grapefruits. And you should see, Sandy, since I signed up, I've had e-mails from men all over the country, and some of them sound pretty great."

"If they're so great, what are they doing looking for women online? Forget I asked that," Sandy said, recalling how handsome Ian had looked the morning he'd announced he was leaving her for Kerri Franklin. "Okay. So, this guy you're going out with tonight . . ."

"His name is Jack Whittaker, he's fifty-five, his wife died last year of leukemia, and he has his own business selling widgets, or something like that. Anyway, he's from Palm Beach, and he's stopping in Torrance on his way to visit friends in Naples, and he suggested having a drink and getting to know each other."

"So why would you want me hanging around?"

"Well, because of Liana Martin." Rita smiled her sweetest smile, the one that brought dimples to her cheeks. "In case this guy turns out to be a psycho killer or something."

Sandy laughed. She and Rita had clicked from the moment they'd met in the staff room at the start of the school year, and she'd quickly become Sandy's closest friend in Torrance, the only good thing that had happened to her since leaving Rochester.

"Actually, what I was thinking was that we could already be having drinks when he shows up. And then, if I decide I like him, I could give you some signal, you know, like I could wink or toss my head." Rita tossed her head back, then grabbed her neck in pain.

"No, I can't do that. He'll think I'm having a spasm. But, anyway," she continued over Sandy's laughter. "How about I'll scratch the side of my nose, and you'll beat a hasty retreat?"

"I can't."

"Yes, you can."

"Maybe next time."

"How about next week? I'm meeting this guy in Fort Lauderdale."

"You're kidding."

"I told you, this service is terrific. What do you say? If he has a friend . . ."

"Maybe."

"Great."

"I said, maybe." Sandy shook her head, half in amazement, half in admiration. "Do I not make myself clear?"

"'It's a new world, Goldie,'" Rita said.

"What?"

"It's a line from *Fiddler on the Roof.*"

"You're quoting *Fiddler on the Roof*?"

"The drama department did a production of it last year. It was fabulous. You wouldn't believe what good voices some of these kids have. Count Dracula, for instance. He played the tailor, and he was fabulous."

Sandy tried picturing Victor Drummond as a poor Russian tailor. Surprisingly, it wasn't much of a stretch. "Can I use your phone?"

Rita pulled the old-fashioned, black telephone across the tall counter, almost knocking over several bottles full of cotton balls and tongue depressors. "I can't believe you don't have a cell phone."

"I hate the damn things."

"You need one. What if there's an emergency?"

"Someone can always find me."

"What if *you're* the one having the emergency?"

Sandy ignored the question. "You have a home number for the Drummonds?"

Rita crossed to the small desk wedged into the corner under the window overlooking a side alleyway. She pulled the school directory out of the top drawer and quickly located the Drummonds' phone number. "What are you going to say to them?"

"First of all, are they aware their son hasn't been in class since Tuesday?" Sandy said as she dialed. "And that he has a rather nasty cut on his arm? And that I think someone should have a look at it."

"A psychiatrist?"

"That would be my recommendation."

"Which I'm sure will be welcomed with open arms," Rita said.

The phone rang five times before the Drummonds' answering service clicked on, and Sandy left a short message asking them to contact her as soon as possible. "Nobody's ever home for these kids. No wonder they're so lost."

"You're saying we should all give up our jobs and be stay-at-home moms?"

Sandy shrugged. "I don't know what I'm saying."

"Kerri Franklin is a stay-at-home mom."

Sandy rolled her eyes toward the recessed ceiling. "Obviously there are no easy answers."

"Sure I can't change your mind about going out with me later?"

"My cue to leave." Sandy got off her chair, opened the door, and stepped into the hall. "Be careful tonight."

"I will."

"I mean it. If you have even a twinge that something's not right with this guy, you get out of there immediately."

"Yes, Mother." Rita stuck her thumbs in her ears and wiggled her fingers.

Sandy laughed and closed the door. Seconds later, she was marching down the wide corridor of the main building toward the exit, inhaling the smells inherent to all high school corridors: perspiration, dirty socks, and cloying cologne, mouthwash, and disinfectant. The concrete walls were painted a dull yellow and covered with framed photographs of students who'd attended classes over the twelve years the school had been in operation. There were pictures of the football, baseball, and basketball teams, as well as a glass cabinet devoted to their trophies. There were also photographs of the short-lived chess club, the shorter-lived debating club, and a whole section devoted to the drama department's various productions. Sandy scanned the pictures for one of Victor Drummond, but the only photos from *Fiddler on the Roof* were of Tanya McGovern, Amber Weber, and Liana Martin as the milkman's three marriage-able daughters, and one of Greg Watt as their beleaguered father, Tevye. Truly, the Fiddler from Hell, Sandy thought, her eyes return-ing to the picture of Liana Martin.

Where was she anyway? What had happened to her?

"So what do you think?" a voice asked from somewhere behind her, and Sandy jumped. "Sorry, didn't mean to scare you."

Sandy spun around to find Gordon Lipsman, the school drama teacher, watching her through disconcertingly crossed brown eyes, a grin spreading from one side of his big, square head to the other. "Gordon. I didn't hear you."

"Sneakers." He indicated his shoes with a lowering of his eyes. "Very sneaky."

Sandy forced a smile onto her lips. Gordon Lipsman was one of those people whose eagerness to be liked made it almost impossible to comply, the kind of person who gave stereotypes a bad name. He spoke with an ersatz British accent that was more annoying than authentic, because as far as anyone knew, he'd been born right here in Torrance. Now forty, he'd never married and, until recently, had been living with his widowed mother and more than a dozen cats in a house on the outskirts of town. His mother had died in February, resulting in a mild emotional meltdown and the postponement of this year's musical offering, reputed to be *Kiss Me, Kate.*

"I see you've been admiring our Drama Hall of Fame."

"It's very impressive." Sandy began a silent count of the cat hairs covering Gordon Lipsman's blue-and-white-striped seersucker jacket. And was that ketchup on his sleeve? "I had no idea Greg Watt could sing."

"Oh, he's full of surprises, that one. He was an absolutely splen-did Tevye, although his father didn't take too kindly to the idea of his son wasting valuable time onstage when he thought he should be out working. He made it quite clear that Greg was not to partake in any more such flights of fancy. Although I don't think those were his exact words."

"I'll bet."

"I've been hoping to change his mind. He'd make a wonderful Petruchio, don't you think?"

"I didn't realize the drama department was doing a show this year."

"Oh, yes. My mother, may she rest in peace, would have wanted it that way. And *Kiss Me, Kate* was one of her favorite shows." Tears filled his eyes, only to vanish in the very next breath. "I was thinking of your daughter for the lead. She's such a pretty girl. Do you think she might be interested in trying out?"

"I guess you'd have to ask her."

"I was hoping you might intercede on my behalf."

"I'll mention it to Megan," Sandy offered. Then: "What about Tim?" Getting involved with the drama club might be just the ticket for drawing Tim out of his shell, she was thinking. He liked the theater, and maybe getting a part in the school play would help boost his confidence. Why hadn't she thought of this before?

"Tim?"

"My son."

"Oh, yes. Tim. Quiet chap. Doesn't say much. Well, I'm afraid he's all wrong for Petruchio, of course, especially if Megan agrees to play Kate. It wouldn't do for a brother and sister to play lovers, after all. No, that would never do. But there are lots of smaller roles. He's certainly welcome to audition on Monday." Surprisingly strong hands fluttered nervously to his face, landing at the tip of his bulbous nose.

Sandy thought of the caricature that Greg had drawn of the man, the way it had captured his essence in a few crude strokes. "Is that blood?" she asked suddenly.

The color immediately drained from the drama teacher's face. "Blood? Where?"

"On your sleeve."

Gordon stared at the stain on his cuff, then slowly raised it to his nose, sniffing at the offending blotch as if he were an animal. "Spaghetti sauce," he pronounced after a moment's pause. He held out his arm, as if offering her a chance to confirm his assessment.

"I should get going." Sandy turned to leave, tripping over her feet in an effort to avoid Gordon Lipsman's outstretched hand, and collapsing into him. They stumbled toward the wall in a kind of free-floating, spastic tango. "I'm so sorry," she said when she was finally able to extricate herself from his clammy grasp. She turned, surreptitiously brushing away several stray cat hairs that had jumped from his jacket to her pink cotton blouse. Joey Balfour was standing about twenty feet away, a cell phone in his hand, extended toward her.

For one crazy second, Sandy thought that a call had come through for her on his line, and that he was offering his phone to her as a courtesy. Only when he ran laughing down the corridor did Sandy realize what had actually happened.

By the time she got home, a photograph of her in Gordon Lipsman's arms was plastered all over the Internet.

chapter eight

"Megan, Tim. Your father's here."

Megan glanced slowly toward her locked bedroom door, then looked back at the unsettling image filling her computer screen.

A familiar high school corridor. A man in a blue-and-white-striped seersucker suit. A woman in a conservative, pink cotton blouse and navy, pleated skirt. His arm encircling her waist. Her back arched, her head thrown back. What could actually pass as a smile on her face. It looked as if they were dancing, Megan thought, although her mother had insisted they most assuredly were not. Megan grinned. While it was decidedly strange to see her mother in the arms of anyone other than her father—and especially the unlikely arms of dorky Mr. Lipsman—she thought her mother looked pretty, and she welcomed even the hint of a smile on her lips. It had been several months since Megan had seen her mother's face register anything but sorrow. Although that was better than nothing at all. Often there was just this vacant stare. Megan knew when she saw that faraway gaze in her mother's eyes that she was peering into the past, trying to figure out how everything had gone so terribly wrong.

It wasn't your fault, Megan wanted to assure her in those moments, but she didn't because, deep down, she thought it might be her mother's fault after all. If only she'd dressed a little sexier or made some effort to tame her unruly curls. If only she hadn't been so eager to voice her opinions, if she'd interrupted her husband less, gone along more. Maybe then he wouldn't have spent so much time in distant chat rooms. Maybe he wouldn't have connected with Kerri Franklin. Maybe they'd still be a family.

Megan sank back in her chair, blew a series of imaginary bubbles with her lips. Her mother had mentioned that Mr. Lipsman wanted her to try out for the part of Kate in the school's upcoming production of *Kiss Me, Kate,* and maybe she would. Especially if Greg Watt, who she thought was really cute, could be persuaded to play Petruchio.

Her mother would undoubtedly be horrified at the knowledge she found anything even remotely attractive about Greg Watt and question Megan's sanity. A girl her age had better things to think about than boys like that, she'd say.

And what could Megan offer in her defense? That she alone was able to see through the bad-boy facade, that she saw beyond the arrogant set of his jaw and the cockiness of his strut, that she liked the way his shoulders mimicked the calculated swagger of his hips, the way his jeans hugged his slender thighs and tight rear end? Oh, sure. That would go over well.

Tight *rear end*? Megan repeated silently, feeling herself blush. Who her age talked like that? Still, she could barely bring herself to *think* the word *ass,* let alone say it out loud. She was her mother's daughter in that regard, she thought with a sigh, deciding that if her mother hadn't been such a prude, such a stickler for decorum and proper language, her father might now be sitting in front of the TV, eating a sandwich, and not waiting impatiently by the front door to take her and her brother out for dinner. She turned back to the computer, pressed a key, and watched the image of her mother in Mr. Lipsman's arms instantly evaporate. Would that it were so easy to make problems disappear in real life, she thought, reluctantly picturing Liana Martin.

Where was she? What had happened to her? It had been four days since anyone had seen her.

She returned to the main menu, clicked onto MSN, pressed several more keys, then sank back in the chair, refusing to dwell on unpleasant possibilities, preferring instead to imagine herself in Greg's strong, muscular arms. He'd protect her from harm, she thought, feeling his imaginary warm breath wrapping around her own, his lips lowering slowly, teasingly, to hers. The kiss that followed was both urgent and tender, as his hands gently cupped her face, just like they did it in the movies, Megan thought, wondering if Greg had ever entertained such fantasies about her.

It wasn't entirely out of the question, she decided. Even though she was a year younger and a grade behind him, and they'd never actually had a real conversation—"Hi. How ya doin'?" was about the extent of it—she'd noticed the way he looked at her each time she passed him in the halls. And once, just a couple of weeks ago, she'd caught him staring at her in the cafeteria, and he'd turned away quickly, obviously embarrassed at having been discovered, and tossed a piece of cake across the table at his friend Joey Balfour, who retaliated by hurling the contents of his cup of Coke in Greg's face, and the next thing you knew, there was this major food fight going on, and both Joey and Greg ended up being suspended for two days. Megan shook her head, wondering why Greg bothered wasting his time with a cretin like Joey Balfour. She knew that although they might appear similar on the surface, Greg was nothing at all like Joey, who was crass and crude and just plain dumb. Greg was none of those things. Deep down, he was sweet and smart and sensitive. Not to mention sexy. Megan was determined to get to know him better. And if it took auditioning for a part in Mr. Lipsman's next musical extravaganza, well, then, that's exactly what she'd do.

She glanced back at the computer screen and frowned, as she did each time she saw the message that had been sitting there since Tuesday.

SAMPSONS BEWARE! DELILAH'S ON THE PROWL!

DELILAH's out **CRUISING** the halls, and she's bigger and better than ever. Well, maybe not better. But certainly **BIGGER**. And she's got a new handle—no, not a love handle, although we bet she has lots of those too**!!!!** It's a nickname. And it's not **DELI**. Although we kind of like that one. No, this handle comes courtesy of **MRS. SANDRA CROSBIE,**
(Torrance's own **Ginger Rogers!**
Check out that hilarious picture of her and **Loony Lipsman**)

the jilted wife of that handsome scoundrel, **Dr. Ian,** who you know from previous e-mails is currently making house calls to Torrance's resident **sex pot,**
     KERRI FRANKLIN,
who just happens to be **DELILAH's** mother.
     THAT'S ONE HOT MAMA!!!!
We'd sure love to get into those short shorts she wears.
And speaking of shorts, **DELILAH's** new handle is really **SHORT.**
So short, it's just an initial. **DEE.**
That's **BIG D,** to you, fella.
     You're from BIG D, my oh, yes!!!!!!
Remember that old song? My Daddy used to sing it all the time. Except there's a new set of lyrics now. They go—**DRUM ROLL, PLEASE!!!!!**—(and get out your dancing shoes, Mrs. Crosbie)—

Yes, I'm in Deli, where every hole is smelly,
And the boys all eat her after class,
Yes, you're in Big D, my oh, yes,
I said, Big D, stinky hole, double chin, and a big fat ass!!!!!!

"Oh, God," Megan whispered. Not only had that awful posting been there for days, but now someone had added to it. *Torrance's own Ginger Rogers! Check out that hilarious picture of her and Loony Lipsman. Get out your dancing shoes, Mrs. Crosbie!*

What was the matter with her mother anyway? Why did she always have to inject herself into the middle of everything? Wasn't it bad enough she was a teacher at Megan's school, so that Megan never had any privacy, never any space of her own? When she went to school, there was her mother; when she came home, *there* was her mother. And if her continual presence wasn't bad enough, did she always have to go sticking her nose into everyone else's business? Didn't she realize that every time she butted in where she didn't belong, she exposed her family, her *daughter,* to potential ridicule? Was that why her father left? Because he couldn't stand the fact she was always *around*?

Megan could still hear her mother ranting when she'd seen the picture upon her return from school this afternoon: *There was no such thing as privacy anymore! Someone was always lurking with a camera! Some idiot was always eager to post the picture! The bullies were everywhere!* That quickly segued into another of her familiar tirades: *If you didn't conform to their rigid dictates of what was acceptable, you didn't survive! If a girl didn't fit into a size two pair of jeans, if she didn't wear her hair long and straight, if her nose wasn't small and upturned, and her breasts large and round, she was a loser. Or worse, an object of scorn and ridicule, like Delilah Franklin. If a boy lacked six-pack abs, if he dressed differently, like Victor Drummond, or was quiet and sensitive, like Brian Hensen, then he was a weirdo, or worse, a homosexual. Since when had the standard of beauty become so narrow? Since when had young people become so intolerant? Why did everybody feel compelled to look and sound exactly the same? Why was everyone struggling so hard to be someone else? Were they so unhappy with who they really were?*

Megan pushed her long, straight hair away from her perfect, oval face. She understood the pain behind her mother's outrage, discerned the echo of the question she was really asking: *How could your father leave me for a woman like Kerri Franklin?* But while Megan recognized the truth of her mother's remarks, sometimes she wished she would just shut up.

Still, she couldn't help but feel sorry for Delilah, who'd never done anything to deserve the kind of abuse that was regularly heaped on her. Of course, the girl did nothing to help her cause. Surely she could go on a diet, try to lose a few pounds, make more of an effort to fit in. Was she really as oblivious as she seemed?

Megan suddenly wondered what would happen if, God forbid, her father actually married Kerri Franklin. That would make Delilah her stepsister, and could she possibly imagine a worse fate? She'd worked so hard all year to make friends, and she was so close to being accepted into Torrance High's inner circle, to being an actual confidante of Tanya and Ginger and Liana—where *was* Liana?—and to think of the ridicule she'd be subjected to if she and Delilah were actually to become family! No, it was too awful to contemplate.

Just as it was too awful to think about what might have happened to Liana. The school was rife with rumors: she'd run off because she was pregnant and Peter had refused to marry her; she'd died during a botched abortion; she'd eloped with some older guy she'd met on the Internet; she'd been raped and strangled by a sexual predator, her body dismembered and scattered throughout the Everglades, like pieces of discarded, stale bread.

Megan closed her eyes, her fingers absently scrolling down the screen, as she tried not to picture Liana Martin's voluptuous body serving as alligator fodder. When she looked up again, the offensive e-mail had been replaced by another posting.

UPDATED FAGGOT LIST
Victor Drummond
Perry Falco
Jason O'Malley
Brian Hensen
Tommy Butterfield
Donny Slaven
Rick Leone
Ron Williams
Tim Crosbie

"Oh, God," Megan said again, seeing her brother's name at the bottom of the list. She felt instantly sick to her stomach. Had Tim seen it? Of course he'd seen it. "The whole school has seen it," she whispered.

There was a knock on her bedroom door. "Megan," her mother said. "Didn't you hear me call you? I said your father is waiting."

Megan felt her mother lingering on the other side of the door. "I'll be right there."

A second's hesitation, then: "Well, hurry up."

"Two minutes." Surely her mother and father could spend a few minutes alone together without fighting.

Her mother would have a fit when she saw this latest posting, Megan knew, snapping off the computer without going through the appropriate channels, and hearing it groan in protest. She'd assume

Joey and Greg were responsible, just as they were responsible for posting that stupid picture of her and Mr. Lipsman, and that awful song about Delilah. Were they?

Well, obviously Joey. But surely not Greg.

Megan pushed herself away from her desk, grabbed her purse from the floor, and threw it across the shoulder of her white-and-green-striped cotton dress, then opened the door to her bedroom. She could hear her parents arguing even before she reached the living room.

"He looks fine," her mother was saying.

"He looks like a punk," her father countered. "I told you I was taking them to the golf club for dinner. You know that means a shirt and tie."

"How would I know that? I've never been there."

Silence. Megan could almost see the pinched expression on her mother's face and her father's fists clenching at his sides. The golf club was an especially thorny issue between them. Her father had argued that the cost of joining the expensive club was justified because of all the professional contacts he'd make, and her mother had acquiesced against her better judgment. The ink was barely dry on his deposit check when he'd moved out.

Now her father stood in the middle of the small, rectangular-shaped living room, shaking his head sadly, as if he were a helpless bystander at the scene of a horrific accident, trying to come to terms with what he'd just witnessed.

"Daddy, hi," Megan said in greeting. She forced one reluctant foot in front of the other, praying there'd be no further eruptions.

"Sweetheart." Her father's arms surrounded her, and she felt her body stiffen involuntarily, her own arms freezing at her sides. She knew her mother was watching them. If she returned her father's embrace, as she was desperate to do, her mother would take it as a betrayal, and her mother had been hurt enough. "You look gorgeous, as usual."

Megan smiled her appreciation. So do you, she was thinking. Her father was one of those biologically blessed men who actually got better looking with age. He had a full head of thick, dark blond hair, eyes that were clear and blue, and lips that were soft and inviting. Women had always found him attractive. Even her friends considered him "hot." "Are we ready to go?" Megan asked. "I'm starving." She wasn't, but she thought it was probably a good idea to leave as soon as possible.

"No, we aren't ready," her father said. "Your brother has to change first."

Megan glanced across the room to where her brother, Tim, sat slumped across the red velvet sofa, his sneaker-clad feet dangling over the armrest, kicking at the air as if it were water. Tim had their mother's mouth and their father's eyes, while his hair was an interesting combination of both—the same dark blond as Ian's, but with Sandy's stubborn curl. He was wearing a crinkled white shirt and baggy khaki pants. Tall, gangly, still not comfortable in his skin, he had no concept of his budding good looks, and therefore no idea of his potential power. "How about your blue blazer?" Megan suggested. "And that tie Grandma sent you for Christmas." She bit down hard on her lower lip and closed her eyes, although not fast enough to miss the flash of pain that streaked across her mother's face. Her mother had been disappointed when they'd been unable to travel back north for the holidays because of Ian's "busy schedule."

("Busy schedule, my rear end," she'd railed later.)

"Ties are stupid," Tim muttered.

"They're a sign of respect."

Megan knew her brother was thinking, Who are you to talk about respect? She also knew he'd never say such a thing out loud. "Hurry up, Tim," she said before anyone could say anything. "I'm starving."

With exaggerated slowness, Tim arched his legs into the air and lowered his feet to the cold tile floor.

The floor—another sore point, Megan thought. Her mother had wanted to tear up the ugly, white squares and replace them with warmer, bleached-hardwood strips, but her father had insisted any renovations to the unimaginative, three-bedroom bungalow would have to wait another year. Now her father lived in a brand-new, modern apartment near the downtown core. Megan had chosen not to tell her mother about the apartment's bleached-hardwood floors.

Tim finally managed to push himself off the sofa. He slouched from the room as if he were swimming through molasses.

"And comb your hair," Ian called after him.

"His hair is fine," Sandy said.

"It's way too long," Ian argued. "He looks like a punk."

Megan felt her stomach cramp. "Can we just go?"

"What do you think, Megan?" her father asked.

"I think his hair looks nice," Megan replied truthfully, avoiding his gaze.

"Of course you do." Her father's voice radiated disappointment, as if she'd let him down.

Megan stared at the now empty sofa, thinking that none of the furniture they'd brought down from Rochester suited the house. Everything was too dark, too heavy. It made the house feel claustrophobic. It made you want to get out.

She glanced at her mother, then quickly turned away, hoping to hide her sudden anger. What was the matter with the woman, for God's sake? Didn't she want her husband to come back? Why was she wearing that stupid purple sweat suit that made her look hippy, even though she wasn't? Was she purposely trying to look as unattractive as possible? Couldn't she have worn some makeup, or at the very least a little lipstick?

"Sweetheart?" her mother asked. "Are you okay?"

"Fine," Megan said. "Just hungry."

"Tim," her father called. "What's taking you so long? Get your ass out here."

Megan winced, felt her mother do the same.

"It takes a few minutes to put on a tie," her mother reminded him.

"Not if he did it more often."

"Then we probably should have stayed in New York" came the pointed retort.

Megan held her breath.

"Actually, I've been giving some thought to moving back to Rochester once the school year is over," her mother continued.

She had? Her mother hadn't said anything about that before.

"What are you talking about?" her father asked.

"Well, there's really nothing to keep me here."

Was this some sort of ploy on her mother's part? Did she think that by threatening to go back to New York, she'd force her husband to come to his senses?

"What are you talking about?" he repeated. "What about the kids?"

"They'll come with me."

Is that what she wanted? Megan asked herself. To go back to Rochester? Now, when she was growing more popular every day, when it was only a matter of time before Greg asked her out?

"What about your job?" Ian was demanding. "Don't you have a contract?"

"I'm sure that, given the circumstances, they'll understand."

"The circumstances," Ian repeated knowingly. "So this is about getting back at me."

"This isn't about you."

"You don't think you're being just a little bit selfish?"

"Excuse me? *I'm* being selfish?"

Tim came bounding back into the room, jacket half-on, half-off, tie dangling, no doubt propelled into action by the sound of his parents bickering. "Okay. I'm ready."

"You aren't taking my kids anywhere," Ian said, as if Tim were invisible.

"I think they're old enough to make that decision for themselves."

What would she decide? Megan wondered. Did she really want to start in at yet another new school, to leave her friends, leave Greg?

Her cell phone sounded inside her purse. Megan reached inside the canvas bag, lifted the phone to her ear. She heard the voice on the other end of the line, tried to absorb the words she was hearing even as she felt the color drain from her face.

"What is it?" her mother asked, instantly at her side.

Megan dropped the phone back into her bag, stared at her mother through a thickening layer of tears. "That was Ginger Perchak," she whispered. "They found Liana."

Her mother stared at her without speaking, as if she already knew what was coming next.

Megan sank into the nearest chair, stared out the front window at the growing darkness. "She's dead."

chapter nine

Sheriff John Weber sat in his police cruiser at the side of the quiet residential street and tried to keep the bile from rising in his throat. In his almost twenty years in law enforcement he'd seen a lot of terrible things—the mangled corpses of car-accident victims, the slashed torsos of drunken brawlers, the swollen faces of battered wives that punctuated each and every Super Bowl. He'd seen victims of hunting accidents, of sexual assault, of willful neglect and abuse. He'd seen teenagers puke their guts out, wives cry their eyes out, children scream their lungs out. He thought he'd seen it all.

But he'd never seen anything like this.

A young girl, a girl he knew personally, a girl whose parents he knew well, a girl on the cusp of womanhood, her whole life ahead of her, with everything to live for—God, was there no cliché that didn't apply?—lying in a makeshift grave about half a mile from where Ray Sutter had run his car off the road a few days earlier, half her head blown away by a bullet fired from close range, the rest of her feasted on by animals and insects, so that it would take the coroner days, if not weeks, to determine what other tortures she might have endured. Hell, he wouldn't have known for sure it even *was* Liana Martin if Greg Watt hadn't recognized the MOVE, BITCH T-shirt she was wearing. Greg had been part of a group of kids organized and led by Cal Hamilton, who'd reported it was either Greg or Joey Balfour who'd first come upon the suspicious mound of earth. John made a mental note to have his deputies question all three again later in greater detail, as well as Ray Sutter. (Could there have been a more sinister reason he'd been on that particular road earlier in the week?) Of course, the girl's T-shirt was filthy and covered with blood, and he couldn't imagine a lady like Judy Martin allowing her daughter to own such a thing, let alone wear it to school. He thought of Amber. Parents have so little control over their children's lives once they reach a certain age, he realized, fighting back the threat of tears.

Not the first time tonight he'd had to struggle to keep his emotions in check.

But even the sight of Liana's rotting corpse hadn't been as awful as Judy Martin's beautiful face contorting with grief when she heard the news of her daughter's grisly death. John glanced over at the Martins' neat white bungalow, with its black-and-white-striped awnings and ornately carved front door. He saw himself approaching the house, watched the front door open as he was reaching for the bell, saw the look of hope in Judy's eyes turn quickly to trepidation and then, even faster, to horror, as she digested the terrible news. John doubted he'd ever be able to shake the image of the poor woman falling back against her husband's chest, as if she'd been pushed, her body caving in against itself, like a collapsible chair. He saw her knees give way and her body sink to the floor like an anchor, her husband's impotent arms unable to sustain her fragile weight. He heard the silent scream emanating from her twisted mouth. In seconds, he'd watched her age a lifetime. Her daughter's lifetime, he realized now, with a sad shake of his head.

It had been almost an hour since they'd found Liana's body. He'd had to call the coroner for Broward County, make the necessary arrangements, and wait until the girl's body had been taken away before driving over to the Martins' house, convinced they'd no doubt have heard the news already. As soon as Liana's body had been pulled from that shallow grave, he'd seen members of the search party mumbling into their cell phones.

But as it turned out, nobody had wanted to be the first person to break the news to Howard and Judy Martin. They'd left that dubious honor to him. He'd also had to tell the Martins that, as yet, there were no suspects in their daughter's death, although now that this was officially a murder investigation and no longer just a case of a teenager gone missing, his department would have to revisit every aspect of the case. That meant reinterviewing all Liana's friends and acquaintances, as well as her fellow students and teachers—what was it Delilah had said about her science teacher having a thing for young girls?—and other, more peripheral characters like Cal Hamilton and Ray Sutter. John knew he'd probably end up talking to the whole town personally before the week was up. His shoulders slumped. He was tired already.

He checked his watch, thinking he'd better start right away—the mayor had already phoned twice since Liana's body had been unearthed, the first time stating his desire to be kept in the loop, the second time wondering whether they should call in the FBI. John had reminded the mayor that he knew more about the citizens of Torrance than any FBI agent could and urged him to be patient. "I'll handle this," he told him, deciding to go home and grab a shower. He couldn't very well invite himself into people's homes wearing the same sweat-and-dirt-stained uniform he'd been wearing when he pulled Liana out of the soggy ground.

"You can't wear that," he could almost hear Pauline sneer, remembering that they were supposed to be having dinner tonight with Sarah and Frank Lawrence. But surely even Pauline would understand these were rather special circumstances. And anyway, he had no appetite. Even the thought of food made him queasy.

John sat in silence for several minutes, trying not to think of the missing girl from neighboring Hendry County. Was it possible Candy Abbot was buried somewhere out there as well, that a madman was on the loose in south-central Florida, preying on young girls, and that this was only the beginning? John buried his head in his hands, refusing to speculate. He was too old for this, he thought, too old and too ill-equipped. True, he had a staff of smart and eager young deputies, and they would work their tails off trying to find Liana's killer, but they had even less experience in this sort of thing than he did. He also had an ambitious young mayor staring over his shoulder and second-guessing his every move. Hell, it had barely been an hour and the man was already wondering what was taking so long.

John knew that in real life, unlike on TV, despite how focused and intense the police effort, most crimes were solved by the perpetrator turning himself in or, more likely, by accident. John shook his head, intent on ridding his mind of all unwanted thoughts and images before heading for home.

The first thing he intended to do when he got there was tell his daughter how much he loved her.

The house was dark.

John heard the television blasting as soon as he stepped inside the front door. This was nothing new. The television was always blasting. "Pauline?" he called out, flipping on the light switch by the door to illuminate the so-called great room—a living-dining-family room combined. Other than its size, there was nothing particularly "great" about it. It was a simple rectangle, and the furniture, while expensive enough, was altogether too floral for his taste. They rarely used the dining room. And John couldn't remember the last time the three of them had sat on the awkward leather sectional in the arbitrarily designated family area to watch TV together.

He glanced toward Amber's bedroom at the front of the house, but her door was closed, and there was nothing—no sounds, no sliver of light—to indicate she was inside. "Amber?" he called, wondering if she'd heard the news about Liana, and hoping she hadn't gone out. "Amber? Amber, are you there?"

When she still didn't answer, he proceeded to the kitchen, dropping the large bag from McDonald's he'd picked up on his way home onto the gray granite countertop. The bag contained a Big Mac, several McChicken sandwiches, and three large orders of fries that he hoped would be enough to appease Pauline for having to cancel their dinner plans, and while he'd had the girl behind the counter double-bag the order and then place the whole thing in a larger plastic bag and knot it, not even that had been enough to keep the unmistakable odor from reaching his nose. *Eau de McDonald's,* he thought, and might have smiled had the circumstances been different.

"Pauline?" he called, louder this time, as he walked toward their bedroom at the back of the house. He doubted she could hear him over the noise of the TV, and wondered why he bothered. Pauline insisted that years of listening to loud music as a teenager had done significant damage to her eardrums, and she couldn't hear the TV unless it was played at top volume. But since she had no trouble hearing anything else, John secretly believed she did it to annoy him.

Sometimes, when he wanted to go to bed early and she was still watching one of her favorite programs—as far as he could determine, they were all her favorites—he'd have to sleep in the tiny guest bedroom at the front of the house. He didn't mind doing this, despite the fact that the bed was only a double as opposed to a king, and it wasn't as comfortable as the one in his own room. Still, he didn't have to share it, and the guest room was one of the few rooms in the house that didn't contain a TV. The other rooms all had television sets, including the kitchen and master bathroom. This wasn't his idea. He'd never been much of a TV watcher. Pauline sometimes accused him of being a snob, but the truth was even simpler than that: he had a hard time following most of the programs. As a child, he'd suffered from a mild form of attention deficit disorder, and he still found it difficult to focus on any one thing for any length of time. Probably not the best attribute for a man in his position, he thought. Luckily, his attention span had never been severely tested.

Until now.

"Pauline?" He entered the bedroom, his eyes moving back and forth between the image of a beautiful young woman with long blond hair and large full breasts as she bounced provocatively across the giant-screen TV, and the empty, unmade bed across from it. That the bed was unmade didn't surprise him. That Pauline wasn't in it did. Was it possible that Pauline had heard the news about Liana and, knowing that he'd probably be tied up for most of the night, already canceled their plans for dinner and taken Amber out, simply forgetting to turn off the television? "Pauline?" he said again, grabbing the remote control from the midst of the green-and-yellow floral sheets and snapping the damn thing off.

"What are you doing?" came the immediate response. "Don't do that."

John's head shot toward the hallway. "Pauline?"

"I'm watching that."

Pauline emerged from the walk-in closet off the hall between the bedroom and the bathroom, securing a gold loop earring as she walked. Her shoulder-length, chestnut-brown hair was pulled back into a bun at the nape of her neck, and she was wearing what appeared to be a new blue dress. At least John thought it was blue. He was color-blind, as well as having ADD, so it could have been black. And he assumed the dress was new because he couldn't recall having seen it before. Pauline always claimed that, for a deputy sheriff, he was alarmingly unobservant. He hadn't had the heart—or maybe it was the nerve—to tell her his professional faculties were actually highly astute, that despite his color blindness and ADD, his failure to notice things was largely confined to her.

Not that she wasn't an attractive woman—she was. At forty-three, she was tall and reasonably slender, with bright eyes and a smile that was as engaging as it was seldom seen.

"You're late," she said, grabbing the remote from his hand and clicking the television back on. "You'd better get out of those dirty clothes and into the shower. I told Sarah we'd meet them at seven-thirty and it's almost that now."

"You haven't heard?"

"Heard what?"

"About Liana."

Pauline said nothing, her attention momentarily diverted by what was happening on the TV. "Would you just look at that face," she directed, pointing at the screen. "She tries to tell people she hasn't had any work done, but who's she kidding? Any woman over fifty who doesn't have lines has had a face-lift."

"Pauline," John said, louder than he'd intended, causing Pauline's shoulders to stiffen. "We found Liana's body."

"Yes, I know." Pauline lowered her eyes to the ivory-carpeted floor. "*Mon Dieu*, you didn't take off your boots."

"My boots?"

"You're getting muck all over the carpet."

"You know about Liana?"

Another stiffening of her shoulders. A slight straightening of her back. "Sarah called to tell me about it twenty minutes ago."

"Then what the hell are you doing?"

"What do you mean, what am I doing? I'm getting dressed to go out." Her nose sniffed at the air. "Is that McDonald's I smell?"

John raised his voice higher to compete with the raised voices on the TV. "I brought you some McChicken sandwiches." This whole conversation was becoming surreal, as if he were an unwitting participant in one of those ghastly reality series his wife loved so much.

"Why would I want a McChicken sandwich when we're meeting Sarah and Frank for dinner?"

"Because we aren't meeting Sarah and Frank for dinner," he exploded, responding to the challenge in his wife's voice. "Because a young girl has been brutally murdered—"

"A young girl we barely knew—"

"We knew her."

"Barely."

"We know her parents."

"Who have always looked down their noses at us. Don't think they haven't."

"Howard and Judy Martin are—"

"—lovely people, I know. Spare me. They're total snobs, and the only time they ever have anything to do with you is when they need something."

"Their daughter has been murdered."

"Brutally, yes, I know. Tell me, is there any other way?"

"For God's sake, Pauline. Do you ever listen to yourself?"

"Don't make me out to be the villain here," she snapped. "I haven't done anything wrong. I'm sorry the poor girl is dead. I really am. But what can I do about it? Disappointing our friends by not going out to dinner isn't going to bring her back."

"I can't," John said, shaking his head in disbelief.

"What do you mean, you can't? Why not? What can you possibly hope to accomplish tonight?"

"I don't know. But I have to try."

"So you'll try after dinner. Don't you have a staff for this sort of thing?"

"They're already out there. Think about it, Pauline. How would it look for me to be eating in a restaurant when everyone else is working round the clock?"

"Since when have you cared about how things look?"

"That's not the point."

"You raised it," she reminded him.

"Sean Wilson's already on my back—"

"Sean Wilson's a little pipsqueak."

"He's the mayor, Pauline."

"Yes, the tiny, perfect mayor. I know. Please. You could squash him with your bare hands."

"The point is that I can't go out to dinner with Sarah and Frank," John reiterated. "The point is that I don't *want* to go out to dinner with Sarah and Frank, that I don't *want* to delegate this to my deputies. A young girl has been murdered, and it's *my* job to try to find out who did it."

"Oh, for God's sake," Pauline scoffed. "Her boyfriend probably did it."

"Her boyfriend?" Had Pauline heard something he hadn't? "Why do you say that?"

Pauline waved toward the TV. "Because it's always the boyfriend." She paused, uncertainty crossing her face for the first time. "Isn't it?"

"Well, we'll be looking into that possibility, of course, but . . ."

"But?"

John paused, weighing just how much to tell her. "I think we might have a lunatic on our hands."

"What?"

"This is just conjecture at this point, so you can't say anything to anyone. The last thing I want is to cause a panic."

"What are you talking about? What do you mean, a lunatic?"

"There's a second girl missing."

"What? Who?"

"A girl from Hendry County. No one we know."

"So we don't know her disappearance has anything to do with Liana," Pauline said.

"That's right."

"Lots of girls disappear."

"Yes, they do."

"She probably just ran away."

"Probably."

"Why would you even think there's a connection?" Pauline asked, a hint of anger in her voice.

"Instinct," John answered honestly.

"Have your instincts never been wrong?"

"They've been wrong many times."

"But you don't think they're wrong this time," Pauline said, reading the look in his eyes.

"No. I don't."

"*Merde.*" Pauline sank to the bed, kicked off her open-toed shoes. "You think we're dealing with a serial killer?" she asked after a pause.

"I don't know."

"Do you think it could be someone we know?"

"I don't know."

"Do you know *anything*?"

"I know that until we find Liana's killer, we have to be extra-cautious, especially where Amber is concerned. Where is she anyway?"

"What do you mean, where is she? Isn't she here?"

Immediately, John tore from the room, hurling himself through the kitchen and great room toward Amber's bedroom at the front of the house. He pushed open the door to her room with his open palm.

A thin figure bolted from the bed.

"Amber! Thank God." John crossed over to the bed in two quick strides and took the young girl in his arms. "Didn't you hear me call you?"

"No," Amber said, pulling out of his grasp and tucking her long brown hair behind her ears. "I lay down for a few minutes. I guess I fell asleep." She glanced from her father to her mother. "What's the matter?"

"We thought you might have gone out," John said.

"So?"

"We don't want you going anywhere without telling us. At least for the time being. And definitely not alone."

Amber stared at her father through eyes that looked as if someone had colored in two round circles with an emerald-green crayon. "Because of what happened to Liana?"

"You know?" Pauline asked from the doorway.

"It was on the Internet."

John's head snapped toward the computer on Amber's desk. "What? Where?"

"On my e-mail."

"Who sent you an e-mail about this?"

"Who didn't?" came Amber's response.

"Show me," her father directed.

Wordlessly, Amber approached the computer on the desk across from her bed. She was wearing a pair of baggy khaki pants and an oversize, checkered shirt. *If she really thinks her body looks so damn good this skinny, why does she take such great pains to hide it?* John wondered as Amber accessed her e-mails.

There were thirteen of them, all saying essentially the same thing—Liana Martin was dead. She'd been shot through the head. It was gross, GROSS, **GROSS**. One e-mail—unsigned—said she'd been raped and decapitated. Another, sent by Victor Drummond, said Liana's body had been drained of blood.

"That's rubbish," John told his daughter, who'd returned to her queen-size bed.

"I thought so," Amber said. "But she was shot, right? Shot through the head?"

"Yes."

"Was she raped?"

"We don't know yet."

"And you don't know who did it?"

"Your father thinks it might be the work of a serial killer," Pauline said.

"Pauline, for God's sake!" John exclaimed. "What did I say about . . . ?"

"A serial killer?" Amber's green eyes grew even wider, accentuating the gauntness of her cheeks.

"There's another girl missing," Pauline continued, ignoring her husband's disapproval.

"What?"

"Okay, this stops right here and now," John said firmly. "You aren't to repeat this to anyone. Do you understand?" But even as he spoke the words, he knew it was hopeless. Already he could hear Pauline gossiping on the phone to her friends. Already he could read the e-mails Amber would soon be posting on the Web.

"Of course," Pauline and Amber replied in unison. "*Oui.* Okay."

"It's just a theory at this point. There's nothing to be gained from getting people all riled up," he said. "But until we catch this guy, I don't want you going out anywhere alone. Is that clear?"

"What if you don't find him?" Amber asked.

John shook his head. He didn't have an answer for that one. "Just do me a favor and be extracareful, okay?"

Amber nodded.

"When you're not in class, you're at home. I'll drive you to school in the morning and Mom will pick you up."

"What?" Pauline said.

"There's auditions for the school play on Monday," Amber protested. "They're doing *Kiss Me, Kate,* and Mr. Lipsman wants me to audition for the part of Kate's sister, Bianca."

"All right," John agreed, after a nod from his wife. "As long as you're not alone. And call when the audition's over and you're ready to come home."

Amber shrugged her agreement.

"And eat something," John heard himself say. "You weigh two pounds, for God's sake. If somebody grabbed you, you wouldn't stand a chance."

Huge green orbs rolled toward the ceiling.

"Your father bought McDonald's," Pauline offered, and John felt strangely grateful for her support.

Amber stared at her parents as if they'd both suddenly stripped themselves of all their clothing and were standing naked before her. She looked appropriately horrified.

"There's a Big Mac, some McChicken sandwiches, and fries," John continued in spite of this.

"Are you kidding me?"

"Do I look like I'm kidding?"

"I don't eat meat. You know that."

"Then have the fries."

"I don't eat fried food."

"Just what *do* you eat?" John demanded angrily.

"John," Pauline warned.

"I eat lots of things."

"Like what? *What?*" he demanded, knowing this was the wrong tactic to take, but unable to stop himself. Rita Hensen, the school nurse he'd consulted when Amber's weight had dipped precariously low, had told him that eating disorders were almost impossible to treat until the girl was ready to do something about it herself, and even then, it was probably something she'd struggle with all her life. It was pointless to yell at her. Society had already done too good a job at bullying girls into believing that the ideal woman looked like a prepubescent boy.

And then there were the women on the opposite end of the spectrum, John thought. Women like Kerri Franklin, who looked more like plastic dolls than human beings.

Although he had to admit—he liked to look.

What the hell was wrong with everybody?

When had looking like a real woman ceased to be a viable option?

"I don't want to have this discussion," Amber said, lying down and pulling the covers over her head to signal an end to the conversation.

"Amber. . . ."

"John," his wife urged. "Leave it alone." She pushed him gently from the room.

John understood that the only thing Amber felt she could control was her weight. The world was a big and terrifying place, especially for girls on the verge of womanhood.

In light of what had happened to Liana Martin, he thought, who was he to disagree?

chapter ten

I heard you were the one who found Liana's body," Delilah said as Cal Hamilton ushered her inside the darkened bungalow. Outside it was a sunny and warm afternoon—the warmest Saturday this month, the radio announcer had proclaimed on the drive over—but inside the icy, air-conditioned house it might as well have been the middle of the night. Or so it seemed to Delilah, whose eyes took several seconds to adjust to the dramatic change in light. She tugged on the hem of her loose white shirt, self-conscious about the stubborn roll of flesh that spilled over the low-rise waistband of her jeans. She hated the jeans' uncompromising cut, the unflattering way they dissected her midriff, adding bumps to already unsightly bulges, emphasizing that which was already exaggerated enough. Why couldn't someone design clothes that actually fit real people—according to recent studies, more than half the population of the United States was significantly overweight—and not just the Amber Webers and Megan Crosbies of this world? When had the majority of purchasers become an undesirable demographic? Where was the sense in that?

Not that anything made much sense these days.

"Pretty grisly sight," Cal said as he led Delilah toward the kitchen at the back of the ultratidy, little house.

Delilah snuck a peek into the tomblike living room, where the furniture, like wary sentinels, stood guard. She wondered if anyone actually ever sat in the uncomfortable-looking, straight-backed sofa or high-backed wing chairs and hadn't been surprised, on previous visits, to find the lampshades still covered in plastic. At first she worried that it was dangerous to have plastic wrap so close to a lightbulb, but she quickly concluded that those bulbs were probably never turned on, so what difference did it make? Her mother claimed the plastic would eventually warp the shades, but Delilah doubted Cal Hamilton would notice. It was too dark.

In the kitchen, as in every room she'd seen, the blinds were pulled tight, although the sun had managed to slip between several uneven slats and was spraying rays of light, like lasers, across the mustard-colored ceramic tiles of the floor.

"What happened? Did you, like, step on her?" Delilah crossed over one beam of light, then came to an abrupt halt between two more when Cal stopped suddenly and spun around.

Cal Hamilton shook his mop of wavy blond hair, a derisive sound escaping the natural snarl of his lips. Clearly he found the question idiotic. "A couple of the boys saw a mound of earth they thought looked suspicious. We decided to check it out."

"And you found Liana?"

"No. We found the Pillsbury doughboy." Cal's voice dripped sarcasm and impatience in equal measures.

Immediately Delilah's eyes filled with tears. She lowered her canvas tote bag to the round kitchen table and stared at the floor, suddenly grateful for the oppressive darkness. As much as she'd grown used to—even inured to—the hateful taunts of her classmates, she'd never been good with sarcasm. It sliced through the folds of flesh between her ribs with the effortlessness and efficiency of a sharp blade aimed directly at her heart, especially when wielded by an adult. Even though Delilah didn't much care for Cal Hamilton—she found him crude and egotistical—still, she wanted him to like her. Something else that didn't make a whole lot of sense.

"Of course it was Liana," Cal said, his voice softening. "Although she wasn't exactly looking her best." He paused, cocked his head to one side. A wave of blond hair fell seductively across his forehead. "You gonna ask me how she looked?"

Delilah shook her head. "No."

"Good. 'Cause she looked god-awful."

Delilah swallowed, feeling her throat go all dry and prickly, causing her next words to scrape against her throat. "Somebody said her head was missing."

"Somebody's exaggerating. As usual." Cal smiled. "Only half her head was missing." He slapped his hands against his thighs. *Ba da bum*. "Anyway, much as I'd love to stay and continue this discussion, I gotta run."

"Oh, sure. I didn't mean to keep you."

"There's beer in the refrigerator, and liquor in the dining-room cabinet." He winked to let her know he was kidding. "And don't answer the phone if it rings. Let voice mail take it." He crossed to the back door at the end of the counter. The door opened into the carport at the left side of the house.

"Is Mrs. Hamilton home?" Delilah asked. Silly question, she thought immediately. Why else was she here?

"She's sleeping."

Delilah stole a look at her watch. It was barely two o'clock in the afternoon, and while she knew that grown-ups often took naps in the daytime—Grandma Rose nodded off for precisely twenty minutes at four o'clock every day, and God forbid you did something to disturb her—Fiona Hamilton wasn't that much older than she was—was she even thirty?—and so it seemed odd that she was always sleeping. She'd been sleeping on the two previous occasions she'd been here, Delilah remembered, wondering if the woman was suffering from some kind of medical condition, and hoping it wasn't contagious. I have enough problems, she thought, feeling selfish and guilty in equal measures.

"She had kind of a rough night last night," Cal said, and winked again.

Delilah tried not to catch the meaning of that wink, although she felt an unexpected, and highly unwelcome, fluttering between her legs. What was the matter with her? Was she actually titillated by the vague boasting of this steroid-bound cretin?

"Anyway," he continued, "routine's the same as last time. Make yourself comfortable. Don't play the TV too loud—"

"I brought a book," Delilah interjected, holding up her copy of *Cry, the Beloved Country*. Mrs. Crosbie had instructed the class to have the first half of the novel finished by the end of next week, but she intended to read the whole thing. That is, if she could turn on a light.

"—use your cell if you want to talk on the phone," Cal continued as if she hadn't spoken, "and if my wife wakes up before I get back, make sure she doesn't leave the house."

"Is your wife all right, Mr. Hamilton?" Delilah asked before she could stop herself. She was aware of the rumors regarding Fiona Hamilton being a battered wife.

Cal Hamilton looked uneasily from side to side, as if debating with himself whether to answer her question or send her flying across the room. "No," he said finally. Then after an even longer pause: "It's not that she's sick exactly, but . . ."

Delilah held her breath. But . . . ? she asked silently.

"She's just not quite right," he continued, as if he'd decided he could trust her. "In the head, I mean. Not that you have to worry about anything," he added quickly. "She's not violent or anything like that."

"Violent?" The word popped from Delilah's mouth and ricocheted off the kitchen walls, like a steel ball in a pinball machine.

"I said she's *not* violent," Cal stressed, then laughed. "Hell, she's as timid as a church mouse, for Christ's sake. She just has all these phobias she's trying to deal with."

"Phobias?"

"Irrational fears," Cal qualified. "At least that's what her shrink says."

"She sees a psychiatrist? Where?" Delilah knew there were no psychiatrists in Torrance, although she thought the town could probably use one.

"Well, not here, that's for sure," he said, as if reading her thoughts. "Back in Miami."

"What kind of phobias?"

"You name it, she's got it." Cal shook his head. More blond hair fell across his forehead. "Let's see. She's afraid of heights, afraid of snakes, afraid of crowds. She's claustrophobic, agorphobic—"

"Agor*a*phobic," Delilah corrected, then bit down hard on her tongue. Probably not a good idea to correct him, she was thinking as a cruel smile stretched slowly across his lips and his hands formed loose fists at his sides.

"Yeah, that's it. Ago*ra*phobic," he said. "She's afraid to go out-side the house."

"Technically it means a fear of the marketplace. I read about it in *Cosmo*."

"Is that so?" He pushed the hair away from his face. "She tries, you know. That's part of the problem. Poor girl gets it into her head that she's gonna go out, and she takes off without me, and pretty soon she panics and starts running around like a chicken with its head cut off. People find her, they have to call me, she gets all humiliated. We have to start all over again from square one. That's why she's a little self-conscious and uncomfortable with people, why she doesn't say a whole lot, and why sometimes what she *does* say doesn't make a whole lot of sense. Anyway," he said loudly in the same breath, the word punctuating the air like an exclamation point, "I really gotta go." He checked his watch. Delilah noticed it was a Rolex and wondered how he could afford such an expensive item. She concluded the watch must be fake, then wondered how much of anything he'd told her was genuine. "I'm runnin' a little late." Cal opened the rear door that led directly into the carport. "Be back in a couple of hours. Take care of my girl."

"Don't worry about anything," Delilah said, watching him about to climb into his shiny red Corvette, only to pause for several sec-onds and stare into the backyard of the house next door. "Forget something?" she asked, but he ignored her. In the next instant, he was behind the wheel and backing onto the street. She'd always wanted to own a car like that, Delilah thought, catching sight of Megan Crosbie sunning herself in a skimpy white bikini in the next yard, and remembering the Crosbies lived next door. So that's what Cal Hamilton had been looking at, she realized with a shake of her head. She closed the kitchen door, wondering if a man would ever look at her that way.

Got to lose a few pounds first, sweetie, she heard her mother say in that hopeless nasal twang she'd been unable to shake, despite repeated voice lessons. It seemed vocal cords, unlike other, more pliant parts of the body, were remarkably resistant to alteration. Her mother could plump up her lips all she wanted, but the sounds that escaped them would stubbornly remain the same.

Delilah shrugged as she opened the refrigerator door, then shrugged again as she perused the contents. Milk, orange juice, beer, more beer, a few green apples, some limp celery, a leaf of pale green lettuce that was turning brown at the edges, more beer. She checked the freezer, found three large boxes of DoveBars, all open. "Better not," Delilah whispered, closing the freezer door before she gave in to temptation, and deciding on water instead. Her grandmother had told her that if she drank a glass of water every time she felt like eating, she'd be less hungry, and therefore less inclined to overeat. With fresh determination, Delilah crossed to the sink and poured herself a glass of water, inadvertently glancing between the slats of the blinds covering the small back window and staring into the Crosbies' backyard just as Megan Crosbie sat up in her deck chair and began applying sunscreen to her slender thighs. She's so pretty, Delilah thought. Bet she never had to choose between water and a DoveBar. But she didn't begrudge Megan her long legs and tiny waist. Megan had always been, if not exactly *nice* to her, then at least never overtly *mean,* even though she had more reason to be nasty than the other kids, considering it was Delilah's mother who was responsible for Megan's father leaving home.

Megan finished smoothing on her sunscreen, then glanced toward the Hamilton house, as if she knew she was being watched. Instinctively, Delilah raised her hand and waved, but her wave went unanswered as Megan adjusted the angle of her lounge chair and lay back down, surrendering to the sun's warm rays. Delilah sipped at the water in her glass, knowing the slight had been unintended, that Megan couldn't possibly have noticed her standing there behind the closed blinds. Why were the blinds shut anyway? she wondered. Why was the house always so dark? Was Fiona Hamilton afraid of the sun as well as being *agorphobic*? She laughed and turned away from the window.

The woman, more apparition than human being, was standing in the entranceway to the kitchen, her thin arms hanging limply at her sides, her bare toes peeking out from underneath the bottom of her white nightgown. Long, sandy hair fell loosely past her shoulders, swamping an already fragile face, and accentuating the intensity of her large, blue-green eyes.

Delilah gasped at Fiona Hamilton's unexpected appearance. The glass of water she was holding slipped from between her fingers and crashed to the tile floor, shattering instantly.

"Oh, no," the woman cried, although she didn't move.

"It's okay. I'll clean it up." Delilah was immediately on her hands and knees in the pool of spilled water, stretching in all directions to retrieve the sharp pieces of broken glass. "I'm so sorry. I didn't hear you come in."

"What have I done? What have I done?"

"You haven't done anything," Delilah said quickly. "I was just a little startled, that's all."

"You're bleeding."

Delilah looked at her hand. Blood was indeed dripping from a small cut on her index finger. Was Fiona afraid of blood too? "It's nothing." She wiped her finger on her jeans, held it up again. "See? It's fine." The finger immediately resumed bleeding.

"Oh, God. Oh, God."

"Mrs. Hamilton, it's really just a little cut." Delilah pushed herself to her feet, quickly discarding the pieces of glass she'd collected into the bin underneath the sink, then turning on the cold-water tap and holding her finger beneath the water's icy flow. It stung, but she held it there, afraid that should she remove it, it might start bleeding again, and then Fiona Hamilton might collapse altogether. "Should you be out of bed?"

The woman glanced over her shoulder, then back at Delilah. She said nothing.

"Mrs. Hamilton, are you all right?"

"You broke the glass."

"I did. I'm sorry."

"Oh, God. Oh, God."

"It's all right. I'll replace it."

"Those are Cal's favorites."

"What?"

"The glasses. He'll be so upset."

"They're just ordinary glasses, Mrs. Hamilton. They're not expensive. We have the same ones at home. You can buy them at Publix."

"Oh, God. Oh, God."

"I tell you what: I'll call my mom, get her to pick up a new one right away," Delilah offered, pulling her fingers away from the tap water and retrieving her bag from the kitchen table, then ferreting around inside it for her cell phone. She quickly pressed in the numbers and lifted the small phone to her ear.

"Oh, God. Your purse." Fiona pointed to the small red fingerprint in the middle of Delilah's canvas bag.

"It's okay. It's okay. It's an old bag. No big deal. . . . Hello, Grandma Rose?" For the first time that Delilah could remember, she was actually glad to hear her grandmother's voice. "Is my mom there? Could you get her, please?"

"Kerri!" her grandmother shrieked directly into the receiver.

Delilah pushed the phone away from her ear, regarding the young woman trembling in the doorway. Her whole body was shaking, Delilah realized. Was she more afraid of the blood, the broken glass, or how her husband might react? It was just a cheap glass, for God's sake. Did Fiona overreact this way to everything?

"She's not answering," Delilah's grandmother announced after several seconds. "I don't know where she is."

"Could you try again?"

"Why? Is there a problem?"

"I'm at the Hamiltons'. I broke a glass."

Fiona started whimpering.

"You what?"

"It was an accident."

"Honestly, Delilah. You're like a bull in a china shop."

Thank you for that, Delilah thought, trying to decide which woman she'd rather deal with—the witch on the telephone or the nutcase in the doorway. "Look, they're the same glasses we have in the kitchen. I need Mom to go to Publix as soon as possible and bring me a replacement."

"Why can't you go?"

For a minute Delilah wondered the same thing. Surely she could just run to the store for a few minutes. Fiona Hamilton was an adult, not a little girl. Except that this adult was standing there trembling, clearly unhinged by the sight of a broken glass and a cut finger, so how could she leave her alone? "I can't, Grandma Rose. Please, could you just ask my mother to do this for me?"

Silence.

It took Delilah several seconds to realize her grandmother had hung up. "Thank you. I appreciate that," she said to the silence that followed. She returned the cell phone to her bag, forced a smile onto her lips. "My mom'll be here soon."

Fiona nodded gratefully, ran her hands up and down her bare arms.

"Are you cold? Would you like some coffee? I could make some. That'll warm you up."

Fiona shook her head. "Cal doesn't like me to drink coffee."

Delilah wondered whether the caffeine in coffee heightened her various fears.

"He doesn't like the smell of coffee on my breath," Fiona explained without prompting.

Delilah nodded as if she understood, even though she didn't. She'd heard people talk about "coffee breath," but personally, she'd never found it offensive. And anyway, Cal wasn't home. He wouldn't be back for a couple of hours. Surely the smell would be gone from her breath by then. "How about some tea then?"

Again Fiona shook her head.

"What about a DoveBar?"

Even in the dim light, Delilah could see Fiona's eyes brighten. "A DoveBar?"

Delilah opened the freezer with a pronounced flourish and extricated an ice cream bar from the top package.

"Oh, no. Those are Cal's," Fiona warned, the light in her blue-green eyes fading, as if on a dimmer.

"I'm sure he wouldn't mind."

"No, I couldn't."

"Of course you can. In fact, we'll both have one." Delilah pulled a second bar out of the package, handed the first one to Fiona. "Go on. I'll tell him they were so good, I had two."

"He won't believe you."

Delilah almost laughed. "Are you kidding?" Was the woman blind as well as phobic? "Come on. It's good for you." Delilah tore the wrapping off the bar of ice cream, bit off a chunk of succulent, dark milk chocolate. "Mmm. Delicious. Go on. Have a bite."

Fiona stared at the ice cream bar in her hands without moving.

"Tell you what. Let's shed some light on the proceedings." Delilah was moving to the window before Fiona could object. "It's a beautiful day out there. It's sunny. It's warm." She pulled open the blinds over the sink. "There. Much better." She spun around, the smile on her face freezing as the sun shone spotlights on the deep bruises covering Fiona's arms and neck. "My God. What happened to you?"

The DoveBar dropped from Fiona's hands. It bounced off her bare toes and rolled under the table. "Oh, God. I shouldn't be here."

"What are you talking about? You live here."

"I should be in bed."

"Why should you be in bed, Mrs. Hamilton? Are you sick?"

"I shouldn't be talking to you."

"Why not?"

"He doesn't like me talking to strangers."

"I'm hardly a stranger, Mrs. Hamilton. I'm . . ." What was she exactly? A neighbor? The babysitter? What exactly was the woman so afraid of? "I'm a friend."

"He'll be very angry when he finds out I was down here."

"How will he find out? I won't tell him."

"He'll know."

"How will he know?" Delilah's eyes searched the room for hidden cameras.

"I'll tell him."

"What?"

"During inspection. He'll ask, and I'll have to tell him."

"No, you won't. You don't have to tell him anything. What do you mean, 'during inspection'?" What was Fiona talking about?

Fiona Hamilton stared at Delilah as if she were speaking a foreign language.

"Mrs. Hamilton," Delilah broached gently, nodding toward the woman's bruises. "Did your husband do this to you?"

"What? No. Of course not."

"Because if he did, you don't have to stay with him. We can call the sheriff. You can have him arrested."

"No. I could never do that."

"But—"

The doorbell rang, followed immediately by a loud knocking at the front door.

"Oh, God. He's back."

Was it possible? Delilah wondered. Had Cal Hamilton snuck back, parked his car on the street? Why?

"He'll be so angry," Fiona was wailing. "I'll never pass inspection."

"What are you talking about? What inspection?"

The knocking grew more insistent.

"Oh, God. Oh, God."

"Delilah!" a distant voice called from the front of the house.

"It's my mother," Delilah said, releasing a deep breath of air, and reaching over to pat Fiona's shoulder as she brushed past her, feeling the other woman shrink from her touch. She cut quickly through the living room to the front door, opening it to find her mother on the other side, arm extended, glass in hand.

"I took it from our kitchen," Kerri said instead of hello. She was wearing the shortest pair of white shorts Delilah had ever seen, and her considerable cleavage was spilling out of her black-and-white-striped, V-neck T-shirt. "What the hell is going on?"

"I don't know," Delilah whispered, taking the glass from her mother's hand. "But whatever it is, it's weird." She heard footsteps behind her, turned to see Fiona Hamilton disappearing down the hall to her bedroom, heard the door shut behind her.

"Yeah? Well, I don't think you should come here anymore," her mother said. "Not with all this crazy shit going down."

"What crazy shit?" Had something else happened? Her mother hadn't seemed unduly concerned before.

"There's been another incident."

"What kind of incident?"

Her mother took a deep breath. "Another girl is missing."

11

KILLER'S JOURNAL

Well, that was an exciting weekend.

From the minute the first reports hit the grapevine about another missing girl, all hell broke loose. The whole town of Torrance erupted, like a volcano, everybody spilling their crazy theories in all directions and trying to outrun rampant speculation. Was there any connection between this girl and Liana Martin? Was it true there was yet another girl, a runaway from Hendry County, who'd disappeared before Liana? Was it only a matter of time before the rotting corpses of young women started sprouting up like errant crops all over Alligator Alley? Was a maniac on the loose in South Florida? And if so, was said madman a stranger or someone everybody knew?

Soon every man whose whereabouts couldn't be confirmed by at least three reliable witnesses—which most assuredly did *not* include any members of his immediate family—was considered suspect. Seemingly every male between the ages of seven and seventy was hauled in by the sheriff and his deputies for questioning.

Nothing.

The sheriff looked exhausted. I saw him briefly yesterday afternoon, although he didn't see me. He was coming out of the gun store—apparently, there's been a marked increase in the number of guns sold—and I can report he looked drawn and haggard. Surprising for a man of his girth. He looked as if he'd had the shit kicked out of him, which might not be such a bad thing—he could stand to lose a few pounds—except that his complexion had gone all pale and pasty. Not a good look for him, I thought, and might have waved had he been looking in my direction. But he wasn't. No, he was staring at the rear passenger tire of his police cruiser, which was looking a little flat, courtesy of a nail someone had maliciously poked into its side.

You could almost hear him thinking: a dead body, another missing girl, and now this, the final indignity—a flat! I watched him reach inside the front seat and pull out his walkie-talkie. And he grumbled something into the speaker and shook his head, then leaned against the side of the car and waited for someone to come to his aid. Which I suppose they did eventually. I didn't wait around to find out.

I had things to do.

It's interesting what happens to a small town when tragedy strikes. When Liana Martin first went missing, the denizens of Torrance were naturally concerned and sympathetic. You heard only the nicest things about Liana and her family. *Liana was the lovely oldest daughter of two of Torrance's beautiful elite. The Martins were upstanding citizens and involved, caring parents.* When their child's body was pulled from the ground, everybody mourned.

And then the whispers started: *Is it true she was wearing a* MOVE, BITCH *T-shirt when they found her? That's kind of asking for it, wouldn't you say? She was always a handful, that one. Her mother could never control her. I heard she was seeing some older guy from Miami. I heard she had a taste for kinky sex.*

It's called blaming the victim, and from everything I've read, it's a common response to calamity. It seems that blaming the victim is a defense mechanism, a way people have of distancing themselves from disaster. If the victim can somehow be held accountable for her fate, well, then—whew!—the rest of us don't have to worry. We don't smoke, so we'll never get cancer. We wouldn't walk alone after midnight, so we'll never get raped. We'd never wear a MOVE, BITCH T-shirt, so what happened to Liana could never happen to us. I don't think people intend to be mean. I think they just want to feel safe.

Which, of course, they aren't.

Not from the true crazies of this world.

Do you really think there's a maniac on the loose in South Florida? Do you think it's a stranger or somebody we know?

Well, let's see. Who do we know? Who do we suspect?

Right away, the name on top of everybody's list—Cal Hamilton.

Well, why not? Cal's a relative stranger to these parts, and he's big and strong and has that sly smile. What's that? A killer smile, you say? And he has an eye for the ladies, not to mention that poor—abused?—wife of his that hardly anybody ever sees. And he was away on Saturday afternoon when that girl disappeared. And didn't somebody spot his car in the area where she was last seen? And wasn't he the one who found Liana's body? And, I don't know—he just looks like somebody who'd shoot a girl in the head, don't you think?

Or how about Joey Balfour? He was with Cal Hamilton when they found Liana. Supposedly he was the one who stumbled on that suspicious mound of earth. Or was that Greg Watt? Doesn't really matter. They're more or less interchangeable, aren't they? Two big, stupid lugs who've been involved in more than their fair share of mischief over the years. Yes, it's true they come from good, hardworking families, but remember when they vandalized all those expensive foreign cars at the dealership? And wasn't Joey involved in some sort of rape thing a few years back? Yeah, we know it was only statutory rape and the charges were dropped after the girl left town, but still . . .

How about Avery Peterson? What? The science teacher? You heard he has a taste for young flesh? Well, only him and half the country, for Pete's sake. Can't hang a man for that. If you ask me, Gordon Lipsman's a lot more suspect. He's creepy, and he lived with his mother and all those cats. Aren't cats the devil's disciples? And don't forget Leonard Fromm, currently the esteemed principal of Torrance High, but who in his youth was a world-renowned surfer dude? He's been a little strange ever since his wife ran off with her personal yoga instructor. For that matter, there was something very strange about that yoga instructor.

Talk about strange—what about Brian Hensen? He hasn't been quite right ever since he found his father hanging from the shower rod. Or Victor Drummond? Maybe his vampiric fantasies were no longer enough to satisfy him. You know that Liana's body had been drained of blood.

And what about that boyfriend, Peter Arlington? I hear they'd been fighting. Does anybody really believe he was sick that day? Did he see a doctor?

And speaking of doctors, what about Dr. Crosbie? Obviously going through a midlife crisis of some kind. I mean, any man crazy enough to leave that sweet little wife of his for a windup doll like Kerri Franklin has got to have a few screws loose. Loose screws being part of the good doctor's problem, wouldn't you agree? Anyway, he's pretty new to these parts—he's from New York, for God's sake. Need I say more?—and he's got no alibi for Saturday afternoon. Says he was in his office, catching up on some paperwork. Do you buy that?

And what about old Mr. Calhoun, young Mr. Frickey, middle-aged Mr. Rodriguez? What about the butcher, the baker, and the candlestick maker? What about the man standing on the corner or the man crossing the street? It could be any one of them.

Which one?

It seems that no one is immune from suspicion or safe from gossip. And it's so interesting how gossip assumes a life of its own, creates its own reality. Interesting too how things can start out in one direction and end up somewhere else entirely. Like Liana Martin. She started off for home and ended up in the ground.

So I guess all the panic and conjecture when another girl went missing wasn't entirely out of line, although if you ask me—and, of course, nobody did—it was a lot of fuss over nothing. The missing girl, whose name is Brenda Vinton, was from Collier County, which is directly to the west of Broward and is considered one of the state's fastest-growing counties, encompassing 2,006 square miles (exactly 787 more square miles than Broward). According to the latest census, the population of Collier County has increased by 65 percent in the last decade. (I like to keep track of such things.) Collier is famous for its cypress trees, and since most of Collier is taken up by the Everglades, the vast bulk of the development has been along the Gulf of Mexico on the west coast. Approximately two thousand Seminole Indians live in Collier, although I doubt you'll find any of them in a big city like Naples, where Brenda Vinton is from.

Anyway, Brenda Vinton is this pretty, sixteen-year-old girl whose parents reported her missing when she failed to come home from her piano lesson on Saturday afternoon. She was only about half an hour late, but people were already jittery in Naples because some pervert had been going around exposing himself to children, and another pervert—maybe it was the same pervert, nobody was quite sure—had tried to force a ten-year-old girl into his car the previous week, but had been frightened off by the girl's screams. The good people of Naples had also just heard about Liana Martin's murder, and so when Brenda Vinton failed to return home at the appointed hour, everyone was understandably concerned. A search party was organized immediately, and someone alerted the media, and next thing you knew, South Florida was in a panic, convinced it had another serial killer—we've had several—on its hands.

Which I guess they do.

Except that I don't consider myself a serial killer. Not really. I think of serial killers as people with misplaced God complexes who strike at random, trolling the streets for targets who unwittingly fulfill their sick fantasies. These people are social outcasts whose overwhelming and sadistic sexual urges can ultimately be satisfied only through killing. They won't stop killing until they're caught.

That isn't me.

First of all, I don't strike at random, although I recognize it may seem that way to some, especially now, in the beginning stages of my work. (Because it *is* work.) And my victims are hardly selected at random. No, I have a plan, carefully thought out, and even more carefully put into action, and my victims have all carefully been chosen. Even Candy Abbot, who didn't exactly fit the mold, was part of my overall plan. She was my test case, if you will, a regretful, if necessary, casualty of war. (Because it *is* war.) I needed to see if my plan was feasible, if the chloroform would work, if the house where I intended to stash my victims was as appropriate a prison as I imagined. But obviously, I'm learning as I go along. Some things will have to be modified—such as always keeping bottles of water on hand—and I have to give more thought to emergencies and allow for the unexpected. But all things considered, Candy Abbot was a positive experience, at least for me. (I doubt she'd agree.) Not to mention, she gave me the confidence to take my plan to the next stage.

Enter—and exit—Liana Martin.

That was a tense time, just before her body was recovered. The sheriff had all his officers out in force, and they'd already organized several search parties, none of which had turned up anything. There was talk of spreading out, of going farther afield, maybe even calling in the FBI. This had me understandably nervous because I dreaded my secret hideaway being discovered. Not that it's such a secret. I mean, how can it be? The house sits at the end of a large field, clearly visible from the road, if you look hard enough. Although I've discovered that people don't really look very hard, even when they're searching for something. They think they are, but actually they're just going through the motions, poking around, waiting for something to pop out at them. And that field, that old house, have been neglected for so long that people no longer see them as anything but backdrop. Like in the movies.

Still, I began to worry. If Liana's body wasn't discovered soon, the sheriff would be forced to enlarge the area of his search, and he might stumble across the field and the house, and then it would be game over. At least temporarily. I'd have to go back to the drawing board, and I doubted I'd ever again find a place so perfect for what I had to do. Not to mention the time it would take to relocate and begin again. No, I definitely didn't want that.

So when the search teams gathered, I made sure to drop a few quiet suggestions. There were quite a few of us in the various search parties, and everyone was talking at the same time, vying for position of alpha male, suggesting this area and that as a good place to start, and pretty soon it was impossible to decipher who had suggested what, so I was able to steer us subtly toward the field where I'd buried Liana's body. Once there, it didn't take a lot of effort to angle the group toward the actual grave site, and then—lo and behold!—there she was.

Okay. I admit it. That part was fun. Seeing the looks of wary anticipation on the faces of the others when that suspect mound of earth was discovered, those looks becoming grimaces as a limp hand was uncovered, and then the gasps of horror as Liana's body was pulled from the ground. God, she was a mess! Time and the animals had done their job all right, and no amount of expensive gloss would have helped those once sassy lips. Of course, I mimed shock and outrage, the same as everybody else. I threw my hand over my mouth and pretended I was about to be sick. And to be truthful, the smell of nearby vomit was almost enough to do the trick. It's funny how just that odor is enough to induce nausea. Anyway, I took half a dozen deep breaths, the way my mother used to tell me to do when I was a child, and I was okay.

What is it they say? Mother is always right?

What do they know? What does anybody know?

They didn't even realize I was there.

I'll tell you what *I* know, and that's that I don't have any misplaced deity complex. I'm not the least bit interested in playing God, thank you very much. And I certainly don't get any weird sexual thrill out of either killing or watching people die. As I've already explained, the part of this whole thing that I enjoy is the buildup, the game-playing. (Because it *is* a game.)

Which brings me back to Brenda Vinton.

Brenda Vinton is one of those vacuously pretty girls you see everywhere these days. Long hair, pert little nose, expressionless eyes. Hardly a heartstopper, at least judging from the picture I saw on one of those ubiquitous flyers that papered the state almost as soon as she went missing. Although maybe she just doesn't take a good picture. Some people are like that. They're beautiful in person, but they don't photograph well. In pictures, they appear awkward and stilted, void of personality and character.

On the other hand, some people aren't good-looking by any stretch of the imagination, yet they photograph beautifully. You see a picture of them and you think, That person is gorgeous. But then you see them in real life, and there's nothing special about them at all. In fact, often they're rather plain. This is certainly true of many of the top models, those glorious faces you see on the covers of fashion magazines. They seem stunning on the surface, but really they're just the highly paid, high-cheekboned receptacles of someone else's vision, a bunch of blank canvases awaiting the right combination of paint and proper lighting. They need an outsider's hand to bring them to life.

Of course, sometimes an outsider's hand brings death.

Ask Liana Martin.

But we're talking about Brenda Vinton now. And she has one of those faces that won't age particularly well, at least judging by her mother, whom I saw in that ludicrous press conference she threw, tearfully thanking all those volunteers who gave up their weekend to search for her darling daughter. Mrs. Vinton's face—round and uninteresting, with soft, bovine lips and small, deep-set eyes that kept filling up with tears—registered an ever-shifting combination of relief, anger, and embarrassment, sometimes all three at the same time. Occasionally Mrs. Vinton would glance behind her at her former husband and his new wife, a girl who looked young enough to be his daughter—he should really be ashamed—and she'd grimace, although I doubt she realized she was doing so. I had to laugh. People betray themselves so easily. The smallest of gestures give them away.

So, there was Mrs. Vinton on the steps of some civic building, probably City Hall, torn tissue in hand, thanking the police force and the volunteers, stealing peeks at her husband and his young wife, and saying how sorry she is for all the trouble her daughter has caused. Brenda is remorseful, she says repeatedly, adding that they'll be seeking help for her. She takes a final glance at her former husband, whose scowl is barely contained by his tight smile. And then the press conference concludes, and she is gone.

Brenda, of course, was nowhere to be seen throughout these proceedings. Too ashamed, her mother explained.

I don't buy that. I don't think little Brenda is the least bit ashamed. After all, she got what she wanted, which I suspect was a break from her mother, who's no doubt been way overprotective since her husband abandoned her, as well as some attention from her neglectful father, who's no doubt been busy of late with his new wife. Not to mention that for more than twenty-four hours, hers was the name on everyone's lips, the face on every telephone pole and television newscast, the subject of every prayer.

And where was little Brenda while all this was going on?

She was holed up in some crummy, local motel, drinking Coke and eating potato chips while following reports of her disappearance on TV. She hadn't meant any harm, she insisted to police officers after the chambermaid discovered her still in bed when she went in to change the sheets on Sunday afternoon. She hadn't planned to run away. She certainly hadn't realized the furor her disappearance would cause. It was a spur-of-the-moment kind of thing. She'd just finished her piano lesson and was on her way home to study for a test on Monday, and she was worried because she hadn't read any of the books that were going to be on the test, and she was afraid she wasn't going to pass, and then her mother would be angry and probably wouldn't let her go to the Killers' concert taking place next weekend in Fort Lauderdale, even though she'd stood in line for five hours to get tickets and spent all the money she'd gotten for her last birthday to get a halfway decent seat, and it really wasn't fair, and she hated being a kid, and she hated school, and she especially hated having to take piano lessons on a Saturday morning when all her friends got to sleep in, and she just decided, right then and there, totally impromptu, not to go home and study for that stupid test, but to go to some motel and just veg out for a few hours. And that's what she did. Except later, when she turned on the TV, there was her picture and the news that she'd vanished. And she didn't know what to do. And no, since you ask, she didn't realize her mother would get that bent out of shape. How was she to know the commotion her being a few hours late would cause, that the whole city would be out looking for her? Yes, of course, she'd heard about that poor girl in Torrance who'd gotten herself killed, but that was halfway across the state, for heaven's sake, and why would anyone think one thing had anything to do with the other? She's sorry, okay?

Well, no, it's not okay. And I have half a mind to pay Brenda Vinton a visit, teach her what happens to stupid little twits who cry wolf. Except her mother's probably watching her like a hawk right now, and it'd be way too risky. And it would mean all that driving, and more time wasted when there's already been enough time wasted because of that silly girl. Because of her, I'll have to delay the next phase of my plan. People are way too uptight right now. They're on red alert, as it were. The mayor's on the warpath. A few big-city reporters have been nosing around. Everywhere I go, people are looking over their shoulders, peering into the windows of cars they don't recognize, picking their kids up from school. I observe them when they don't know they're being watched. I listen in when they're talking. I understand what they're feeling. I'm one of them after all.

Or so they think.

And so I understand it would be foolhardy to proceed at this point, that it would be prudent to wait, at least another few weeks, until people have relaxed their guard, at least a little, and the reporters have returned to their big-city newspapers, the mayor has stopped pontificating for the cameras, and the sheriff and his deputies have gone back to their usual routine of handing out speeding tickets and enforcing the noise bylaws.

Besides, I already have the next girl picked out, so there's no rush, although I would have preferred to have kept to my original schedule. But, as I stated earlier, I have to be prepared for the unexpected, for the deus ex machina, however unfair. And looking on the bright side, this way I'll have more time to anticipate, which, as I've said before, is my favorite part.

Maybe when I'm done with the good people of Torrance, I'll take a drive over to Naples and pay Brenda Vinton a little visit. We'll see. I have lots of time to decide.

chapter twelve

O kay, people, we don't have a lot of time," Mr. Lipsman announced, waving his hands in the air, as if he'd stumbled into a horde of angry bees. He looked around the three-hundred-seat auditorium, beckoning about a dozen malingerers standing at the back of the large space to come forward and join the approximately fifty other students gathered in the front couple of rows. "Come on, people." He clapped his hands, swatted at the air again, paced impatiently back and forth in front of the raised platform.

Megan watched his performance from her seat on the left aisle of the second row. She'd heard Mr. Lipsman had once had aspirations to be an actor, but that his mother had disapproved of so frivolous a career, and so he'd never pursued it. Now, as Megan watched his oversize gestures and near operatic sighs, she concluded he'd missed his calling. It was a shame, she thought, feeling almost sorry for him—almost, because he was such a doofus it was hard to sustain much sympathy for any length of time. Still, she concluded, it must be terrible to spend your life doing something that was, at best, a second choice, and to watch others, many less talented than yourself, assume the mantle that might have been yours, had you only had the courage of your convictions and the determination to follow your dreams. As well as the stamina to stand up to your mother, she added, flipping her long brown hair over her shoulder with fresh resolve, and swiveling around in her seat as the group of wayward seniors sauntered slowly down the aisle toward the front of the auditorium.

Greg Watt was not among them.

Megan suppressed her own sigh of disappointment. She'd been hoping Greg would show up for the auditions, despite gossip his father had put his foot down, insisted his son stop wasting his valuable time on such "pansy-assed pursuits." At least, that's what she'd overheard Joey Balfour telling a group of boys in the hall this morning. What was the matter with parents anyway? Were they all so pathetic and self-absorbed? Oh, they made a big show of claiming that all they cared about was their children's happiness, but when push came to shove—and it was always the parents who did the pushing; kids only shoved back when cornered—the only people's happiness that really mattered was their own. Mrs. Lipsman hadn't wanted her son to be an actor, so he'd compromised both his talent and his ambition, settling for the role of high school drama teacher instead. Mr. Watt frowned on his son's more artistic interests, insisting Greg devote his time and energy to the family business. And *her* mother had decided she wanted to return to Rochester, blithely assuming her son and daughter would automatically acquiesce to her wishes. Well, Megan wasn't about to give in on this one. She wasn't going to leave Florida, she'd decided over the weekend. And it didn't matter that she hadn't wanted to come here in the first place, or that she missed her friends up north, or that Liana Martin had been murdered.

"It's not safe here," her mother had argued.

"It's safer here than in New York," she'd quickly countered.

And then another girl had gone missing, and her mother had been positively apoplectic. They hadn't even buried Liana, she'd railed, and now a second girl had disappeared. A third, if you believed the rumors. And then it turned out Brenda Vinton hadn't been kidnapped after all, so all her mother's crazed rants about a serial killer on the loose, preying on young girls, were nothing but conjecture. Statistics said that it was far more likely that Liana Martin had been killed by someone close to her than by an itinerant sociopath. So no way she was moving back to Rochester, Megan had insisted, continuing to press her point even after she understood its irrelevance. She knew, perhaps even better than her mother, that the real reason her mother wanted to leave Torrance had nothing to do with serial killers and everything to do with straying husbands. Could she blame her?

Megan looked toward the end of the aisle where Delilah Franklin sat hanging over the end of her plush, red velvet seat, waiting for Mr. Lipsman to proceed. The girl filled the room like a stray cloud, her very presence threatening to ruin everyone else's fun. Why does she have to be everywhere I go? Megan wondered, knowing she was being unfair. The poor girl had every right to go wherever she wanted, and she was obviously here because she wanted to be in the school play.

It was also obvious, from the distance the other students kept from her—the several seats on either side of her and those directly behind her were jarringly empty—that none of the other students welcomed her presence. And truthfully, Megan couldn't imagine what part she'd be right for. With any luck, Mr. Lipsman would feel the same way, and Delilah would be consigned the thankless job of painting scenery or sewing costumes. Hadn't that been her job last year?

This was a dumb idea, Megan thought, as Mr. Lipsman began handing out copies of the script. She shouldn't have come. She didn't really want to be here. She had no interest in appearing in the school play, even if she was handed the starring role.

At first it had appeared the production would be canceled. It had already been postponed once, after the death of Mr. Lipsman's mother, and after Liana's body was discovered, the principal had toyed with the idea of shelving it altogether. But Mr. Lipsman had made an impassioned speech about the need for hope over despair, claiming the play would take the students' minds off their grief and fear, et cetera, et cetera, all of which was just an elaborate way of saying, "The show must go on."

"Let's make *Kiss Me, Kate* our tribute to Liana Martin," the principal had subsequently proclaimed over the loudspeaker, encouraging all students to involve themselves in the production in some capacity, be it on the stage or behind the scenes.

"Much better for the students than grief counseling," Mr. Lipsman was overheard to say, although counseling was also offered.

Megan couldn't understand how going ahead with *Kiss Me, Kate*, would do anything for Liana's memory, nor did she pay a visit to the grief counselor who was brought in, despite her mother's encouragement. She had no interest in discussing Liana's death with a stranger. Nor did she feel like talking about the murder with anyone she knew, especially her mother, who kept pressing Megan to tell her how she felt, asking her over and over if she was all right, until she was dizzy and felt like screaming. "I'm here if you want to talk about it," her mother said.

But Megan had always been more comfortable with silence. Unlike most girls her age, she preferred keeping her thoughts to herself. If you didn't acknowledge your feelings out loud, you didn't have to deny them later. In any event, she much preferred the anonymity of the Internet, which allowed her to share her anxieties without revealing her voice. Clearly, many others felt the same way.

Isn't it awful? one person wrote. *Isn't what happened to Liana the most awful thing?*

Poor girl, wailed another. *Poor, poor girl.*

And yet another: *My heart breaks. My soul bleeds. This is truly the end of the world.*

Of course, there were other postings of a completely different sort:

She was a bitch.

Who gives a shit?

She got what she deserved.

Undoubtedly the authorities were tracking the writers of these missives and would be able to determine who'd sent them. Not that such a discovery was likely to amount to much. Megan assumed that anyone smart enough to kidnap someone in broad daylight, murder her, dispose of the body, and then elude capture for this long wouldn't be stupid enough to leave so obvious a trail. Sheriff Weber and his deputies had questioned the entire town, some people more than once, and had yet to turn up anything concrete. Except, of course, Liana's body, which the coroner had yet to release. There was talk of a funeral, or at the very least, a memorial service, to be held later in the week. Megan didn't want to go. But how could she not?

Would Liana's killer be there? she wondered. Would he bow his head in prayer like the rest of the mourners and whisper words of condolence to the bereaved family? Would he stand next to the grave as Liana's body was, once again, lowered into the cold ground? Would he stand next to her, brush up against her shoulder?

Megan shook her head, determined to dislodge the uncomfortable thought. She glanced toward the back of the auditorium, hoping Greg Watt had snuck inside and was even now standing there, hands on his hips, smirk on his lips, surveying the scene. But the three sets of auditorium doors were closed, and Greg was nowhere to be seen. It appeared that everyone who planned to audition was already here. Her eyes returned reluctantly to the front of the theater.

Considering the number of people, it was quiet. Everyone looked vaguely shell-shocked. Ginger Perchak and Tanya McGovern huddled together in the front row, fussing over their scripts. Amber Weber sat in the row behind them, mouthing some lines of dialogue to herself. Brian Hensen sat several seats to her left, arm extended toward Mr. Lipsman, waiting for his copy. Farther back sat Peter Arlington, his arms wrapped around his chest, eyes staring resolutely at the floor. Victor Drummond was there, as was his ghoulish friend, Nancy, the one with the raccoon eyes and weird piercings. There were other students whose faces Megan recognized, although she didn't know their names. Even Joey Balfour was in attendance, for God's sake, although Joey had made it clear he was there only because he considered actresses—even those at the high school level—to be both uninhibited and oversexed, and hoped he might get lucky. "As a tribute to Liana, of course," he insisted, and everyone laughed in spite of themselves. Judging by the way several of the freshmen girls were looking at him now, he might be right, Megan thought, wondering if that was the way she looked at Greg Watt.

A copy of the script suddenly dropped into her lap. "Please have a look at the part of Kate," Mr. Lipsman intoned solemnly from somewhere above her head. He opened the script to the appropriate page, his fingers touching hers. Megan quickly withdrew her hand, dragging the backs of her fingers along the front of her jeans, as if to rid them of his touch. Mr. Lipsman was still standing over her. When she raised her eyes to his, he winked.

"Mr. Lipsman," Delilah called from her seat at the far end of the first row. "You forgot me."

Mr. Lipsman extended a script toward her without bothering to turn around. "Sorry about that." Once again he winked at Megan, as if to say he shared her revulsion, as if to say he was one of them.

Megan felt an unexpected twinge of sympathy for Delilah as the ungainly girl rose from her seat. That twinge grew into an outright ache as Delilah tripped over a stray foot that appeared suddenly in her path to send her sprawling across the laps of several horrified students.

"What the hell . . . ?"

"I'm sorry," Delilah quickly apologized.

"Have a nice trip?"

"Get off of me!"

"I'm really so sorry."

"See you next fall."

"*Get off.*"

Delilah struggled to her feet, smoothing her long, black peasant skirt across her hips. The skirt would have looked fashionable on anybody else. On Delilah, it looked like a collapsing tent.

"I saw England," Joey Balfour recited in a grating, singsongy voice. "I saw France. I saw Big D's underpants. Oh, wait a minute. What am I saying? She isn't wearing any."

"Oh, yuck," someone said as everybody laughed.

"Gross," echoed somebody else.

Megan waited for Mr. Lipsman to put a stop to the cruelty, but he continued to hand out copies of the script as if unaware anything untoward was happening.

"I didn't get my copy," Delilah reminded him sheepishly in her little-girl voice, as the last of the scripts was distributed among the students.

"Well, I'm afraid that's the last of them. I guess you'll have to share." Mr. Lipsman scanned the rows for volunteers.

No one raised a hand.

"She can share mine," Megan said after a pause, watching Delilah's face light up with gratitude.

At the same time, the faces of Ginger Perchak and Tanya McGovern darkened. *What am I doing?* Megan wondered as Delilah moved gracelessly toward her. Now she'd have to change seats, and she'd been perfectly comfortable where she was. And Ginger and Tanya probably wouldn't talk to her now. She should have sat with them in the first place, instead of sitting off by herself, hoping Greg would show up.

This was all her mother's fault, she decided as she moved over to let Delilah sit down. Her mother was always saying that the most important thing in life was to be kind. The Golden Rule. *Do onto others as you would have them do onto you.*

Somebody should have told that to whoever killed Liana.

"Thanks," Delilah said, burrowing in against Megan's side, her thighs spilling over the boundaries of her narrow seat, pressing against Megan's. "What part should I look at, Mr. Lipsman?"

"Have a look at the chorus," Mr. Lipsman said.

"The whole chorus?" Joey Balfour asked to more laughter.

Megan would have laughed too, but she stopped herself when she felt Delilah's body stiffen.

"All right. That's quite enough of that," Mr. Lipsman said in a belated attempt at disapproval. "Is anyone here familiar with this play?"

Megan raised her left hand. "I saw it on Broadway a few years ago."

"She saw it on Broadway," Joey mimicked, and Megan saw Ginger sneer.

What's the matter with me? she thought. *Why can't I keep my big mouth shut?*

"I've never been to a Broadway play," Delilah whispered, smiling at Megan as if they were the best of friends.

God, get me out of here, Megan prayed.

"Does anyone realize that this musical is based on a play by William Shakespeare?" Mr. Lipsman continued. "Can anyone tell me its title? Megan?"

Megan shook her head, although she knew the answer. *The Taming of the Shrew,* she said in her head as Mr. Lipsman said the words out loud. He went on to explain the plot, and how the musical differed from the original. He said he'd listen to everyone read first, narrow down his selections, then hold the singing auditions later in the week. "Ginger," he said. "Why don't we start with you. The part of Kate." Ginger rose from her seat and climbed the several steps to the stage. "And, Brian, why don't you give Petruchio a try?"

"I thought that was my part," a voice boomed from the back of the auditorium.

All heads swiveled toward the voice except for Megan's, which remained bowed, her eyes focused resolutely on the script in her lap. She didn't have to turn around to know Greg was here, and if she looked, she knew her face would betray her instantly. She took a bunch of deep breaths to calm the suddenly erratic beating of her heart.

"Are you okay?" Delilah asked beside her, sounding just like Megan's mother.

"I'm fine," Megan hissed. "Why wouldn't I be?"

"You looked flushed is all."

Had she always talked so loud? "I'm fine," Megan repeated, as Greg whisked by her, stopping at the front row beside Tanya.

"This seat taken?"

"Be my guest." Tanya smiled as Greg sank into Ginger's now empty seat.

Megan feigned indifference as Greg extended his muscular, long legs in front of him. She was thinking that if it hadn't been for Delilah, and by extension, her mother—because if it hadn't been for her mother's stupid Golden Rule, Megan would never have invited Delilah to share her copy of the script, and the seat beside her would have been empty—then Greg might have chosen to sit next to *her*.

She felt Delilah's mouth drawing closer to her ear, felt her warm breath brush up against her skin, like a cat against a bare leg. "He's such a jerk," Delilah whispered. "I hate him. Don't you?"

"No. Why would I hate him?" Megan asked, a touch too loud, and Greg turned his head toward her, as if aware they were talking about him. Megan felt her cheeks redden and a line of sweat break out along her forehead.

"Are you okay?" Delilah asked again.

Megan closed her eyes. If she asks me that one more time, I'll kill her, she thought, focusing all her attention on the stage, listening as Ginger and Brian mechanically read their lines, then read them again after some direction from Mr. Lipsman.

"Thank you," Mr. Lipsman said, when they were through, telling them they could take their seats, but to please stick around. "Tanya and . . ." His eyes scanned the room.

Not Greg, Megan prayed silently, although he was the logical choice. Please not Greg.

". . . Peter," Mr. Lipsman concluded. "Let's hear the two of you, shall we? Oh, and Greg," he continued unexpectedly as Megan held her breath, "I'll be calling on you and Megan in about ten minutes, and I see you don't have a copy of the script, so why don't you go over it together at the back of the auditorium until I call you?"

Greg was instantly on his feet. "Coming?" he asked Megan as he walked past, continuing to the back of the auditorium without looking back.

Megan climbed awkwardly over Delilah's legs. "Poor you," she heard Delilah say as she raced up the aisle after him, then, "Mr. Lipsman, I don't have a script now."

Megan slowed her steps as she neared Greg's side. His back was to her. She felt unsteady, light-headed, as if she might tumble over with the slightest shift in air currents. You're being silly, she told herself, grabbing the back of the nearest seat to steady herself. He's not even that cute. Look at him, for God's sake. He's like this big, dumb hulk. He probably doesn't have a brain in his head. Except it wasn't his brain she was looking at, she realized, her eyes glued to the curve of his buttocks underneath his tight jeans.

"This all right?" He pointed toward the last row, then slid into a seat before she had time to reply.

"Fine," she said anyway, lowering herself into the seat next to him, and opening the script to the appropriate page. So far, neither had actually looked at the other.

"Could you bring the script a little closer?" he asked.

Megan transferred the pages to her other hand. "I think this is the section he wants us to read."

"Yeah?"

"That's what the others are reading."

Greg leaned forward, studied the text. Seconds later, she felt his attention shift, and she knew he was looking at her. Staring at her, actually. Damn, she thought. I should have sat on his other side. My left profile is so much better than my right. Damn, damn, damn.

"So, you're Kate, are you?" he said seductively.

"Apparently." Megan was relieved her voice sounded as steady as it did.

"Yes, well, *apparently*," he repeated, sounding just like David Caruso in *CSI: Miami*. "I've been sent to tame you."

Megan felt her cheeks blush bright red. But instead of dropping her gaze to her lap and fiddling with the script, she cocked her head coquettishly to one side and looked him straight in his dark brown eyes. "Really?" she heard herself say. "You think you're up for it?"

A slight pause. Brown eyes sparkled. Then: "Oh, I'm always up for it."

What on earth was she supposed to say now? Megan wondered. She was reciting lines from a script she'd yet to read. Did she tell him she was new at this sort of thing? That she'd never been good at improvisation? That she was still a virgin, for God's sake? That there'd been this one guy back in Rochester she thought was cute, but her family had moved away before their encounters in the backseat of his car could progress very far? That she found Greg almost unbearably attractive, and that her mother would have a fit at the very idea of the two of them together, which, of course, only made him that much more appealing in her eyes? What was wrong with her?

"You busy this Saturday night?" he was asking.

"What?" Had she heard him correctly?

"A bunch of us were thinking of getting together. Holding kind of a vigil for Liana."

"A vigil?"

"Kind of."

Was he asking her out? Was *kind of a vigil* the same thing as a date? "I'm not busy."

"Good." He reached over and closed the script she was holding, then he took her hand, began absently sucking the tips of her fingers.

Megan felt a charge, like an electrical current, travel from her palm to her shoulder and quickly pulled her hand away. "Don't you want to study our lines?"

"Nah," he said, leaning his head back against the seat and closing his eyes. "It's in the bag."

chapter thirteen

It's in the back," Rita was saying. "Behind the bar, turn right at the Budweiser sign."

"You're sure you don't want to just get out of here?" Sandy checked her watch as she inched her way out of the narrow booth. "They're obviously not coming."

"What are you talking about?"

"They're ten minutes late. They're not coming."

"They're only five minutes late. They'll be here. You saw the traffic on I-95. It's Saturday night, for Pete's sake."

"There's always traffic on I-95. They should have been prepared. *We* were."

"So they're not Boy Scouts. Now go powder your nose, will you? They'll be here before you get back."

"And if they're not?"

"We'll order drinks, stick around another fifteen minutes, then head back to Torrance," Rita offered.

Sandy nodded. "Order me a green-apple martini." She headed for the washroom at the back of the popular, oceanside singles' haunt, wondering why all these places looked so much alike. And it didn't matter whether you were in Rochester, Torrance, or Fort Lauderdale, in the middle of a busy downtown street or surrounded by a white, sandy beach. To paraphrase Gertrude Stein, a bar was a bar was a bar. There was loud music, there were dim lights, there were neon signs, there was booze, and there were a bunch of lonely men and women pretending to be otherwise. Restless men cheating on their boring wives, bored wives looking for a little outside attention, divorcées hunting for their future exes, teenagers pretending to be of legal drinking age, forty-year-olds acting like teenagers. The men looking to get laid, the women looking to be loved. What was that saying? Men dangle the possibility of love to get sex; women dangle the possibility of sex to get love? Something like that. Sandy was too tired to remember it exactly. What difference did it make anyway? The simple truth was that some people would go home tonight happy, and some would not. And then there were some who shouldn't have gone out at all.

People such as herself.

What was she doing here?

Hadn't she initially refused to accompany Rita to Fort Lauderdale? Hadn't she insisted she had no interest in meeting some guy, no matter how nice Rita's date had assured her he was, because, after all, Rita's date was just some guy she'd contacted through an Internet dating service and was only meeting in person for the first time tonight? If he turned out to be a creep, chances were good his friend would be a creep as well, and Sandy needed another creep in her life like she needed a hole in the head. Hadn't she told Rita she didn't think it was a good idea to drive all the way to Lauderdale— all right, it wasn't *that* far—when a murderer was on the loose, and that they should be home watching out for their children?

Except that their children didn't want them watching out for them. Their children were the ones pushing them out the door. Too much hovering only made them more nervous than they already were, or so they claimed. And they were busy tonight anyway, going to this vigil one of the kids had organized for Liana, to which parents were definitely not invited. Thank God, Sandy thought. The memorial service on Wednesday had been more than enough anguish for one week, and Sandy had had to deal with the continuing emotional fallout of Liana's gruesome death both at home and in class. All that acting out: the anger, the tears, the frustration. Helplessness masquerading as restlessness. Restlessness growing into willfulness. Willfulness translating into noise. So much noise.

Selfish as Sandy knew it was, she'd had enough of teenage angst. She had enough of her own. She couldn't answer their questions. She didn't know why these things happened or if—when?—they might happen again. She didn't know anything. Except that she needed a break, a time-out from grief and fear, even if it meant driv-

ing to the Atlantic Ocean to get it. Besides, it wasn't as if she and
Rita were planning to stay out all night. They'd be back in Torrance
well before midnight, which was when Sandy had told Megan and
Tim they had to be home. So, there was nothing to worry about,
nothing to feel guilty for.

Except Sandy *was* worried, and she felt guilty as hell. As late as
five o'clock that afternoon, she'd called Rita and told her she wasn't
going to Fort Lauderdale. And then Ian had phoned and suggested
getting together next week to talk, and she assumed (yet again—
how stupid could she be?) that he'd finally come to his senses and
realized what an idiot he'd been (*she* was the idiot!) and he wanted
to discuss coming back. She was silently rehearsing her already well-
rehearsed response—he'd hurt her badly, things could not simply
return to the way they'd been, there were obviously major issues
they'd have to deal with, a marriage counselor was probably a good
idea—when he'd said something about hoping they could keep their
divorce as amicable as possible (was there a *bigger* idiot in the entire
universe?), and she'd hung up without saying a word. Then she'd
called Rita back and told her she'd changed her mind about tonight,
and now here they were, in the latest, trendiest bar in Fort Lauderdale, where the smell of beer and whiskey competed with the
smell of surf and sand. Not only were they the oldest women in the
room, by at least a decade, they were also the most overdressed.
Who wears a silk cocktail dress to a bar these days? Sandy wondered, noticing that every other female in the room was wearing
tight-fitting, low-rise jeans that highlighted their taut, bare midriffs.
Of course, every other female in the room was under thirty, had
never given birth, and wore a size two, not to mention dangerously
high, open-toed stilettos, and see-through tops that exposed a
shocking amount of amplified cleavage. The only thing shocking
about Sandy's cleavage, she thought, securing the top button of her
red-and-white print dress, was that she'd considered showing it at
all.

"Look at you—you're gorgeous!" Rita had exclaimed with perhaps a touch too much enthusiasm when she'd picked Sandy up at
her door.

Sandy waved the compliment aside. She was presentable—maybe.

"You're gorgeous," Rita insisted, as Sandy had been hoping she would.

"I'm not gorgeous. I'm frumpy and flabby and flat-chested."

"Wow. That's a lot of F-words."

"You want another one?" Sandy asked sweetly.

Rita patted her freshly coiffed brown bob and blinked several times, as if it were a strain keeping her eyes open under the weight of all her mascara. "Come on. Our Prince Charmings await. Let's get this show on the road."

So now their show was on the road, but their dates were no-shows. Why was she surprised? Sandy approached the bar of trendy Miss Molly's Ocean Bar and Grill, pulling back her shoulders as she neared a group of men approximately her age. Maybe I don't look so bad, she was thinking. Hardly gorgeous, but definitely present-able—maybe. She smiled as she walked past the quartet at the bar. Not one of them so much as glanced in her direction. "Well, yes, now that you mention it, I *am* waiting for someone," she muttered to herself, pushing open the door to the tiny burgundy powder room. "Prince Charming should be here any minute." She stood in front of the large, gilt-edged mirror behind the white enamel sink, pleasantly surprised by what she saw. True, she was unlikely to be mistaken for a woman in her twenties, nor was she as *gorgeous* as Rita insisted, but she was indeed quite presentable. More than present-able actually. "You look pretty damn good," she told her reflection, tugging at a few wayward curls and reaching into her purse for her lipstick.

The tipsy sound of giggles from the other side of the door announced the impending arrival of several other patrons, and before Sandy could move out of the way, three young women, each closing in on six feet, all with long, straight blond hair and low-cut tank tops, blue jeans, and high heels, were crowded around her at the mirror. For an instant Sandy thought they might be triplets. It was only upon closer (and furtive) inspection that she saw that two of the girls had brown eyes while the third's were brilliantly blue, and that one girl bit her cuticles to the quick while the others boasted long, French-manicured nails. It was also apparent that two of the girls had implants. And one girl's smile was shier than the others', possibly because her teeth weren't as blindingly white as her friends'. Sandy decided she liked her the best.

The blue-eyed woman entered the stall behind them as the brown-eyed girls—was this really what Van Morrison had in mind?—began playing with their hair. "What do you think?" one asked the other. "Up or down?"

"I like it down. That's a neat shade of lipstick."

It took Sandy a second to realize that the young woman was talking to her. "Oh, thank you."

"What's it called?"

Sandy checked the bottom of the metallic, pink tube. "Passion Peach."

"Yeah? I like it. Like your ring too," she added with a nod toward the diamond eternity band on Sandy's left hand.

The ring had been a gift from Ian on their tenth wedding anniversary. It had replaced the thin gold band that was all they'd been able to afford when they got married. "Thank you," Sandy said again, thinking that eternity didn't last as long as it used to. *I was hoping we could keep our divorce as amicable as possible,* she heard Ian say. "Would you like it?" She pulled it from her finger.

"What?"

"My ring. Do you want it?"

The girl laughed. "What do you mean?"

"My husband wants a divorce, an *amicable* one apparently, so it looks like I won't be needing it anymore." Sandy held out her hand. "Really. You can have it."

Now the girl looked nervous. "Oh, no. I couldn't do that." She glanced toward her friend. Both girls glanced toward the stall.

"You're right," Sandy said, slipping the ring back on her finger. "Sorry. I didn't mean to be so weird."

"Oh, no. You're not weird," the girl lied.

"It really *is* a lovely ring," said the other. "You could probably sell it on eBay."

"That's right. I read that one of those girls from *The Bachelor* sold her engagement ring on eBay after that bastard dumped her."

"Did she?" Sandy had no idea what the girl was talking about, although the words *bastard* and *dumped* echoed in her ears as she hurried from the room. She heard the young women giggling even before the powder room door was fully closed.

"What was *that* about?" she heard one of the women say.

"What *was* that about?" Sandy asked herself out loud, looking around self-consciously in case anyone had overheard. But no one was looking at her, and nobody had noticed she was talking to herself, and if they had, they didn't care. This whole evening was a disaster, she and Rita had obviously been stood up, and it was time to cut their losses and run. She'd down her green-apple martini and leave, she decided as she made her way through the crowded room, people pushing past her as if she didn't exist. I might as well be invisible, she was thinking. A figment of my own imagination.

It was then that she saw them.

The Princes Charming. Middle-aged and pale-skinned. One balding, the other wearing what was obviously a toupee. Rita's date was the one with the hairpiece. At least Sandy assumed he was Rita's date because he looked like an older version of the Internet picture Rita had shown her. Actually he looked old enough to be that guy's father. He was wearing a dark green golf shirt decoratively sprinkled with floating white tees, and he was sitting with his arm casually draped across the burgundy leather banquette, his fingers stretching toward Rita's shoulder. He was animatedly talking and Rita was laughing, as if she were actually having a good time. Was she? Oh, God, Sandy thought. I'm not ready for this.

Rita saw her and waved. "Sandy," she called, loudly enough that several nearby patrons looked up from their drinks. "I was wondering what happened to you."

Sandy approached the booth as both men made halfhearted attempts to stand up.

"This is Ed," Rita said, introducing the man next to her. Sandy realized he wasn't much taller than Rita. "And this is his friend Bob."

Bob turned his balding head toward her, and Sandy noted he had a serious, pleasant face. Late forties, maybe fifty. Not handsome exactly, but definitely attractive. "Nice to meet you," she said, sliding into the booth beside him.

"This, of course, is my friend Sandy," Rita said. "Didn't I tell you she was gorgeous?"

Bob smiled his agreement. His smile said he was pleasantly surprised.

"Rita tells us you're from New York," Ed said.

"Well, Rochester, actually."

"I'm from New Jersey originally."

"Really? How'd you end up in Florida?"

"Came down with my first wife on a holiday, honeymooned here with my second, met my third in Miami, moved my practice down here—"

"Ed's a dentist," Rita interjected.

"It's on my profile," Ed said.

"You've been married three times?" Sandy asked, sipping on the green-apple martini in front of her. She didn't recall anything on the profile he'd posted on the dating website that mentioned he'd been married so many times.

"Four actually, but who's counting?"

Sandy swiveled toward Bob. "And you?"

"One marriage. One divorce."

"Same as you," Rita said, as if pointing out something they had in common.

"I'm not actually divorced yet," Sandy reminded her.

"She still hasn't seen a lawyer, if you can believe it. Bob, talk some sense into her. Bob's a lawyer."

"A divorce lawyer?" Sandy took another sip of her drink.

He shook his head. "Corporate and commercial. But I could recommend someone if you'd like."

"No, thank you. That's all right."

"I've already given her the name of a good divorce lawyer—Marshall Hitchcock in Miami. Do you know him?"

"'Fraid not."

"He's supposed to be really good."

"Can we talk about something else?" Sandy asked, taking a longer sip of her martini, feeling it starting to warm her throat.

"You sound just like wife number two," Ed said. "She was always saying that. 'Can we talk about something else? Can we talk about something else?'" he mimicked. "She talked herself right out of that marriage, I'll tell you. My God, get a load of the veneers on that girl." Sandy turned to see the young women she'd been in the powder room with walk by. One of them was laughing, and Sandy couldn't help but wonder if she was laughing about her. "Whoever did her mouth did a hell of a job."

Sandy finished the green-apple martini in one prolonged gulp. Immediately, she felt a lump of panic settle inside her stomach, like a stone in water. She couldn't do this. She couldn't sit in a cramped booth in a crowded restaurant, sipping martinis and making small talk with two men she didn't know and didn't want to know, although Bob seemed nice enough. Quiet and unassuming, maybe even a little modest. He'd actually blushed when Rita had announced he was a lawyer, although maybe he was just embarrassed. Maybe he didn't want to be here any more than she did. Which meant that maybe under different circumstances, he might be worth getting to know. But not now. Not when she was still so raw and unsure, when just the thought of dating curdled her stomach, when the idea of actually being intimate with a man, a man who wasn't Ian—had they ever been really intimate? she wondered now—was as terrifying as anything she could think of, and that included the possibility of a serial killer in their midst. She had to get away from all these people, from Rita with her cute brown bob and overly made-up, overly hopeful eyes; from Ed and his four wives, bad toupee, and talk of veneers; from Bob with his nice, serious face and modest mien; from the triplets; from Miss Molly's Ocean Bar and Grill; from Fort Lauderdale; from Florida.

From herself.

"Sandy?" a male voice asked from somewhere above her head. "Is that really you?"

Sandy turned around and looked up to see a handsome man

with salt-and-pepper hair smiling expectantly down at her. He was tall and slender and casually dressed in dark, pleated pants and a blue silk shirt, and his eyes had the kind of mischievous twinkle she'd always found devastatingly appealing. Normally she wouldn't forget a face that looked as good as this one, Sandy thought, trying to place him. But not only couldn't she put a name to the face, she couldn't insert the face into any previous context. Her mind raced quickly through her years at NYU, and when that cursory search failed to locate him, she went thumbing through her high school yearbook, trying to add lines and experience to otherwise blank eyes and bland expressions. Still nothing. Was it possible he was one of Ian's business associates? Had she met him at one of the dozens of medical conventions she'd attended over the years? Or maybe he was the father of one of her students, either here or in Rochester. Again, impossible. Surely she would have remembered that face.

"You don't remember me, do you?" he stated with the kind of bemused detachment that made him even more attractive.

"Of course I remember you," Sandy lied, climbing to her feet as the stranger embraced her in a welcoming hug.

"Will Baker," he whispered in her ear.

"Will Baker," she said out loud, reluctantly extricating herself from his grasp and staring into his gold-flecked, hazel eyes. She still had absolutely no idea who he was. "How are you?"

"All the better for seeing you again," he said, turning toward Rita and the two men at the table. "Will Baker," he said, extending his hand to both Bob and Ed. "A neighbor from Rochester, from way back when. Would you mind if I stole her away for just a few minutes?" Without waiting for an answer, he took Sandy's hand and pulled her gently toward the exit.

Sandy allowed herself to be led, the smell of the nearby ocean filling her nostrils as soon as they stepped into the cool, night air. It was a beautiful night, she realized, watching the tall palm trees in the parking lot sway to the sound of the surf. Where were they going? Who *was* he? "Who are you?" she asked, coming to a sudden stop next to a bright red Porsche.

"You still don't remember me?"

Sandy thought back to Harrison Street where she'd grown up in Rochester. There were the Maitlands to one side, the Dickinsons to the other. The Dickinsons had a son, but he was already a teenager when Sandy was a little girl, and so it couldn't be him. Nor could he be the Careys' boy. He'd been short and stocky, and even if he'd grown tall and lost his baby fat, he wouldn't have morphed into anything that looked like Will Baker. Besides, his name was Baker, not Maitland, not Dickinson. No Bakers that she remembered had lived on Harrison Street. Nor had there been any on Whitmore Avenue, where they'd moved after Harrison. "We've never met before, have we?"

A sly grin stretched across his mouth. "No."

"I'm not sure I understand."

"You looked like you needed rescuing."

"What?"

"I'm afraid I was eavesdropping, which is how I know your name is Sandy and that you're from Rochester. But I saw the look on your face when Mr. Ed was talking, and I thought, That's much too pretty a lady to be stuck listening to that crap, and so . . ."

"You came to my rescue."

"Forgive me?"

He thinks I'm pretty, Sandy thought gratefully. This beautiful-looking man, who could have his pick of any of the women in that room, and that includes the nubile triplets, picked me, the Ian reject, to rescue. "What else did you overhear?"

"That you're in the market for a good divorce attorney."

"Please tell me that's not you."

"It's not me," he assured her quickly.

"What do you do, that is when you're not rescuing damsels in distress?"

"Stockbroker. And you're a teacher."

"I didn't think we discussed that."

"I believe it was mentioned before you got back to the table."

"Anything else of interest that was mentioned while I was gone?"

"Trust me. There was nothing of interest going on at that table until you arrived."

Sandy smiled. He'd not only rescued her, he was flirting with her. And she was flirting back. She who, mere minutes ago, had found the whole idea of dating to be nausea-inducing. And all it took was one lethal green-apple martini and a handsome face. It seemed she was as easily swayed by a beautiful exterior as her soon-to-be-not-so-amicably-divorced husband.

Will patted the back of the red Porsche. "Care to go for a ride?"

If this is a dream, Sandy thought, it's the best damn dream I've had in years. "I can't leave my friends," she heard herself say.

"Sure you can."

Could she? Sandy wondered. Could she actually get into a stranger's car—how many times had her mother warned her against that very thing? How many times had she warned her own children?—even if that car was a shiny, new, tomato-red Porsche? Could she really be considering going for a drive with a man she didn't know, a man she'd met in a bar, for God's sake, when there might be a lunatic on the loose? (Had there ever been a serial killer who drove a Porsche? She didn't think so. Ted Bundy, for example, had driven a Volkswagen Beetle, and hadn't she once read that vans were the serial killers' vehicles of choice?) The only things she knew about Will Baker were his name and occupation—if they really *were* his name and occupation—and that he was the sexiest man she'd ever laid eyes on. (Take that, Dr. Ian Crosbie and your Barbie-doll clone. I can be every bit as shallow as you can.) Could she do it? Could she? *Could she?* "I'll have to let my friends know."

"Why don't you call them from the car?"

He opened the car door. Sandy glanced back at the bar, then climbed inside.

chapter fourteen

John Weber was pacing back and forth beside his police cruiser. The car was idling in his driveway, and small clouds of gray fumes puffed from the exhaust like smoke rings from a cigarette, polluting the clear, night air. Where was Amber, for Pete's sake? Hadn't she said she'd only be a minute? He checked his watch. It had been more than ten minutes already, and what on earth could she possibly be doing in there? "Give the girl a break," Pauline had yelled from the front door the first time he'd honked the horn. "She's almost ready." But how much did she have to do to get ready? She was going to a vigil, not a party. Or so the story went. Supposedly, a bunch of kids were getting together to mourn Liana in their own way—could it really have been a full week since her body had been found?—with songs and guitars and poems and reminiscences. It was to be less formal and more intimate than the memorial service her parents had held for her on Wednesday.

John didn't want Amber to go. He'd argued that she hadn't been particularly close to Liana, although, yes, they'd acted in *Fiddler on the Roof* together last year. Still, Liana had been almost two years her senior, and they hadn't traveled in the same social circles. And it was entirely possible that someone from her circle had killed her, someone who would probably be there tonight. John would much have preferred Amber to skip the damn thing, which he considered both morbid and excessive. But, as usual, he'd been outnumbered, two to one.

"It's a way for the kids to deal with their grief," Pauline had insisted.

"It just prolongs the misery," John had argued.

"You don't understand" came Pauline's automatic response. Her answer for almost everything these days. *You don't understand.*

And maybe she was right. Maybe he didn't understand. His way of dealing with problems had always been to solve them to the best of his abilities and then put them to rest. He didn't want to spend day after day rehashing what he already knew, asking the same questions that had been asked a hundred times already, or stating the obvious. (Although wasn't that exactly what he and his deputies had been doing all week?) He preferred to define the problem, arrive at a solution, then get the hell away from it as fast as humanly possible. You ran *away* from a fire; you didn't embrace the flames.

Besides, he suspected that along with the songs and the guitars and the poems and the reminiscences, the vigil for Liana would also involve alcohol and drugs. Christ, he remembered his own teenage years. All he'd wanted to do was drink beer, smoke weed, and get laid. Especially get laid. And if it meant having to strum a few wayward bars on a beat-up old guitar, or recite a few treacly poems he neither liked nor understood, well, he'd have been more than happy to oblige, if such displays of male "sensitivity" were what it took to talk little Jenna or Sue out of her tight little jeans. The boys today were no different from how he'd been. Hell, they were worse.

And Amber would be no match for them. With how much she weighed, or *didn't* weigh, one drink would be more than enough to tip the scales of common sense toward reckless behavior. Sixteen-year-old girls were easy enough to manipulate, especially when they were so hungry to fit in that they'd starve themselves to do it. John could see his daughter being coaxed into taking a tiny sip of someone's drink or a toke off somebody's joint. He didn't think she'd ever done drugs, but then how many times had he heard parents blindly insist that their children absolutely did not do drugs—*Never ever, no way!*—and how many times had he caught those same children smoking weed in the park or tripping out on Ecstasy?

At least she was still a virgin. He was pretty sure of that, he decided as he reached through the car's open front window and honked the horn a second time. She didn't have a boyfriend after all, had *never* had a boyfriend, for which he was grateful, although Pauline didn't share his gratitude.

"A girl her age should have boyfriends," she'd fret.

"A girl her age should eat," he'd counter.

Not for the first time, he considered the possibility that Liana's killer would be at tonight's vigil. He knew that murderers often attended their victims' funerals, that it gave them a sense of power, even a perverse sexual thrill. That was why he'd paid close attention to those who'd come to Liana's memorial service, but there'd been so many people in attendance that the crowd had spilled out of the church and onto the street, and while there were a number of faces John didn't recognize, no one had aroused his suspicions. The truth was that, despite his best efforts, he was no closer to finding Liana's killer than he'd been a week ago.

Sean Wilson had called at least once, and lately, two and even three times each day. So anxious was the so-called "tiny, perfect mayor" to see this case solved and "his" town returned to normal that he was beginning to actively interfere with John's investigation.

"Just what is it you expect me to do, Sean?" the sheriff had asked him yesterday afternoon when the mayor had cornered him as he was coming out of his office. Anyone watching the confrontation between the two men—and John had noticed several officers and virtually all the support staff secretly glancing in their direction during their sometimes spirited discussion—would have had a hard time suppressing a smile. The men were an almost comical study in contrasts. Sean Wilson was approximately a decade younger, fifty pounds lighter, and a full foot shorter than John Weber. His hair was thick and dark brown in comparison to John's thinning pate. His olive green suit was neat and stylish in contrast to the sheriff's old and wrinkled uniform. And while John's naturally deep voice underlined the almost girlish pitch of the mayor's excited utterances, the mayor's barbs were deadly nonetheless, spraying the air like pellets from a BB gun. John struggled to maintain his composure and keep his massive hands from reaching for the mayor's tiny, perfect throat.

"I expect you to solve this case," the mayor told him, as if this were something that might not have occurred to John, "and return my town to normal."

"That's exactly what I'm trying to do."

"By doing *what* exactly?"

John dug his fingers into his thighs to keep from throwing a punch at the mayor's head. To think he'd actually voted for the man. "Well, let's see," he began. "We've interviewed, and in many cases, reinterviewed, Liana's family and friends, her ex-boyfriends, her classmates, her neighbors, her teachers, the school principal, Cal Hamilton, Peter Arlington—"

"Yes, what about him?"

"What about him?" John repeated.

"Well, he was her boyfriend. They'd been fighting. Seems like a prime suspect to me."

"Except that Peter's father confirms he picked him up from school the afternoon Liana disappeared, that they went to a ball game in Miami, and that they had to leave the game early because Peter was feeling sick to his stomach. His mother says Peter stayed home from school the next day and that she called from work several times to check on his condition. She says she even came home during her lunch break and found him sleeping."

"I assume you've checked the ticket stubs and the phone records?"

"Of course." John shook his head. Thanks to TV shows like *Law & Order* and *CSI,* these days everyone was an expert on police procedural.

"What about Greg Watt and Joey Balfour?"

"They claim they were together at the time Liana went missing."

"Convenient. Can they prove it?"

"We can't *dis*prove it."

"And Cal Hamilton?"

"Says he was making the rounds of his suppliers."

"And was he?"

"We're still checking that out."

"Maybe we should contact the FBI." Not the first time the mayor had made that suggestion.

Truthfully, John himself had considered calling the FBI several times over the last week, but ultimately dismissed such a call as premature. "I think it's still a little early to be calling in the troops."

The mayor lowered his head, as if afraid to look John directly in the eye. "If we could just put our egos aside for a few minutes—"

"This has nothing to do with egos," John interrupted. *At least not mine,* he fought to keep from adding.

"Face it," the mayor continued, "you're not as young or agile as you used to be. You've got problems at home."

"Problems at . . . What are you talking about?" Did the whole town know about his battles with Pauline, his worries about Amber, his affair with Kerri Franklin? Probably, he conceded silently. Everyone pretty much knew everyone else's business in a town like Torrance. But did people think his inability to control his personal life meant he couldn't do his job?

"You've been doing this a long time," the mayor was saying. "Maybe too long."

"Some might call that valuable experience."

"Others might call it burnout." Sean Wilson paused, as if expecting John to interject, then continued when he didn't. "Besides, you're certainly not used to dealing with crimes of this magnitude. Serial killers are a little out of your bailiwick after all."

"We have no evidence we're dealing with a serial killer," John stated firmly. The truth was that, despite the missing girl from Hendry County and the recent false alarm with regard to Brenda Vinton, only one young woman had actually turned up dead. And while it wasn't his intention to downplay Liana Martin's grisly murder, that one girl had been killed simply wasn't enough to warrant calling in federal agents. Still, his gut told him that a serial killer was *exactly* what they were dealing with, and that it was only a matter of time before the killer struck again.

Maybe even tonight, John thought now, returning to the present as he reached inside the car window to honk the horn, hoping the abrasive sound would be enough to chase away the echo of the miniature mayor's giant doubts about his capabilities. Was it possible the man was right?

The front door of his house opened. Pauline appeared in the doorway, hands on her hips. "What's the matter with you? I told you she's coming."

"So's Christmas."

Pauline shook her head, retreated back inside. "Amber," he heard her call. "Your father's waiting."

As if Amber didn't know. As if he hadn't been standing here for—he checked his watch again—almost fifteen minutes. As if he had all night.

Which was exactly what he had, he realized. What was the rush? According to the mayor, neither he nor his investigation were going anywhere.

Amber suddenly materialized at her mother's side. John stared at her in amazement. She looked exactly as she had fifteen minutes earlier when she'd gone to get ready. The same jeans, the same powder-blue sweater, the same white-and-black sneakers. What had he been expecting? That she'd put on a dress? That she'd change her hair or put on makeup? That she'd miraculously put on ten pounds?

As she skipped down the front walk, he noticed that she had indeed applied a smear of blue shadow to her eyelids and added a rhinestone clasp to her hair, and as she drew closer, he realized she smelled vaguely of lemons, which he assumed was perfume. The scent settled uneasily in his throat. He'd never been particularly fond of perfume. He liked a woman's natural smell and could never understand why they seemed so intent on covering it up.

"You sure you want to go to this thing?" John asked as he and his daughter climbed inside the car. "It's not too late to change your mind."

"Why would I change my mind?" Amber fastened her seat belt and stared out the front window.

John backed the car out of the driveway, waved at Pauline as he drove down the street. But Pauline was already closing the door and didn't see him wave. "Pick up a DVD on your way home," she'd already instructed. "Your choice," she'd said, although he knew whatever he picked would be wrong. She was already angry he hadn't wanted to go out to a movie. "You never want to go anywhere anymore."

"I just think we should be available in case Amber wants us to pick her up early."

"She won't."

"She might."

She wouldn't. John could tell that already from the determined cast of his daughter's surprisingly strong jaw. She was angry at him because he'd insisted he'd pick her up at eleven o'clock, which she thought would make her look like a baby in front of all the other kids, but he wouldn't agree to her going unless she agreed to his terms, and so now she was mad at him, just as Pauline was mad at him, and had there ever been a time in his life when some woman *wasn't* mad at him? The time with Kerri Franklin, he thought, as he spotted Delilah walking alone on the other side of the street. He honked as he angled the car toward her.

"What are you doing?" Amber demanded. "Dad? What are you doing? You're not stopping, are you?"

"She's probably going to the vigil. We might as well give her a lift."

"No. Don't do that."

"Why not?"

"Because," Amber said, rolling her eyes in exasperation as he pulled the police cruiser to a stop and pressed the button to lower the window on the passenger side of the car. Amber flinched noticeably as he leaned his body across hers, pulling in her already concave stomach and holding her breath, the way she used to do when she was a little girl and couldn't have her way.

"Delilah," he said in greeting.

"Hello, there, Sheriff," Delilah said pleasantly. "Hi, Amber. How are you?"

Amber released the air in her lungs and grunted something that sounded vaguely like "Fine," but offered nothing further.

"Can I give you a lift somewhere?"

"I'm going to Pearson Park."

"That's exactly where we're heading. Hop in."

"No, Dad," Amber hissed underneath her breath.

"Gee, thanks. I was getting a little tired." Delilah opened the back door of the cruiser and climbed inside. "My mother said she might need the car, and my grandmother said I should walk. But it's so far," she continued apologetically.

"How *is* your grandmother?" John asked, although he really wanted to ask about Kerri. Does she miss me? Does she ever talk about me?

"She's pretty good for someone her age with a heart condition."

"She's a tough one, all right," John concurred.

Delilah laughed. John watched her in his rearview mirror as she wiped some perspiration from the underside of her double chin. "Oh, by the way, Amber, congratulations," she said.

John's head snapped toward his daughter. "Congratulations? What for?"

"She got the part of Bianca in *Kiss Me, Kate*."

"You did? Why didn't you tell me?"

"I told Mom," Amber said, as if this were explanation enough.

"Well, that's wonderful," John said, trying to disguise his hurt. "Isn't it?"

Amber shrugged. "It's all right."

"I think it's terrific," Delilah enthused. "I knew you'd get the part the minute I heard you read. You were the best Bianca by far."

"Well, isn't that nice to hear?" John said when his daughter failed to say thank you. What was the matter with her? Had she always been so rude? Had she lost her manners along with all those pounds? "What about you, Delilah? Are you going to be in the play?"

"I'm in the chorus," Delilah said cheerfully. "I wasn't really right for any of the major roles. And I'll be helping with painting the scenery and stuff, like I did last year. It was fun." She made several more attempts at conversation, all of which drew little more than a one-word response from Amber, and after a while Delilah sank back in her seat, letting the silence take over.

As soon as they arrived at the park, Amber unhooked her seat belt, threw open the front door, and stepped outside.

"Be here at eleven o'clock," John called after her as she headed toward a group of kids gathering under a nearby banyan tree. "Or call if you decide to come home earlier."

"Thanks so much for the lift, Sheriff Weber," Delilah said.

"Think nothing of it, Delilah. I'd be happy to give you a ride home later."

"Thanks, but I probably won't be staying too long."

"Well, I don't recommend walking home alone."

Delilah leaned over the front seat and smiled, almost gratefully. "I don't think you have to worry about me, Sheriff." She opened her door and got out of the car, hurrying to catch up to Amber.

Mutt and Jeff, John thought, as Delilah waddled up to Amber's side. Amber immediately picked up her pace, clearly embarrassed to be seen with Delilah. Why was it socially acceptable to look skeletal, John wondered, but not well-fed? He watched Amber blend into the group of kids under the banyan's spreading branches, while Delilah remained on the outside. He heard somebody sing, "Oh, no, it's Big D! I can tell!" and wondered what that was all about. He saw another group of kids gathered at the far end of the large park and watched the two groups start to drift together. He wondered where they'd settle, and if he should make his presence felt, then decided against it. He'd already assigned several officers to keep an eye on things, make sure nothing got out of hand, and to call him if anything looked even vaguely suspicious.

It would be dark soon, John knew, watching his daughter fade into a silhouette. He hoped she wouldn't disobey him, that she'd be there waiting for him at eleven o'clock. Why couldn't she be sensible and leave early, like Delilah?

Although he didn't like the idea of Delilah walking home in the dark alone. She might be an unlikely victim for attack, but she was still vulnerable. Maybe he'd drop by Kerri's house on his way to the video store, tell her he didn't think it was a good idea for her daughter to be out walking alone at night.

Except that wasn't the real reason he was here, he recognized, as he pulled the car to a halt in front of Kerri's house some ten minutes later, exiting the vehicle before he changed his mind. He knew he was being foolish, that Kerri had no romantic interest in him anymore, that she probably wasn't even home. It was Saturday night, as Pauline had already pointed out, and Kerri was undoubtedly out with Ian Crosbie, and John would be stuck talking to that miserable mother of hers. He shouldn't be doing this, he thought as he walked up the path to her house and knocked loudly on the door.

"He's here," John heard Rose shout from inside the house. Had she been watching him from the living room window?

"About time," Kerri said with a laugh as she pulled open the front door. She was wearing black capris and a pink, V-necked jersey that matched her bright pink lipstick. Her blond hair was half-up, half-down, and John wondered if this was deliberate, or if she hadn't been able to make up her mind. "John!"

"Kerri."

"Is something wrong? Has anything happened to Delilah?"

"Delilah's fine," he assured her quickly.

"Well, of course, she's fine," Kerri's mother, Rose, said from the sofa in the living room. "She's a goddamn Sherman tank, for God's sake. I told you you didn't have to worry about her. Come on in and sit down for a few minutes, why don't you, Sheriff?"

"I guess I can do that." John stepped into the living room and sank into the leather chair across from the tan sofa in which Rose was securely nestled. A lace doily slid from the top of the chair onto his shoulder, and he jumped, as if it were a spider.

"A little jittery, are we, Sheriff?" asked Rose.

John removed the errant doily from his shoulder, setting it onto the glass coffee table in front of him. "I'm fine, Rose. And you?"

"Surviving," she said wearily, as if the very act of survival required a superhuman effort.

John thought her continuing survival was probably harder on those around her, but didn't say so. Instead he said, "Glad to hear it."

"What brings you by?"

John looked toward Kerri, who had remained standing. She was staring at him expectantly. "Well, I saw Delilah earlier," he began, his voice at odds with his thoughts. What he was thinking was *Kerri's home, and it's a Saturday night.* "Actually, I gave her a lift to the park." *And since it's Saturday night and she's not out with Ian Crosbie, maybe that means the good doctor has returned to his wife, which would mean Kerri is once again available.* "I offered to pick her up at eleven when I go to get Amber, but she said she probably wouldn't be staying that late." *And we wouldn't have to get into anything serious. Just the occasional tryst, the occasional kind word out of those wildly exaggerated lips.* "And I just wanted to warn you that we still have a murderer out there, and it's probably not such a good idea for Delilah—or you, for that matter—to be out by yourself alone at night until we catch this guy."

"That's so sweet of you," Kerri said, "to worry about us."

"Why are you really here?" said Rose.

"I'm sorry?"

"You didn't drive over here to warn us about Delilah. The girl's a Sherman tank," Rose repeated, obviously enjoying the image.

"Mother, I wish you wouldn't say things like that."

"So why is it you haven't caught this guy yet?" Rose asked, ignoring her daughter's admonition. "You can be replaced, you know." She winked, as if to convey she wasn't referring only to his job.

John tried not to react, although he wondered briefly if Rose had been talking to the mayor.

"Do you have any leads?" Kerri asked, perching on the arm of the sofa.

"Not really," John admitted.

"What about Cal Hamilton?"

John was getting a little weary of people second-guessing him. "What *about* him?" he asked, his professional curiosity overtaking his personal angst.

"Just that there's something really peculiar about him. I had to run over there last week when Delilah was babysitting his wife—"

"What do you mean, 'babysitting his wife'?"

"He doesn't like to leave her alone, claims she has all these phobias, but I don't buy that for a minute. I think there's something really creepy going on over there."

"Like what?"

"I don't know. All I know is that I had to take a glass out of my own cupboard and rush it over there because Delilah accidentally dropped a glass on the floor—"

"A Sherman tank, I tell you," Rose interjected.

"—and Mrs. Hamilton panicked, and Delilah said she's obviously terrified of her husband, and she wouldn't be surprised to discover a bunch of dead bodies buried underneath the house. I told her I don't want her going over there anymore, but she says that someone has to look out for poor Mrs. Hamilton. Can you do something, John?" Kerri continued, his name sounding almost musical on her tongue.

"Not unless Fiona Hamilton files a complaint."

"Can't you get a search warrant or something?"

"On what grounds?"

"On the grounds that he probably killed Liana Martin."

"'Probably' isn't good enough, I'm afraid."

The doorbell rang.

Kerri jumped to her feet and tottered toward the front door on three-inch platforms.

"Pizza man," John heard somebody say.

"You're late," Rose yelled. "I'm starving."

"Mother, be nice," Kerri said as Ian Crosbie entered the room, a large pizza box in his hands.

"I hope you remembered the double cheese."

"Do I ever forget your double cheese?"

Rose giggled like the proverbial schoolgirl. "You know the sheriff, don't you, Ian?" she asked playfully, as John rose from his seat.

"Of course." Ian handed Kerri the box in order to shake John's hand. "Is there a problem?"

"Just dropped by to say hello."

"He gave Delilah a lift to the vigil," Kerri offered as explanation.

"Your kids go?" John asked the doctor.

"As far as I know."

What kind of an answer was that? John wondered. *As far as I know.* Why *don't* you know? You're their father, for God's sake. A father should know where his children are. Especially now, when there was a murderer walking around.

"Thanks for stopping by, John," Kerri told him as she walked him to the door.

"Take care," he told her. On his way home, he decided three things: one, that there'd be no more impromptu visits to Kerri Franklin; two, that he didn't like Dr. Ian Crosbie; and three, that he was personally going to take a closer look at exactly what the good doctor had been up to since his arrival in Torrance.

chapter fifteen

So, what do you think Mom's up to tonight?" Tim asked his sister as they hurried toward the park. She was walking quickly, and her ponytail swung back and forth like a pendulum.

"What do you mean?" Megan asked impatiently. "You know what she's doing. She went to Fort Lauderdale with Rita. Can't you walk any faster than that?"

"No, I can't. My foot's sore."

"Why's it sore?"

"I don't know. It just is. Why are you in such a hurry?"

Megan slowed her pace. What was the matter with her brother? It had taken him forever to get dressed. He'd eventually appeared in a pale blue, button-down shirt and fashionably ripped, stonewashed jeans, only to spend another ten minutes in front of the mirror in the hall on his hair—he kept glancing at her as if checking for her approval—only to have it end up looking exactly the same as before he'd started, the stubborn, dark blond curls refusing to unwind no matter how hard he tugged and pulled. At first she thought there might be someone at the vigil he was trying to impress—in truth, she was surprised at how quickly he'd agreed to come—but ever since they'd left the house he'd been dragging his feet, both literally and figuratively. Now they were almost twenty minutes late, although maybe that was okay. Better late than early. It wouldn't do to look too eager. *Treat 'em mean to keep 'em keen.* Isn't that what Liana once told her? (Had Liana been too mean? Had someone killed her because of it?) On the other hand, if she was *too* late, Greg might decide to leave, or worse, to hook up with another girl. It was a delicate balancing act, this man-woman thing, one she'd have to learn to master.

One her mother had *never* mastered, she realized, gradually resuming her previous pace. Talk about your learning disabilities. And was such a deficiency hereditary? Did her mother's incompetence in this area mean her social encounters with the opposite sex were doomed from the start? That she'd never be a success with boys? That any relationship she might have with a man was bound to fail? Was she destined to follow in her mother's footsteps, tripping over her own feet at every turn? "Just be yourself," her mother always counseled. But look where that advice had gotten her. No, if there was one thing Megan *had* learned, it was that "yourself" was never quite good enough. "Why do you think Mom's up to something?"

"Well, for starters, she was all dressed up."

Megan did a quick check of her own outfit—jeans by former Spice Girl Victoria Beckham, its blue crown insignia provocatively sewn into one of two back pockets, tight yellow jersey proclaiming the wearer a JUICY GIRL. "That horrible red-and-white silk thing? She's had it forever."

"You told her she looked nice."

"What was I supposed to say? That she looked like a tablecloth?"

"I thought she looked pretty."

Megan shrugged. To each his own, she thought. "Why else?"

"She didn't give us a very hard time about going out tonight."

"Are you kidding me? We have strict orders to stick together and be home by midnight."

"That's not so bad."

"Are you kidding me?" Megan asked again. What was the matter with her brother? Did he really think that spending time with his sister and being home by midnight *on a Saturday night* was okay? Were the kids right about him? Was he gay? "What else?"

"I don't know. She just seemed a little nervous to me."

"So? She's always nervous."

"Maybe. I just . . . Forget it."

"Just what?"

"Do you think maybe she has a date?"

"A date? You can't be serious."

"Why can't I?"

"Because she's not divorced yet."

"Neither's Dad," Tim reminded his sister.

"True. Can't you hurry up?"

"What's the rush? Liana's not exactly going anywhere."

Megan stopped abruptly in her tracks. "What did you say?"

"You heard me."

"I can't believe you said that. You're supposed to be so sensitive, for God's sake. Mom's always warning me to be careful what I say to you, 'cause you're so damn sensitive."

"I'm not so sensitive."

"Obviously. Jeez. How could you say that?"

"It was a joke."

"Yeah, well, it wasn't very funny."

Tim lifted his shoulders, then lowered them in an exaggerated shrug. If only he wouldn't slouch, Megan thought. He always looked as if he were about to fall over.

"Who would she have a date with?" she demanded as Pearson Park came into view. "She doesn't know anyone in Fort Lauderdale."

"Maybe Rita does."

Once again Megan stopped in her tracks. Was it possible? Could her mother really be out on a date? And if so, why was Tim the one to intuit it and not her? "No," she decided out loud. "She would have told me."

"Did you tell *her* about Greg Watt?"

"What?"

"No, *Watt*. Funny name, I know, but—"

"What are you talking about?"

"Don't you mean, *Watt* am I talking about?"

"So, help me, God, Tim. This is *so* not funny."

"It isn't?"

"What *about* Greg Watt?"

"Who? What? *Watt?*" Tim asked, then laughed out loud. "Sorry. Couldn't help myself."

"Tim, I swear . . ."

"No, don't do that. Greg might not approve."

"Where is this coming from?"

"Are you kidding? Where *isn't* it coming from?"

Megan felt her heart drop into her stomach. "It's on the Web?"

"Flashed on my computer screen as I was getting dressed. Couldn't believe my eyes."

So that's what had taken him so long to get dressed. That's what had accounted for all those sidelong glances as he was fixing his hair.

"Congratulations. You're famous," Tim continued. "Apparently you two put on quite a show at the audition. And I don't mean on the stage."

"I don't believe this."

"Then it's true? You were really making out with that muscle-bound moron?"

"No, of course it's not true. And he's not a moron."

"He's the mother of all morons. He probably posted that story on the Web himself. You really let him suck your fingers?"

"Oh, shit." Megan began spinning around in circles, torn between continuing toward the park and running for home. "Don't you dare say anything about this to Mom."

"What am I going to say to her? That you begged me to attend the vigil of some girl I couldn't stand so that you could be with some jerk *she* can't stand?"

"I did not beg you, we weren't making out, and what do you mean, you couldn't stand Liana?" Megan asked, trying to keep up with the sudden shifts in the conversation. "Since when?"

Again Tim shrugged. "Since always."

"Why didn't you like Liana?"

"Because she wasn't a very nice person."

"She was nice to me."

"Yeah, well, you were in the minority, believe me."

"I *don't* believe you," Megan insisted, pointing across the street at the large gathering of young people. "Everyone loved Liana. All these people are here to honor her memory."

"They're here because it's the only game in town. Where else are they gonna go? It's a happening, Megan. We're here to sing and dance and get high."

"That may be why *you're* here," Megan protested, having a hard time picturing Tim doing any of these things. But then, she was starting to think she didn't know her younger brother very well at all. He'd changed in the months since their father had moved out. "But it's not why *I'm* here."

"No, *you're* here to meet Greg Watt."

"I most certainly am not."

"Really? You better tell *him* that."

"What?" Megan spun around. Greg was crossing the street toward her, wearing an oversize, orange-and-black football jersey, his massive shoulders moving in rhythmic coordination with his slender hips. He had a self-satisfied grin on his face that bordered on idiocy. Why did she find him so damned attractive?

"There's my Kate," he said, swooping her into his arms. "Hi, jerk-off," he said to Tim before effortlessly scooping Megan into his arms and tossing her over his shoulder. "Bye, jerk-off."

Megan squealed, half in terror, half in delight, her hands slapping at Greg's back, her ponytail reaching for the ground. "I'll meet you back here at a quarter to twelve," she called to Tim as Greg proceeded across the street and into the park. "Put me down, Greg," she cried, but her voice sounded unconvincing, even to her own ears.

"Quiet, up there," he said, then bellowed at the crowd, "Make way for Petruchio and his woman."

Megan allowed her body to go limp. It was useless to argue. Her protests only fueled Greg's recently ignited dramatic fire. Besides, as much as she wanted to be upset with him—*had* he posted that story about them on the Web?—she found his antics charming, even thrilling. No one had ever picked her up and thrown her over his shoulder before. No one had ever called her his "woman" and paraded her around for all to see. Everyone was watching them. And while such behavior might not be considered strictly appropriate under the circumstances, no one seemed to mind. This was a vigil, after all, not a funeral. They were here to celebrate, not mourn. Still, should she really be enjoying herself quite this much?

A girl was dead. A girl she'd liked and admired. Although it was becoming increasingly clear that not everybody felt the same way. Certainly her brother hadn't. And how many others? she wondered. How many were here tonight just to sing and dance and get high? How many had come because it was "the only game in town"?

Megan lifted her head to see some sixty or seventy kids arranged in a large, free-floating circle, some talking softly, others laughing loudly, some with cigarettes dangling from their lips, others with candles waiting to be lit, some swaying to the random strumming of a handful of guitars, others swaying in passionate embrace. From upside down, she saw ghoulish Victor Drummond puffing on a joint that was then pried from his lipsticked-red lips by his equally ghoulish friend Nancy, who took several long drags before passing it on to Tanya McGovern. Megan wondered if it was wise of them to be smoking weed so openly when she was pretty sure she'd spotted several police officers patrolling the outskirts of the park. But Victor was already rolling another joint and seemed blissfully unconcerned with the so-called long arm of the law. Greg spun around and suddenly Brian Hensen popped into view. He was sitting off by himself, staring at Delilah Franklin, who was about twenty feet away, trying to engage Ginger Perchak in conversation. Closer to the main path stood Peter Arlington. Peter was kicking at the grass and staring vaguely into space, as if afraid to make direct eye contact with anyone. He'd probably gotten wind of what people were saying behind his back, that illness could be faked and fathers persuaded to lie for their sons. Megan didn't know Peter well, but she knew he'd been crazy about Liana, and she couldn't imagine him doing anything to hurt her.

She wondered what it felt like to have half your face blown away. She wondered if Liana's killer would ever be caught.

Megan sensed movement out of the corner of her eye. "Who's that?" she said, lifting her chin to get a better view of a large pineapple palm in the distance off to her right. "Is that Mr. Peterson?" She wondered what her science teacher would be doing in the park, lurking in the shadows. Was he there to spy on them, to report any indiscretions to the principal? But her question was drowned out by the sound of the guitars.

"You say something?" Greg asked.

"I thought I saw Mr. Peterson."

"Peterson? Where?" He spun her around.

"Wait. Put me down. You're making me dizzy."

Greg gently lowered her to the ground as a tremulous male voice began singing "Tears in Heaven." "I don't see him."

It took Megan a few seconds to reorient herself and locate the large pineapple palm. "I thought I saw him over there."

"Don't see anyone."

"Guess it wasn't him," Megan said as several boys emerged from behind the tree, pushing and shoving one another.

"Hey, Petruchio," Joey Balfour suddenly called from the middle of the crowd. "Saved you a seat over here, man."

"Catch you later," Greg called back, taking Megan by the hand and leading her away from the gathering.

"We won't be able to hear the speeches from over here," Megan protested weakly.

"Think we'll miss anything?" He led her toward a bench at the far end of the park, then pulled a joint out of the pocket of his jeans, prepared to light it.

"You really think that's a good idea? The area's crawling with cops, and if that *was* Mr. Peterson—"

"He'll tell your mother?"

"Or post it on the Web," she said pointedly.

Greg returned the joint to his pocket, leaned back against the green wooden slats. "I had nothing to do with that."

"Who did?"

"Could have been anybody."

"Joey?"

"Joey? Nah. My money's on Ginger."

"Ginger? Why would she do something like that?"

"I saw her watching us. And you got the part of Kate and she didn't."

"You swear it wasn't you?"

Greg smiled. "I swear," he said easily. "Gentlemen never kiss and tell."

"You're not a gentleman," she reminded him, although, strangely enough, she believed him. "And we didn't kiss."

"Yeah. I was kinda hoping we could do something about that tonight."

He leaned forward. Megan found herself holding her breath as his face drew closer and his mouth touched down gently on hers. She felt her lips start to tingle, the sensation spreading quickly across her body, like a rash, and she drew back. "You really think it was Ginger who posted the story?" she asked, turning away and looking at her feet, her voice barely audible.

His hand moved to her chin, guided her face back to his.

Megan closed her eyes and tilted her head, but instead of pushing his tongue down her throat, as she was half-expecting—he was a jock after all, and what did jocks know about finesse?—he planted a series of delicate kisses on her eyelids, sending her body into fresh spasms of shock and delight. If he doesn't kiss me again, she was thinking—on the lips and right this minute—I'm going to explode. And then he *was* kissing her, full on the mouth, and still she felt she was about to burst wide-open. She fought the urge to throw her arms around him and wrestle him to the ground. Who would have thought he'd be such a good kisser? she wondered as she only reluctantly came up for air.

"You want to lie down?" he asked.

"What?" *Watt?* she heard her brother echo. Megan's head shot from side to side.

"What's the matter?"

"My brother—I thought I heard his voice."

"I didn't hear anything."

Megan jumped to her feet. "I should go look for him."

Greg stood up, pressed his torso into her back. "Your brother's a big boy. He can take care of himself."

"It's just that I promised my mother we'd stick together."

"Are you always Mama's good little girl?"

Damn it. What was her mother doing here? Was she going to let her ruin everything? "Not always." Megan turned around, her mouth reaching for his. His arms wrapped around her as he lowered her to the ground. She shouldn't be doing this. Not here. Not now. They were moving way too fast. She'd get grass stains on her new Victoria Beckham jeans.

It was the last thought that brought her to her senses and back to her feet. "Wait, stop."

"What's the matter?"

"We shouldn't be doing this."

"Why not?"

"It's just not right. Not here. Not now."

"Where then?" he asked logically. "When?"

"No, you don't understand. We're moving way too fast." She decided to omit the part about getting grass stains on her Victoria Beckham jeans.

"I've always been a sucker for speed," he said, pushing himself off the ground. "Come on, Kate. What's your problem?"

"For one thing, my name's Megan, not Kate."

"I know that."

"The point is, you don't know *me*," Megan told him, thinking if she could just keep talking, she might be able to forget about the feel of his lips, the taste of his tongue. "And more important, since that doesn't seem to bother you a whole lot, I don't know *you*." She knew she'd give anything for him to kiss her again.

Instead, Greg plopped down on the bench, supporting the back of his head in the palms of his hands. "What do you want to know?"

"I don't know," Megan admitted, lowering herself onto the seat beside him. She hadn't thought that far ahead. "Tell me about yourself."

"Nothing to tell. Like they say, what you see is what you get."

"I don't think so."

"You don't?"

"I think you're way more complicated than that."

He shook his head. "Anybody ever tell you, you think too much?"

"My father used to tell my mother that."

"Yeah? Not so much anymore, I guess. Sorry," he apologized before Megan could react. "I guess that was a pretty dumb thing to say."

"It's okay. I mean, it's not exactly a secret that my parents have split up."

"I like your mom."

"You do?"

"Yeah. I give her a hard time and everything, but . . . she's cool."

"Cool?"

"And she's a good teacher."

Megan felt a surge of pride. She thought of her mother in her red-and-white silk dress and wondered what she was doing right now. "What about your parents?"

His body stiffened beside her. "My father is your typical farmer. He's a mean son of a bitch." He smiled, as if he'd just paid his father the highest of compliments.

"And your mother?"

"Dead. Two years ago. Cancer."

"I'm so sorry."

"Yeah, well, what is it they say? Shit happens?"

"You must miss her."

"Not so much anymore . . . You want to know what I miss?" he continued, unprompted. "I miss the way she used to sing when she was making dinner." He laughed.

"Did she have a good voice?"

"She was good at everything she did."

"I guess that's where you get your talent."

"Maybe." It was his turn to get to his feet. "So, I guess we should go join the others."

"We could sit here a little while longer," Megan offered, not wanting to leave.

"No, we should go. You're right. This isn't the time or place."

Megan stood up, waited for him to take her hand in his. But he was already walking away from her, and he didn't look back or slow down.

chapter sixteen

Where had his sister disappeared to now? Tim wondered, his eyes scanning the shifting crowd. He checked his watch, pressing the button on its side that illuminated the large dial, noting it was almost eleven o'clock. Where had she gone this time?

He peered through the darkness at the shadowy forms. Despite the tall, overhead streetlights that circled the park like a halo, and the smaller, more ornate gas lamps that lit up the various inner pathways, it was difficult to make out the individual faces of those still present. A number of kids had started wandering off about half an hour ago, having grown restless after more than two hours of well-intentioned, if badly executed, songs and pleasant, if boring, reveries, and those who remained had begun breaking off into smaller groups, which had made it harder for him to keep track of Megan.

Not that he wanted to. But what choice did he have? Someone in his family had to start behaving responsibly. And wasn't he the man of the house now? Wasn't it up to him to make sure everything was okay, that life continued on as normal a course as possible? Except what was normal anymore? Did anybody know?

He certainly didn't.

Young girls were murdered and their killers moved on, while fathers left home, also moving on—if not *in,* at least *not yet*—with every teenage boy's wet dream. Except, of course, his father was far from a teenager, Tim thought ruefully, kicking at a small stone with the pointed toe of his black leather boot and watching it skip across the dry grass. And shouldn't a man that age know better? And now his mother had taken off for Fort Lauderdale with her best friend, who just happened to be the school nurse, but who sure hadn't been dressed like the school nurse when she'd arrived at his house earlier tonight. And how long would it be before he was able to wipe the image of her plump, crinkly breasts spilling out of the top of her too short, too tight dress from his mind? God—what had she been thinking? What did people actually *see* when they looked in the mirror? Or didn't they look?

"Keep an eye on your sister," his mother had urged on her way out the door, undoubtedly the same advice she'd given Megan. "Keep an eye on your brother," he could hear her whisper, and he found himself wondering what she was doing at this exact moment, if she was having a good time, and that if she was on a date, if she was conducting herself in an appropriate manner.

Unlike his father.

Unlike his sister.

What did Megan think she was doing tonight anyway? And with Greg Watt, of all people. It was bad enough she'd allowed that overgrown celery stick to pick her up and toss her over his shoulder as if she were some weightless sack of potatoes, but then to make out with him in plain sight of everyone, in the middle of what was supposed to be a tribute to a murdered friend! Did she really think no one could see her? Just because she and Greg had gone to the other side of the park didn't mean they were invisible. Besides, somebody would have seen them even if they'd gone to the other side of the moon. Had she no sense of decency? No sense of decorum? No sense, period?

And then, mercifully, something had happened. He'd been too far away to see what it was, too far away to hear what was said, but clearly, *something* had happened, somebody had said *something,* and suddenly Greg and his sister were no longer clinging to each other like overgrown vines, and Greg was walking one way and Megan the other, and Tim hadn't seen them together again all night.

Nor was Megan with him now, Tim realized, not sure whether he was more relieved or worried as he caught sight of Greg and Joey in the middle of a group of jocks playing an improvised game of touch football. They were seemingly oblivious to the group of kids still sitting in a circle listening to Victor Drummond's execrable rendition of the old Beatles classic "Strawberry Fields Forever." Was Megan part of that group?

She didn't appear to be, Tim realized, trying to spot his sister in the dim light. But Megan wasn't among those either swaying to the music or waving their burnt-down candles against the cloying air. She had no interest in strawberry fields, Tim thought gratefully, thinking he'd never really liked that song. Stupid thing made no sense at all.

Not that anything did.

The sweet smell of reefer wafted toward his nose and he peered through the darkness at a group of kids passing a joint around beneath a large pineapple palm. For whatever reason, the cops had left them alone, probably deciding they were less likely to get into trouble if they were high on weed. Or maybe they were just too stupid to realize what was going on right underneath their noses.

Tim saw Ginger Perchak and Tanya McGovern and a few other girls crying softly as they waited for their toke, and he wondered if they were crying for Liana or themselves. He thought it interesting that even now, more than a week after Liana's body had been pulled from the ground, girls were still bursting into tears at the slightest provocation, or sometimes no provocation at all. Sometimes all you had to do was look at them the wrong way—was there a right way?—and they'd start to cry. And no one berated *them* or called *them* names. No one questioned *their* sexual orientation. Why were girls allowed—even expected—to show their emotions, no matter how trivial the situation, and boys forced to maintain their composure, no matter how serious? Where was the fairness in that?

"It's all right to cry, you know," his mother had told him after his father had left, her own eyes overflowing with tears. But it *wasn't* all right. He knew that without being told, even as he heard Megan sobbing in her bedroom. His father had lost his moral compass, and as a result their world had been turned upside down. Now he had to be vigilant, on the alert, ever watchful. If he wasn't strong, if he turned his head away, even for a moment, if he allowed his eyes to cloud over with tears, as his mother's eyes continued to do when she thought nobody was looking, how would he ever find his way again? How would he be able to lead them out of the darkness?

Once again Tim illuminated the dial of his watch, knowing even before he checked the time that only a few minutes had passed since the last time he'd looked. Where the hell was Megan? She wasn't with Greg and she wasn't with either Ginger or Tanya, and it was getting late, and they had to be home in an hour, and surely she hadn't wandered off somewhere on her own. Surely she wasn't *that* stupid.

And then suddenly the night air was filled with the most beautiful sound. A girl was singing, her voice as pure and clear as a cold mountain stream. *Can you save me in the morning?* she was singing, her voice gaining strength and purpose with each mournful refrain. *Can you save me in the morning?*

Tim turned toward the sound.

I've got to sit back down and quench my thirst. Before I cross that line, could you draw it first?

Tim found himself holding his breath. The singer was Delilah Franklin.

All around him, people began shifting their positions, cocking their heads, turning toward the sound. Whispers of disbelief wafted through the air. "Who's that?" someone whispered. "Is that really Delilah Franklin?" asked somebody else. "She must be lip-synching," proclaimed a third.

"Holy crap!" shouted Greg, dropping the football in his hands and pushing his way into the circle. "Is that Big D I hear singing?"

Delilah instantly fell silent, lowering her head and staring at the ground, as if praying it would swallow her whole.

"What's going on here?" Joey Balfour demanded, appearing breathless at Greg's side. "Sounded like a pig in heat."

"Shut up, Balfour," Greg said.

"I thought for sure another chick was being butchered."

"Jesus. I said, shut up."

"And I say, fuck you," retorted Joey.

"And I say, everybody's said enough," interrupted Victor Drummond. "We're supposed to be honoring Liana's memory, not acting like a bunch of assholes."

"Yeah, well, you'd be the expert on assholes, wouldn't you now, faggot?" Joey said.

There was a collective intake of breath. Tim watched Victor grab his guitar and slowly push himself to his feet. Tim wondered for an instant if Victor was going to swing the guitar at Joey's head, but Victor only turned his back and began walking away. "Party's over," he said over his shoulder.

"Oh, no, it ain't," Joey called after him. "Haven't you heard? It ain't over till the fat lady sings? Oops," he added. "The fat lady *did* sing."

There was laughter from those still sitting.

"Guess that means we can all go home," Joey continued. "The fat lady has definitely sung."

Tim waited for Greg to tell Joey to shut up again, to encourage Delilah to continue with her song. One word from him and all the ridicule might stop. But instead, he laughed along with the others, then shrugged his massive shoulders, as if to say, Sorry, I tried, then returned to his football game.

Delilah remained seated for several seconds, her head bowed. Tim wondered what she was thinking as she slowly struggled to her feet, then moved away from the group. "The fat lady has sung," a boy shouted from somewhere to Tim's right.

"Party pooper," a girl called after Delilah.

And then another burst of song, this time from the other side of the rapidly unwinding circle. It was quickly spread throughout the park by myriad disparate voices: *Every party needs a pooper. That's why we invited you. Party pooper. Party pooper.*

The unforgiving voices chased Delilah out of the park and onto the street. Tim watched her run across the road and disappear around the corner, feeling sorry for her in spite of himself. He didn't want to feel anything but scorn for the daughter of the woman who was responsible for breaking up his family. He shook his head, hoping to rid himself of such ill-placed sympathy. It didn't matter that Delilah had the voice of an angel. What mattered was that she was fat and awkward, and that made her an easy target. And being anywhere in her proximity made that person a target as well. No—Tim couldn't afford the luxury of sympathy.

"Wow," a girl said from behind his back. "Who knew she could sing like that?"

Tim spun around, found himself staring into the face of Amber Weber. "Yeah," he said, unable to say more. He'd always been shy around girls, and Amber Weber wasn't just any girl, she was the sheriff's daughter, and while she might be really skinny, she was also really tall, at least two inches taller than he was, and pretty, and he'd never known what to say to really pretty, really tall girls whose fathers were sheriffs, so what he said again was "Yeah."

"It makes you feel kind of sorry for her," Amber continued, as if she could read his thoughts.

"Yeah."

"Too bad she's so fat. She'd have made a great Kate. Sorry," Amber apologized immediately. "I know Megan will be fabulous in the part. I'm really looking forward to working with her."

"Yeah." Was she flirting with him? Tim wondered. She'd never said more than two words to him before, even though they were in most of the same classes together. "Have you seen her?"

"Your sister?"

"Yeah."

Amber looked around. "No. I saw her before," she said, then stopped without completing the thought.

Tim completed it for her. *With Greg,* the thought continued.

"How come you didn't try out for the play?" she was asking.

Tim shrugged.

"You should have. It's fun. Maybe you could talk to Mr. Lipsman. It might not be too late. You could be in the chorus or something."

"I don't think so," Tim said.

"Musicals just not your thing?"

Tim shook his head. What was she implying? That because his name had made that stupid faggot list it meant he was supposed to like musicals?

"Do you know what time it is?" Amber asked.

What was the matter with the watch she was wearing? Tim wondered, checking his wrist. Wasn't it working?

"That's so cool," Amber said, pointing to the illuminated dial.

"It's almost eleven."

"Damn. I have to go. My father's picking me up." She pointed to the opposite end of the park. "You want a ride home?"

Tim would have loved a ride home. His leg had been bothering him all day and standing around half the night hadn't helped matters. Not to mention he was bored and tired and mad at Megan. Where was she anyway? "Can't." He thought he saw a hint of disappointment flicker through Amber's eyes. Was it possible? "I could walk you over there," he offered, the longest string of words he'd put together all night.

"That'd be great. I'm a little nervous. You know."

"Yeah."

They started ambling through the park, sidestepping the kids still clinging to the edges of their disbanded circle, now barely a semicircle really, and trying to avoid being hit by the careless football whizzing past their heads. "Hey, jerk-off," Greg called after him. "Leaving without saying good-bye?"

"You see my sister?" Tim asked.

Greg made no response.

Tim wondered for an instant whether Greg had heard him, but the slight sneer tugging at Greg's lips confirmed he had, and that there was nothing to be gained by asking the question again. He toyed with the idea of giving Greg the finger, then quickly thought better of it. His mother had enough to worry about without him coming home with a body full of broken bones. Again he wondered what his mother was doing, and whether she was on her way home. Fort Lauderdale was approximately an hour's drive away. That meant she and Rita should be heading for the highway if they planned on making it back home before midnight.

"*He's* the jerk-off," Amber whispered, touching his elbow.

Tim felt a bolt of lightning travel from his arm directly to his penis. He had to stop for a minute, his legs unable to proceed.

"Are you okay?" Amber asked, touching him again.

If she didn't stop, Tim thought, he'd be a paraplegic before he reached the sidewalk. "Yeah," he grunted.

"Something wrong with your leg?"

"I hurt it earlier," he managed to croak out.

"Yeah? How'd you do that?"

"Tripped," he lied. He couldn't very well tell her he'd been trying out some moves from a kung fu movie he'd seen on television the previous night and had gotten twisted inside his own feet before crashing to the floor. It had looked so easy, he was thinking. And it might come in handy if he ever had to protect his mother or sister from . . . what? And who was he kidding? He couldn't get out of the way of his own feet, for God's sake. How would he be able to protect anybody else?

"You have to be more careful," Amber said.

"Yeah."

This time she kept her hands to herself and they walked the rest of the way in silence, Tim's eyes perusing the premises, hoping to catch sight of Megan. Amber's father's police cruiser was parked on the street when they got there, her father waiting beside it.

"Hi, Dad," Amber said, pulling away from Tim's side. "This is Tim. Tim Crosbie."

Tim watched the sheriff's eyes narrow as he extended his hand. "Ian Crosbie's son?"

"Yes, sir." Tim felt his fingers crunch inside the bigger man's sturdy grip. His hand went quickly numb.

"Tim's mom teaches English," Amber said. "I get her next year."

If we're still in Florida, Tim added silently.

"Can we give you a lift home, Tim?" the sheriff asked.

"No, thank you, sir. Thanks anyway."

"Tim's waiting for his sister," Amber explained. But the sheriff was already getting back into his car.

"What about Delilah?" Tim heard him ask.

"She left already." Amber opened the passenger door and climbed into the front seat beside her father, offering nothing further. She turned back and waved as the car pulled away from the curb.

Tim stood on the sidewalk, watching the car until it was absorbed into the horizon, rubbing the elbow Amber had touched with the hand her father had mangled. What was that all about? he wondered. Had her sudden interest in him meant she was, in fact, *interested,* or had she just been interested in a chaperone, someone to make sure she made it to the other side of the park safely and in one piece?

"Who knows?" he said, as he began his return trek through the park. *Who the hell ever knows what goes on inside a woman's head?* he could hear his father muttering.

He was almost halfway through the park when he saw a lone figure leaning against a large royal palm, staring into the bushes beyond the nearby path. "See anything interesting?" Tim asked, approaching cautiously.

"What's your idea of interesting?" came the measured reply.

Tim shrugged. He was sorry he'd asked. He should have known better. Brian Hensen was a weird one. "I understand our mothers are out on the town together."

Brian angled his shoulders toward him without changing the position of either his hips or his feet. Tim thought that must be hard to do. "Guess so."

"Your mother has friends in Fort Lauderdale?" Tim tried to make his question sound as casual as he could. He leaned against the side of the tree, hoping to get some information about what exactly his mother was up to while simultaneously taking the weight off his sore leg.

"Not that I know of. Why?"

"I thought that's where they were going."

"Yeah? She didn't say." Brian reangled his shoulders back to their original position. He stared into the distance. "I think they had dates lined up," he said after a lengthy pause.

Tim's mouth went dry. "What makes you think that?"

"I've been reading her e-mails. She's signed up with some online dating service."

Tim was more shocked by Brian's audacity than by the fact Rita Hensen was using a dating service to meet men. But what shocked him most of all was that his mother was somehow involved. He checked his watch again, although this time he didn't bother illuminating the dial. "They should be home by midnight."

"Yeah? Don't hold your breath."

Tim realized he was doing just that, and he released the air in his lungs in one prolonged, and painful, exhalation. "You seen my sister?"

Brian shook his head. "Not for a couple of hours."

Tim pushed himself away from the tree. He had to find Megan. Where *was* she? And what was his mother doing going out with men she met through an Internet dating service? Was this her way of get- ting back at his dad, some twisted idea of payback? Women were so confusing, he thought. Maybe he should just go live with his father. It would probably be a whole lot easier.

Except that his father didn't want him. Hadn't he made that per- fectly clear by moving out?

"My mom told me your dad committed suicide," Tim said, then thought he probably shouldn't have. He and Brian weren't exactly friends, despite their mothers' best efforts. This was probably the longest conversation they'd ever shared.

"She's right."

"She said you were the one who found him."

"Right again."

Tim couldn't tell from the sound of Brian's voice whether he was angry. Brian tended to sound the same no matter what he was say- ing, his voice flat and surprisingly deep for one so slight. Although he wasn't really as slight as Tim had once thought, he realized, not- ing the size of Brian's muscles beneath his tight, gray T-shirt. While his complexion was still an otherworldly pale, lending him an almost fragile air, he'd bulked up considerably in recent months. Tim wondered if he'd been working out and thought of asking him about his exercise routine. Instead he said, "What was it like? Find- ing him, I mean."

"It was pretty gross," Brian replied matter-of-factly. "I mean, he'd hanged himself, you know, and his eyes were bulging out and his tongue was off to one side, kind of like this." This time his whole body swiveled around to face Tim. He jerked his head to one side, thrust his tongue out of his mouth, and widened his eyes so that their whites all but glowed in the dark.

Tim took an involuntary step back.

"I thought I might try it sometime," Brian continued. "I don't mean kill myself, of course. Just a minor blackout. I hear some people really get off on it."

Tim began backing away. He'd gotten enough of a charge from Amber Weber simply touching his arm. "I should get going. Gotta find Megan," he said, stumbling on his sore leg and falling on the ground.

Brian extended his hand to help Tim up. "That was very cool," he deadpanned.

They heard a rustle in the bushes up ahead, saw a man emerge and walk along the path toward them, the light from one of the lamps casting shadows across his bald head.

"Mr. Peterson," Tim gasped. "What are you doing here?"

"Just keeping an eye on things," the science teacher replied with a sly smile. "Making sure they don't get out of hand." He nodded toward Tim's hand, still in Brian's.

Tim immediately pulled his hand away. "I fell," he stammered. "Brian was just helping me up."

Mr. Peterson's smile spread to his eyes. "Have a nice night, boys." He continued on down the path.

Behind Tim, Brian was laughing.

Tim spun around, almost falling a second time.

"Careful there," Brian warned, then laughed again.

"What's so funny?"

"You should have seen your face."

"You know what he was thinking, don't you?"

"Who cares what he was thinking?"

"Shit," Tim muttered. Were the rumors true? Was Brian gay?

"You want to know what I think?" Brian asked.

"Not especially."

"I think you should go find your sister," Brian said anyway. Then he laughed again.

chapter seventeen

Sandy was wondering how one human being could be so stupid. Especially one who was supposed to be so smart. Or at least smart enough to have been entrusted with the impressionable minds of several hundred young people, minds she was supposed to be developing, shaping, guiding. Who was she to guide anybody?

What had she been thinking? How had she gotten herself into this mess?

She did a quick recap of the evening's more salient events: at seven-thirty, Rita had picked her up; by eight-thirty they were pulling into the parking lot of Miss Molly's Ocean Bar and Grill in Fort Lauderdale; at approximately nine o'clock, their dates had arrived; several minutes of excruciating conversation later, Will Baker had miraculously appeared; less than fifteen minutes after that, she was speeding down the highway in his bright red Porsche, laughing and stealing looks at the disarmingly handsome and charming man whom she might have thought too good to be true had she been thinking at all. What was it they said—if something seems too good to be true, it usually is? Why hadn't she thought of that before she agreed to get in his car, before she used his cell phone to call Rita and tell her she wouldn't be coming back, asking her to apologize to Bob and Ed on her behalf, and saying she'd speak to her in the morning?

"I'm sorry. I think we have a bad connection," Rita had answered calmly as Sandy pictured her excusing herself from the table. "What do you mean, you'll call me in the morning?" she demanded moments later. "Where the hell are you?"

"I'm with Will," Sandy responded, as Will smiled and reached over to pat her hand. His hand lingered on her thigh, and Sandy felt—and quickly dismissed—the first pang of doubt about what she was doing.

"Well, I'm not exactly thrilled, but I can't say I blame you. He's very cute."

"I agree."

"Is he going to drive you back to Torrance?"

"I assume so."

"Maybe you better find out."

"Don't worry. I'll call you in the morning." Sandy hung up before Rita had a chance to say anything else.

"So, everything okay? Your friend not mad at you for leaving her with those two yahoos?"

"Oh, they weren't so bad." Actually Sandy had found Bob pleasant enough and felt a stab of remorse for having ditched him so cavalierly. He deserved better. "And Rita's cool. She'll handle it."

Rita's *cool*? Sandy repeated silently. Since when had she started speaking like one of her students? What was happening? First she'd deserted her best friend for a handsome stranger. Now she was tossing out unfamiliar words like *cool*. It was a slippery slope she was traveling on, she thought, wondering if they were headed anywhere in particular or just cruising around. "Beautiful night," she said instead of asking, settling into the tan leather bucket seat. "Beautiful car."

"Beautiful night. Beautiful car. Beautiful girl," Will said with an easy smile.

Sandy smiled too. How long had it been since anyone had referred to her as a *girl*? And while she would certainly have bristled had either Ed or Bob used that appellation earlier, she found it downright thrilling coming from Will. She leaned her head back, luxuriating in the recklessness of what she was doing. She'd always been such a good girl, such a stickler for playing by the rules. And where had it gotten her? It had gotten her to Torrance. It was definitely time for a change. "So, are you from Florida originally?" she asked, wishing she'd been able to come up with something fresher.

"Is anyone?" he asked in return.

"Practically everyone in Torrance was born there."

"Torrance?"

"Where I live," Sandy explained. "It's about an hour west of here."

"Isn't that where that girl was murdered last week?"

A second pang. "Yes. You know about that?"

"Just what I read in the papers. They find the guy?"

"Not yet."

Will was silent.

"So, where *are* you from?" Sandy asked.

"Chicago."

"Got tired of the long winters?"

"Got tired of the hassles with my ex. Decided it would be in everybody's best interests if I relocated."

Sandy felt yet another pang of doubt jab at her side. That's silly, she told herself. So what if he has an ex-wife? What did she expect? That he was without a past, without flaws? Besides, wasn't she a soon-to-be-ex herself? *Ex*-wife, soon-to-be-*ex*, what *ex*actly had she been *ex*pecting? *Ex, ex, ex, ex,* she repeated silently, enjoying the harsh sound. "Do you have children?" she heard herself say.

"Two boys. One's seven, the other's nine."

Which meant he was probably younger than she was, Sandy realized, a fourth pang poking her squarely in the ribs.

"You?" Will asked.

"A boy and a girl. Megan's seventeen; Tim's sixteen," she added reluctantly, wondering how much younger than her Will might be. Five years? A decade? And what did that mean exactly? That he had a thing for older women? That he considered age unimportant? That he was as blind as a bat without his glasses?

"Really? You must have had them very young."

"I was ten actually," Sandy said.

Will laughed. "A child bride."

"Just about."

"And what happened?"

"We grew up."

Will nodded. "Yeah. It happens to the best of us."

"Apparently."

"What's he do?"

"He's a doctor."

"Well, that works out great for you."

"It does? What do you mean?"

"You can soak him for all he's worth."

Sandy detected a slight hint of anger behind Will's expansive smile. Another pang. "I'm not interested in soaking him."

"That's what they all say in the beginning. Then they change their minds."

"They?"

"You put him through med school?"

"Yes. But then he put me through teacher's college later on."

"You still come out ahead."

Sandy heard herself sigh. She turned away, stared out the window at the passing scenery. A row of high-rise condominiums was blocking out any view of the ocean beyond. She thought of Rita, wondered how she was managing with Ed and Bob. She owed her friend an apology, she decided. Maybe she'd pick up a plant from Publix or a box of chocolates. The thought of chocolates made her stomach rumble. She crossed her hands over her stomach self-consciously.

"I take it the divorce wasn't your idea," Will said.

Was it that obvious? "No. It wasn't."

He touched her hand. "Doesn't mean it wasn't a good one."

Sandy smiled, feeling the tension in her body ease. "Where are we going?" she asked as he turned left at the next corner.

"Thought we'd stop for a bite to eat."

Good idea, Sandy thought, as her stomach rumbled again. The sports car picked up speed. Within minutes, they'd left the ocean far behind. "There doesn't seem to be a lot of restaurants in the area," Sandy noted, her eyes scanning the quiet residential streets.

"Who said anything about restaurants?" He turned right, then left, then left again into the parking lot of a modest-looking, twenty-story, white building. He pulled into a space marked 602 and turned off the engine. "Here we are."

"Here we are where?"

"Be it ever so humble." He jumped out of the car, quickly coming around to her side and opening her door.

Sandy hesitated. "Will . . ."

"Something wrong?"

"I'm just not sure this is a very good idea."

"What's not a very good idea?"

"This." Did she have to spell it out?

"This?"

Apparently she did. "Going up to your apartment."

"Are you afraid of elevators?"

She laughed. "No. I just thought . . ."

"What did you just think?" He was smiling again. Clearly he was enjoying himself. "You thought we'd spend all night just driving around?"

Sandy realized she hadn't been thinking that far ahead, that she hadn't been thinking at all. "I just don't want you to get the wrong idea."

"And what idea would that be?"

"You know." This was silly. She was behaving like an adolescent.

"You think I want to get you up to my apartment so that I can have my way with you?"

"No. It's not that." Of course it was. Why else did a man bring a woman back to his apartment? She may have been away from the dating scene for twenty years, but no matter how much the world had changed in those twenty years, some things never did, and this was definitely one of those things.

"Okay. Truth time," Will was saying. "And the truth is, I'm starving. I haven't had anything to eat since breakfast, been working like a dog all day, and I stopped at Miss Molly's on my way home, hoping to grab a bite, which was when I overheard your conversation and saw your discomfort and made a judgment call to spirit you away, but now I'm so hungry I'm about to faint, and I can't drive anymore without something in my stomach, and I have some leftover chicken in my fridge, that I made myself, incidentally. Did I tell you I'm a great cook?"

Sandy shook her head.

"Well, I'm a great cook. Come on, Sandy. What's the matter? You trusted me enough to get into my car. What are you afraid of now?"

"I'm not afraid."

"You think I'm a dangerous man?"

"What? No."

"So what's the problem?"

What *was* her problem? Sandy wondered. Her body swayed toward him, although her legs refused to move.

"Look. I tell you what. We'll go inside for two minutes. I'll check my messages, grab a piece of chicken, and then I'll drive you back to Torrance. Okay? How's that? Can't get much fairer than that, can I? You can even wait in the car, if you don't trust me."

Sandy felt her lips relax into a smile. She was being silly, she told herself. Will Baker was a sophisticated man. And she was a grown woman, not some helpless teenager. So, stop acting like one, she told herself, climbing out of the car. "Maybe I'll have a piece of that chicken myself."

"Thought you'd come around."

They proceeded inside the heavily mirrored, white-and-gold lobby of the old building, where an elderly security guard sat behind a high marble reception desk. "Hello, Mr. Baker," the man said, waving as they walked past.

Sandy felt whatever tension remained in her body dissipate. She had nothing to worry about. The security guard knew Will by name. And he'd seen her face. She was perfectly safe.

"Mr. Samuels," Will said as he guided Sandy toward the bank of elevators at the rear of the lobby. "How are things?"

"Pretty quiet. You heard about Mrs. Allen in 1412?"

"No. What happened?"

"Stroke. Last Monday." Mr. Samuels tried snapping his arthritic fingers. "Went like that."

"Sorry to hear that. How's Mr. Allen holding up?"

"Are you kidding? The quiches have already started piling up outside his door. He won't have any trouble, believe me."

Will laughed as the elevator doors opened behind him. "Catch you later, Mr. Samuels." Will pressed the button for the sixth floor.

"It's so easy for you guys, isn't it?" Sandy commented as the elevator doors drew to a close.

"What is?"

"Women."

Will laughed. "Why do you say that?"

"Well, here's poor Mrs. Allen in 1412 who drops dead from a stroke, and before her body even hits the floor, women everywhere are running to their stoves to make Mr. Allen dinner."

"You're saying he shouldn't eat?"

Sandy smiled. "I'm saying that sort of thing wouldn't happen if it had been *Mr.* Allen who'd had the stroke. Mrs. Allen would be fixing her own dinner."

"Real men don't make quiche," Will quipped as the elevator doors opened onto the sixth floor. He stepped back to let Sandy exit.

"But I hear they make a mean chicken," Sandy said, walking beside him down the narrow, gold-carpeted hallway.

"They make excellent chicken." Will unlocked the apartment door and Sandy entered the tiny tan-and-green-striped foyer. "This way." He led her past a small galley kitchen into a sparsely furnished living-dining area that contained a green leather sofa and matching chair, a half-filled bookcase, and a small, glass-topped dining-room table with two high-back, black leather chairs. Large squares of beige ceramic tile covered the floor. There were no area rugs, no paintings on the off-white walls, no photographs or knickknacks of any kind. "Make yourself comfortable. I'll be right back."

Sandy walked to the bank of windows that made up the apartment's east wall and stared across the street at another tall building. Welcome to the big city, she thought, feeling an unexpected rush of exhilaration. She'd forgotten how much she missed cramped spaces in tall buildings, she realized with a laugh, hearing Will moving around in the kitchen. "Can I do anything to help?"

"Not a thing."

"How long have you lived here?"

"About a year."

"It's very nice," she said, mentally redecorating, replacing the green leather furniture with something softer, painting the walls a warmer, more inviting shade. Actually the apartment wasn't unlike the one she and Ian had lived in just before she'd gotten pregnant with Megan. It was about the same size and shape, although it had fewer windows and the floors were cheap wood, not expensive tile. They'd been happy enough there, she thought. Of course she'd thought they were happy enough right up until the moment he'd announced he was leaving her for another woman.

Kerri Franklin winked at her from the reflection in the glass. Sandy closed her eyes, opening them only when she felt something stir behind her. She turned around just as Will reentered the room, a drink in each hand.

"Green-apple martini, right?"

"Oh, God, no. I couldn't."

"Sure you can. Chicken's gonna take a few minutes to heat up."

"We don't need to heat it up. I'm sure it's delicious cold."

"Who's the chef here?" he reminded her.

Sandy was about to remind *him* that he said they'd only be a few minutes, but she decided against it. She didn't want to sound ungrateful, since it was obvious he was going to all this trouble to impress her. Hadn't Ian once complained she didn't know how to have fun, that she was always the first to leave a party, the one who put a damper on everyone else's good time?

"Come on," Will was saying. "Have a few sips and try to relax. I'll check my e-mails and then we can eat."

Sandy nodded, taking a few tentative sips of her martini to prove she wasn't a spoilsport, then watched him walk from the room. She took another sip of her drink, thinking that if his chicken was half as good as his martini, she was in for a real treat. She sat down on the sofa, feeling the silk of her dress immediately stick to the leather of the seat, and she crossed and uncrossed her legs several times, trying to get comfortable. She took another sip of her martini, which tasted far more of green apples than it did vodka, so there was probably little danger of her getting drunk, she decided, taking another. She looked around for a table on which to deposit her glass, but there wasn't one, so she took another sip instead, and then another and another, each sip longer than the one before, until she realized she'd finished half the glass. What the hell? she thought, downing the rest. Nobody was going to accuse her of not knowing how to have fun.

"Hey, Sandy," Will called from the other room. "Come here. You've got to see this."

Sandy lowered her now empty glass to the floor, then stood up, feeling the room spin around her. "Whoa," she said, grabbing the back of the sofa and pausing until the spinning stopped.

"Sandy," he called again.

"Where are you?"

"The bedroom. Turn right at the hall."

The bedroom, Sandy repeated, turning left instead and finding herself in the kitchen. I'll just check on the chicken, she thought, leaning over and sniffing at the air as she pulled open the oven door.

The oven was empty.

Sandy pulled back, the sudden motion creating ripples in the still air. Maybe she'd misunderstood, she thought, fighting to clear her head. Hadn't he said the chicken was heating up?

"Sandy," he called again. "What's going on?"

"Coming." She proceeded down the hall toward the bedroom, even as a nagging voice was telling her to hotfoot it out the door. "I thought you said the chicken was heating up," she told him from the doorway.

"I said it would take *a few minutes* to heat up," he corrected her. "I'm preheating the oven now."

"Oh." Had the oven felt warm?

"Anybody ever tell you you have a very suspicious nature?"

"Sorry." She shifted her weight from one foot to the other, fighting the almost overwhelming urge to sink to the floor.

"You okay?"

"I think that drink went right to my head."

"You drank the whole thing?"

"Probably a mistake."

"You want to sit down?" He looked toward the king-size bed that took up most of the room.

Sandy noted the navy satin sheets and shook her head. Bad idea, she thought, as the room spun around her. "You said you wanted to show me something?"

Will pointed at the computer on the narrow desk across from the bed. "Take a look at this."

Sandy approached the large, flat-screen monitor, her eyes widening as she absorbed the image on the screen. "Oh, my God."

"Can you believe the kind of stuff people send you?"

Sandy stared openmouthed at the image of a man and a woman, both naked, the woman bending forward from the waist as the man cupped her breasts from behind, his huge erection positioned strategically at her rear end.

"Great ass, huh?" Will said.

Sandy wasn't sure if it was the feel of Will's hands suddenly cupping her own breasts or his easy use of the word *ass* that did it, but suddenly, she was pushing him away and propelling herself toward the bedroom door.

"What are you doing? Where are you going?" he asked, grabbing her hand and pulling her back, pressing her open palm against the front of his pants.

Sandy yanked her hand away as if he'd just placed it on a hot stove. "I'm out of here."

"Don't be silly. What'd you come here for?"

"I thought we were having chicken," Sandy sputtered, knowing how ridiculous she sounded.

"Oh, come on," he said, dekeing around in front of her and blocking her exit. "Nobody's that naïve."

"Apparently somebody is. Look. I'm sorry if I gave you the wrong impression." Was he going to let her out of here?

"The wrong impression? You've been coming on to me all night."

"What? How can you say that?"

"You got into my car, didn't you?"

"Yes," Sandy admitted, feeling her stomach start to swirl along with her head. "That wasn't too smart. I admit that. But now I'd like to go home."

"To Torrance?"

"Yes. To Torrance."

"Where that girl was murdered." A statement this time, not a question.

Sandy found herself holding her breath.

"Think she was stupid enough to climb into a stranger's car?"

"Oh, God." Sandy's stomach started doing flip-flops against her heart.

"Think all she was expecting was a nice chicken dinner?"

What was he saying? That he'd murdered Liana Martin and was about to kill her as well? Would the police find her rotting corpse in some distant swamp with half her head blown away? The thought propelled her into action. She pushed him out of the way and raced for the apartment door.

He was right behind her. "You want out?" he demanded, once again blocking her exit. "Fine. You want out? Get out." He reached behind him and opened the door. Immediately, Sandy bolted toward the elevators, his voice in hot pursuit. "You're pathetic. You know that? You want to know why I picked you tonight? I picked you because I thought you were a sure thing. An old bag like you— I thought you'd be grateful."

How could she have been so stupid? Sandy wondered as she stepped inside the waiting elevator. How had she gotten herself into this mess? She was at least an hour's drive from Torrance; she didn't have a cell phone to call for a taxi, which would likely cost her a week's salary; she couldn't very well call Rita and ask her to drive all the way back to pick her up, especially after deserting her earlier; she was drunk and feeling sick to her stomach, and her kids would be horrified when they saw her. Please let them be asleep when I get home, she prayed. Please don't let them see me.

She checked her watch, but the dial was spinning and the num-bers refused to settle. "He's right," she said as the elevator doors opened into the lobby. "You are pathetic."

"You say something?" asked old Mr. Samuels from behind the reception desk.

"I was wondering if you could call me a cab," Sandy said. Then she threw up all over the gold-flecked marble floor.

18

KILLER'S JOURNAL

I didn't feel so hot this morning so I stayed home and rested. Not sure what it was. Fatigue maybe. Or some bug I picked up. I hear there's something going around, which doesn't surprise me. There's always something going around. It's kind of scary when you think about everything that's out there, all these microbes and bacteria, exotic viruses, weird and deadly strains of flu, all of them just hiding, biding their time, waiting for just the right moment to make their presence known.

Sort of like me.

I don't get sick often so I knew something was wrong the minute I got out of bed. My legs felt wobbly and unsteady, as if the floor were on a tilt. I was nauseous and dizzy and had no appetite. My muscles felt as if they'd been transformed into flaccid rubber bands, incapable of sustaining my weight. "I just don't feel like *me,*" my aunt used to say whenever she got sick, and for the first time I understood what she meant. So since it's Sunday, and there was no urgent reason for me to push myself, I chose to give myself the morning off. I deserved a rest after all. I needed time to recharge my batteries, regain my strength. There's still so much to be done.

Maybe it was last night. All that celebrating in the park. A celebration of death, as it were. I followed the proceedings carefully. I confess it gave me a thrill. Maybe that's what made me so light-headed this morning. Maybe I was suffering a celebratory "death hangover." If so, hopefully it's the first of many.

So what was I doing all morning as I lay in my bed? Was I thinking, plotting, selecting, anticipating, remembering, letting my imagination run wild? Well, yes. All these things. I'm a very creative person, even if this is something that is rarely acknowledged and certainly never encouraged. People tend to pigeonhole you. They think they know you. They grow complacent with their perception of who they think you are. They don't want that perception challenged or altered. They don't want to know more.

The truth is they don't know anything.

Take my aunt for example.

She thought she knew me.

She was wrong.

Have I mentioned I killed her?

Shame on me, although truthfully, I feel no shame. Not anymore. I did for many years. Too many years, I realize now. Oh, not for killing her. No way. She deserved what happened to her. No, the shame I'm talking about was the shame I carried with me while she was alive. God, how she used to terrorize me! How she loved to make me feel guilty! How ugly and worthless she made me feel! She was one of those people who truly deserves to die. And she was my first. My virgin kill, as it were.

I've already alluded to some of my experiences with my aunt: the time she took me to a neighbor's birthday party and almost let me drown, the way she subsequently transferred the blame to me, the vacations she ruined, the swimming lessons she insisted I take, the waterskiing disaster, her taunts, that grating hyena-like laugh. *You big baby. Where are you, scaredy-cat? Come on, chicken liver.*

You might have thought things would get better as I got older, but that would be underestimating my aunt's eagerness to interfere, her ability to infiltrate and infect the minds of others. Even my own mother's.

Nothing I did was ever good enough. My failures were magnified, my successes ignored. Every disappointment I suffered was good for a laugh. Who's laughing now? I wonder.

I've replayed that afternoon so many times in my mind, I sometimes worry that I'll tire of it, that one day the memory might grow
stale, or that it might start skipping, like a defective CD, and I'll
inadvertently omit an important part, a small tidbit perhaps, but
one meant to be savored. I don't want to leave anything out. I don't
want to forget even the smallest detail of that day. That's why I've
chosen to create a permanent record. I'm carving these memories in
stone, so to speak.

Tombstones.

Even though my aunt was my first kill, it remains my most satisfying. What is it they say about sex and love? That sex is always
more fulfilling when love is involved? Does the same hold true of
murder? And is hate as powerful as love? I think it is. In fact, I think
it's more powerful.

Certainly, killing Liana Martin was infinitely more rewarding
than killing Candy Abbot.

Just as my next kill will be even more satisfying than doing away
with Liana Martin.

There's one kill in particular I'm looking forward to.

Her time is drawing near. Each day brings me one day closer.

But I'm getting ahead of myself, and if I'm going to get the most
out of these recollections, I have to be accurate, I have to make sure
I'm in the moment. There can be no outside distractions. I have to
return to that hot and humid July day, almost three years ago.
Almost three years? God, it doesn't seem possible. What is it they
say? Time flies when you're having fun?

So, okay. Here goes. I was alone in the house. Reading, enjoying
the air-conditioning and the solitude. And suddenly there she was.
Banging at the door, demanding to be let in. I ignored her, focusing
all my attention on the book in my hands, and after a minute it got
quiet, and I thought she'd gone away. I remember allowing myself a
sly smile, but the smile quickly disappeared with the sound of a key
turning in the lock. I heard the front door open and close, the sound
of footsteps approaching.

"Oh. You're home," she said, clearly startled to see me. Her
short, dark hair was frizzy with the humidity, and the underarms of

her blue sundress were stained with little half-moons of perspiration.

"Yes," I acknowledged with a nod.

"Why didn't you answer the door when I knocked?"

"I didn't hear you."

"How could you not hear me?"

"How did you get in?"

She waved her key in front of my face. "Your mother thought I should have one. In case of an emergency."

"Is there one?"

"Is there one what?"

"An emergency."

"Don't be smart," she said, an expression I've always found faintly ridiculous. Why would you tell somebody not to be smart? Unless of course their smarts made you look stupid.

"What are you doing here?" I asked.

"Your mother borrowed my good black heels, and I need them for tonight."

"Do you have a date?"

"Actually, yes, I do."

I laughed. "Poor guy."

"You're certainly one to talk," she said, and although I wasn't sure exactly what she meant by that—truth be told, I'm still not—I knew it was meant to be insulting. "What are you reading?" She grabbed the book out of my hands, roughly flipped through several pages. "Aren't you a little old for comic books?"

"It's a graphic novel."

"It's a glorified comic book. Honestly! At your age. Don't you have anything better to do with your time?"

"Don't you have to get ready for your date?"

She checked her watch. It was one of those Rolex knockoffs that don't fool anybody. I mean, all you have to do is feel them to know they aren't real. They don't even look real, if you ask me. Kind of like fake boobs. She had those too. "I have lots of time."

"Good. Because I think my mother might have been wearing those shoes when she went out."

"What?"

"I'm pretty sure she was wearing those shoes." Actually I was sure of no such thing. I rarely paid any attention to what shoes my mother might or might not have been wearing. I only said that to upset my aunt, and was gratified to see it had.

"Where did she go? When will she be back?"

"I have no idea. She didn't say."

"Those are expensive shoes. She better not be wearing them to go grocery shopping," she railed.

I shrugged, returned to my book. Seconds later, my aunt was rushing up the stairs to my mother's bedroom. I heard a closet door opening above my head, items being tossed carelessly to the floor.

"Found them," my aunt announced angrily, appearing at my side seconds later, waving the shoes menacingly close to my head.

"Then you should be happy," I said.

"Why did you tell me she was wearing them?"

"I said she *might* have been wearing them."

"Now I'm all hot and flustered." She said this as if it were my fault.

"Can I get you something to drink? A Coke or some juice?"

She plopped herself down on the sofa. "A Diet Coke."

That was it. No please or thank-you. No "That would be nice." I got up from my chair and went to the kitchen. "You know, they say Diet Coke isn't good for you," I called back. "Supposedly it alters your brain waves."

"Then I guess you have nothing to worry about," she said, then laughed that awful hyena-like laugh.

At that precise moment—2:22 in the afternoon exactly, according to the digital clock on the stove—I decided to kill her. Actually, I'd been thinking about it for months, maybe even years, planning what I would do if I ever got the opportunity, thinking of ways to dispatch her with a minimum of fuss and a maximum of pain. At least for her. I wanted her to suffer in death, as she had made me suffer in life.

"We don't have any Diet Coke," I lied, moving several cans to the back of the fridge. "How about a gin and tonic?"

Did I mention she was a heavy drinker?

"Now that's a good idea," she said, probably the nicest thing she'd said to me in years.

"Trust me," I said, removing the bottle of tonic from the fridge and locating the gin in the cabinet below the sink, expertly combining the two.

There were always lots of pills around the house. I rifled through several kitchen drawers, found an old prescription bottle of Percodan, crushed the six remaining pills, then emptied them into her gin and tonic. Talk about altering your brain waves. Then I returned to the living room and handed her the drink.

"Took you long enough," she said. Not "Thank you" or "You're so kind."

"You're welcome," I said, watching her down half the glass in one gulp.

"Not bad," she pronounced, taking another sip, then leaning back, lapsing into silence, seemingly lost in thought. She took another sip, made a face, lowered the glass to the floor.

"Something wrong?"

"Tastes bitter."

"Isn't it supposed to?"

"You probably put in too much tonic."

"I can add some more gin," I offered helpfully.

She looked toward her almost empty glass, then jumped to her feet. "No, that's all right. I should get going."

"Why don't you stay awhile?" I urged in my most conciliatory voice. "We don't get much opportunity to talk these days."

"You want to talk?" She seemed surprised, maybe even flattered.

"How are you managing these days?" I asked.

"How am I managing? What kind of question is that?"

"How's your job at the bank?"

She made a clucking sound deep in her throat, her mouth folding into a frown. "It's awful. If Al hadn't been such an idiot about finances, I wouldn't be in this position. Anyway, I better go and make myself beautiful."

"You already *are* beautiful," I told her, almost gagging on the words.

She smiled, patted her frizzy hair. "Why, thank you. That was very sweet." She leaned over to kiss my forehead, stumbled slightly. "Oh," she said, touching the side of her head with the shoes in her hand.

"Something wrong?"

"I just got a little dizzy all of a sudden."

"Maybe you should sit down."

"No. I'll be fine." She took several steps toward the door, then stopped, her body swaying.

"Maybe I should drive you," I volunteered.

"Don't be silly. I'm perfectly fine. I just stood up too fast, that's all." She reached for the door handle, missed it by several inches.

I was right behind her. "Okay, look. I'm supposed to be meeting somebody in half an hour." Another lie. I wasn't meeting anyone. "You can give me a lift as far as your place."

She neither agreed nor offered any protest as I reached across her and opened the front door, then guided her toward her dark green Buick. True to form, she sloughed my hand from her elbow and rebuffed my attempt to open her car door. "What do you think you're doing?"

"Just trying to help."

"You can help by keeping quiet."

So the drive back to her house was silent. The only sound was the increasingly ragged sound of her breathing. I kept a close eye on both my aunt and the road. One of the reasons I chose to accompany her was to make sure that no innocent people were mowed down along the way. It was my aunt's demise I sought. No one else's.

Of course, that was then. This, as they say, is now.

Anyway, by the time she pulled into the driveway of her small, two-story, wood-framed house with its bright red door and chipped white paint, she was wobbly, and she seemed almost grateful when I offered to accompany her inside. She even let me carry her shoes. "I don't know what's wrong with me," she kept saying. Then, more accusingly: "There must have been something off with that gin."

The front door opened directly into the living room. The furniture was that ultramodern crap, all sharp angles and strange shapes. Mostly red. She loved red. "I think you should lie down for a while," I said as we walked through the tiny dining area to the steep staircase beside the kitchen at the back. Upstairs were two small bedrooms and one bathroom. I assumed I'd find what I needed in at least one of those rooms. If not, there was always the kitchen.

"Just a second," I said as we reached the top of the stairs.

"What?" Her look was as accusatory as her voice.

"This," I said simply. Then I pushed her with all my might.

It happened so fast it was almost a blur. I've had to learn to slow the fall down, as if I were pressing a slow-motion button in my head, so that I can truly enjoy the sight of her as she flew backward through the air, her feet swooping up toward her head as her arms shot out from her sides like wings, her back crashing against the thin red carpet that ran up the middle of the hard wooden stairs, her body bouncing between the steps and the wall as she continued falling until she reached the bottom, landing with both her hands flung above her head, her legs splayed indelicately, exposing the white panties beneath her blue linen sundress.

She was moaning and semiconscious when I reached her side. Blood was pouring from her left ear and her eyes were rolling back and forth in their sockets. I couldn't be sure whether she was about to black out or come to, so I knew I had to work fast. I quickly removed her beige sandals and replaced one of them with one of her black, high-heeled shoes. "Shouldn't wear such high heels," I scolded. "Don't you know they're killers?"

I hurled her other shoe against the wall and watched it leave a scuff mark in the white paint before bouncing down several steps, eventually landing five steps short of the floor. Then I raced back up the stairs and put her sandals in her closet. That's when I found what else I was looking for.

A large plastic bag.

It was wrapped around a pair of black silk pants, pants she'd recently gotten back from the cleaners and had probably intended to wear on her date that night. I tore the bag from the hanger, careful to make sure there were no telltale pieces of plastic left lying about, then carried the bag down the stairs to where my aunt lay. Her eyes were closed as I lifted her head into my arms, then began carefully slipping the bag over her head.

Her eyes suddenly opened wide. "What are you . . . ?" she managed to sputter before I got the bag fully over her nose and mouth. In her already weakened and precarious state, she was no match for me. I think she was probably dying anyway, but I couldn't take the chance that she might linger until her date arrived and managed to get her to the hospital in time to save her life. And ruin mine.

So I held on tight, feeling her squirm, watching the breath slowly seep from her body, her eyes growing wider with each agonizing breath. At least I hope it was agonizing. I believe I actually felt her heart stop, but I held on for another five minutes before carefully removing the plastic bag from her head and closing her eyes with my fingers. I knew that everyone would assume she'd taken a nasty tumble down the stairs in those ridiculously high heels and died as the result of the fall. Everyone knew she enjoyed a drink or two in the afternoon. No one would be probing any deeper.

Don't go looking for trouble. Isn't that what they say?

And I was right. They didn't. Her death was quickly classified as accidental. The sheriff, out of respect for my family, decided against an autopsy. What was the point in cutting her up? It was perfectly obvious what had happened to her. What could be gained by prolonging everyone's grief? Such are the joys of small-town life. And death.

We buried her next to my uncle. Everybody mourned. Including me, of course. I believe I even managed a few tears.

So that's it. One down.

Fast forward almost three years later. Two more girls are dead. That makes it three down.

And more to come.

I'm feeling better already.

chapter nineteen

Megan was feeling sick to her stomach. And not because she'd eaten something disagreeable, which she hadn't, because she had absolutely no appetite and was seriously considering never eating again, or because she'd had too much to drink, which she hadn't because she didn't like the taste of alcohol and so had never felt the slightest temptation to get drunk, or even because she'd smoked too much weed, which she hadn't, because all she'd had were a few puffs, and besides, everyone knew that marijuana didn't upset your stomach. No, she was feeling queasy because she'd made a fool of herself with Greg Watt in front of half the school at last night's wake, and then he'd ditched her, also in front of everybody, and she still had no idea what she'd said or done wrong. One minute they were having a nice conversation about his mother, and the next minute he was walking away, and that was the end of it. He'd avoided her for the rest of the night. Or at least for the next hour, which was all the neglect she could stand, and so she'd gone home without telling anyone she was leaving, left without Tim, whose side she'd promised to stick to like glue, and snuck out of the park and walked home. Alone, at night, in the dark, with a murderer on the loose, as her mother had reiterated—how many times?—after Tim had shown up at their door at almost the same moment their mother had arrived home in a taxi. And now Megan was grounded. No going out for the next month, except to school and for rehearsals, which her mother insisted she attend, ostensibly because she didn't think it fair to deprive poor Mr. Lipsman of his leading lady, but more probably because Megan had been so willing to forgo them. And now her cell phone had been confiscated and her computer removed from her room. Which was probably a blessing in disguise, Megan thought, considering the gossip that was probably circulating right this second in chat lines throughout America, and *that,* more than anything, was what was making Megan feel sick to her stomach. That and what her mother would say if and when she found out about Greg Watt.

Not that her mother was one to talk, Megan decided. She hadn't exactly looked all that great when she'd arrived home at just minutes before midnight. Megan had watched Sandy slowly extricate herself from her taxi and teeter toward the front door as if she were sidestepping pieces of broken glass. She'd only had a few seconds to wonder what had happened to Rita when to her horror she saw Tim rounding the corner. "Mom?" he'd called out. "Is Megan home?"

"What? What do you mean? Isn't she with you?" And then the front door was opening and closing, and the hysteria was rising, before crashing down around all their heads. "What do you mean, you don't know where she is? What do you mean, you couldn't find her? Did you look? Did you look everywhere?"

And stupid her. Stupid for thinking that simply by announcing her presence, her mother would be so glad to see her, and so relieved to know she was safe and sound and not in the clutches of some slavering maniac, all would be forgiven.

All was definitely not forgiven.

After the initial euphoria, the frantic kisses on her cheek, the trembling fingers clutching proprietarily at Megan's sides, Sandy's face had grown dark and angry. "What do you mean, you left without telling your brother? You were supposed to stick together. Why weren't you together? Where were you? Who were you with? What do you mean, you walked home by yourself? Don't you know there's a killer out there? I can't believe you're that stupid. What aren't you telling me?" And then, without waiting for an explanation: "You're grounded."

Of course Megan had tried to change her mother's mind, but each protest of innocence had served only to cement her guilt. Sandy, while clearly not herself—even a mouthful of Altoids hadn't been enough to disguise the alcohol on her breath—was perceptive enough to know when her daughter was hiding something from her, and she would not be coddled, mollified, or thrown off course. Ultimately, Megan had fled to her room in tears.

When Sandy had knocked on her door some fifteen minutes later, Megan had assumed she'd had a change of heart and had come to apologize. Instead, her mother had unhooked her computer and unplugged her phone, as well as seized her cell phone from her purse. Instead of an apology, she'd announced, "I'm very disappointed in you, Megan." Which meant that she was expecting Megan to apologize to *her*.

Apologize and explain.

How can I explain? Megan wondered now, picturing herself in Greg's surprisingly gentle arms, his fingers twisting around her hair, his tongue teasing the inside of her mouth. She could still taste the beer and cigarettes on his breath, could hear the hurt in his voice when he talked about his mother. She'd felt so close to him. Was that it? Had she strayed too close? "I'm such an idiot," she moaned, falling back on her bed and staring up at the quietly rotating ceiling fan.

"Okay, sweetheart. Have a good time. And be careful," she heard her mother telling Tim as the front door opened and closed.

She should go out there and apologize, Megan decided. Get it over with. Act suitably contrite and hope her mother would relent or, at the very least, give her back her cell phone. Sandy would ask a few questions that were none of her business and Megan would flatter her with a few well-placed lies—"You were right, Mom. I never should have gone to Liana's wake. I didn't realize how upsetting it would be. Of course I should have said something to Tim, but he was talking to some boys in his class, and I know how concerned you've been about him not having any friends, and I didn't want to interrupt them—you know how easily embarrassed he gets and I knew he'd insist on walking me home—and, yes, I realize now how stupid it was, and I'm really very sorry. I promise I'll never do anything that stupid ever again. Can you forgive me?"

Oh, and by the way, what were you doing last night that you came home in a taxi, and why did you smell like liquor, and where was Rita? Answer me that before you take anything else away from me.

Okay, so maybe not in those exact words, Megan was thinking as the phone rang, then rang twice more before Sandy finally picked it up. Megan stood still, waited for the sound of her mother's voice.

"Rita, hello," her mother said, although she didn't sound too glad to hear from her friend. "I've been meaning to call you all day. . . . Yes, I'm fine. I'm sorry you were so worried."

So, her mother's behavior had caused Rita concern. What had she done?

"I would have called you last night when I got home, but it was late and . . . No, it didn't go exactly the way I'd hoped." Sandy paused. Megan could almost feel her sneaking a peek over her shoulder, making sure no one was listening. "Actually, it turned out I *didn't* know him," her mother continued, raising Megan's interest even further by lowering her voice. Megan took several baby steps into the hallway. "Yes, I know what I said, what *he* said, but he wasn't a former neighbor after all. In fact, I'd never seen him before in my life."

Seen who? What was her mother talking about?

"Yes, I know it was reckless. Trust me, I know. I've been kicking myself all night."

What had her mother done?

"I know. I know."

What did her mother know?

"You don't want to know," her mother told her friend.

Yes, we do, Megan answered silently. We most definitely want to know.

"Well, we drove around for a little while," Sandy obliged. "Did I tell you he drove a Porsche?"

Her mother had gone for a ride with someone who drove a Porsche?

"Yes, I know that shouldn't mean anything, but what can I say? I'm shallow and I was impressed."

Me too, Megan thought, inching closer, trying to picture Sandy in her red-and-white print silk dress in the passenger seat of a Porsche.

"And then he said something about being hungry, and I assumed we were going to a restaurant, but then he said he had some chicken at his apartment. . . . I *know* it's the oldest line in the book, you don't have to tell me that, but it's a book I haven't read in a very long time. And he was being so sweet, and he made me feel, I don't know, as if he was completely innocent and that if I didn't come up to his apartment, then *I* was the one with the problem."

Megan released a deep breath of air. For the first time in a long while, she understood exactly what her mother was talking about.

"Yes, I went," Sandy continued. "And, no, of course there wasn't any chicken. At least none that I saw. But, no, nothing happened. I mean, he tried, and when I refused, he got a little insulting, more than a little actually. I think 'pathetic' was one of the kinder words he used."

Megan gasped, then threw her hands across her mouth. How awful, she thought. Her mother was hardly *pathetic*.

"And he threw me out of his apartment, and then *I* threw up in the lobby. . . . Yes, I guess you could call it poetic justice, except it didn't feel that way at the time. It just felt awful. So I took a cab home. . . . No, of course I wasn't going to call you. After abandoning you the way I did? Not a chance. I may be shallow and stupid, but I'm not totally insensitive. Besides, I didn't have a clue where I was. How'd the rest of your evening go, by the way?"

So, let's get this straight, Megan thought. Her mother had ditched her good friend to run off with some stranger in a Porsche, then risked her life for a piece of chicken, then thrown up in the lobby of a strange apartment building, then climbed into another stranger's cab? *Her* mother? The same one who'd lectured her about walking home from the park alone when there was a murderer on the loose? The one who'd taken away her phone and computer privileges and grounded her for a month? *That* mother?

"I'm glad you had a good time. Was Bob terribly upset when I didn't come back?"

Bob? Who was Bob? There was a Bob?

"I guess I should call him and apologize. Do you have his number? . . . Good. . . . No, I am definitely not interested in any more double dates. I'm clearly not ready to be dating. I shouldn't even be allowed out of the house, for God's sake."

And yet *she* was the one who was grounded, Megan thought.

"Yeah, okay. I'll talk to you later. Sorry again about last night." Sandy hung up the phone. "Megan," she called out. "I think you might be a little more comfortable in here."

Megan rolled her eyes, half in defeat, half in admiration. "How long have you known I was there?" she asked, coming into the living room and plopping down on the sofa.

"Not long. How much did you overhear?"

"Pretty much everything."

Sandy nodded. She was wearing jeans and a pink T-shirt with the outline of a big red heart in its center, and her hair was freshly washed and hanging in loose, wet curls around her face. "I guess that makes my humiliation pretty much complete."

"Did he really say you were pathetic?"

"Among other things."

"He sounds like a creep."

"He was."

"Was he good-looking?"

"Very."

"As good-looking as Dad?"

Her mother sank back in her chair. "Different," she said after a pause. "Younger."

"Wow," Megan said, not sure whether to be filled with anger or admiration. "I guess that makes everything all right then."

"Are you being sarcastic?"

"What do you think?"

"I think I'm not in the mood for sarcasm."

"Well, I don't think it's fair for me to be punished when you behaved worse than I did."

"It *doesn't* seem fair, does it?"

"No. It really doesn't."

Sandy pushed herself to her feet. "Yeah, well, there you go. I'm thirsty. Can I get you something?" She walked toward the kitchen.

Megan was right behind her. "What!"

Sandy was already leaning into the open fridge. "Let's see. We have Coke or ginger ale, or there's orange juice."

"What do you mean, 'Yeah, well, there you go'?"

"It's kind of self-explanatory."

"You're saying I'm still grounded?"

"Yup."

"*Yup?* Since when do you say *yup?*"

"I'm sorry, sweetie," Sandy apologized, pouring herself a glass of juice. "But I thought I made myself very clear. You had strict instructions to stay with your brother. And you were very foolish to walk home by yourself under the circumstances."

"Not as foolish as getting into a stranger's car and going up to his apartment," Megan protested.

"True enough."

"So, how come I'm the only one who has to suffer?"

"Trust me. You aren't the only one who's suffering."

"I'm the only one who's grounded."

"Yeah, well . . ."

"*There you go?*" Megan repeated. "You're such a hypocrite."

"No," Sandy said kindly, refusing to rise to the bait. "I'm your mother. And I love you more than anything in the world, and whether you think it's fair or not, I get to set the rules." She walked back into the living room, sipping on her drink, Megan on her heels.

"What if I tell you I want to go live with Dad?" Did she?

"Do you?"

"Maybe."

A look of pain settled in around her mother's tired eyes. "Then I hope you'll think it over very carefully."

"He wouldn't ground me."

"Maybe not."

"He's not a hypocrite like you are."

Her mother said nothing, although the pain in her eyes spread to her mouth, tugged on its corners. She sank into a nearby chair.

"I wonder what Dad would say if I told him about what you did last night."

"I imagine he'd have himself quite a chuckle."

"He'd think you were pathetic," Megan said pointedly. "So would Kerri." She brought her shoulders back and raised her chin. "So do I."

The glass of juice began shaking in her mother's hand and she lowered it to the floor.

"No wonder he left you," Megan added, furious at not being able to provoke her.

"Okay, Megan. I think you've said enough."

"I don't think so."

Her mother nodded, looked Megan squarely in the eye. "Well, then, I guess you better give it your best shot."

Megan's eyes instantly filled with tears. "Damn it. Is this the way it always is?" she heard herself wail. "Doesn't it get any better? Any easier? Are guys always such jerks?" She buried her head in her hands, burst into a flood of angry tears as Sandy quickly rose to her feet and drew her into her arms. Megan burrowed deeply into her mother's side, inhaling the fresh scent of lavender from her still damp hair.

"Some things get better," Sandy said, kissing her forehead. "Some things get worse. And nothing is ever easy. But not all guys are jerks."

"Dad's a jerk."

"No."

"Yes, he is. Why are you protecting him?"

"You're right. He's a jerk."

Megan laughed through her tears.

"He wasn't always a jerk," her mother qualified. She guided Megan back to the sofa, sat down beside her, and began stroking her hair.

"Was Dad the first guy you had sex with?" Megan broached.

Her mother's hand froze. "Oh, God. I don't think I'm ready for this conversation."

"Was he?"

Sandy fell back against the sofa. "I take it you don't mean kissing."

"Mom," Megan said, stretching the word into three syllables.

"Yes, he was the first man I had sex with."

"So then, he's the only one?"

"Oh, God. I really *am* pathetic."

"No, you're not. Jessica Simpson was a virgin when she got married."

"Who?"

"Jessica Simpson. You know, the singer. *Daisy Duke. The Newlyweds.*"

"What?"

"She was married to Nick Lachey, and she was a virgin till her wedding night."

"Oh."

"I mean, she and Nick eventually split up, but still—"

"Are you having sex, Megan?"

"What?"

"Is that why you left the park early, to be with some boy?"

"No. Are you kidding me? No way."

Her mother's shoulders slumped with relief. "Good. I mean, it's not that I don't expect you to have sex one day. Sex is a very beautiful thing, especially when two people love each other. But you're so young and there's so much time."

Megan rolled her eyes. "Oh, God. I don't think I'm ready for this conversation."

Sandy laughed. She was so pretty when she laughed, Megan thought.

"I'm really sorry," Megan said. "For all those awful things I said. I just said them because I was mad."

"I know."

"I love you."

"I love you too."

"Could I have my phone back?"

"Not a chance."

"Didn't think so."

"It was worth a shot," her mother said as the doorbell rang. "You expecting someone?"

Megan shook her head, rose to her feet. "I'll get it." She crossed to the front door, peered out the peephole. "You're not going to believe this," she said, pushing the door open, and thinking how strange it was that doors in Florida opened outward instead of inward. You could knock some unsuspecting visitor unconscious if you weren't careful. Her father had explained it had something to do with hurricanes, and it had made sense at the time, but she couldn't remember his explanation now.

"Who is it?" Sandy was asking.

"Hi, Megan," Delilah Franklin said, entering the small foyer. "Hi, Mrs. Crosbie. Sorry to bother you at home this way."

Sandy scrambled to her feet. "Delilah," she acknowledged, a worried look creasing her brow. "Is something wrong?"

Megan knew her mother was wondering if something had happened to Ian, whether he'd had a sudden heart attack or been hit by a car. "Is my father all right?" Megan asked in her stead.

"As far as I know. Why? Did something happen?"

Sandy's shoulders slumped. "What can we do for you?"

"I was wondering if you'd seen Mr. or Mrs. Hamilton today."

Megan and Sandy both looked in the direction of the house next door. "No," they answered together. "Why?"

"Just that I was supposed to baby . . . to come over and keep Mrs. Hamilton company for a few hours this afternoon, but I've been ringing the bell for ten minutes, and nobody answers."

Sandy shrugged. "I guess they went out."

"I guess." Delilah shifted from one foot to the other as if she was hoping to be invited inside to wait for their return.

Please don't invite her to stay, Megan pleaded silently.

"I guess I'll come back later."

"You probably should call them first," Sandy suggested.

"Yeah. It's just strange, you know." Delilah turned to leave, then stopped just as Megan was about to close the door. "I wasn't going to go back there anymore. It's kind of creepy there, you know? But I felt kind of sorry for Mrs. Hamilton. Have you ever talked to her?"

"Not really."

Delilah hesitated. "Well, I guess I'll see you guys at school."

"See you at school," Sandy repeated, as Megan closed the door.

chapter twenty

Can I tell him what this is about?" the young woman was asking.

John Weber leaned his considerable bulk against the high counter of the reception desk, his eyes scanning the series of closed doors that comprised the well-lit inner office. "Just tell him the sheriff needs a few minutes of his time. Oh, and Becky," he said to the girl he'd known since she was two years old, and whose chubby, freckled face had barely changed in the twenty years since, "tell him I haven't got all day." He looked around the crowded waiting room. It was eight-thirty on a Monday morning and already half a dozen people were there.

"Dr. Crosbie," he heard Becky whisper into the intercom. "Sheriff Weber is here to see you. . . . Uh, I don't know. He wouldn't say." She raised her head, smiled shyly. "Dr. Crosbie says if you'll just have a seat, he'll see you as soon as he's through with his patient."

"Thank you." John looked toward the gray-walled reception area's only vacant seat, between an elderly woman who was rocking back and forth in obvious distress and a man who hadn't stopped blowing his nose since John had walked through the door. While he might be able to remember their names given enough time and effort, he didn't really know either of them beyond a casual hello. The same was true of the three middle-aged women and one man whose strained, unhappy faces were buried deep inside their magazines. There was a time, and not all that long ago either, when John knew virtually everybody in town. Now they all looked vaguely alike, one face blurring into the next. John felt no connection to any of them, he realized, and wondered whether such disaffection was a sign of the times or more proof that he was getting too old, too complacent, to do his job properly. He approached the window that overlooked the street, trying not to see the mayor's pinched expression reflected in the tinted glass.

Ian Crosbie's office was located on the second floor of the relatively new, three-story building on Church Street, so named because of the proliferation of churches in the area. John tried to remember the last time he'd been to church, other than for a wedding or a funeral. Liana Martin's memorial service had taken place just around the corner. Although technically, he hadn't actually been inside that church. There'd been so many people that day, the crowd had spilled out onto the street. He'd staked out a spot to the right of the front steps, the better to watch those coming by to pay their respects. Or get their jollies.

He'd seen nothing out of the ordinary. If Liana's killer had been among the mourners, he'd aroused no undue suspicions. If anything, it was the people who *hadn't* shown up that afternoon who'd tweaked John's interest the most. People like Dr. Ian Crosbie.

"Sheriff Weber?" a petite dishwater blonde in a nearby chair was asking. She pushed herself away from the white-trimmed, pearl-gray wall and squinted at him through one eye that was swollen and pink.

"Mrs. Marshall," he acknowledged, giving himself an invisible pat on the back for remembering her name.

"Are you feeling all right, Sheriff?"

"I'm fine, thank you."

"That's good. We wouldn't want our sheriff getting sick."

"Thank you, ma'am."

"Especially now."

"I understand."

"We're counting on you, Sheriff."

She didn't have to say for what. John understood she was talking about finding Liana Martin's killer and returning the town to its former tranquillity. "I'm doing my best."

"I'm sure you are."

"Any leads?" The woman beside Mrs. Marshall leaned forward in her royal-blue chair, tucked shoulder-length, mousy-brown hair behind one ear.

Try as he could, John was unable to produce the woman's name. "The investigation is ongoing," he told her, which was a fancy way of saying *No, no leads,* and they both knew it.

The man who'd continuously been blowing his nose suddenly sneezed. Everyone quickly blessed him. "Actually you don't have to say *Bless you* when you have a cold," the man said, blowing his nose again.

"Really?" Mrs. Marshall asked.

"According to my mother."

"I never heard that," said Mrs. Marshall, returning to the latest issue of *In Style* magazine.

John knew it was the latest issue because his wife had the same one at home, and Pauline was always first at the drugstore when the new magazines came out. She felt it was her duty to keep abreast of the latest styles, as well as keeping tabs on Jennifer and Brad and Angelina and Paris and those famous pin-thins, Nicole and Lindsay, and why did he even know these people's names? Was there some weird virus going around, and had he been infected along with the rest of the nation? Celebrity-itis, he thought, clearing his throat to hide the laugh that had almost escaped. He wondered if the good doctor could do anything about that.

"Thanks, Dr. Crosbie. Bye, Becky," chirped a familiar voice as the door to the inner office opened and Tanya McGovern stepped into the reception area. "Sheriff Weber," she said with a smile. "What are you doing here? Are you okay?"

"I'm fine, Tanya, thank you. And you?"

"I haven't been sleeping very well these days."

"That's quite understandable."

"My mother thought I should have some sleeping pills, so Dr. Crosbie wrote me a prescription."

"We'll all sleep better once this madman is caught," Mrs. Marshall opined.

"Any leads?" Tanya asked.

"The investigation is ongoing," the woman beside Mrs. Marshall answered before John had a chance.

"Well, I better get to school," Tanya said, already halfway out the door.

"Take care." John returned to the window, watching Tanya as she left the building and climbed into a waiting van. Was that Greg Watt behind the wheel? he wondered, pressing his forehead against the cool glass. But the car turned the corner before he was able to make a positive identification.

"John?" a male voice said from behind his back. Not Sheriff Weber, as should have been the case given the nature of their relationship, or lack thereof, but, rather pointedly, *John*.

"*Ian*," the sheriff said in response, turning around and smiling at the involuntary wince that flashed across the good doctor's handsome face. Ian Crosbie was wearing a blue-and-black-checkered shirt underneath his open, white lab coat and a pair of neatly pressed black trousers that accentuated his slim hips.

"Is there a problem?" the doctor asked. "Are you ill?"

Ill, not sick, John noted. "No, no. Not *ill*. Nothing like that. I'm afraid I just need to ask you a few questions."

The doctor looked suitably chagrined. "Could it possibly wait until later? As you can see, I'm very busy this morning."

"I'm afraid this can't wait. I've tried several times to get ahold of you already."

"Yes, I'm sorry about that, but—"

"—you've been very busy. I understand. This shouldn't take long."

Ian Crosbie sighed, lifted his hands into the air, as if to say, What can you do? "If you'll excuse us for just a few minutes," he apologized to his patients as he led John into the inner sanctum.

"You're looking well, Becky," John told the receptionist as he followed the doctor down the narrow hall, past two rooms where patients were already waiting, into a third room at the back. Ian Crosbie immediately sat down in the large, brown leather chair behind his exceedingly tidy oak desk and motioned for John to occupy the smaller one on the other side. A mistake, John thought, choosing to remain standing. He'd become aware early in his career that peering down on his opponent gave him a strong psychological edge. And he wondered when exactly he'd started thinking of Ian Crosbie as his opponent.

"What can I do for you, Sheriff?" Ian plucked a red ballpoint pen from a mug filled with such pens and began tapping it against the side of his desk.

So it was *Sheriff* now. "I need to ask what you were doing on the afternoon that Liana Martin disappeared."

The pen fell from Ian's hand, hit the desk, rolled between two framed photographs of his children, and dropped to the gray-carpeted floor, where it bounced out of sight. "Excuse me?"

"Monday, April—"

"I know what day it was."

"Then perhaps you can tell me what you were doing that afternoon."

"Is this a joke? I've already been questioned about this."

"No, Dr. Crosbie. I assure you it's not a joke." John watched the color drain from Ian's tanned cheeks and tried not to smile. It wouldn't be professional to betray his enjoyment of the good doctor's all-too-obvious discomfort.

"Well . . . I was here. I've already told that to one of your deputies."

"Yes, I believe it was Deputy Trent you spoke to last week," John said, pulling his small notebook out of his shirt pocket and reading from his notes. "He says you claimed your office was closed that afternoon."

Ian became even more flustered. "It *was* closed. I had some paperwork to catch up on. What are you implying?"

"So much paperwork you canceled your patients?"

"I didn't have any patients booked for that afternoon."

"Really?" John flipped forward several pages. "According to your receptionist, whom another of my deputies talked to a couple of days ago, you told her to cancel your appointments that afternoon because of a family crisis." John had assigned an officer to interview Becky after running into Ian at Kerri's house.

"Well, it wasn't a crisis exactly. My wife was upset about something regarding our son—"

"Your wife? That would be Sandy Crosbie?"

"Well, we're separated, of course, but—"

"She doesn't remember being upset about anything." Actually he hadn't talked to Sandy, but he had a pretty good instinct he was right about this.

"That's because she's *always* upset about something. Look, Sheriff, I don't understand where this is going. I'm beginning to feel a little like a suspect here."

"Whoa, slow down a minute, *Ian*. Who said anything about you being a suspect?"

"Then why the third degree?"

"Just doing my job. I mean, try to see it from my point of view." John glanced around the book-lined room. "Clearly you have a very busy practice. Yet you chose to cancel your patients that afternoon and send your receptionist home. Why is that?"

"I told you I had a lot of paperwork to catch up on."

John smiled. "You might want to rethink that one," he said slowly.

There was a pause, followed by a shake of the head, a nod of defeat. "All right, look. We're both men here. I'm sure you understand about these things."

"What things?"

Another pause. A slight pursing of his lips. "I was with someone."

Not altogether unexpected, John thought. "Kerri Franklin?"

Yet another pause. A roll of his eyes. "No."

Now *this,* this was unexpected. John shook his head, half in outrage, half in admiration. He'd come in here on a fishing expedition. He hadn't expected to actually catch anything. "Liana Martin?" he asked, almost afraid to hear the doctor's response.

"Liana Martin? No! God, no! She was a child, for God's sake."

"She was eighteen," John reminded him.

"I didn't even know Liana Martin."

"Who then?" John reached over to grab a pen from the mug on Ian's desk. "I'll need a name."

"Look. It's a little embarrassing."

"It'll be more than a little embarrassing if you don't give me a name. I already have a witness who can place you on Liana Martin's street around the time she disappeared."

"What? That's crazy!"

"Is it?"

"I don't even know where she lived, for God's sake. There's no way I was there."

"If you don't know where she lived, how do you know you weren't there?"

"Because I was *here*." Dr. Crosbie realized he was yelling and quickly lowered his voice. "I was here."

"Who were you with, Ian? Is she a patient?"

"A patient? No, of course not. You think I'm nuts? You think I want to lose my license over a piece of ass?"

It was John's turn to wince. He'd always hated unnecessary crudeness, although he supposed he was as guilty of it as anybody. "Then who?"

"It's nobody you'd know."

"I'll need a name to corroborate your story."

Another pause. Ian Crosbie pressed the fingers of his right hand against his temple, as if he had the worst headache in the world.

And perhaps he did, John thought, deciding to sit down and make himself comfortable after all. He sat back, stretching his long legs out to one side. "A name?"

"Marcy. Marcy Grenn. Look, do you have to . . . ?"

John jotted down the unfamiliar name. "Address?"

"She lives in Boca. She's married," Ian admitted sheepishly. "The only address I have is her e-mail."

This just keeps getting better and better, John thought. "You're saying you met her online?"

"I don't appreciate your tone, Sheriff."

"Sorry. I didn't realize I had one."

"My personal life is none of your business."

"I'm investigating a murder, Dr. Crosbie."

"Which I had absolutely nothing to do with, no matter who says they saw me on Liana Martin's street the day she disappeared."

John pretended to scribble something in his notebook. In truth, nobody had come forward claiming to have seen the good doctor on Liana Martin's street that afternoon. He'd just thrown the accusation out to provoke Ian further, see where it might lead. And what do you know? It had led him to Boca Raton and a married woman named Marcy Grenn. Sometimes, he thought, feeling a sudden surge of energy, this job was downright fun. "I'll need that e-mail address."

Ian Crosbie quickly jotted down the address on a piece of prescription paper and handed it across the desk. "I trust you'll keep this information confidential."

"I don't think this exactly qualifies as doctor-patient privilege," John told him, pocketing the piece of paper along with his notepad, then returning the pen to its former home.

"Look. I'm just asking you to be discreet," Ian said. "There's no reason anybody else has to know about this, is there?"

"Nice talking to you, Ian," John said, rising to his feet. "I'll be in touch." He walked from the office, saying a pleasant good-bye to Becky and the people in the waiting room, knowing the whole town would soon be whispering about his unscheduled visit with Ian Crosbie. He'd contact this Marcy Grenn in Boca, he was thinking as he climbed into his cruiser, even though he was pretty certain Ian was telling the truth about her. There was no point in saying anything about her to Kerri, he decided as he pulled away from the curb and headed toward the highway. She'd just accuse him of being jealous and spiteful, acting more from sour grapes than genuine concern. In the end she'd believe what she wanted to believe. People always did.

"Mr. Peterson," John said to the balding science teacher as he slid into the booth across from him. "Mind if I join you?"

"Sheriff," the man replied, looking just past John's head toward the washrooms at the back. Even though it was a Monday night, Chester's was filled to capacity. Avery Peterson was sipping on a gin and tonic. An untouched Coca-Cola sat in the middle of the polished wooden table, a slice of lemon balancing precariously from the rim of the tall glass. "Actually, I'm with someone. She's just 'powdering her nose.'"

"That's all right. I won't be here long. I just need to ask you a few questions, if you don't mind."

Avery Peterson shrugged. "I thought I answered all your questions last week."

"These are new ones. Mr. Peterson—"

"Avery," the science teacher interrupted.

John nodded. He had no desire to be on friendlier terms with the middle-aged Romeo. He'd seen the *someone* he was with, a young woman named Ellie Frysinger, who'd graduated from Torrance High only two years earlier and who now worked at the mall selling discount clothing. What the pretty, young woman saw in this nondescript, balding lothario was beyond John's comprehension. And yet rumor had it he'd been involved with a surprising number of eager young women ever since his rather acrimonious divorce five years earlier.

"I hear he's hung like a horse," Pauline had confided the other night over a dinner of Kentucky Fried Chicken.

"I believe that falls under the category of too much information," John had testily replied, tossing his untouched drumstick to the plate. Did women really consider such things important? he'd wondered then as he wondered now. He'd always liked to believe that they were less superficial than men, but increasingly he wasn't so sure. Being the fairer sex didn't make you the better one. Vulnerability didn't necessarily equal sensitivity.

Now John was having a hard time looking at the science teacher—his *daughter's* science teacher, for God's sake—without thinking of horses. It was the last thing he wanted to be thinking about after an exhausting day spent driving back and forth to Boca Raton, although Marcy Grenn had been both pleasant and cooperative. She'd confirmed Ian's story, even showed him the e-mails they'd exchanged after connecting in a chat room some weeks earlier. Her husband was always away on business, she'd confided, and she enjoyed the occasional diversion. She was smiling when she told him not to lose her e-mail address. John, while tempted, had driven away from her town house thinking that he and Dr. Crosbie already had one woman in common, and he wasn't about to make it two.

There was an accident on the highway and he'd spent over an hour stuck in traffic, then had a fight with Pauline over absolutely nothing, before heading over to Chester's to reinterview Cal Hamilton. After all, his impromptu visit with Ian Crosbie had yielded a virtual treasure trove of information, albeit ultimately useless as far as Liana Martin's case was concerned. He thought maybe he'd be able to loosen Cal Hamilton's tongue as well.

Except that when he'd gotten there, Cal Hamilton had already left. According to the bartender, he'd stormed out of Chester's over an hour ago without a word to anyone and had yet to return. John had been sitting at a table on the other side of the bar, nursing a beer and waiting for him to come back. It was almost nine o'clock. Pauline had already called twice to ask when he was coming home, and he'd been just about to leave when he saw Avery Peterson come in with Ellie Frysinger.

"We've had reports you were seen in Pearson Park the night of Liana Martin's wake," the sheriff began.

Avery Peterson didn't flinch. "That's right."

"Mind telling me why you were there?"

The science teacher shrugged. "I was just curious."

"Curious?"

"About who would show up, what they had planned, that sort of thing."

"You knew it was supposed to be a 'kids only' event?"

"Just watching out for my students. In case anyone got carried away."

"Anyone ask you to do this?"

"Lenny and I discussed it earlier."

"That would be Leonard Fromm?"

"Our esteemed school principal, yes. That would be him."

"And if I were to call him right now, he'd confirm this?"

Avery Peterson retrieved his cell phone from his jacket pocket, offered it across the table. "Be my guest."

"Several people reported you lurking behind the bushes," John said, ignoring the phone.

Avery Peterson returned it to his pocket and smiled. "I was trying to be discreet."

"What was your relationship with Liana Martin?" John asked pointedly.

"I beg your pardon?"

"Answer the question please, Avery."

"She was my student."

"Nothing more?"

"Such as?"

"Well, it's no secret that you like your women on the young side."

"Is that a crime?"

"No, but murder is."

Avery Peterson laughed. "Please tell me you didn't really say that."

There was the muffled sound of a police siren. John shrugged. "That would be *my* cell phone," he announced, extricating it from the rear pocket of his pants. "The siren was my daughter's idea." He pressed the correct button and lifted the phone to his ear.

"John," the woman's voice shouted before he had the chance to say hello. "You have to get over here right away."

In the background John heard banging and yelling. "Kerri?"

But before she had a chance to answer, the line went dead in his hands.

chapter twenty-one

What the hell do you think you're doing?" the man demanded, advancing angrily, swatting the phone from Kerri's hand with a furious flick of his wrist.

Kerri felt the sting of his fingers as the phone flew into the air, then crashed to the floor, the piece of plastic at the back of the receiver coming loose and disgorging the batteries inside. They rolled across the rose-colored carpet, coming to rest under the white, pleated dust ruffle of her queen-size bed. "I've called Sheriff Weber," she told him, shielding her face in case he got tired of swinging at inanimate objects and started taking his frustrations out on her. She'd invested far too much time and money on her face to have it casually destroyed by some moron who was mad because he couldn't find his wife. "He's on his way."

Cal Hamilton sneered, "I've seen the sheriff in action. Trust me. He doesn't move that fast."

Maybe not for you, Kerri was thinking, although what she said was "I really think you should go now."

"Not till I get what I came for." He folded one muscular forearm over the other, planted his feet a shoulder-width distance apart.

Mr. Clean with hair, Kerri thought, although his white T-shirt was covered with grime, and even from a distance of several feet she could smell the liquor on his breath. "I told you. She's not here."

"Then where is she?"

"How the hell would I know?" Kerri asked impatiently. "I've never said two words to the woman."

"No, but your daughter has."

"And she already told you she has no idea where your wife is."

"The little pig is lying, and so are you." Cal pushed a small chair out of his way and inched closer.

Kerri took an involuntary step back, angry at herself for allowing this man to intimidate her in her own home. Three husbands had already tried that. Three husbands had been sent packing. If only Delilah hadn't answered the door. "It's Mr. Hamilton," Kerri could still hear her daughter's little-girl voice announce warily as she opened the front door.

And then it was chaos.

Cal Hamilton, whom Kerri had always considered cute in a thuggish sort of way, and Delilah, looking especially lumpish in her unflattering denim cutoffs, had exchanged heated accusations and denials, eventually waking up the sleeping giant that was Rose, who began yelling down from her upstairs bedroom, ordering everyone to shut the hell up. When it came to intimidation, Kerri thought, not without a trace of admiration, no man could hold a candle to her mother.

Delilah and Kerri had raced upstairs as Cal began taking the downstairs rooms apart, tossing heavy furniture aside as if it were weightless, then tearing through the kitchen and the hall closet before bounding up the stairs and bursting into Kerri's bedroom. She'd managed to shout out only a few words to the sheriff before Cal had furiously slapped the phone from her hand. Hopefully John was on his way. With any luck he'd get here before Cal did any real damage.

Her mother and daughter had locked themselves in Rose's room, but all it would take was a few swift kicks from Cal's black leather boots to bring the door crashing down. Unless Delilah had managed to push her mother's heavy dresser from its place against the wall opposite Rose's bed to barricade the door. Which was entirely possible. Her daughter was hardly a delicate flower, and all that extra weight should be good for something, Kerri thought, then immediately felt guilty. It wasn't right to have such unkind thoughts about your own flesh and blood. Although it was hardly surprising. She was her mother's daughter after all.

"Last time, Kerri," Cal warned now. "Where the fuck is she?"

"Last time, moron," Kerri answered steadily. "I have no fucking idea."

It was then that he hit her, a hard smack across the face with his open palm that sent her sprawling across the top of her billowing white comforter. Kerri didn't move. She was thinking that she should have seen it coming. She'd been in situations like this before, tense standoffs with drunken men who weren't above using their fists to win an argument. Her first husband had beaten her so badly when she was pregnant with Delilah that he'd sent her to the hospital with two cracked ribs and a fractured wrist. Six months after their daughter's birth, another beating had broken Kerri's nose.

The first of her cosmetic procedures, she thought now, reaching up to feel that Cal hadn't damaged anything. What was taking John so long? And why wasn't Delilah coming to her rescue? Surely she could hear what was going on. Surely she knew her mother was in trouble. Surely if she'd actually been able to drag the dresser in front of the bedroom door, she could push it away again.

And then Kerri heard her daughter's halting, little-girl voice ordering Cal to step back, and miraculously, she felt him comply. "Hey, girl," she heard him say. "Don't do anything stupid now." And when she turned her head and looked toward the bedroom door, she saw Delilah standing there, her arms extended, a gun at the end of her trembling fingers.

"Get your hands up in the air," Delilah ordered, and again Cal did as he was told. "Are you all right?" Delilah asked her mother.

Kerri nodded. "Sheriff Weber's on his way." Where on earth had Delilah gotten a gun?

"Look, just tell me where my wife is and I'll get out of your hair," Cal offered, as if his visit were nothing more than a pesky intrusion.

"How many times do we have to tell you we don't know where she is?" Kerri said.

"She knows," Cal insisted, staring at the weapon in Delilah's hand. "She was there today. My neighbor saw her."

"What are you talking about?" Kerri glanced back at her daughter.

"I *was* there," Delilah confirmed. "I was there yesterday too. Just like I was supposed to be. I knocked. I rang the bell. Nobody answered."

"You're a lying bitch."

"What have you done to her?" Delilah asked, her voice so low her words were barely audible.

"What have I done to her?" Cal repeated incredulously, swaying from one foot to the other. "I haven't done anything to her, you stupid cow. At least not yet."

"Don't move," Delilah warned. "I'll shoot you if you take another step." Several tears escaped her eyes to fall the length of her cheek.

Could Delilah do it? Kerri wondered. Could her daughter actually shoot another human being?

Cal's abrupt laugh answered the question for her. "Who are you kidding, lard-ass? You're not going to shoot anybody." He pushed past Delilah and was down the stairs before the trembling girl had figured out how to remove the safety catch. The front door slammed shut behind him.

"Oh, my God," Kerri wailed, hearing his car squeal out of their driveway. "Give me that before you kill somebody." She grabbed the gun from her daughter's shaking hands. "Where did you get this thing?"

"It's mine," Rose announced, suddenly appearing in the doorway, clutching her green chenille bathrobe to her chest. "Give it to me."

Her mother had a gun? What the hell was going on? "Since when have you had a gun?"

"It was your father's."

"Do you have a license for it?"

"How do I know?" Rose asked impatiently.

Kerri dropped the gun into her mother's outstretched hand. What a night this was turning out to be. First Ian had canceled their date without explanation, then Cal Hamilton had shown up at her door and torn the house apart, then her daughter had turned into John Dillinger, and now her mother was making like Ma Barker. "You'd better hide it before the sheriff gets here."

"What difference does it make?" Rose said dismissively. "It's not loaded."

"It's not loaded?" Delilah asked.

"Of course not. Don't be stupid."

"Just put the damn thing away, will you?" Kerri watched Rose shuffle back to her room. It was amazing that after all these years her mother still had the ability to astound her.

"Are you all right?" Delilah asked. "Did he hurt you?"

"No. He's not nearly as tough as your daddy was." Kerri held out her arms. Delilah rushed into them, almost knocking her over. "Thank you, sweetie. You were very brave." She kissed her daughter's forehead, tasted the nervous perspiration that clung to her skin. Delilah's arms snaked around her, tightening their grip with each breath. Kerri quickly extricated herself from her daughter's painful grasp, began smoothing down the hair extensions that had become messed during the fracas.

"He killed her," Delilah whispered. "I know he did."

"But that doesn't make any sense," Kerri protested. "I mean, why would he come over here, tearing up the place looking for her, if he killed her?"

"To throw us off the scent."

"Dear God. What an imagination you've got. You think he killed Liana too?" Kerri joked, trying to laugh. But the laugh died in her throat when she saw the look on her daughter's face. "I think you've been watching too much television," Kerri said. "You honestly think Cal Hamilton is a serial killer?"

"Maybe. Or maybe he killed Liana to make it look that way."

The doorbell rang.

"Your knight in shining armor has arrived," her mother called out from across the hall.

"Did you put the gun away?" Kerri asked as she walked past her room.

"What gun?" Rose asked from her bed.

"I could use a drink," Kerri said.

"Something you're not telling me?" John asked as Kerri was walking him to his car some forty minutes later. They'd gone over the events of the evening several times in those forty minutes, and he'd questioned both her mother and daughter about what had happened. Nobody had mentioned the gun. Was that what he was referring to?

"I'm pretty sure we told you everything."

He nodded, although the expression on his face said he wasn't sure he believed her. "You're sure you're okay?"

"I'm fine." Even in the dark, Kerri was aware of the sheriff's eyes on her body as she moved, and she casually increased the already exaggerated sway of her hips. She knew how John Weber felt about her, that he'd been lusting after her since the sixth grade, even before she *had* hips, for God's sake. Certainly before she had breasts, she thought, pulling her shoulders back and pushing her twice-augmented bosom forward.

She didn't even remember what her own breasts looked like anymore. She just remembered her mother's scalding assessment of their inadequacies. "Flat as a pancake," her mother had repeatedly pronounced. "You better find a guy who likes pancakes." There were the constant put-downs, the continual comparisons to her sisters that all but guaranteed their future estrangement. "Ruthie has such lovely breasts," her mother often said. "She gets them from me. Unfortunately, you and Lorraine take after your father's side of the family, although at least Lorraine has nice legs."

Kerri ran her hands along her once-heavy thighs. A lot of lunges and a little liposuction had leveled the playing field rather nicely, although the principal players had long since left the field. Both of Kerri's sisters had managed to escape their mother: Ruthie had moved to California a decade ago, calling only when she needed money for another stint in rehab. Lorraine had taken the easy way out and died.

Kerri glanced back at the house, saw her mother watching her from her bedroom window. She's just waiting for us *all* to die and then she can die happy, she thought.

"I'll station someone out front," John offered as they reached his cruiser. "Until I get Cal into custody."

"I appreciate that." Kerri listened as John phoned in his request for a deputy. He'd always taken such good care of her, she was thinking as he returned his cell phone to the pocket of his pants. He'd liked her in all her various incarnations: flat or busty, thin or lush-lipped, chunky-thighed or chiseled. And he was a good, surprisingly agile lover. Too bad their timing had always been slightly off, that she'd married three losers, two of them named Danny, that he'd married that witch Pauline. And while Kerri had eventually turfed all her husbands out on their ears, she knew John Weber, for all his ostensible bravado, would never work up the courage to leave his wife.

Why was she even thinking such thoughts? She and John Weber hadn't been lovers for years. She hadn't even thought of him in those terms since the night she'd turned on her computer and found herself engaged in suggestively witty banter with a successful, if disenchanted, doctor from upstate New York. Pretty soon they were exchanging photos and phone numbers, then actually meeting in Miami for the first of several trysts. During their second rendezvous, he'd confessed what her mother already suspected: he was married. But her mother, far from chewing her out about the futility of carrying on another dead-end relationship with a married man, was suddenly advising her on how best to get her false nails hooked even deeper inside the doctor's pliant flesh. "Give him the blow job of his dreams," she'd pronounced in most unmotherly terms. After their next passionate encounter, the good doctor had announced his intention to relocate to Torrance. Five months after he'd set up his new practice, Rose had told her daughter to pull the plug on their relationship. "One more blow, then out you go," she'd rhymed with a cold smile, as if she were Johnnie Cochran delivering his final summation to the jury in the O. J. Simpson trial. *If the glove doesn't fit* . . . Kerri's swollen lips had worked one last miracle, then she'd tearfully bid the man of her mother's dreams adieu. And waited. Six weeks later, Ian Crosbie had walked out on his wife and family. Rose had assured her it was only a matter of time until he proposed.

"You're not seeing Dr. Crosbie tonight?" John asked, as if reading at least part of her thoughts.

"Not tonight," Kerri said, thinking she detected a hint of something in John's tired eyes, as if he knew something she didn't.

"We're not joined at the hip, you know." Where was Ian tonight anyway? she wondered. He hadn't offered any reason for breaking their date, other than that he'd had a hard day and wanted to get to bed early. Kerri had thought of paying him a surprise visit, but she'd always hated surprises herself. They had a nasty way of backfiring. "So what's the next step?" she asked, blaming the incident with Cal for her growing sense of unease.

"Think I'll go pay Cal Hamilton a little visit."

"You think he went home?"

John shrugged. "Wherever he is, I'll find him."

"What do you suppose happened to his wife?"

"Too early to say."

"You think she ran off?"

"Maybe."

Kerri shook her head in mounting frustration. When had John Weber become so damned circumspect? One of the things she'd always liked about him was that he was so uncomplicated. "Do you think Delilah could be right about him?" she ventured, reluctant to see him leave.

"Do I think Cal's a serial killer?"

"*Do* you?"

"Guess I'll have to find out." He opened the cruiser door, climbed into the front seat, and turned on the car's engine.

"John . . ."

The car window lowered with a push of a button. "An officer will be here any minute. You sure you don't want me to drive you to a hospital?"

"No, I'm okay. I know a good doctor."

John threw the car into gear. "Get back in the house and lock the door," he directed. "Don't open it for anybody until you hear from me."

"What if you don't find him?"

"Go on inside," John said again, pointing toward the upstairs bedroom. "You don't want to give your mother heart palpitations."

Kerri sighed, a sigh that said, Don't be so sure, and John smiled, which made Kerri want to reach in and kiss him, but she didn't.

Rose was obviously watching their every move, and the last thing Kerri wanted was to reactivate her mother's venomous tongue. Rose had been much less critical of her since she'd started seeing Ian. True, she'd transferred some of that poison to Delilah, but Delilah was somehow able to slough off her unkind remarks in a way that Kerri had never been able to do. Besides, maybe her mother's harsh barbs were what Delilah needed to spur her on, get her thinking about her weight, her hair, her *everything*, Kerri thought, returning to the house. Didn't the girl ever want to go out on a date? Didn't she want a boyfriend? Didn't she want to have sex? Kerri shuddered. The last thing she needed to be thinking about right now was her daughter having sex.

"What'd the sheriff say?" Delilah asked as soon as Kerri stepped inside.

"He's gonna station a man outside the house until he finds Cal." Kerri closed the door behind her, then locked it. "Bring me a chair from the kitchen, will you?" she instructed her daughter, who promptly did as she was told. Kerri secured the back of the chair under the door handle. "Just in case," she said, although she doubted such meager precautions would be sufficient to keep an enraged Cal Hamilton out.

"I like Sheriff Weber, don't you?" Delilah said.

"'Course I like him."

"But his daughter's a real pill."

"Takes after her mother." Kerri walked into the living room, began retrieving some of the doilies Cal had tossed to the floor.

"I'll straighten up. You sit down." Delilah quickly gathered up the remaining doilies, returned each to its former position. "Are you going to call Dr. Crosbie?"

Kerri sank into the sofa and checked her watch. "It's kind of late. I don't want to wake him."

"It's not that late, and I'm sure he'd want to know what happened."

"I don't know. He said he was going to bed early."

"Mom, for Pete's sake. He loves you, doesn't he?"

Does he? Kerri wondered.

"Well, I think you should call him. Tell him what happened." Delilah handed her mother her cell phone.

Kerri hesitated. What was she so afraid of? "You're not going to stand here and listen, are you?"

"Oh. Oh, no. No, of course not." Delilah quickly retreated into the kitchen.

Kerri took a deep breath, then pressed in Ian's number. Of course he'd want to know what had happened here tonight. And he'd undoubtedly be so concerned, he'd hop in his car and come right over, she was telling herself as the phone rang once, twice, three times, before being picked up.

"This is Ian Crosbie," came the familiar, recorded message. *"I can't come to the phone right now, but if you leave your name, number, and a short message, I'll get back to you as soon as possible."*

Kerri clicked off before the beep, lowered the phone to the cushion beside her, assuring herself that Ian's not picking up didn't necessarily mean he wasn't home. It just meant that he'd gone to bed early, exactly as advertised. So why the concern? Why was she feeling so tentative?

"Kerri," her mother called from upstairs. "Kerri, what's happening?"

Kerri pushed her platinum hair extensions away from her unlined face, rubbed her lifted brow, and closed her "done" eyes, a deep sigh leaving her enhanced bosom to escape her swollen lips. "I have no idea."

chapter twenty-two

John sped away from Kerri's house at more than twenty miles over the limit. He wasn't worried about pedestrians. Since Liana's body had been discovered, no one went for a casual stroll after dark anymore. Besides, he had to put some space between himself and Kerri before he did something stupid. Just the smell of her had been so damned intoxicating, and the way she'd leaned inside the car, displaying her breasts as if they were pots of bright flowers sitting on a windowsill, offering them to him like fancy canapés on a silver platter. For a moment, he'd actually thought she might be trying to seduce him, but then she'd mentioned that asshole Dr. Crosbie, and the name had flooded through his veins like ice water. *I know a good doctor,* she'd said.

He'd been tempted at that moment to tell her everything he'd discovered about the "good doctor," but instead he'd pressed his foot to the pedal and taken off into the night. Kerri Franklin's love life was none of his business. His business was to apprehend law-breakers, and Cal Hamilton's behavior tonight had definitely crossed the line from the merely objectionable into the downright criminal. You didn't tear up a woman's house and terrorize her family, you didn't slap her around, demanding answers she didn't have, just because your wife had finally awakened from her stupor, come to her senses, and run the hell away.

Which was his assessment of what had probably happened regarding Fiona Hamilton.

And now he was only minutes from the Hamilton house, and he prayed that Cal would be there and he wouldn't have to have his deputies spend half the night driving around looking for him. He also hoped Cal had calmed down enough to take stock of his situation and was even now preparing to turn himself in without any further unpleasantness. A night in jail would undoubtedly sober him up. And as mad as Kerri was, chances were good she wouldn't press charges if Cal apologized and promised never to do it again.

Unless Delilah's suspicions proved to be true and Cal Hamilton had slaughtered not only his wife but Liana Martin too—and possibly even Candy Abbot?—John thought, the dull buzz of a headache beginning to circle his eyes like a dying fly, which meant the man was either a deranged serial killer or a cold, calculating murderer.

Somehow neither description fit.

Cal might be an arrogant jerk, but he wasn't crazy. Nor was he very bright. While John found it entirely plausible that Cal was indeed *capable* of killing his wife, especially if he'd been angry or drunk or, more likely, both, John didn't think Cal had the brains to try to disguise what he'd done by showing up at Kerri's door sometime later, demanding to know her whereabouts. And while he might be heartless enough to kill a succession of innocent young women in order to divert suspicion from himself in the death of his wife, John didn't think he was clever enough by half to have concocted such a scheme. Such premeditation required an active intelligence, an imagination Cal Hamilton sorely lacked.

John had been dealing with the criminal mind for a long time, and while he'd never personally overseen a case involving a serial killer, he knew two things for sure: one, most criminals weren't very smart, and two, none of them ever thought they were going to get caught.

He also knew that predators were notoriously good at hiding their sick cravings from the community in which they lived. How many reports had he read, how many cases had he followed, how many newscasts had he seen, wherein clearly shattered friends and neighbors lined up to voice their shock and disbelief when a psychopath was uncovered in their midst? How similar were the statements they gave to the police and the press? *He was so quiet, so unassuming. We never had the slightest idea he could do something like this.*

Cal Hamilton was anything but unassuming and quiet. Furthermore, he looked as if he had something to hide, and as a result you suspected him of anything and everything. And while it was true

that the most obvious suspect was often the right one when it came
to solving homicides, John couldn't believe this would prove to be
true in the brutal slaying of Liana Martin. It was too easy, and nothing in John's life had ever come easy. Although it would make for a
pleasant change, he thought as he rounded the corner of Old Country Road and pulled to a stop in front of Cal Hamilton's bungalow.

The normally dark house was lit up like the proverbial Christmas
tree. All the lights in the place appeared to be on, although the
blinds were down, as always, and two cars were parked in the driveway, as well as several more on the street. John recognized the white
van that had picked up Tanya McGovern from the doctor's office, as
well as Joey Balfour's old blue Pontiac and the red Chevy that Ray
Sutter had recently driven off the road not far from where Liana's
body was later unearthed. What was everybody doing here?

"Sheriff," he heard a woman call softly as he headed up the walk-
way.

His first thought was that it was Fiona Hamilton, that she'd
returned home to find her house ablaze with lights and filled with
strangers and had been hiding in the shrubbery ever since, waiting
for everyone to leave. But when he turned around, he saw that the
woman tiptoeing toward him in her bare feet wasn't Cal's missing
wife but rather Sandy Crosbie, his next-door neighbor.

"What's happening?" she asked, tucking her chin-length hair
behind her ears. She was wearing yellow pajamas under a long, pink
cotton robe. "Have you found Fiona?"

John shook his head. "May I ask how you knew she was missing?"

"Are you kidding? Cal stormed over here about an hour ago, asking if we'd seen her. I told him Delilah Franklin had been by yesterday, asking the same thing, and he just took off. Naturally, my kids
were on the Internet the minute he left. And a bunch of people are
in there now, trying to organize a search party. Everybody's talking
about a serial killer."

Jesus, John thought. A search party. In the dead of night. "Look,
the fact that Fiona's missing doesn't mean she's dead. There's a very
good chance she left of her own accord."

"Do you really believe that? She's such a meek little thing." A phone rang in the distance. Sandy spun toward the sound. "Oh, dear. That's my phone again. It's been ringing all night. Everybody wants to know what's happening."

"Please tell them that any speculation at this point is both premature and counterproductive. Now, if you'll excuse me . . ." John broke from her side and approached Cal's front door. He rang the bell several times, then knocked loudly. "What the hell's going on in here?" he barked as Greg Watt opened the door.

Greg Watt, dressed all in black, stepped back and allowed John entry. "Sheriff's here," he announced without answering the question.

"About time," Cal barked from the living room. "Get your ass in here, Sheriff, and tell me what we're going to do about finding my wife."

"*We're* not going to do anything," John said evenly, although the sight of Greg Watt, Joey Balfour, Peter Arlington, and Ray Sutter forming a protective circle around Cal Hamilton was enough to make him want to scream. What were these guys doing here? He knew they were all regular patrons of Chester's, and that Cal, Joey, and Greg had been part of the search team that had discovered Liana's body, so maybe it made sense that Cal had contacted them to ask for help in finding his wife, but was that really Gordon Lipsman sitting off by himself in the corner? "What the hell are you doing here?" he asked his daughter's drama teacher.

"I was in private rehearsals with Greg and Peter for the school play when Joey called him and said Fiona Hamilton had gone missing," the teacher explained with an indignant stiffening of his back. "Greg said they'd meet him here, and I decided to tag along. In case I could be of assistance."

"And you?" John asked Ray Sutter. "Please tell me you haven't been driving under the influence again."

Ray Sutter, roughly forty years old and in need of a good shave, turned his droopy eyes toward the sheriff. He had a long, lived-in face and a head of unruly brown hair and always looked as if he'd either just crawled out of bed or was looking for one to climb into.

"I heard about Fiona," he said, the slight slur in his voice capsizing his valiant attempt to sound wounded by the sheriff's suspicions. "Thought I'd stop by, volunteer my services."

John's gaze shifted toward Peter Arlington.

"Obviously, if Mrs. Hamilton's disappearance has anything to do with Liana's murder, then I want to be involved," the boy offered without waiting to be asked.

Talk about the blind leading the blind, John thought, motioning to Cal Hamilton. "Okay, that's it. You're coming to the station with me."

"What for? We can talk here," Cal said.

"You're under arrest, Cal."

"What?"

"What are you talking about?" Joey Balfour pushed a lock of dark, greasy hair away from his forehead. John immediately noticed a cut above his left eye and a small bruise by the side of his mouth. "You're arresting a man because his wife is missing? On what charge?"

A few days ago, John might have been upset at the effrontery of a punk kid mouthing off to him in this fashion. But tonight he found such teenage posturing amusing, even comical. "Assault," he barked, watching Joey take a step back. "Speaking of which, what happened to your face?"

Joey raised a hand to his chin. "Walked into a door," he said out of the side of his mouth.

"That bitch told you I assaulted her?" Cal demanded.

"What bitch?" Gordon Lipsman asked, the color draining from his face.

"You found her?" Ray Sutter said.

John ignored them both. "Do you deny barging into Kerri Franklin's house and striking her?" he asked Cal.

"I barely touched her, for Christ's sake. Did she tell you that psycho kid of hers threatened to shoot me?"

Greg laughed.

John shook his head. The evening was moving beyond the ridiculous into the surreal. "Let's talk about this at the station, shall we?"

"Shall we? *Shall we?*" Cal mimicked. "Are you crazy, Sheriff? My wife is missing and there's a killer on the loose."

"We'll talk at the station," John repeated.

"I'm not going anywhere until you tell me what you're going to do to find my wife."

"Exactly how long has your wife been missing?" John asked, trying to diffuse the situation before taking Cal into custody.

"I called her from work. She didn't answer the phone. I came home. She wasn't here."

"So, you're saying she was here when you left for work," John reiterated.

"Yes."

"Which means she's only been gone a few hours. She could be at the movies."

"She's not at the movies."

"You seem awfully sure."

"I *am* sure." Cal Hamilton began angrily pacing back and forth in the confined space. "She hates movies. She doesn't have any money. She doesn't like crowds."

"Maybe she doesn't like *you.*"

"What are you suggesting?"

"That we need to continue this discussion at the station."

"I'm not going anywhere."

"I'm not giving you a choice." John placed his hand purposefully over the gun in his holster.

"Shit," Cal said. "Another gun."

"Come on, Sheriff," Ray Sutter intervened. "The guy's upset. Surely you can understand that."

John recalled how upset Ray Sutter had been the night he drove his car into the ditch not far from where Liana's body was later discovered. And now, here he was again. "Oh, I understand *that*. What I *can't* understand is what you guys are still doing here. I'm tempted to arrest the lot of you."

"We're just trying to help," Gordon Lipsman said.

"What's that old show-business expression?" John asked pointedly. "Don't call us, we'll call you?"

Gordon Lipsman blanched. He looked toward his brown, tasseled loafers.

"Look, there's not much anyone can do tonight," John continued. He didn't want trouble. Not from the town drunk, a couple of teenage toughs, and a wimpy, high school drama teacher. Where was his backup anyway? He'd called for another car on the drive over. What was taking so long? "Go home, people. Get a good night's sleep. If you feel you have to do something, you can check out the mall on your way home."

"My wife isn't at the goddamn mall. I'm telling you—"

"And I'm telling *you:* You're under arrest. Now turn around and put your hands behind your back," John instructed, unhooking his handcuffs from his belt to show he meant business. He'd hoped it wouldn't come to this, but clearly some show of force had become necessary. "Come on, Cal. Don't make this any harder than it needs to be."

"Fuck you," Cal said, even as he turned around and extended his arms behind his back.

Thank God, John thought as he slipped the cuffs around Cal's thick wrists. He made a mental note of the scratches on Cal's hands, wondering if they'd come from tearing up Kerri's place or something more sinister.

"Is that really necessary, Sheriff?" Gordon Lipsman asked, his eyes still on his shoes.

"Go home," John said again, waiting until they'd left the house before ushering Cal outside. A police cruiser pulled up as the last of their cars departed. About fucking time, John thought, leading Cal to the curb. What he said was "Read Mr. Hamilton his rights and take him to the station. The charge is assault."

"You're not coming?" Cal asked John as the second officer pushed him into the backseat of the cruiser.

"I think we could all use some time to cool off and calm down," John said. "I'll see you in the morning. Maybe by then, Mrs. Hamilton will be back to bail you out."

"And if she isn't?"

"We'll file a missing persons report and start looking."

"I bet you wouldn't be so relaxed if it was *your* wife who was missing," Cal said from the backseat of the cruiser, and John might have smiled had Cal not added ominously, "Or your daughter."

"What's that supposed to mean?"

"Just thinking out loud." Cal Hamilton sank back in his seat, stared out the front window, refused to acknowledge the sheriff further.

"Lock him up," John directed the other officer with a loud knock on the hood of the car with the palm of his hand.

"You have the right to remain silent," he heard the deputy say as he threw the car into gear.

"Yeah, yeah, yeah," Cal said dismissively as they pulled away from the curb.

For several minutes John stood staring at the pavement, debating whether he should go down to the station and question Cal further. But he doubted he'd learn anything more of value tonight, and he knew he should probably go home, try to get a good night's sleep. If Fiona Hamilton was, in fact, missing, then he had an exhausting day ahead of him. It wouldn't take long before the press got wind of her disappearance, and pretty soon he'd be up to his eyeballs in reporters from neighboring counties, and the mayor would be on his back again, deriding his instincts, his dedication, his ability. John had been in law enforcement almost twenty years, and twits like Sean Wilson were still questioning his worth. Maybe because he routinely questioned it himself, John realized, understanding that if a serial killer was indeed in their midst and he apprehended him, then he'd no longer be regarded as an overweight, over-the-hill sheriff of a backwater, little southern town. Was that really how others saw him? he wondered. And did he have the strength to alter that perception?

A woman's voice sliced through the night air. "Sheriff?"

He turned toward the sound. "Mrs. Crosbie."

"Please call me Sandy."

He tried to smile. "What can I do for you, Sandy?"

"Is everything all right?"

"For now. I may need to speak to you again tomorrow."

"Of course. Anything I can do to help. Sheriff," she began again before he could turn away.

"Yes?"

"That phone call I had before . . ."

"Yes?"

"It was from Rita Hensen."

The school nurse, John thought, picturing the tiny woman. It had been John who'd unwound the cord from around her husband's neck three years ago, and the sight of his lifeless body hanging from the shower rod was something he doubted he'd ever be able to completely erase from his memory. "Is there a problem?"

"Well, I'm not sure whether I should be telling you this . . ."

"Telling me what?"

"I don't want to get Brian into trouble. He's a very sweet boy, very sensitive, and I'm sure he hasn't done anything wrong, but with everything that's been happening . . ."

"Mrs. Crosbie . . . Sandy," John corrected. "What is it you're trying to tell me?"

"Rita just called. She's very upset."

"Has Brian done something?" This was like pulling teeth, John thought. Except more painful.

"That's just it. She's not sure. He won't talk to her."

"So what makes her think anything's wrong?"

Again Sandy hesitated. Then the words tumbled out in a rush, as if spilled from a glass. "Well, he's been very uncommunicative ever since Liana's vigil. Clearly something has been bothering him, but he wouldn't discuss it. At first Rita thought the whole thing had just churned up memories of his father's death. He hasn't been sleeping well. He's up at all hours. Sometimes he leaves the house in the middle of the night."

"What happened tonight?" John asked, knowing there was a more specific reason for Rita's call.

"Brian went out earlier without telling her where he was going. He was gone for well over an hour, and when he came back, he headed straight for the bathroom. Rita heard the water running for the longest time, and when he finally came out, she saw that he'd rinsed out his shirt, and . . ."

"And?"

"And she thought that was very curious because he never does stuff like that, and that's when she saw a few red drops on the floor and realized it was blood."

"She's sure it was blood?"

"That's what I said. She said she's a nurse, she knows what blood looks like. She also said there were bruises on Brian's hands and scratches on his face."

"He could have tripped. He could have gotten into a fight. He could have walked into a door," John ventured, thinking of Joey Balfour. What a night this was turning out to be. "There are any number of reasonable explanations. We shouldn't go jumping to conclusions." But even as he spoke the words, John was wondering if it was possible that Brian Hensen was somehow involved in Fiona Hamilton's disappearance, that he'd somehow managed to lure her from her home, that he might actually have killed her, that this shy, sensitive seventeen-year-old boy whose father had committed suicide three years earlier could also have murdered Liana Martin and Candy Abbot. Was it possible?

"That's what I tried to tell her," Sandy said.

"What?"

"What you said—that there were any number of explanations, that she shouldn't go jumping to conclusions."

"What was Brian's explanation?"

"There wasn't one. When Rita questioned him about it, he called her a bunch of names and stormed out of the house."

"Does she have any idea where he went?"

Sandy shook her head. "He took the car. She's beside herself because she thinks he might have been drinking."

"Shit," John said. How many times had he said that tonight?

"I didn't know whether to tell you."

"You did the right thing."

"I don't want to get Brian into trouble."

"Sounds like he's already in trouble."

"What are you going to do?"

"Find him," John said simply.

"And then what?"

John shook his head. He hated conversations that ended with *And then what?*

chapter twenty-three

He spent the better part of the next hour driving through the carelessly laid-out grid that was Torrance. Whoever had designed this place should be shot, John thought, knowing no formal planning had been involved in the town's creation, that Torrance had more or less designed itself, beginning as a few widely scattered homesteads and expanding as its population increased. It followed no particular course, spilling like loose flesh from the top of a girdle into whatever empty spaces it could find.

John executed another perfect three-point turn at the end of yet another dead-end road, shaking his head in bemused wonderment at his ineptitude. It wasn't as if he didn't know his way around. He did. But it was late, he was getting tired, there were no streetlights, and the starless sky was the kind of dark your eyes never got used to. How was he supposed to find anyone?

It was ironic, he thought, that he'd begun the evening searching for one man and was ending it looking for another. On one end of the search was Cal Hamilton, a brute and a bully, all balls and no brain. On the other was Brian Hensen, smart, shy, and sensitive. Could one be more different from the other? And was there a link between the two? Was it possible that Brian Hensen was in any way connected to Fiona Hamilton's disappearance, and by extension to Liana Martin's death? God, he hoped not. Surely that family had suffered enough already.

Once again his thoughts returned to that afternoon three years ago when he'd answered the phone to hear the flat tones of a four-teen-year-old boy summoning him to a modest house on Cherry Drive. "Sheriff Weber," the voice had said without inflection, "this is Brian Hensen. Could you come over, please. My father is dead. I can't cut him down."

The senior Brian Hensen's face was remarkably similar in shape and bone structure to that of his son, although Brian's face was delicate where his father's had been coarse, his hair lighter, his skin fairer, his eyes a paler shade of blue. Neither could be considered handsome—their noses too broad, their chins too weak—but they were perfectly respectable faces nonetheless. There was just something missing, a focus perhaps, and in its place lingered a sense of distraction that had been passed from father to son.

The senior Brian Hensen had suffered from depression all his life, succumbing to its ravages three years earlier, as one succumbs to any terminal illness. Some people had turned up their noses, called him a coward, said he chose the easy way out. But mental illness had robbed Brian Hensen of choices. Would people be so judgmental about someone who died of pneumonia, John wondered, or gave in to the constant and debilitating pain of cancer? Pain was pain, he thought, his eyes searching the deserted roadside for any sign of Brian's black Civic.

He'd been worried about Brian ever since he'd found him clinging to his father's lifeless body, his skinny arms wrapped around the man's muscular thighs, trying to hold his legs up, to take some of the weight off his broken neck. "I couldn't cut him down," the boy kept repeating, a pair of useless scissors discarded on the white tiles nearby.

Indeed, it had been difficult for even John and his deputy to cut through the twisted sheet the senior Hensen had used as a noose, even more difficult to remove that noose from around the bruised folds of his flesh. His skin had taken on a bluish hue, and purple lined his lips.

And if *he* could still see Brian Hensen's body hanging lifeless from his shower rod, he who was used to the sights and smells of death, what must it be like for a sensitive young boy on the verge of manhood, unformed and unsure, still trying to figure out who he was and what he wanted from life? Did he want life at all? Or had he inherited his father's suicide gene along with all the others? John knew that depression often ran in families, like long legs and brown eyes, and that suicide could be as contagious as chicken pox. He'd worried about Brian taking his own life. He hadn't even considered the possibility he might take someone else's.

John turned right, the headlights of his cruiser catching something suspect beneath a large banyan tree off the side of the road. He immediately pulled the car to a stop, grabbed his flashlight from the glove compartment, and jumped out of the vehicle. The night was growing cooler, although the air was still heavy with humidity. Even still, the sweet odor of marijuana took no time reaching his nostrils. He inhaled, experienced a vicarious thrill. It had been twenty years since he'd last enjoyed a toke. The memory warmed and comforted him as he advanced, his hands relaxed at his sides. There'd be no need for guns here, he thought as he approached the young man sitting beneath the tree in the high grass. In his experience, smokers of marijuana were far more mellow and much less likely to resort to violence than their drunken counterparts. "Victor," he said, staring down at the young man whose ghostly white face required no extra lighting.

"Sheriff," Victor acknowledged without any effort to disguise what he was doing. He took another drag off his hand-rolled cigarette and stared into the night.

"What are you doing here, Victor? Aside from the obvious."

Victor's head shook slowly from side to side. "The obvious is all I'm doing," he replied after a pause.

"You know it's against the law," John said, feeling like a total hypocrite. What he really wanted to do was pull up a patch of earth and join him.

"I'm not hurting anyone."

"Except yourself."

Victor laughed. "Come on, Sheriff. You really believe that?"

"It's against the law."

"You gonna arrest me?"

John focused his flashlight on the surrounding area before circling it back to the road. "Where's your car?"

"Didn't bring it."

"You walked here from home?"

"It's not that far."

"A couple of miles."

"Cardio," Victor said with a sly smile. "It's good for you."

"Not if you get eaten by an alligator, it's not." Again John circled the surrounding area with his flashlight.

"Don't worry, Sheriff. I'll protect you."

"I appreciate that."

Victor took another drag off his joint. John debated telling him to put it out, but the cigarette had already burned all the way down to Victor's fingers and all that remained was one last drag, which Victor took, stretching it out as long as he could and holding it in his lungs until he was forced to exhale. "Good stuff," he croaked.

"What are you doing out here alone?" John asked, expanding his original question.

"Nothing" came the reply, as expected. "Just thinking."

"About what?"

"Stuff."

"Your parents know where you are?"

Victor laughed.

John nodded understanding. From what he knew about Victor Drummond's parents, he doubted they cared much where their son was, only that he was out of their hair.

"You see Brian Hensen tonight?"

Victor shook his head. Jet-black hair fell across his powdery white forehead. "Brian? No. Why?"

"What about Fiona Hamilton?"

"Who?"

John sighed. This was getting him nowhere. "Okay, look. I'm taking you home now."

"Cool." Victor wiped the grass from the back of his skinny black jeans as he pushed himself to his feet. He followed John to his car, climbed in the front seat. "I've never ridden in a police cruiser before."

"Not exactly the thrill of a lifetime."

"Don't sell yourself short, Sheriff." Victor leaned back and closed his eyes. "Sell yourself short, Sheriff," he repeated with a girlish giggle. "Does that qualify as alliteration?"

"Damned if I know."

"Guess I'll have to ask Mrs. Crosbie about it tomorrow."

John pulled away from the side of the road, did a U-turn, and headed toward Victor's sprawling, split-level home not far from the mall. It was rumored that Wayne Drummond had made a killing in the stock market when everyone else had been losing his shirt. There'd even been some talk of insider trading, but no formal charges had ever been laid. Since such matters were out of his jurisdiction and beyond his understanding, John had never taken much interest in any of it. But he'd never cared for either Wayne or his snooty wife, Wendy. Wayne and Wendy, he repeated silently now. Did that qualify as alliteration?

"I understand you and Liana Martin were pretty close," John ventured as they neared Victor's house.

Victor opened his eyes, turned them toward the sheriff, although his head remained steady. "We were friends. I told you that already."

"You didn't tell me you were *close* friends."

"Because we weren't."

"I heard otherwise."

"You heard wrong."

"You didn't have a crush on her?" John pressed.

"Crushes are for teenyboppers."

"Really? I heard she had one on you."

Victor straightened up, looked directly at John. "She did?"

"Her mother seemed to think so."

The flicker of a smile quickly passed across Victor's lips, then just as quickly disappeared. "Her mother's wrong. Liana had a boy-friend."

"What do you think of him?"

"Peter? Not much. Is he a suspect?"

"Everybody's a suspect."

"Really? I heard he has an airtight alibi."

"What about Brian Hensen?" John asked, seeking to regain control of the conversation.

"He's okay. Why do you keep asking about Brian?"

They passed the mall. It was then that John thought he spotted a black Honda Civic off by itself at the back of the large parking lot. He brought the cruiser to a sudden stop. Victor's house was just down the next street. "Think you can manage alone from here?" he asked the boy.

"Sure thing, Sheriff." Victor hopped out of the car, then leaned back inside, his white face highlighted by the darkness, like a full moon. "Thanks for the ride."

"Go to bed," John said, watching Victor turn down the street before he made another U-turn and headed back to the mall's entrance.

The area was illuminated by a series of tall, bright lights that stood at regular intervals throughout the parking lot. Normally the lot was filled to capacity, the mall being pretty much the main gathering spot in town. But it had closed an hour ago, and the only cars remaining were those parked on the other side next to the movie theater. Except for the one car John had spotted off by itself, just out of the glare of a tall lamppost. He'd almost missed it, caught just a glimpse of it as he was driving past. And now he couldn't see it at all. Had he imagined it? He advanced slowly, about to give up when he saw the car again. It appeared to be empty, so he parked a suitable distance away, then climbed out of his car and approached cautiously, keeping his hand close to his holster. This time there was no mellowing smell of marijuana to greet him.

As he got closer, he saw nobody behind the wheel, nor were any amorous bodies bopping around in the backseat. Even a casual glance inside the car revealed no one. Not until his face was right up against the car's tinted side window did John see the boy's body sprawled across the front seat. "Sweet Jesus," he muttered, grabbing the door handle and trying to yank it open.

The body inside sat up and shrieked.

John screamed as well, his hand extricating his gun from his holster and aiming it at the window.

"No!" the boy shouted. "Stop! Don't shoot!"

It took John several seconds to calm down and gain control of his breathing. "Open the fucking door," he ordered when he could find his voice.

"Don't shoot," the boy said again, inching forward on the seat and releasing the lock.

Immediately John pulled the door open, dragged the boy from the car, and spun him around. "What the hell were you doing?" John demanded angrily, returning the gun to his holster.

"Sleeping?" the boy asked, as if he were no longer sure, as if he couldn't be sure of anything. Tears dropped the length of his cheek and dripped from his chin. The sharp smell of urine indicated he'd wet his pants.

"Something wrong with your bed at home?"

Brian Hensen wiped the tears from his face, smoothed back his fine, dishwater blond hair. "Did my mother send you?" he asked meekly.

"She's worried about you," John said, evading the question.

"I'm fine." He glanced at the front of his pants. "I *was* fine," he corrected, "before you scared me half to death."

"You scared me too. I thought you were dead."

As Brian turned toward the light, John saw the cut on his forehead and the bruise at the side of his mouth that Sandy Crosbie had mentioned.

"What happened to you?"

"Nothing."

"Don't tell me 'nothing.' You've obviously been in a fight."

"It was nothing."

"Who was it with?"

"No one."

"Come on, Brian, don't give me that crap. I'm not your mother. I'm the damn sheriff. And trust me, it's not a good idea to lie to the sheriff. Now tell me what happened to you or I'm gonna have to haul your skinny butt off to jail."

"On what grounds?"

"On the grounds that I can." John smiled.

"Why are you smiling?"

"Because I'm thinking about what I'm going to do to you if you don't start talking." He paused to allow his words time to sink in. "Your mother said she caught you washing out a bloody shirt."

"My mother should mind her own business."

"You *are* her business."

"I'm not a child."

"Then stop acting like one."

"I cut myself. I was bleeding. My mother once told me that if you don't get the blood out of something quickly, it stains."

"Whose blood was it, Brian?"

"What?" He seemed genuinely startled. "What are you talking about? It was mine."

"How'd you cut yourself?"

"Walked into the branch of a tree."

"Yeah, and Joey Balfour walked into a wall," John said, suddenly putting it all together. "You and Joey got into it tonight, didn't you?"

Brian said nothing. Another tear slid down his cheek and he rubbed his nose with the back of his hand. John saw that the backs of his knuckles were swollen and bruised.

"What were you and Joey fighting about?"

"He's an asshole."

"That he is. Set the scene for me," John directed.

"What do you mean?"

"Where did the fight take place?"

"Near Pearson Park."

"What were you doing there?"

"Hanging out."

"Alone?"

"I was talking to a couple of kids."

"Names?"

"What difference does it make? Just kids from school."

"Indulge me," John said.

Brian hesitated. "Perry Falco. We're in most of the same classes together."

"And?"

"And?" Brian repeated.

"You said you were talking to a couple of kids."

"I don't know their names."

"You said they were kids from school."

"It's a big place. I don't know everybody."

John knew Brian was lying, although he didn't know why. He decided to try another approach and circle back later. "So, okay. You're hanging out with Perry Falco and a couple other kids when Joey walks by."

Brian nodded.

"Was he alone?"

"Yeah."

"Greg Watt wasn't with him?"

"No."

"What direction was he coming from?"

Brian shrugged. "What difference does it make?"

"Okay. So what happened then?"

"He started in on me."

"What do you mean? He hit you?"

"He called me a name."

"What name?" John already had a pretty good idea. He'd seen the messages on his daughter's computer. He'd heard the whispers.

"He called me a faggot," Brian confirmed.

John doubted that was all there was to it. "What else?"

"Nothing. He called me a faggot, so I hit him. Then he jumped me, beat the crap out of me. No surprises there."

"And what did Perry Falco and the others do while this was going on?"

"Nothing."

"They just stood around and watched you get the shit kicked out of you?"

"They took off. It was my fault," Brian added quickly. "I started it. There was no reason for anyone else to get involved."

"Four against one. Seems to me the only one who would have gotten hurt was Joey Balfour."

"Can I go home now?"

"Why are you lying to me, Brian?"

"I'm not lying."

"It was just you and Perry, wasn't it?" John asked softly. "The two of you were in the park when Joey surprised you."

Brian took a deep breath, looked toward the concrete. "We were just talking," he said quietly. "But Joey kept saying he saw us kissing. I tried reasoning with him, but that was a total waste of time. Then he said it was no wonder my dad killed himself, that he'd rather be dead than have a faggot for a son." Brian took another deep breath, sucking in the night air, like water from a straw. And then another, as if he couldn't get enough. "That's when I hit him."

"And that's when Perry took off?"

"I don't blame him for running away. Joey would have started in on him next."

John released a deep breath of air. "You see anyone else tonight?"

"Like who?"

"Fiona Hamilton."

"Who?"

"Never mind."

"Can I go now?"

"If you promise to go straight home."

"I promise."

"And stay there."

Brian nodded, although he didn't move. "You won't tell anyone, will you? About me and Perry in the park? I mean, we were just talking, but . . ."

"Don't worry about it."

"I mean, it's one thing if it comes from Joey," Brian continued. "Nobody really believes anything he says anyway."

"I won't say anything," John assured him. "Now go home. Get some sleep. And stay out of the park."

John watched Brian get back in his car and drive off. Then he climbed back into his cruiser and headed for home.

chapter twenty-four

"All right. Quiet, people," Gordon Lipsman was saying to the assembled cast of *Kiss Me, Kate* as he lifted fluttering hands into the air and pointed his index fingers toward the ceiling.

Megan wondered if he was pointing at anything in particular, although she wasn't interested enough to look. Probably it was just another of Mr. Lipsman's arsenal of meaningless tics and affectations. He preened, he pouted, he pointed to the ceiling. Sometimes he twirled around in a series of ever-shrinking circles; sometimes he swooped back and forth in front of the stage like a giant, white bat, before sinking into one of the auditorium seats, and sighing deeply. Yesterday Megan had wondered what all the circling and sighing was about. Today she no longer cared. She just wanted to get the rehearsal over with so she could go home.

"Has anybody seen Greg?" Mr. Lipsman asked, spinning around on his heels, as if Greg had just entered the room and was even now creeping up behind him.

"He's not here," Delilah said, stating the obvious from her seat in the far corner of the front row.

"What do you mean, he's not here?" Gordon Lipsman checked his watch. It was almost four o'clock. "Wasn't he in school today?"

"I don't think so," someone said.

"I didn't see him," said someone else.

"He called me this morning," Tanya McGovern volunteered. "Said his father needed him at home today." She smiled in Megan's direction. The smile was smug and self-satisfied. It said, I know something you don't.

Megan yawned noticeably, as if to say, I couldn't care less where he is or why. But the truth was, she did care, and she suspected everybody knew it. Monday had been bad enough. Her first day back in class after Liana's vigil. Everybody was talking about her. She'd heard the whispers in the corridors, seen the eyes that trailed her down the hall, the not-so-subtle shakes of disapproving heads. She knew they were reading from Tanya McGovern's script, that they were saying she'd made a fool of herself, that she'd betrayed her friend's memory by making out with another friend's boyfriend, even though Tanya had never said a word to her before about being interested in Greg, and Greg himself had dismissed Tanya as being way too easy. So, in one night she'd lost everything: a potential boyfriend, her so-called girlfriends, her reputation, and her self-respect. And she still didn't understand why. She didn't understand what had happened.

One minute she and Greg had been kissing passionately; the next, he was walking away. Was she that bad a kisser? Had he been repulsed by her ineptness, her obvious lack of expertise? Had he been looking for more of a challenge? Had he just been toying with her? Had he decided she simply wasn't worth the effort? She knew he'd been interested. What had changed his mind, and changed it so abruptly?

He'd spent Monday ignoring her, going so far as to sit on the other end of the aisle during yesterday afternoon's initial read-through of the play. Today's rehearsal would have involved their first big scene together, and she'd been hoping to clear the air. She wasn't looking for a confrontation, just an explanation. If an apology was necessary, she'd make one, although she didn't know what she had to apologize for. What had she done that was so awful? All right, so maybe a vigil wasn't the most appropriate place for igniting a new romance, but other kids had been making out that night as well, and no one was shunning *them*.

Megan had been staring out her bedroom window last night when Greg's white van had pulled onto her street, and for one heart-stopping moment, she'd thought he might be coming over to see her. But instead, he and Mr. Lipsman had emerged from the car's front seat, along with Peter Arlington from the back, and they'd all raced up the front path to Cal Hamilton's house, disappearing inside seconds later. Joey Balfour's car was already parked in the driveway behind Cal's sports car, and soon a beat-up red Chevy arrived, and then the sheriff. Not long after, everybody left. Greg had left the house and climbed into his van without so much as a backward glance.

Megan had spent the hours between midnight and 2 a.m. trying to banish him from her brain, and when that didn't work, the hours between two and four trying to think up clever things to say, assorted ways to recapture his attention. She'd imagined him responding to her overtures in a variety of ways, some warm and friendly, others indifferent, even hostile. She'd tried to anticipate everything that could possibly happen. What she hadn't anticipated was nothing happening at all. She hadn't considered his simply not showing up. She'd even washed her hair and worn her new black jersey with the scooped neckline. "Isn't that a little low-cut for school?" her mother had asked.

So what did Greg's absence mean? That his father had really needed his help at home? Or that he was dropping out of the production altogether, that he no longer wanted to play the strutting Petruchio to her willful Kate? Damn it, she thought. He was the only reason she'd auditioned for the damn play in the first place. And now she was stuck sitting here in the school auditorium with a bunch of kids who were treating her as if she had some kind of communicable disease, and the only person who was being nice to her was Delilah Franklin, which only made things worse. Maybe her mother was right. Maybe it was time to move back to Rochester. Clearly she didn't belong in Torrance. Did she belong anywhere?

Mr. Lipsman brought his right index finger to the bridge of his nose, pushed back a pair of invisible reading glasses. "All right. I guess we'll have to proceed without him." He signaled for Amber and several others to join him on the stage. "In the meantime, Tanya, why don't you see if you can get ahold of him. Maybe he can persuade his father to spare him for a few hours."

"I'll try his cell," Tanya offered, retreating to the back of the auditorium, Ginger Perchak at her side. Several weeks ago she would have been right there with them, Megan thought wistfully.

"Do you think his father is giving him a hard time about being in the play?" Delilah asked, sliding into the seat beside Megan.

"How should I know?" Megan snapped, staring straight ahead.

"Sorry. I thought you two were . . ."

"Were what?"

"You know."

"I *don't* know. And we're not."

"Sorry," Delilah apologized again, slinking down so low in the seat she was almost lying down. Megan could almost hear the seat groan. "I just thought—"

"Don't think."

"Sorry," Delilah said yet again. "So, did you hear about Brian Hensen and Perry Falco?"

"What about them?"

"Joey caught them making out in the park last night."

Megan had heard the rumors, read the fevered e-mails. "Joey's a jerk."

"You don't have to tell me that."

"Then why are you, of all people, spreading this kind of malicious gossip around?" But even as she asked the question, Megan knew it was unfair. Delilah was a human being after all. She liked gossip as much as the next person, and for once, she wasn't its target. It was so much nicer to identify with the victor than the victim.

"I'm sorry."

"For God's sake, stop apologizing."

"Sorry," Delilah muttered. Then, just as Megan was deciding she'd had all the *sorry*s she could take, and that she was going home, Delilah asked, "What do you think happened to Fiona Hamilton?" Fiona's disappearance had the whole town talking.

"I have no idea."

"Did you know her very well?"

Megan shook her head. "I didn't know her at all."

"She lived next door to you."

"So? I hardly ever saw her."

"Do you think Liana's killer got her?"

Megan shook her head. She'd had a similar conversation with her mother last night, except then she'd been the one asking Delilah's questions. Now she gave her mother's answer: "I think she probably just ran away."

"I hope you're right," Delilah said.

It was four o'clock on Tuesday afternoon and Fiona Hamilton still hadn't turned up. There was talk of calling in the FBI. A major sweep of the area was planned for tomorrow.

"I can't find him," Tanya suddenly announced, clomping down the aisle, Ginger an eager puppy at her heels. "He's not answering his cell." They plopped down into the seats across the aisle from Megan. "I left him a message."

Mr. Lipsman sighed, then made a clucking sound with his mouth. "Can I have the chorus onstage, please?"

Immediately Delilah was on her feet.

"God, look at that cow," Tanya whispered, loud enough for everyone to hear, as Delilah mounted the several steps to the stage.

"Elephant is more like it," Ginger concurred.

They glanced toward Megan, as if daring her to join in, to say something that would demonstrate her solidarity with them. She realized that a few nasty words would be enough to get her back in their good graces, that Tanya was giving her this chance to reenter the inner circle. This is my opportunity to make things right, she was thinking. To make up for getting the part of Kate over both Tanya and Ginger. For making out with Greg. It would be so easy. All she had to do was reference a suitably unattractive animal, utter something like "What a pig!" She certainly didn't owe Delilah anything just because the girl had been nice to her. Or because one day the two social outcasts might end up as stepsisters. She opened her mouth to speak, her lips curling around the words *Oink, oink,* when she heard her mother's voice in her ear. *If you can't say something nice about someone, don't say anything,* the voice advised. Followed by another of her favorite platitudes: *Do onto others as you would have them do onto you.* Megan closed her mouth as both Tanya and Ginger turned away from her with disappointment, the opportunity of renewed acceptance evaporating as suddenly as it had appeared. Megan rose from her seat and rushed up the aisle to the back of the auditorium.

"What a loser," she heard Tanya proclaim.

"Don't go far, Megan," Mr. Lipsman cautioned as she pushed through the door into the corridor, heading for the nearest exit.

"Rehearsal over already?" a voice asked from somewhere beside her.

Megan didn't have to turn around to know who was speaking. She stopped in her tracks, counted silently to ten before answering, "No. It just started."

"So where are you going?" Greg asked.

Still Megan refused to turn around. She was afraid that if she did, she would burst into tears, so relieved was she by his presence, by the fact he was speaking to her. "Mr. Lipsman's working with the chorus, so I thought I'd go outside for a few minutes, get some air."

"Air sounds good," Greg said, falling into step beside her.

Megan concentrated all her energy on breathing in and out. She was trying to remember the things she'd worked out in her head the previous night to say to him, all those clever observations and retorts, but her mind had gone totally, numbingly blank. So she decided to say nothing, to let Greg take the lead. Not until they stepped outside did she even glance his way, and only then because he stepped purposely in front of her. Even with the sun shining directly in her eyes, she could see that his face was scratched and one eye was swollen almost shut and ringed in purple. When he smiled, his split lip veered precariously to one side. "My God, what happened to you?" It seemed that half the student population was covered in bruises. What was the matter with everyone?

"My father and I had a slight disagreement."

"What about?"

"He's not crazy about my choice of extracurricular activities."

"He hit you because he doesn't want you to be in the play?"

"School musicals aren't high on his list of priorities."

"So he beat you up?"

"He tried."

"Looks like he succeeded. Have you seen a doctor?"

Greg shrugged off the potential seriousness of his injuries. "It's nothing."

Megan fought to keep her hands at her sides. What she wanted was to reach out and caress those bruises, to plant a series of tender kisses up and down the side of his cheek. "I can't believe he did that to you."

"It's not the first time."

"Have you ever told anybody?"

"I'm telling you."

Megan felt strangely flattered, although part of her wondered what would have happened had she not been the first person he ran into. Would he have confided in Tanya instead? "I meant somebody like the sheriff."

"Sheriff's got his hands full right now, wouldn't you say?"

"Why don't you let me call my father? I'm sure he'd see you without an appointment."

"Why don't you sit down beside me and just talk to me awhile. That's all the medicine I need." Greg took her elbow, led her toward a royal palm tree in the middle of a small triangle of grass about thirty yards from the school. They sank to the moist earth, his hand still on her arm.

"What do you want to talk about?" Megan asked warily. What she really wanted to say was, What the hell's the matter with you? Why the sudden need to talk? Why did you abandon me in the park?

"I don't know," he admitted with a smile.

"I saw you last night."

"You did?"

"At Mr. Hamilton's."

He nodded. "Pretty scary about his wife going missing."

Megan didn't really want to talk about Fiona Hamilton. "What were you and Peter doing with Mr. Lipsman?"

"We were rehearsing a song over at his place."

"Really? What was that like?"

"A little weird. He lives in this big old house he used to share with his mother, and it's still filled with her things, not to mention thousands of cats."

"Thousands?"

"Well, ten anyway." Greg smiled, then winced.

"It hurts when you smile?"

"Old man packs a wallop."

"I wish you'd let my father take a look at it."

"I have a better idea."

"Which is?"

"You could kiss it and make it better."

Megan found herself holding her breath.

"That's what my mother used to do when I was a kid," he added sheepishly.

Megan said nothing. What kind of game was he playing? Had he and Tanya concocted this little plan together? Kiss her, dump her, don't talk to her for days, then see if she's stupid enough to let you kiss her again? Besides, hadn't they been talking about his mother the last time they'd been together, right before he'd left her standing in the park alone? "What's going on?" Megan heard herself blurt out.

"What do you mean?"

"You know what I mean," Megan said, unable to stem the flow of words that were suddenly bursting from her mouth. "You haven't said two words to me since the vigil, and now all of a sudden, here you are, acting all sweet and lovey-dovey." Lovey-dovey, she repeated silently. *Lovey-dovey?* Where had that ancient expression come from?

"Lovey-dovey?" he repeated, smiling despite his obvious discomfort.

"You left me standing there in the park by myself, feeling like a complete idiot."

"I know," he acknowledged after a brief pause.

"Why did you do that?"

"I don't know."

"What do you mean, you don't know? One minute everything's great, and the next minute you're not talking to me. Why?"

"Because I'm an idiot. Guess my dad's right."

Megan shook her head. "No. You're not getting off the hook that easily." There followed a long pause, during which Megan wondered if she'd ruined everything and Greg was preparing to get up and walk away again. What would she do then? Run after him? Or count herself lucky and watch him go?

"You scared me," he said unexpectedly.

"I don't understand."

"Neither do I."

"How did I scare you? What did I do?"

"It's what you didn't do."

"What didn't I do?"

"You didn't treat me like some big, dumb jock who doesn't know his ass from a hole in the ground."

"That's because you aren't."

"Which is exactly what I mean."

"You're losing me again."

"That's precisely what I was afraid of."

"What was?"

"Losing you."

Megan's head was spinning. "What are you talking about? You're the one who walked away."

"Preemptive strike. Isn't that what they call it?"

"You were afraid of losing me so you dumped me. Is that what you're trying to tell me?"

"Pretty stupid, I guess."

"Pretty cowardly. You didn't even give me a chance."

"Consider yourself lucky."

"Why?"

"Because I was going to seduce you."

"What?" No one had ever talked about seducing her before. It made Megan feel grown-up.

"You heard me. I'd been planning it since that afternoon in the auditorium. Thought you were ripe for the picking."

Megan tried to feel insulted, but what she really felt was flattered. And excited. "So what stopped you?"

"You did. The way you stood up to me, told me to slow down, that I was gonna have to get to know you, that you were gonna have to get to know *me*. And next thing I know, you got me talking about my mother and shit I never talk about. Which got me thinking." He grinned. "And I don't like thinking. I'm not used to it."

Megan smiled too, then quickly forced her mouth into a frown. "So you hooked up with Tanya instead."

"Tanya? No way. Been there, done that. We're just friends."

Thank God, Megan thought. "Does she know that?"

"She knows. She's just giving you a hard time 'cause you got the part of Kate."

So now what? Megan wondered, inching closer to his side. "You were really going to seduce me?"

"Trust me. You were done for."

"And how were you going to accomplish that exactly?"

A sly grin stretched across Greg's mouth, threatening to reopen the cut on his lower lip. "For starters, I was gonna touch you right here." He brushed his fingers against the side of her neck.

Megan felt a tingle spread across the top of her spine to travel down her back.

"And then I was going to kiss the side of your mouth, like this." He lowered his face to hers, his lips gently touching down on her own. The tingle spiraled into Megan's breasts. "And then, here," he continued, kissing first one eyelid, then the other. "And then, here," he said, his lips returning to her mouth, where he kissed her again, harder this time.

"Careful," she told him, feeling the raised edge of the cut on his lip. "You're injured."

"Feels better already."

Megan heard her breath emerge in a series of shallow bursts. "And then what were you going to do?"

Greg pulled back, his finger drawing a line along her flesh from her chin to the top of her scooped-neck jersey. "I was gonna look into those big, trusting eyes and suggest we get the hell out of there."

"You think I would have gone?"

"You tell me."

"Megan!" a voice called out. "What are you doing out here?"

Megan jumped at the sound of her mother's voice. Reluctantly, she turned around, saw her mother cutting across the pavement from her portable classroom, and quickly scrambled to her feet. "Mom, hi. I didn't know you were still here."

"Hi, there, Mrs. C.," Greg said as he pushed himself into a standing position, wiped some loose grass from the seat of his jeans. "Working late?"

"Just getting a few things ready for tomorrow. You?"

"We were running some lines," Megan said.

"From the play," Greg added.

"What happened to your face?" her mother asked Greg.

"It's nothing," he demurred.

"We should get back inside," Megan said.

Her mother's wary eyes moved from Megan to Greg then back again. "Probably a good idea," she said.

chapter twenty-five

They must think I'm a complete idiot, Sandy thought as she watched Megan and Greg disappear inside the school's heavy side door.

We're just running some lines.

From the play.

Lines, maybe, Sandy thought. But from the play, my . . . behind. Greg Watt! Good God, what was her daughter thinking? Assuming she was thinking at all. Which she probably wasn't.

Not that Sandy had any right to question her daughter's common sense or her dubious taste in men, not when her own recent behavior was decidedly suspect. She thought of that fiasco with Will Baker, cringing at the memory of that awful night. She'd climbed into a car with a total stranger, for God's sake! She'd gone up to his apartment! At least Megan had an excuse for her recklessness of late: she was seventeen years old. Teenagers were expected to do stupid things. When else in their increasingly complicated lives would they ever have that luxury? Not to mention, a classmate had been brutally murdered, shaking Megan's subconscious belief in her own immortality. It was only natural she'd do a little acting out.

But Sandy was closing in on forty, which qualified her as middle-aged—dear God, she was middle-aged!—which meant she no longer had the inexperience and ingenuousness of youth on her side. Naïveté no longer flattered her. And in light of her own track record where men were concerned, who was she to tell anybody anything? So, it probably wasn't the best time for another mother-daughter talk. Megan had already assured her she wasn't having sex. She had to bite her tongue, say nothing to Megan unless asked for her opinion, and even then, to keep her opinion of Greg Watt to herself. She knew that nothing whetted the appetite of a rebellious teenager more than a disapproving mother.

Not that she entirely disapproved of Greg. True, he was no intellectual, but neither was he stupid. Behind the brutish bravado lay a lively, active imagination, and a genuine, creative talent. Besides, intelligence didn't necessarily translate into decency, and it was a mistake to confuse the two. Ian Crosbie was an undeniably intelligent man. Look where that had gotten her.

Sandy waited another minute before entering the main building. She passed the closed doors to the auditorium, wondering how long her daughter's flirtation with Greg Watt had been going on, and whether he'd had anything to do with Megan's early exit from the park the night of Liana's vigil.

Thoughts of Liana led to thoughts of her death and led back to thoughts of Greg Watt. Greg and Liana had been part of the same circle. No one would have thought twice about seeing them together. Plus he'd been part of the search team that had uncovered her body. Not to mention he'd been over at Cal Hamilton's house last night, after Fiona had supposedly disappeared. And he was certainly strong enough to have overpowered two unsuspecting women, even if they'd put up a fight. Speaking of which, where had he gotten those cuts and bruises on his face? Sandy stopped dead in her tracks. What was she thinking? Did she really believe Greg Watt was capable of murder? "That's insane," she muttered. "You're being ridiculous."

"My mother always used to say that when she wanted to talk to an intelligent person, she talked to herself," a voice said, approaching from behind.

Sandy did a slow turn around. "Mr. Fromm," she said, addressing the gangly school principal. He was approximately fifty years old, stood well over six feet tall, and carried all his weight on the front of his feet when he walked, so that he always looked as if he were about to fall over. Sandy thought this was probably the result of a youth spent surfing the oceans of the world in search of the perfect wave. The wild comb-over of sun-bleached hair only served to enhance the image of the stoned surfer dude, as did his preference for oversize Hawaiian shirts, such as the wild red-and-orange floral print he wore today. Sandy was hard-pressed to recall ever seeing him in a jacket and tie. "How are you today?"

"I'm wonderful. And you?"

"Just fine, thank you."

"Just fine?" he asked, giving those two words a completely different spin. "I understand you've been going through a difficult time lately."

"Well, it hasn't been the easiest of times for any of us."

"True enough. Awful business," he added, looking from side to side, as if he were afraid he was about to be decked by an unexpected swell of water. "Well, should you need anything . . ."

"Thank you." Sandy noted the look of fear that flashed briefly through the principal's sleepy gray eyes, as if he suddenly realized she might take him up on his offer.

"Right, then, well . . . ," he said, already drifting from her side.

Sandy continued on down the hall toward Rita's office. She wanted to ask Rita about Brian, who'd skipped his morning English class. But when she got there, the door was locked and the office was dark. Obviously Rita had left. Sandy thought it strange they hadn't talked to each other all day, especially in light of Rita's desperate phone call of the night before, and she wondered if Rita was embarrassed. Or maybe she'd figured out it was Sandy who'd called the sheriff and she was angry. Or maybe she was still a little peeved about the way Sandy had deserted her on Saturday night. Sandy decided to phone her later, maybe even stop in and see her on her way home.

She started back down the corridor, her eyes glancing toward the auditorium as she passed by. She was almost at the exit when she heard a door open behind her, then heard footsteps running in her direction. She turned around, saw Delilah Franklin sprinting toward her with surprising speed and grace.

"Hi, there, Mrs. Crosbie."

"Delilah," Sandy acknowledged as the girl reached her side. "Is something wrong?"

"No. Mr. Lipsman just realized he left some sheet music at home, and he needs it ASAP. I volunteered to go get it." She held up the key to his house.

"Does he live nearby?"

"He's over by Admiral Road."

"Admiral Road?" Sandy tried—and failed—to picture the street, give it context. "Isn't that kind of far away?"

"I guess."

"Do you have your car?"

Delilah shook her head. "It's my mother's car, and she's using it today."

Sandy tried not to let her face register discomfort at Delilah's mention of her mother. I'm getting pretty good at this, she thought, feeling a slight twitch building at the side of her mouth.

"Besides, my grandmother says I need the exercise."

"Why don't you let me give you a lift?" Sandy offered, wondering, What is the matter with me? It was one thing to be polite. It was another to be stupid. True, she was Delilah's teacher, and as such, she had some responsibility for her welfare. But did she really have to go out of her way to be nice to the daughter of the woman who'd stolen her husband? Was she hoping word of her generous spirit would filter back to Ian, that he'd look at her in a new, more flattering light, that he'd change his mind and come back to her? Or was she simply hesitant about returning to an empty house?

Technically, of course, the house wasn't empty. Tim would be there, although probably locked in his room with his computer and his video games, so not a whole lot of company there. And Megan would probably avoid her when she got home from rehearsal, reluctant to talk about anything, lest the conversation veer toward Greg Watt. Sandy sensed that even Rita wouldn't be overjoyed to see her, should she drop in unexpectedly. So, a few minutes spent chauffeuring Delilah back and forth would serve to keep the solitude at bay at least a few minutes longer.

"That'd be great," Delilah enthused. "You're sure you don't mind?"

Sandy shrugged, leading Delilah to her white Camry in the teachers' parking lot.

"This is a nice car," Delilah said as she dragged the seat belt across her chest.

"It's getting old," Sandy said. Ian had taken the silver Jaguar when he'd left. She hadn't protested. Damn thing spent more time in the shop than it did on the road anyway. "But it still runs great. It's a good car," she said, thinking she could be describing herself.

"It's very comfortable."

"That's me," Sandy said, pulling out of the lot and onto the street.

"What?"

"Dear me," Sandy amended quickly. "I'm not sure how to get there."

"Turn right at the corner," Delilah directed. "Then just go straight till you hit Citrus Grove. Then make another right."

Sandy did as she was told, extricating a pair of oversize sunglasses from her purse as they headed due west along New School Road. Even though it was technically rush hour, only a few other cars were on the road. "It was pretty hot today," she remarked, thinking that the weather was a safe bet for conversation.

"Getting warmer," Delilah agreed. "I kind of like it when it's cold though."

"Yeah? Me too." Even without turning her head, Sandy could see the big grin that overtook Delilah's round face, as if she'd just paid her the highest of compliments. "You look very nice today," she offered, watching the grin spread wider, disappearing into Delilah's ears. Not the truth exactly, but not quite a lie. The truth was that Delilah looked *presentable*. No more, no less. She was wearing a white shirt and a pair of loose-fitting jeans, and her hair was neatly combed and pinned at the sides. She wore no makeup, and her skin was clear, her eyes bright.

"Can I tell you something?" Delilah asked, continuing before Sandy had a chance to respond. "I'm on a diet." She rolled her eyes, as if embarrassed by her confession. "My mom bought me this really pretty new sweater, but it's a little small, and I'm determined to lose some weight so I can wear it."

"That's very commendable. But go slowly. They say you should only lose one or two pounds a week."

"Really? That's not very much."

"No, but it adds up. Lose two pounds a week and you've lost a hundred pounds in less than a year. Not that you have to lose anything like a hundred pounds," she added quickly.

"I was thinking of twenty-five. Keep going straight," Delilah said when Sandy hesitated at the light.

"That's more than enough."

"At two pounds a week, that should only take me about three months."

"That's right. And you have a much better chance of keeping the weight off if you do it slowly."

"You've never had a weight problem, have you?"

"No," Sandy admitted. "Although I was never happy with how I looked either. I was so skinny growing up, and I always wanted bigger breasts."

"Oh, you can buy those," Delilah said so casually that Sandy laughed out loud. "I think Citrus Grove is the next intersection."

"What happens after I make the turn at Citrus?" Sandy checked to make sure she wasn't speeding.

"You go about half a mile, then turn left."

"This would have been a very long walk."

"My grandmother says exercise is good for me."

"You obviously know the area well."

"I've lived here all my life," Delilah reminded her.

"You like it?"

"It's okay. I'd kind of like to go to California one day."

"Yeah? What's in California?"

"Movie stars," Delilah said with a girlish giggle.

"You like movies?"

"Yeah. My mother and I used to go all the time. Not so much anymore. Turn left here."

Sandy gripped the wheel tighter as she left the main road. Guess Kerri doesn't have a whole lot of time to take her daughter to the movies these days, she was thinking as she drove past the rows of orange trees that lined both sides of the gravel road. It was interesting how quickly the town became a series of rural side roads.

"Now turn left, then right again. I think that's Mr. Lipsman's house over there." Delilah pointed to a neat little house in the middle of a manicured patch of grass at least two hundred yards from its nearest neighbor.

"No way you could have walked here," Sandy said as she pulled the car into the narrow driveway.

"It's farther than I thought," Delilah agreed. "I probably would have had to hitchhike back."

"Which wouldn't have been a very good idea. You just can't go climbing into cars with strangers." Sandy bit her tongue. Who was she to talk about getting into cars with strangers?

"Oh, I pretty much know everybody in this town. Besides"— Delilah looked down at herself—"I don't think I have anything to worry about. Well, I'll just run and get the stuff."

"Do you know where it is?"

"Mr. Lipsman said he's pretty sure he left it in the front hall." Delilah hesitated.

"You want me to come with you?"

"Would you mind?" Delilah asked without a second's pause.

Sandy opened her car door and climbed out. The two women approached the two-story, white clapboard house with the fading black shutters. A large, gray cat sat in front of closed lace curtains in one of the downstairs windows.

"It looks nice," Delilah said without conviction.

"It looks like the kind of house Mr. Lipsman would live in with his mother."

"I hear she's buried out back."

"What? Who? His mother?"

Delilah nodded. "Apparently she wanted to be buried under her favorite lemon tree in the backyard."

"I don't think you're allowed to bury people in your backyard." Even in Florida, Sandy added under her breath.

"That's what everybody says anyway."

Sandy's eyes drifted around to the side of the house as they neared the front door. Was it possible? she wondered. "I don't believe it," she said as Delilah pushed the key into the lock and pulled open the front door. Immediately several cats were at their feet, a fat, black-and-white one brushing against Sandy's bare calves.

"Oh, careful. Don't let them out," Delilah squealed.

Sandy corralled the wayward cats with her feet, wishing she'd worn pants today and not a skirt, returning the cats to the front foyer as Delilah closed the door. Immediately Sandy was overwhelmed by the smell of dank air and Kitty Litter.

"Mr. Lipsman doesn't like air-conditioning," Delilah said. "He says that next to smoking, it's the worst thing for your lungs."

"As opposed to breathing in cat hair all night."

"Mr. Lipsman's a little odd. But he's nice," Delilah added quickly.

"He's odd," Sandy concurred.

"I don't see any sheet music. Do you?"

Sandy glanced around the foyer, a few particles of dust swirling like confetti in the small pool of light coming from a portal-shaped side window. All she saw was an orange cat stretched across an old Queen Anne chair, and another tabby scratching at the legs of the antique end table beside it. On the table was a silver-framed photograph of a stern-looking woman in a stiff-collared black dress, her gray hair pulled into a tight bun at the back of her head.

"That must be his mother," Delilah whispered.

"She looks like a barrel of laughs."

Delilah giggled. "Where do you think Mr. Lipsman left the sheet music?"

"Why don't you check the kitchen. I'll look in the living room," Sandy suggested, and Delilah left her side.

The cats followed Sandy into the living room, where there were more cats. Besides the one in the window, Sandy counted two on the dark green velvet sofa, and another on the heavy, gold brocade armchair that stood beside it. A baby grand piano filled whatever space was left, the closed top of the piano covered with photographs, most of them of Gordon and his mother, going all the way back to his childhood. Even in the fading light of the late-afternoon sun that filtered through the musty lace of the curtains, Sandy could see how little the man's face had changed over the years. Even as a small child, he'd looked like a middle-aged man.

His mother was a completely different story. Originally a pretty, if not downright beautiful, young woman, she'd grown coarser with the years, her smile losing its vitality, her eyes losing their spark. In one of the earlier pictures, she posed happily in a chic blue dress, her arm around an equally pretty girl, probably her sister, their teenage smiles barely strong enough to contain their obvious glee, and over here was another picture of the same young women dancing together at a party.

Sandy's eyes moved from one picture to the next. There were photographs of Gordon and his mother when Gordon was a baby, pictures of Gordon as a toddler, positioned between his mother and his aunt, pictures of Gordon's mother and her cats. Somewhere along the way the smiles turned somber, then disappeared altogether.

There were other pictures as well. Candid photographs of the students at Torrance High: Ginger Perchak and Tanya McGovern sharing a secret; Victor Drummond staring idly off into space; Greg Watt laughing at something Joey Balfour was saying; Liana Martin leaping joyously across the stage. They'd obviously been taken during last year's rehearsals for *Fiddler on the Roof,* Sandy realized. Still, they gave her the creeps. "Delilah?" she called out, suddenly eager to get out of there. "Delilah?"

No answer.

Sandy walked quickly from the living room and down the narrow hall, toward the kitchen at the back. Delilah was standing by the kitchen window, staring out at the backyard. "Delilah?" Sandy asked. "Is something wrong?"

Delilah's voice, when it finally emerged, seemed to be coming from another room. "Which one do you think it is?"

Sandy sidestepped a box of Kitty Litter to reach Delilah's side. She stared into Gordon Lipsman's empty backyard. "What are you talking about?"

"I count four lemon trees. I think it's the bushy one on the end. Which one do you think it is?"

It took Sandy several seconds to understand what Delilah was talking about. "I assure you, Delilah, that Mrs. Lipsman is not buried in the backyard," she said, although she was sure of no such thing. "Now, let's just find the sheet music and get out of here."

"Oh, I found it." Delilah spun around, holding up the papers. "They were on the counter."

"Good. Then let's get out of here. Now."

They'd been driving for almost ten minutes when Sandy realized they were going in the wrong direction. A recent turn had brought the late day's sun directly into her eyes, which meant they were heading due west when they should be going east.

"I think we were supposed to turn left back there," Delilah said at roughly the same moment. "Not right."

"I thought you said to turn right."

"No, I said, turn left and then right. I think."

Sandy quickly turned the car around, headed back toward the last intersection. Ian was always telling her she had no sense of direction, that left to her own devices, she couldn't find her way out of a paper bag. And the visit to Gordon's house had spooked her. That picture of Liana Martin, looking so vibrant and alive. "Okay. I give up," she said, after driving around for several more minutes and seeing nothing but orange groves. She pulled the car to a stop at the side of the road. There wasn't another car in sight. "Where the hell are we?"

"I think we should turn left at the next intersection," Delilah offered.

"Are you sure?"

"No."

"Great."

"Maybe we should just wait here for another car."

"Have you seen a car in the last five minutes?" Sandy asked testily. "I thought you knew where we were going."

"I'm sorry, Mrs. Crosbie. I messed up."

"No, I'm sorry," Sandy apologized quickly, watching Delilah's lower lip quiver. "This isn't your fault. I'm the one who's driving." She took a deep breath. "So you think I should turn left?"

"I'm not sure."

"Well, might as well give it a try." Sandy turned left, continued down the road, passing one fruit grove after another. Just when she thought it was probably time to consider making another turn, the sudden pressure of Delilah's hand on her arm stopped her.

"Stop the car," Delilah whispered.

"Why? Do you know where we are?" Sandy pulled the car to a stop, turned toward Delilah. "What's the matter?" she asked when she saw the look on the girl's face. Delilah was staring out the front window, her eyes wide, her skin ashen. "Delilah, what's the matter?"

"I think I saw something."

Sandy's eyes did a quick 360-degree turn. "What did you see?"

"It looked like a hand."

"What?"

"It looked like a human hand," Delilah said, her voice a shout. "Oh, God. It looked like a hand." She turned toward Sandy, her eyes brimming over with tears.

"Okay, calm down. Calm down," Sandy advised, though her own heart was beating so fast it felt as if it might take flight. "Where do you think you saw it?"

"Back there. About fifty feet."

Sandy threw the car into reverse and slowly backed it up about fifty feet.

"Keep going," Delilah urged through tightly gritted teeth. "There!" Her hand shot to her right, her fingers slamming against the car window. She cried out, closing her eyes and burying her face in her lap. "Is it a body?" she asked as Sandy stopped the car and opened her door. "No. Don't go out there!"

Sandy said nothing as she slowly proceeded around the back of the car, her eyes warily searching the long grass at the side of the road, afraid of what they might find. At first she saw nothing out of the ordinary. Grass, earth, some discarded, half-eaten oranges, flies. Lots of flies. And then, a flash of something shiny reflected by the sun. A wedding ring, she realized, seeing the flesh around the ring and recognizing a human hand.

Sandy's hand shot to her mouth in an effort not to scream as she stumbled back to the car. "Do you have a cell phone? Please tell me you have a cell phone."

Delilah quickly handed Sandy her cell. "What is it? What did you find?"

Sandy pressed in 911. "There's a woman's body lying by the side of the road," she informed the emergency operator, as the color drained from Delilah's cheeks. "No. I have no idea where I am. Somewhere out past Citrus Grove." She promised to stay on the line until the police arrived. Then she lowered the phone to her lap and gathered an increasingly distraught Delilah into her arms.

"Is it Mrs. Hamilton?"

"I don't know." Sandy held the sobbing girl in her arms as they waited for the sheriff to arrive, trying to decide what would be worse—if the body they'd discovered was Fiona Hamilton, or if it wasn't.

chapter twenty-six

You want to tell me what you were doing out here?" John Weber asked as police began cordoning off the area. He was trying to get his mind around the fact that the woman he was talking to had her arm around the daughter of the woman her husband had left her for. That was almost as shocking to him as the body the two of them had discovered lying in the tall grass. A body he assumed was Fiona Hamilton, although he wouldn't be 100 percent sure until her husband made a positive ID. As had been the case with Liana Martin, there wasn't a whole lot left of the woman's face. Still, the hair color was the same, and the body appeared to be relatively intact. It shouldn't be too hard to make a positive identification.

"I'm sorry," Sandy Crosbie said. "What?"

John leaned into the front seat, his left arm resting on top of the open car door. "I asked what the two of you were doing out this way."

Sandy sat behind the wheel of her car, her face streaked with tears. She stared blankly at the windshield, Delilah's head buried against her side, and said, "We were at Gordon Lipsman's house."

"What were you doing there?"

"Mr. Lipsman forgot his sheet music at home," Delilah said, pushing herself into a sitting position, although one hand still clung to Sandy's navy skirt. "I offered to go get it. Mrs. Crosbie said it was too far to walk . . ." Her voice broke as she glanced out the side window, saw the police moving around the body. "What are they doing?"

"Collecting evidence," John told her, although truthfully, he wasn't sure there was much to collect.

"Is it Mrs. Hamilton?"

"We don't know."

"Oh, God," Delilah cried, as if understanding the implications of that remark.

"So, Mr. Lipsman asked you to fetch his sheet music, and Mrs. Crosbie offered to give you a lift. Is that correct?"

"She said it was too far to walk," Delilah repeated.

"You're quite a long way from the Lipsman house," John remarked.

"We made a wrong turn," Delilah said.

"We got lost," Sandy said at the same time.

Clearly both women were in shock, John concluded, deciding to save any further questions he might have until later. "Okay, I'm going to have Officer Trent drive you both home." He signaled to one of his deputies. "I'll bring your car back later."

"What about Mr. Lipsman's sheet music?" Delilah asked, panic sweeping through her voice. John saw that the papers in question were crushed in the palm of her right hand.

"It's okay." He reached in and extricated the sheet music from Delilah's clenched fist. "I'll see that he gets them."

"Did you know that Gordon Lipsman has a picture of Liana Martin in his house?" Sandy asked as she was being led from her car.

"No, I didn't," John answered. What kind of picture? he wondered, deciding to go see for himself later on. "Are you going to be okay, Mrs. Crosbie?"

Sandy nodded, although she looked far from sure.

"All right. Look, I'll be by later. In the meantime, please don't talk to anyone about this. At least until we've located Cal Hamilton." Cal had been released from jail this morning after his boss, old Chester Calhoun, had posted his bail. He'd been ordered not to leave town and to stay away from Kerri Franklin and her family.

"Do you think he did this?"

"I think we have to ID the body before we ask any more questions," John said. Seconds later, he watched as Deputy Trent tucked the two women into the backseat of his cruiser and drove off. "So, what do we have?" he asked, approaching an officer leaning over the body, his hand covering his nose and mouth.

The young deputy jumped to his feet. "Looks like a gunshot to the head. Same as Liana Martin."

"Any identifying marks on the body?"

"A small tattoo on her left ankle. Looks like *Property of* . . . I couldn't make out the rest."

John wondered if Fiona Hamilton had a tattoo. She hardly seemed the type, although that *Property of* business was rather ominous. He wondered if Candy Abbot had had a tattoo. But Candy Abbot had been missing for months, and if this was her body, that meant she'd either been kept alive until several days ago or that her body had been stored in a freezer. Both were possibilities, he realized, although neither felt right. "Anything else?"

"No, sir. No shell casings or stray bullets."

Which meant she'd probably been killed elsewhere, John concluded, then dumped here for someone to stumble across. Her killer hadn't even attempted to bury the body this time, which meant either he'd been interrupted, was getting cocky, or that he'd wanted her to be found quickly. And if he'd wanted her to be found quickly, that raised another interesting question.

Why?

An hour later, John drove Sandy's car back to her house, followed by another officer, who pulled his cruiser into Cal Hamilton's driveway behind Cal's splashy red Corvette. Sandy greeted John at her front door. "I think he's home," she said instead of hello, glancing at the house next door. "The music's been blasting for the last twenty minutes."

John signaled for the other officer to approach. "Stay inside and keep away from the windows," he directed Sandy.

"You think there'll be trouble?"

"Hopefully not."

"Mom?" Sandy's son approached, stopping behind his mother. "What's going on?"

"Just returning your mother's car," John told him.

"You got towed?" Tim asked incredulously.

"Not exactly," Sandy said.

"Your mother will explain later. Now, if you'll excuse me . . ." John heard Sandy's door close behind him as he cut across her front lawn to Cal Hamilton's house, the music getting louder, more insistent, the closer he got. *I'm sorry, Mama,* Eminem wailed. *Wailed* being the operative word, John thought as he knocked loudly on Cal's door. You couldn't really call that singing. Although he harbored a grudging admiration for the young man's obvious talent. The punk had learned how to channel his anger into something not only productive, but immensely profitable. Wouldn't it be nice if everyone could do the same? Too bad rage was easier to channel than creativity, he thought, feeling his own ire rise as he knocked on the door again, harder this time. "Cal? Cal Hamilton, this is the sheriff. Open up."

"Should we break it down?" his deputy asked.

"Only if you want to get your ass sued from here to kingdom come," John told the overly eager young man with the short, dark hair and soft, wide mouth. "This is a courtesy call, remember? We're asking this man's help in identifying a body, very possibly his wife's. We're not here to make an arrest." *Yet,* he added silently, before knocking a third time.

The music retreated to a dull throb. "Hold your horses," came a voice from inside. "Jeez, what's going on here?"

Even before Cal appeared in the doorway, wearing only a pair of tight-fitting, black jeans and a lopsided smile, John knew he was high on something.

"Why, Sheriff Weber, how nice to see you again so soon. To what do I owe this great honor?"

"Get your shoes on," John told him. "And a shirt. I need you to come with me."

"Are you arresting me again? 'Cause whatever it is, I didn't do it. I've just been sitting here all day listening to music and minding my own business."

"You're not under arrest."

"Good." Cal slammed the door in John's face.

John began pounding on the door as the voice of Eminem returned full force. He was debating whether he should leave and come back later when suddenly the caterwauling stopped and the door reopened.

"I have a bell, you know," Cal said, his eyes as smooth and expressionless as glass. "It's right there." He pointed. "All you have to do is press it." He demonstrated. The melodious sound of bells filled the air. *You are my sunshine*. "Cute, huh?"

"I need you to come with me," John said.

"And why is that?"

"We've found a body," John said with deliberate bluntness. "It could be Fiona."

Cal's reaction was both extreme and unexpected. He staggered back into the main part of the house, as if he'd been struck. "What?"

"Does your wife have any tattoos?" John asked, following after him. Immediately he recognized the cloying smell of hashish. Empty beer bottles were everywhere.

"She has a little one on her ankle," Cal replied after a long pause. "Why?"

"Can you describe it?"

"'Course I can describe it. I know every inch of that woman's body. It says *Property of Cal Hamilton*."

John lowered his head, released a deep breath of air. "I'll need you to make a positive identification."

"You're saying it's her?"

"The body we found has a tattoo on her ankle similar to the one you've just described."

"What do you mean, similar?"

"We'll need you to make a positive ID," John repeated.

"I don't understand. You've met my wife. You'd know if it was her. What are you telling me?" Cal backed even farther into the room, until his legs hit a chair and he collapsed into it. "You're saying she doesn't have a face? That some lunatic blew it away, same as with Liana Martin?"

"If you'd prefer to give us a sample of your wife's hair, perhaps from a brush . . ."

"No." Cal jumped back to his feet, shaking his head as if to clear it. "I want to see her. I want to see her."

John waited as Cal slipped a white T-shirt over his head and stuffed his feet into a pair of black sneakers by the door. "I'll take you to her," John said.

"I already told you, she was alive and well yesterday morning when I left for work." Cal was sitting in the small, windowless room that was used to interrogate suspects. The room was sparsely furnished, containing only a rectangular oak table with a small chair on either side of it. Two similar chairs stood against an unadorned wall. The air-conditioning in the room was kept just above freezing. John reasoned that the more physically uncomfortable a suspect felt, the more likely he was to talk. Cal had started sweating almost as soon as he'd been ushered inside.

A two-way mirror filled the top half of the wall across from the closed door. John knew that Richard Stahl, the sheriff for all of Broward County, was standing on the other side of that glass, watching him. The mayor had called him as soon as he'd found out about Fiona Hamilton and requested he drive up to Torrance to oversee John's investigation.

A week ago John might have felt threatened by the mayor's preemptive actions, even more so by his supervisor's unscheduled appearance. But today he felt curiously sanguine about being judged. While he'd never had much patience for the mayor, whom he considered a pompous ass with a Napoleonic complex, he both liked and respected the sheriff of Broward County. Besides, John had never believed in cutting off one's nose to spite one's face. If Richard Stahl had some fresh ideas that might help solve this case, John was more than willing to listen to them.

Normally he would have preferred to wait at least a couple of hours before questioning a man who'd just identified his wife's corpse. But Cal Hamilton wasn't just any man. He was a hothead who'd already been arrested for assaulting one woman and was probably a wife beater as well. And while he'd seemed genuinely shaken at the sight of Fiona's lifeless form, he'd regained his composure with remarkable speed.

"Did anyone else see her?" John asked.

"Not that I'm aware of."

"Had you been fighting?"

"Everybody fights."

"Not everybody uses their fists."

"You accusing me of something?"

"Her body was covered with bruises, Cal. Old bruises. I'm sure that once the medical examiner has a look at her, he'll find lots of old wounds, maybe even a few broken bones."

"Okay, so I may have hit her a couple of times. Trust me, she gave as good as she got."

"You're saying *she* hit *you*?"

"I'm saying she wasn't exactly a saint. Sometimes I had to protect myself."

"You outweighed her by a good eighty pounds," John pointed out.

Cal made a dismissive sound, somewhere between a laugh and a snort. "She could be pretty fierce when she got angry."

"What was she angry about, Cal?"

"The usual. She thought I was playing around. You know, being unfaithful."

"And were you?"

"It didn't mean anything." Cal glanced toward the recessed fluorescent lights of the ceiling. "What's with the look, Sheriff? You trying to tell me you never cheated on your wife?"

John tried not to flinch. "I'm telling you it takes a special kind of coward to hit a woman."

The same derisive sound as before. "Hey, you can call me all the names you want. A coward and a wife beater and an adulterer. It doesn't mean I killed my wife. I loved that woman."

"You sure had a funny way of showing it."

"To each his own."

"What happened, Cal?" John asked, trying a different approach.

"She'd had enough of the abuse? She told you she wanted out? She threatened to leave you?"

"She wasn't going anywhere."

"Not if you had anything to say about it, she wasn't."

"I didn't have to say anything."

"No, you just had to stop her."

"I sure as hell didn't shoot her," Cal said.

"You own a gun, don't you?"

"Yeah. So what? It's my right under the Constitution to bear arms."

"Is it registered?"

" 'Course it's registered. I'm a law-abiding citizen."

"What kind is it?"

"Forty-four Magnum."

"Pretty powerful weapon."

"Powerful enough to blow a man's head clear off," Cal said, paraphrasing Clint Eastwood's line from *Dirty Harry* and looking directly into John's eyes. "Trust me, Sheriff, if a .44 had been used on Fiona, there wouldn't have been anything left of her face at all."

"That's pretty cold for a man who just lost his wife."

"You expecting tears?"

"Where do you keep the gun, Cal?"

"Nightstand beside my bed."

"You won't mind if we take a look at it?"

"I'm sure you're waiting on the search warrant as we speak," Cal said with a shrug. "You know we're just wasting time here. You know you're dealing with a serial killer."

"What makes you so sure it's a serial killer?"

"Well, it certainly doesn't take a genius to figure it out. He's killed two women already. Maybe more."

John leaned forward in his chair, dug his elbows into the table, intertwined the fingers of his left hand with those of his right. "What makes you think there are more?"

"I said there *may* be more. You're dealing with a nut bar, Sheriff. You really think he's gonna stop at two?"

"What makes you think the same man killed both Liana Martin and your wife?"

"Oh, I don't know. Two women disappear; they turn up a few days later with half their faces blown away. Call me crazy, but it doesn't sound like a coincidence to me."

"Me neither. Could be we have a copycat on our hands."

"Could be."

"I've always found copycats kind of pathetic," John said, hoping to provoke the man across the table. "I mean, it speaks of a certain lack of imagination, don't you think?"

"Cut the crap, Sheriff. We both know you think I killed my wife. So the real question is, Did I try to make it look like it was the work of the same guy who offed the Martin girl, or did I kill Liana Martin too?"

"Which is it?"

"It's neither, you moron."

John felt his body tense. He lowered his arms to his sides, made fists with both his hands. Instinctively he felt that Richard Stahl was doing the same thing on the other side of the glass.

"Shit. I've been raising holy hell ever since Fiona disappeared," Cal continued, "trying to find out what happened to her. I got myself arrested, for Christ's sake. I'd have to be pretty stupid—"

"Or pretty smart," John interrupted.

"You're giving me a lot of credit, Sheriff. You're saying I staged the whole thing?"

"It's possible."

"So I'm either lacking in imagination or swimming in it," Cal said with a laugh. "Better make up your mind."

"It'd be a lot easier if you'd just tell me what went down."

"You want me to do your job for you?"

"I want you to start telling the truth."

"Yeah? Well, the truth is my wife is dead. The truth is if you hadn't been so damned convinced she'd run away and started searching the area yesterday, like I wanted to do, instead of harassing me and throwing my ass in jail, we might have been able to find her before she ended up in a field with half her face blown away.

That's the truth, Sheriff. Now either arrest me or let me go home."

John rose from his seat, turned to face the two-way mirror, and stared into the faces he knew were watching on the other side. Were they wondering the same things? he thought. "Arrest him," he said.

They found the gun in the night table beside the bed, exactly where Cal had said it would be.

"Doesn't appear to have been fired recently," Deputy Trent said, raising the weapon to his long, crooked nose.

"A .44 didn't kill Fiona Hamilton," John said, glancing around the room. Or Liana Martin, he added silently, noting the pale blue of the bare walls and the surprisingly small brass bed. The size of the bed was surprising because he would have thought a man like Cal Hamilton needed more room to stretch out. Then he pictured the dark blue tattoo on Fiona's ankle. *Property of Cal Hamilton*. A double bed would certainly have enforced physical intimacy, kept Fiona closer to his side. The bed was unmade, its dull white sheets pushed to the foot of the bed in a heap, its blue cotton blanket draped carelessly toward the floor. Cal was right about one thing: a .44 would have done significantly greater damage. "Keep looking. Who's to say we might not find another gun?"

Across from the bed was a tall wicker dresser, its top drawers filled with literally dozens of sexy push-up bras and skimpy thongs, crotchless panties, silk teddies, and velvet corsets, as well as a variety of sex toys. John found a ballpoint pen he realized too late was actually a tiny vibrator, and he dropped it back into the drawer as if it had suddenly caught fire. Talk about multitasking, he thought to himself, opening the drawer directly below. It was filled with white cotton panties and plain cotton bras. John checked the sizes, discovered they were the same size as the more risqué underwear. One set for day, and one for night, John assumed, trying not to imagine Fiona Hamilton in either.

"Hey, get a load of this," Deputy Trent said, holding up a set of handcuffs before placing them in a plastic bag.

John pulled open the closet door, rifled through the clothes on the white plastic hangers, finding nothing of interest. They'd been in the house for over an hour and the search had yielded little of significance. Yes, they'd found a gun, exactly where Cal had said it would be, but it was almost certainly not the murder weapon. And, yes, they had handcuffs and a variety of sex toys, but all of them could actually be bought at Wal-Mart, he'd discovered on a recent foray. And even if Fiona had hardly seemed the type to go in for vibrating pens and crotchless panties, what did he know? Especially about women. How well do we really know anyone?

"Hey, John," another deputy called from the hall. "I think we may have something." The young man appeared in the doorway, his round cheeks flushed with excitement, a glint of anticipation in his chocolate brown eyes.

"What have you got?"

"I found these buried at the back of a kitchen drawer. Looks like somebody's been collecting trophies." A charm bracelet dangled from his left hand. "It's just a cheap little thing. Looks like all the charms are pieces of candy. Don't know if it means anything."

John felt his entire body start to tingle. Candy Abbot, he was thinking as he pushed the next words out of his mouth. "What else have you got?"

The deputy raised his right hand, displaying a delicate gold necklace curled inside his gloved palm. "Now I *know* this one means something."

John stared at the necklace. In the center of it was a name, written in gold: LIANA.

27

KILLER'S JOURNAL

I've been trying to come up with some clever names for stores.

You know, something that would draw people in, get them to open their wallets, and, by so doing, stimulate the economy. At the very least, give people a chuckle, a laugh to brighten their otherwise dreary days. You know, like if you're on your way to work and you see something that makes you smile, a cute puppy or some guy tripping over a bump in the sidewalk, and you know how just thinking about that later on will make you smile, well, that's the sort of thing I had in mind. Putting a smile on people's faces. I was in the mall the other day, checking things out, and not only was there nothing in any of the stores that caught my eye, but I realized that even the names of the stores are boring and uninteresting. And I thought, Why can't we be more imaginative? And more intelligent. I mean, take William Shakespeare, for example. He was a big fan of wordplay. He'd have come up with something smart and amusing.

So how about calling a store that sells tennis equipment, The Merchant of Tennis? Or you could call a jewelry store, Romeo and Jewelry; a savings and loan, All's Well That Lends Well; a store that hawks hiking shoes, As You Hike It. You could rename Big Macs, Big Macbeths. You could call an optician, King Leer. Okay, so that's a bit of a stretch. But you get the idea.

It doesn't even have to be Shakespeare, as long as it's clever, as long as the Bard would approve. So, along those lines, I offer Bow WOW, as a dog-grooming salon; SpecialTee Shops, for stores selling T-shirts; and Love's Labour Lost, for offices where people go to collect unemployment insurance. Of course, that last one's Shakespeare again. Funny how in the end, everything comes back to sweet William. What would he do with *The Taming of the Shrew,* I wonder.

Oh, I know. How about *Kiss Me, Kate?*

Okay, so setting up Cal Hamilton was fun.

Kind of makes up for what happened earlier, which, trust me, was not nearly as much fun as I was anticipating. Isn't it interesting how nothing ever goes exactly the way you plan? I mean, you have this picture in your head. You think you have everything organized. You think you have every last detail worked out. You can almost taste how it's gonna go down—I mean, it's not like I haven't done this before, you'd think I'd be used to it by now—but life always throws you a curve.

Maybe I should say death always throws you a curve.

Anyway, I guess I should start at the top, as they say. They, again. They're always saying something. Can't keep their mouths shut, which you might say was Fiona Hamilton's problem. God, who'd have thought that little gal would have so much to say? She always seemed like such a quiet, timid little thing. But once she opened up, wow! It was like she'd been waiting years to tell her story, like she couldn't get the words out fast enough. There was no stopping her. Well, no, that's not exactly true.

I stopped her.

Okay, so first things first: Fiona Hamilton wasn't originally part of my plan. She wasn't even on my radar. No interest in the woman at all. I had my list. Trust me, she wasn't on it.

Why do people say "trust me"? Don't you find that the people who say "trust me" are the very people you shouldn't trust at all? And why should you trust anyone anyway? Don't they say trust is something that has to be earned? Of course, they also say things like "Trust your instincts" and "In God we trust." I have a better one— "Trust no one." Trust me, that's the one to remember.

Hey, I just realized that both Liana and Fiona are names that have five letters, the last two being *n* and *a*. Not only that, but each name has three syllables—Fi-o-na, Li-a-na—plus the second letter of each name is an *i*, only with an *e* sound. How do you like that? Not that I'm saying that's why I chose Fiona, although I confess that now that I've thought of it, I do appreciate the symmetry. No, Fiona was what I believe they call a red herring. She was there to throw everyone off the scent, although the idea of any kind of herring being used to throw people *off* a scent is pretty funny when you think about it. Yes, sad little Fiona Hamilton was a means to an end, really, a way to bide my time and have a little fun in the process. I mean, who amongst us doesn't think Cal Hamilton was due for a little comeuppance? And I just thought it would be fun to get everyone in Torrance to relax a little. I mean, once people think a killer is safely behind bars, they tend to ease up, let down their guard. They're so relieved, they get careless, even stupid. And stupid people make for easy targets.

Did I mention I have my next target all picked out?

But back to Fiona.

Fiona, much as I expected, wasn't a barrel of laughs. Nor was she much of a challenge. Frankly, I was disappointed. She was almost too easy. She wasn't what you'd call a fighter, even when it came to fighting for her life. I guess all those years of abuse had worn her down.

"Cal sent me to get you," I told her. She didn't look especially surprised to see me. She just stood there with this blank look on her face, like she wasn't quite sure who I was. Or maybe she'd learned a long time ago not to ask too many questions. I don't know. I just know I was only in that house a few minutes before I had her unconscious and out the kitchen door. Nobody saw me. That's the good thing about carports.

(I wonder how long it'll be before the science department of Torrance High realizes its supply of chloroform has been, as they say, compromised? Probably not until next year when they start gathering up those stupid frogs for dissection, by which time I won't be needing it anymore.)

Anyway, I had everything ready for her when we arrived at the house. Of course, she was still asleep, so the full impact of my efforts was lost on her, but I can't begrudge her that. And I have to say she looked very pretty when she was unconscious. Quite peaceful. Her face was smooth and unlined, and her hair had been freshly washed and it smelled good, like a medley of peaches and apricots. She was wearing this flimsy little blue nightgown—a nightgown in the middle of the day, for God's sake—and if you looked hard, you could see her nipples. Her breasts were real, and bigger than I expected.

I put her down on the cot, even threw a blanket over her shoulders, because I remember reading that it's always a good idea to cover yourself with a blanket when you take a nap, or you'll get a bad chill. Couldn't have that. Wouldn't want pathetic, sweet-smelling Fiona catching her death.

So, I covered her up, then made sure the plastic bucket beside the cot was clean. I even left a roll of toilet paper beside it, so there'd be no question as to what the bucket was for. Plus I put several bottles of water—plastic, again—at the foot of the cot, in case she was thirsty when she woke up. Then I retreated to my room upstairs to wait and watch for her awakening. Boy, what a letdown that was! I mean, there was no reaction at all. Zero. Zilch. Nada. Nothing. It was amazing. She just opened her eyes and sat up, like she'd been waking up in that room all her life. Didn't even bother looking around. Just sat there, kind of slumped forward, her bare toes not quite touching the floor, as if she were sitting at the end of a dock, dangling her feet over the side. And then after about twenty minutes—twenty minutes!—she finally raised her eyes and started to examine her surroundings. Really slow, like she had all the time in the world, her head turning this way and that, to the right, then the left, her eyes moving up toward the ceiling, then back down to her feet. She saw the bucket, the bottles of water. She didn't react. She just sat there, her eyes absorbing her predicament. Then, instead of jumping to her feet, instead of screaming, instead of running around in circles like the trapped little mouse she was, what did she do? She lay back down and closed her eyes again! She actually went to sleep. Can you believe that?

At first I thought it was some kind of trick, that she was being cagey, that she was smarter than I'd realized. I mean, who wakes up in a strange place and doesn't panic, doesn't at least get up and walk around, try the door, call out for help? Who just closes her eyes and blindly accepts her fate? I'll tell you who—Fiona Hamilton, that's who.

So there I was, up in my hiding place watching, and let me tell you, when I realized she'd actually gone back to sleep, *I* was the one who almost screamed out loud. I mean, how long was this going to take? But what could I do? So I just sat there, waiting for her to wake up again. After a while, I started to get worried. Had I miscalculated, given her too much chloroform? Was she dead? Dead before her time?

And then, after another thirty minutes—half an hour, for Pete's sake!—her eyes fluttered open and she sat back up. And this time, she actually managed to push herself to her feet. She walked to the door—I actually got quite excited—and then, guess what? She just stood there. She didn't even try to open it. She just stared at it for a while, then went back to the cot and sat back down. It was really weird. I couldn't believe my eyes. I still have trouble believing it.

Eventually she opened one of the water bottles at her feet and took a couple of long sips, then she used the bucket. And the toilet paper. Then she looked around for something to discard the paper in, and when she couldn't find it—note to self: buy a small, plastic wastepaper basket—she tossed it into the corner. Then she sat back down again and waited. Did she know what she was waiting for?

As it turns out, she actually thought she was waiting for her loving husband. She thought this was all his doing, if you can believe that. As if Cal Hamilton has the imagination to come up with any of this. But that's what she told me. She said she assumed she'd done something to displease him, and that this was his new way of punishing her.

But I'm getting ahead of myself.

When it became painfully obvious she wasn't going to do anything to move the game forward, well, I have to admit, I almost panicked. I'm on a pretty tight schedule and I have to be careful not to arouse suspicion. I've tempted fate more than a few times lately, taken chances that were quite unnecessary, and I didn't want to get too cocky. I knew that even if Fiona had all the patience in the world, her crazy turd of a husband didn't. I knew he'd be out scouring the town as soon as he realized she was missing. Of course, I didn't realize he'd actually go breaking into houses and assaulting people. That was kind of a bonus.

So I decided I might as well go home, give Fiona a few hours to get hungry and, hopefully, desperate. I know *I* was getting pretty hungry. And I had other things to do. So I left, came back later. And surprise! Fiona was sleeping. Can you beat that? This woman was really starting to freak me out. I mean, what was the matter with her?

Obviously I had to alter the plan. There was no point in blindly following a course of action that was doomed to failure. So, I skipped the next part—the part where I really get to shine—and went right to the last phase. I went downstairs and unlocked the door.

Then I went inside.

If she heard me come in, she didn't acknowledge it. Even after I sat down on the cot, right next to her feet, she didn't budge. No, she just lay there sleeping. I watched her breathe, wondering if she was dreaming, and if so, what about?

I dream all the time, although some people tell you they don't dream at all. They're mistaken. The fact is that everybody dreams, although a lot of people don't remember their dreams. But that doesn't mean they don't have them. Studies have clearly shown periods of deep sleep where we're virtually unconscious, and periods where our subconscious takes over, speaking to us in a variety of symbols we often don't understand and, even more often, don't remember. These "dream times" are called REM. And just because we don't remember these dreams, that doesn't mean they aren't important. Aside from releasing the accumulated stresses of the day, our dreams are trying to tell us something. They're problem-solving. That's why some people keep having the same dream over and over. These are called recurrent dreams, which people continue to have until they figure out what they mean and deal with them.

And while we're on the topic of dreams, I had a really strange one the other night. It was quite upsetting. I was standing on a big stage, speaking to a full house. I don't remember what my speech was about, but whatever it was, it was going really well. I was consistently being interrupted by spontaneous bursts of thunderous applause, and every so often a spotlight would come on in the auditorium and I was able to look into the audience and see the smiling faces. But then suddenly, instead of applause, there was laughter. People started pointing their fingers. At me. And I looked down and saw that I was naked. Completely, bare-assed naked. And they were pelting me with candy wrappers and hard, chewed pieces of gum. Kids were holding up their cell phones and taking pictures of me. And nothing I said could make them stop. I was totally, utterly humiliated.

Of course that's when I woke up. Before I had a chance to redeem myself. Before I could exact my revenge. I like to think that's what real life is for. Redemption and revenge. And if it's a choice between the two, I'll take the latter. It's a lot more fun.

Anyway, I tried to tell a few people about my dream, but no one was interested.

When Fiona finally woke up, about ten minutes after I'd been sitting beside her, she just looked at me and said, "Hi."

"Hi," I told her, putting my arm around her shoulders.

And she leaned her head against mine, and we sat there like that for several minutes, until I was afraid she was going to fall asleep again. And that's when I started to wonder if maybe she suffered from narcolepsy, which is when people just fall asleep in the middle of whatever it is they're doing, not because they're tired, but because something in their brain isn't wired properly. I mean, you've got to admit, something was seriously out of whack here. I asked her if she was hungry, and she shook her head. I asked her if she was scared, and she said no. I asked her why not, and she asked me when Cal would be getting here. I said he wouldn't, that he had no idea where she was. She stared at me for about thirty seconds. You could actually see the moment when everything finally fell into place, and she realized what was happening. That's when she asked me if I was the one who'd killed Liana Martin. I said I was. And you know what she did? You're really not going to believe this one! She smiled, laid her head back on my shoulder.

Well, let me tell you, that was the last thing I'd been expecting, and it really freaked me out. I mean, that's like being in a crowded grocery store and being pushed to the front of the checkout line, except in this case the cashier is the angel of death, and you're yelling, "Me first! Me first!"

"Aren't you scared?" I asked her.

She shook her head. Strands of her hair brushed against the side of my mouth. I smelled apricots.

"How come?"

She shook her head again, as if to say she didn't know.

"Tell me about yourself," I urged. Something in me suddenly wanted to get to know her better.

"Nothing to tell."

"Sure there is. What about your family? Your mother and father."

"Both dead."

"How?"

"Cancer. My mother first, then my father, a couple of years later."

"Any brothers or sisters?"

"A brother. I haven't seen him in five years."

"Why not?"

"He lives in Fresno," she said, as if that explained everything.

I always thought Fresno was a silly name for a city, and I said so. She giggled. Said she agreed.

"Is Fresno where you're from originally?" I asked.

She said it was.

"Is that where you met Cal?"

Again, the answer was yes.

I thought I was going to have to keep asking questions, that it was going to be like pulling teeth to get anything out of her, but that's when she fooled me again, went from being a virtual mute to a veritable Chatty Cathy right before my eyes.

"I met Cal six years ago when my father was sick. He was work-

ing as an orderly in the hospital. I thought he was really good-looking. I guess that must make me seem awfully shallow," she apologized, as if she were the only person in the world to fall for someone
just because they looked good, as if that weren't the way the world
worked. "I'd stare at him when he came to serve my father his dinner. One day, he caught me, asked me to come back when he was
finished working. We started hanging out together. After my father
died, he moved in with me and my brother. But they got into a fight
and Randy said Cal had to move out. So I went with him. We
moved into a basement apartment, but then Cal got into a fight
with the landlord, and we had to leave there too."

"Sounds like Cal gets into a lot of fights," I ventured.

"He's got a temper. He likes things done a certain way. He
doesn't like excuses."

"When did you move to Florida?"

"A couple of years ago. Cal said it was the land of opportunity."

"What did *you* say?"

She shrugged. "It didn't matter to me where we lived."

"You didn't mind leaving your friends?"

"Didn't really have any," Fiona said wistfully. "I used to have a
couple of girlfriends at work—I was a receptionist at this hairdress-
ing salon—but after I quit my job, I pretty much stopped seeing
them."

"Why'd you quit your job?"

"Cal didn't like me working. My father was the same way. He
wouldn't let my mother work, said her job was taking care of him."

"Is it true Cal beat you?"

"Only when I deserved it," Fiona said quickly.

"When was that?"

"When I didn't listen, when I did something wrong, when I gave
him a hard time."

"When was that?"

She blushed. "You know."

"You mean, during sex?"

"Sometimes I didn't do things right. Sometimes he'd hurt me
and I'd cry. He didn't like that. Said it destroyed the mood."

"What sort of things did he make you do?"

"Sometimes he'd take me from the back," she said, her voice a monotone, as if she were reading from a list of groceries. "Or he'd tie me up, poke at me with different things. Sometimes he'd hit me with his belt. Sometimes he used his teeth."

I could barely contain my disgust. "He's an animal."

"I deserved it. I should have tried harder."

"What more could you have done?"

"I didn't always pass inspection."

"What?"

"We had inspection every day."

"I don't understand."

"Cal said it was the only way he could be sure."

"Sure of what?"

"That I was being faithful."

"What are you talking about? What kind of inspection?"

"He'd make me take off all my clothes and lie down on the bed." Tears of shame began to tumble down Fiona's cheeks. "Then he'd look behind my ears, inside my mouth." She took a deep breath. "Between my legs."

Well, I've got to tell you, I almost threw up right then and there. Talk about your sick puppies. You've got to wonder what gets into people. Oh, I know he was probably abused himself as a kid. That's the way it usually works, isn't it? He's just doing what comes naturally. Still, people like that have to be stopped. He's a real menace, a danger to society and all that crap. He deserves to rot in jail.

I like to think I've done my part in that regard.

But to be truthful, my revulsion wasn't directed solely at Cal. I was equally repulsed by his wife. I mean, to give in like that, to acquiesce to such perverted demands, to just lie there and allow yourself to be inspected like a piece of meat! She disgusted me. And I think she must have seen that disgust reflected in my eyes, because she gave me this sad little smile and said, "Are you going to shoot me now?" And then she said, "Don't worry. It's okay." Like she was giving me permission, for God's sake. Like she understood. Like she agreed.

Which was kind of against the whole point.

Anyway, I almost changed my mind. I mean, talk about destroying the mood. But what could I do? I couldn't very well let her go. So I shot her, although the only enjoyment I got out of it was the thought of what was in store for Cal. I'd already planted some of the trophies I'd taken from Liana and Candy in his house. I knew it was only a question of time before the sheriff requested a search warrant and those items were recovered. Then I disposed of the body.

So now Cal Hamilton sits in the county jail, charged with murdering two women, as well as being the chief suspect in the disappearance of a third. Of course he's very vocal about protesting his innocence, says he never even heard of anyone named Candy Abbot, that he's being framed for Liana's death, that he loved his wife. You can bet all the newspapers are full of the story—I even caught something about it on CNN—although nobody believes him. You almost have to feel sorry for the guy. Except of course, nobody does. Certainly not me.

No, I'm quite content to let Cal Hamilton sit on his ass in jail for at least another month. It gives the town a chance to catch its breath, shed the shackles of fear that have gripped it these last weeks, and it stops all the nonsense about calling in the FBI. No, sir. No need for that now. A cold-blooded killer has been put behind bars. Our sheriff is a hero.

Anyway, I now have all the time I need to regroup, and to plan my next moves carefully. The academic year is winding down. In approximately another six weeks, summer will officially begin. In the meantime, there's lots to look forward to: the warmer weather, the holidays, the freedom. Of particular interest is Torrance High's upcoming musical extravaganza. It takes place in four weeks and runs for three nights. The cast is full of eager, young hopefuls, and I intend to choose my next leading lady from amongst their nubile lot. Actually, she's already got the part.

Kiss me, Kate, indeed.

chapter twenty-eight

A month later, Sandy sat in the darkened school auditorium—between a nervous Rita Hensen and a snoozing Lenny Fromm—and waited anxiously for the play to begin. Directly behind her sat Avery Peterson, who'd come alone, and two rows behind him, Sandy's husband, Ian, who most decidedly had not. Practically glued to his side, her arm laced proprietarily through his, was Kerri Franklin, resplendent in a hot-pink jumpsuit and a chunky necklace of brightly colored beads that disappeared into the deep V of her plunging neckline. "Boobs and baubles," Rita had pronounced as Kerri bounced triumphantly down the center aisle, along with her mother, Rose, in funereal black from head to toe. Rose, clearly not pleased to be here, hadn't stopped grumbling since she took her seat. "She's only in the chorus, for God's sake," the woman had muttered loudly. "I don't see why we had to make a special trip."

"We're not here just because of Delilah," Kerri reminded her in a voice that carried for several rows. "Ian's daughter is playing the lead, and we thought it would be a nice opportunity for you to meet her."

Sandy thought Kerri had delivered that last sentence with a little more relish than necessary, and with undue emphasis on the *we*. Clearly the information had been intended as much for her benefit as for Rose's.

"Bitch," Rita whispered, obviously agreeing with Sandy's silent assessment. "Please tell me you finally contacted that lawyer I told you about."

Sandy shook her head. "I haven't quite gotten around to it."

"What do you mean, you haven't gotten around to it?"

"I've been meaning to do it."

"So why haven't you? The man's an inconsiderate asshole."

"He's not an . . ." Sandy stopped, unable to say the word out loud. But why did he have to be here tonight?

Originally, Ian had requested tickets for opening night, and Sandy had decided it would be wiser—and no doubt safer—to attend one of the other two performances. So it was decided: Ian would attend Thursday, Tim on Friday, and Sandy on Saturday. That way Megan would have a family member present for each performance and everyone would be happy.

Sure.

It was one of those ideas that worked well in theory. Unfortunately, like many a good idea, this one hadn't gone exactly as planned. An hour before the curtain was scheduled to go up on Thursday night, Rose Cruikshank had complained of chest pains, and Ian and Kerri had had to drive her to a hospital in Fort Lauderdale, where she'd been examined and released. Obviously she was feeling better tonight, Sandy thought, although she seemed bound and determined to make everyone else suffer.

"God knows we hear enough of that awful caterwauling at home," she groused.

"Stop that, Mother," Kerri scolded weakly. "Delilah has a lovely singing voice, and you know it."

"Then why is she always in the chorus? Why isn't she playing one of the leads?"

The question—which was followed by a loud snort—went unanswered, although everyone within earshot silently supplied the correct response. Simply stated, Delilah wasn't leading-lady material. And it wasn't just her size, Sandy realized. It was something else. The girl was too accessible, too lacking in guile. Like an overgrown puppy, she was just too eager to please. She could have the most glorious singing voice in the world and she would still never be the star of the show. At best, she'd be the overweight, wisecracking sidekick. It was the Megans of this world, the slightly aloof, long-legged beauties, whose pretty faces hinted at a depth that might not be there, and whose voices were no more than pleasant, who would always walk away with the leading roles. Onstage and in life.

It wasn't fair, but then, what was?

Was it fair that her husband had left her for a big-bosomed bimbo, that he'd brought that bloated bottle-blonde to the school play—the school in which she taught, for God's sake, where the patrons were largely her colleagues and students, all there to witness her humiliation? Why had Ian chosen the night of their daughter's final performance to make his own breathtakingly public debut with Kerri Franklin? Everyone knew they were an item. Did he have to rub it in her face?

"Take a good look behind you," Rita was saying. "Then tell me honestly: Do you really want him back?"

Sandy slowly swiveled around in her seat, her eyes doing a quick scan of the auditorium, as if she were looking for someone in particular. She saw the McGoverns and the Perchaks and the Arlingtons and the Falcos. She spotted John Weber and his wife, Pauline. And she saw Ian comfortably ensconced three rows behind her, the world's stupidest grin on his handsome face as Kerri leaned closer to whisper something in his ear. She saw him laugh, saw his hand reaching out to squeeze Kerri's knee. Then he looked up, caught Sandy watching him, and acknowledged her gaze with a small wave of his free hand and a nod of his head.

Good God, he'd actually waved. As if she were no more to him than a casual acquaintance, or a patient he'd run into outside the office. He didn't even have the good sense to remove his hand from Kerri's knee. He really was an . . . a piece of work, Sandy amended silently.

"Well?" Rita asked, as if reading her thoughts.

Sandy closed her eyes and said nothing, understanding her humiliation was complete. Because the answer to Rita's question was yes. She still wanted him back.

"Is this thing ever going to start?" Rose suddenly bellowed. "What's the problem?"

Sandy checked her watch. It was almost ten minutes after eight. She wondered if there was, indeed, a problem, then remembered that Megan had told her Mr. Lipsman liked to start the show a few minutes late because that was the way they did it on Broadway. Megan had also told her that their esteemed director could be found

pacing the halls outside the auditorium throughout the performance. That is, when he wasn't throwing up in the washroom across
the hall. Sandy was tempted to join him.

A host of whistles suddenly erupted from the back of the auditorium. Joey Balfour, Sandy knew, without needing to look.

"Quiet down, Balfour, or I'll toss you in jail," the sheriff barked,
and the auditorium burst into spontaneous applause. It continued
until John was forced to stand up and acknowledge the ovation,
while his wife basked in the glow of his reflected glory. After all, it
was *her* husband who'd calmed the fears of an entire community by
putting a cold-blooded killer behind bars.

Unlike *my* husband, Sandy thought, who'd merely titillated that
same community by bedding Silicone Sally.

"Way to go, Johnny-boy," Lenny Fromm said, suddenly emerging
from his nap and jumping to his feet. Everyone in the audience
immediately followed suit. The only people who remained firmly in
their seats were Rose Cruikshank and Ian Crosbie.

When the lights went up at the end of the evening, Sandy was
finally able to stand up, unknot the cramp in her stomach, and
exhale. "Wow. That was really something."

"It was wonderful," Rita concurred. "Megan was just fabulous."

"So was Brian," Sandy said, watching Ian out of the corner of her
eye as he helped Rose Cruikshank to her feet.

"Yeah. He was pretty great, wasn't he?"

"You both should be very proud," Lenny Fromm said before disappearing into the crowd to accept congratulations. He'd slept
through most of the second act.

"I was so worried that he'd back out at the last minute," Rita
said. "Or that he'd get stage fright or start obsessing about there
being enough oxygen in the auditorium."

"It's okay," Sandy said. "It's over now."

"Yes, it is. It's really over. Oh, God. I've been so scared."

"Scared?" Sandy had been a little nervous for Megan too, but
scared?

"I'm not talking about the play."

"I don't understand."

Rita shook her head, as if to say, Not here. "Do you think we could go to my office for a minute before we see the kids?"

"Of course. Is something wrong?" The two women made their way up the aisle and pushed their way through the crowd milling about the back of the auditorium. Ian and Kerri were already leading Rose toward the dressing rooms. Hopefully by the time she returned, they'd have congratulated Megan and left. "What is it?" Sandy asked again as Rita unlocked the door to her office and they stepped inside.

Rita flipped on the overhead light, locked the door behind her, then burst into tears.

"Rita, what's wrong?"

"I'm so stupid."

"You're *not* stupid."

Rita grabbed a tissue from a nearby container, blew her nose, then dabbed at her heavily mascaraed eyes. "I'm sure you've noticed I've been a little standoffish for the last little while."

Sandy made a face that said, No, you haven't, and Rita countered with one that said, Yes, I have, and you know it.

"Well, maybe a little," Sandy conceded. "I assumed you were mad at me about—"

"I wasn't mad at you. I was mad at myself." There was a slight pause. Rita raised her hands to her mouth, then lowered them, along with her voice. "I thought he did it." The words hit the air like pebbles against glass.

"You thought who did what?"

"Brian." Rita's voice dropped even lower, so that she was whispering. "I thought he had something to do with Fiona Hamilton's disappearance. Oh, God. I've been feeling so guilty. I actually thought my son might have killed Liana Martin."

"What?" Sandy repeated, although in truth there were moments she'd thought the same thing herself.

"I'm such an awful person."

"No, you're not."

"What kind of mother thinks her own son might be capable of murder?"

"You had reason to be concerned," Sandy reminded her, thinking back to the evening of Rita's frantic phone call. "He'd been acting very peculiar. You found him rinsing blood from his shirt."

"Yes, I know I had good reason to be concerned. But even after the sheriff told me about Brian's fight with Joey Balfour, a part of me still wasn't convinced. Even after they found those things in Cal's house and arrested Cal for murder, there was a small part of me that wondered . . ."

"It was a difficult time for all of us."

"Ever since Brian's father died," Rita began, then stopped herself. "Ever since his father *killed himself*," she stated bitterly, "and Brian found him hanging there—"

"Rita . . ."

The tears returned full force. "That selfish son of a bitch. If he wanted to hang himself, why couldn't he have picked a nice big tree in the middle of the Everglades? Did he have to do it in our bathroom? Did he have to do it where his son would walk in and find him?"

"He wasn't thinking clearly."

"He wasn't thinking at all, damn him."

"He must have been in tremendous anguish."

"Fuck that!" Rita said with surprising vehemence. "Fuck his anguish! What about his son? His son who walked into the bathroom and found him hanging there with his tongue sticking out and his face a decidedly unflattering shade of blue. No wonder the poor kid worries about there being enough oxygen!" She collapsed into Sandy's outstretched arms. "He should have been here tonight. He should have been here for his son."

They stood in the middle of the small office, Sandy's arms wrapped around the tiny woman, as Rita cried. After a few moments, the sobs shuddered to a halt, and Rita pushed her shoulders back and lifted her head to smile at Sandy. "But it's okay now. The nightmare's finally over. Cal Hamilton is in jail. The murders have stopped. And my son—my beautiful, crazy boy—was great up there on that stage tonight."

"He certainly was."

"So what if he's all fucked-up? At least he's not a killer. Right?"

Sandy gave her friend another hug. "Teenagers are supposed to be all fucked-up. That's their job."

"Do we ever really grow up?" Rita asked, as they headed back down the hallway.

Sandy shook her head. "Beats me."

"You were fantastic," Rita gushed, pushing her way through the noisy throng of well-wishers filling the long, narrow corridor to take her son in her arms. Brian allowed himself to be hugged and kissed.

"Thanks."

"Aw, isn't that sweet?" Joey Balfour said from somewhere nearby.

"You were wonderful, Brian," Sandy said, shooting Joey a warning glance. "Congratulations."

"Thank you." Brian wiped his mother's kisses off his cheek and glanced toward Perry Falco, who stood in the far corner of the hall, watching him. Brian hesitated, then signaled Perry over. "Mom, there's somebody I'd like you to meet."

Sandy excused herself to try to find her daughter. The area was packed with proud parents and assorted well-wishers. Cast members, most still in costume and full makeup, dashed in and out of the four small dressing rooms, accepting accolades and basking in the glow of their success. Sandy looked for Gordon Lipsman, hoping to congratulate him on a job well done. She'd misjudged and underestimated him, she was thinking. He might be prissy and pretentious, but he was also talented. He deserved a pat on the back, maybe even a hug. She didn't care how many pictures of them ended up on the Internet. "Has anyone seen Mr. Lipsman?" she asked.

"I think he went home," Victor Drummond said, emerging from the closest dressing room. "Said he wasn't feeling well."

Sandy almost didn't recognize Victor without his white powder. He looked so different. We all look different without our masks, she thought. "You were great," she told him honestly, feeling a tremendous sense of pride in all her students.

He nodded shyly. "Megan's in the dressing room down the hall, second to the end."

"Thank you."

The hallway was so congested it took Sandy a full minute to get there. On the way, she exchanged superlatives with John and Pauline Weber as well as with the parents of Tanya McGovern and Ginger Perchak. Everyone agreed that everyone's offspring had done a terrific job. Everyone except Greg Watt's father, who was conspicuous in his absence. "Greg," Sandy said, peeking into the middle dressing room where Greg sat alone, removing his makeup with cold cream. He glanced at her through the mirror as she stood in the doorway. "I just wanted to tell you what a wonderful job you did tonight. You should be very proud."

He smiled. "Sorry about having to kiss your daughter," he said with a sly grin. "Mr. Lipsman made me do it."

"Yes, I could see how much you weren't enjoying yourself."

Joey Balfour was suddenly at Sandy's side. "You're such a faggot," he yelled through the doorway at his friend.

Sandy thought of objecting, then thought better of it. "Congratulations, Greg," she said instead, squeezing past Joey and continuing down the hall.

"So where's the party at?" she heard Joey ask, although she didn't catch Greg's reply.

Sandy continued to the last dressing room, found it as crowded with people as the hall. She took a deep breath, prayed that Ian had already left. "Mom?"

Sandy turned toward the voice. "Tim. What are you doing here?"

He nodded toward Amber, who was already out of her costume and into her sweater and jeans, although she was still wearing most of her stage makeup. That makeup probably weighs more than she does, Sandy thought, as Tim shifted from one foot to the other self-consciously. "Amber invited me to the cast party," he said, his chin down, the words floating into the air from the vicinity of his chest.

"Well, that was very nice," Sandy said, trying not to sound too surprised. "Where is this party?"

Tim shrugged. "Someone's house."

"Good," Sandy said, the slight sarcasm in her voice absorbed by the noise in the room.

"I'll wait for you outside," Tim told Amber, who smiled and fluttered her fingers in the air coquettishly.

Dear God, thought Sandy.

"See you later, Mom."

"Try not to be too late." She fought the urge to tell him to keep an eye on his sister.

"Mom, hi!" Megan called, pushing through the crowd to reach Sandy's side.

Sandy threw her arms around her daughter, hugged her tightly. "Megan! You were so fabulous."

"Careful. You'll get makeup all over you."

"Who cares? I am so proud of you."

"It was great, wasn't it?"

"It really was," Sandy agreed. "I was just amazed. I mean, I knew it would be good, but I didn't realize it would be *that* good."

"Wasn't Greg fantastic?"

"Fantastic," Sandy agreed.

"Too bad his father wouldn't come see him. He's such an . . . a jerk."

"I understand there's a cast party."

"Yeah, well, it's closing night and everything."

"Where is it?"

Megan shrugged. "Somebody's house."

"Great."

"You can stop worrying, Mom. Cal Hamilton's all locked up."

"It's not Cal Hamilton I'm worried about," Sandy said pointedly.

Megan looked away, her face growing sullen.

"It's just that it's easy to get lost in the moment," Sandy continued quietly.

"I won't get lost," Megan said.

"Promise?"

"Hey, Megan! Great job tonight," someone called from the doorway.

"Thanks." The smile returned to Megan's face. "Stop worrying," she told Sandy. "I'm a big girl. I can take care of myself."

Sandy nodded, stroked her daughter's beautiful long hair. "I know you can."

"Mom?" Megan called as Sandy turned away. "You look really pretty tonight."

Sandy's hand flew self-consciously to her hair. She'd spent half an hour trying to smooth it out with Megan's ceramic straightener, but the minute she'd stepped into the humidity, she'd felt the curls and ringlets starting to form. And she'd chewed off what was left of her new, peach-colored lipstick during Megan and Greg's final embrace. "Thank you, sweetheart."

"Mom . . ."

Sandy waited.

"I won't be late."

Sandy was smiling as she left Megan's dressing room and started down the corridor. She had two beautiful children, she was thinking: a daughter who was as smart as she was talented, and a son who was as sweet as he was sensitive. Both on the verge of adulthood. Both with bright futures waiting to embrace them. She had good reason to be proud.

A familiar voice pierced her reveries. "But that's not fair." Delilah stormed out of the dressing room at the end of the hall. "Tell them it isn't fair, Mrs. Crosbie," she said, catching up to Sandy.

Reluctantly Sandy stopped and turned around. "What isn't fair, Delilah?" Kerri Franklin entered Sandy's line of vision, began walking toward her.

"My grandmother isn't feeling well, so they want me to drive her home and make sure she gets into bed."

"Delilah, this really isn't anyone's business," Kerri scolded, as Ian appeared in the doorway of the dressing room.

"I'm going to the party," Delilah insisted.

"You're taking your grandmother home."

"Why can't *you* do it?"

"Because Ian and I have made other plans." Kerri said this directly to Sandy. "Now don't argue with me. After you get your grandmother settled, then you can go to the party."

"Great." Delilah didn't move.

"The faster you get out of your costume and get your grandmother home," Sandy said reluctantly, "the faster you'll get to the party." She looked up, saw Ian smiling at her.

"You look terrific," he mouthed.

Before Sandy had time to digest the remark, he and Kerri had left the hallway.

chapter twenty-nine

So, a bunch of us are going over to Chester's for a celebratory drink," Rita was saying as they walked toward the teachers' parking lot. "You game?"

Sandy shook her head. "I don't think so."

"Ah, come on."

"I'm kind of tired."

"No, you aren't. You're just upset because Ian—"

"I'm not upset," Sandy said impatiently, replaying Ian's unexpected compliment over and over in her mind, like a favorite song. What did it mean? Did it mean *anything*? "Look, I'm sorry. I'm just not in the mood, okay?"

Rita raised her hands into the air in a gesture of surrender. "Okay. Fine. You know where we are if you change your mind."

"Have a good time." Sandy watched Rita climb into her car. Around her, people were talking and laughing, car doors were opening and closing, engines were starting.

"Good night," someone called, and Sandy turned toward the voice. But whomever it belonged to had disappeared, and by the time Sandy turned back toward Rita, her car was already pulling out of the parking lot. Rita honked her horn as she advanced onto the street, and Sandy waved.

"You know where to find us," Rita called through her open window.

"I know where to find you," Sandy repeated quietly, her words echoing against the suddenly still night air. "Alone at last," she said as she walked toward her car. She wasn't sure when she realized hers wasn't the only car left in the lot, but she knew instantly whose old black Mercury it was. Hadn't Victor Drummond told her Mr. Lipsman had already left, that he hadn't been feeling well? What was his car still doing here? "Gordon?" she called out, slowly approaching the vehicle, her eyes flitting cautiously from side to side. "Gordon?"

There was no answer. In the distance she heard the sounds of tires squealing and students laughing. She hoped that everyone would drive safely and behave sensibly, and she said a silent thank-you to the star-filled sky that Cal Hamilton was behind bars and Torrance's recent nightmare was over. One less thing to worry about, she thought gratefully.

Someone had probably offered to drive Gordon home, she decided as she reached his car and peeked inside. Which made perfect sense. He couldn't very well drive himself home if he was feeling sick. Too bad, she thought. He'd worked too hard not to be able to wallow, at least for a short time, in all that admiration and applause. Everyone deserves a good wallow now and again, she thought.

"Sandy?" a voice whispered softly, so softly that Sandy wasn't sure if the voice was real or imagined until she heard it again. "Sandy?"

Sandy's head snapped toward the sound. It seemed to be coming from a row of brilliant red hibiscus bushes growing along the far side of the lot. "Who's there?" Sandy asked, advancing gingerly.

"Help me," the voice urged, floating toward her on soft ripples of air.

Sandy glanced around the now deserted parking lot. "Damn it," she muttered under her breath, feeling frightened and debating whether to turn around and run. This is one of those moments, she was thinking. One of those moments that you see in the movies when the stupid heroine goes snooping where she shouldn't be snooping, and the entire audience is yelling at her not to go, but she goes anyway, sticking her neck out just far enough for some deranged lunatic in a hockey mask to chop it off with a machete. *Don't go. Don't go,* she could hear the invisible audience screaming as she approached the bushes and parted the bloodred blossoms.

"Sandy," she heard again.

"Mr. Lipsman!" she cried out, discovering the drama teacher lying on his back on the ground.

"Please help me." He tried extending his hands in her direction, but succeeded only in flailing about ineffectually, and almost slapping her in the face.

"For God's sake, Gordon. What are you doing there?" Sandy grabbed hold of his hands and tried pulling him to his feet, but his clammy palms repeatedly slipped from hers, and he kept ending up on his back. Eventually he found his footing, only to teeter forward on his toes. His arms shot out at his sides as if he were navigating a tightrope, his body ultimately tumbling into hers. Sandy dug her heels into the pavement as he crashed into her, managing to remain upright from sheer force of will.

"Sorry about that," Gordon said, trying to straighten his red-and-gold-striped tie.

"Are you all right?"

"I'm not feeling very well." He grabbed a handful of hibiscus in an effort to steady himself. "I decided to lie down. Then I couldn't get up." He belched.

The pungent odor of whiskey immediately filled the air. "You're drunk!" Sandy tried backing away from the unpleasant smell, but it had already surrounded her.

"You sound just like my mother."

"Dear God." Again Sandy looked around the empty lot, praying someone else might have lingered, knowing no one had. "Careful," she said as Gordon tottered unsteadily toward her, his hand landing like a lion's paw on her shoulder.

"Did you see *Kate*?" he asked.

It took Sandy several seconds to realize he was referring to the play and not an actual person. "I did. It was wonderful."

"I thought it was smashing. Simply smashing," he pronounced in his ersatz British accent. "Didn't you?"

The only thing smashed here is you, Sandy thought but didn't say. "Do you think you can manage to stay upright?" she asked instead, eager to remove his hand from her shoulder before his weight brought her to her knees.

"Oh, yes. Of course." He withdrew his hand. His body waved back and forth like a metronome. "Your daughter was a revelation."

"Yes. She was wonderful."

"Not wonderful," Gordon corrected. "A revelation."

"A revelation, yes." Sandy looked helplessly toward the deserted street. "What are we going to do with you, Gordon?" Why did she always get into these messes? Why hadn't she simply gone with Rita and the others to Chester's? Why did the drunken drama teacher in the parking lot have to be her responsibility?

"It wasn't easy," Gordon was saying. "Those kids are talented, but they're lazy. They don't want to work. They just want to be stars. Everybody wants to be a star."

"How are we going to get you home?"

Gordon looked vaguely startled. At least Sandy thought he looked startled. His eyes were so crossed, she couldn't be sure. "I have my car," he said, pointing in its general direction and almost falling over.

"Yeah, right. Like you're in any condition to drive. Come on." She took him by the elbow and led him as if he were blind. "I guess I'll have to give you a lift."

"Really? That's awfully kind of you."

What choice do I have? Sandy wondered as she guided him slowly toward her car, then helped him into the front seat.

"To tell you the truth, I'm not feeling very well," he said, as if he were confiding a deep, dark secret.

"Please tell me you're not going to be sick."

"I certainly hope not. My mother would be furious." He laughed, a sharp, girlish cackle that spewed invisible droplets of whiskey into the air. "Of course, Mother is dead." He laughed again.

Oh, God, Sandy thought, climbing behind the wheel and starting the engine. "If you think you're going to be sick, just try to give me some warning, so I can pull over."

"My mother used to tell me to take deep breaths."

"That's a good idea."

"She used to tell me wipe my feet and mind my manners."

"One should always wipe their feet and mind their manners," Sandy agreed, pulling her white Camry out of the parking lot and trying to remember the best way to Gordon Lipsman's house.

Turn right at the corner. Then just go straight until you hit Citrus Grove, she heard Delilah say.

"How are you doing there?" she asked a minute later, watching Gordon's head loll to one side.

"Taking deep breaths," he said, although he wasn't.

Please don't let him be sick in my car, Sandy thought as she turned right at the corner. They drove without incident until they reached Citrus Grove and she made another right turn. If memory served, she was supposed to continue for about half a mile, then turn left.

"Where are we going?" Gordon asked suddenly, sitting up abruptly and looking around, although it was too dark to see much of anything.

"I'm taking you home," Sandy reminded him.

"You could take me to *your* home," he suggested with a grin that was more annoying than endearing.

"No, I couldn't do that."

"Why not? Don't you like me, Sandy?"

Sandy decided the best way to deal with this conversation was not to have it. "Am I going the right way, Gordon?" The last thing she wanted to do—other than exchange flirty banter with a man she found borderline repulsive—was to get lost again. She recalled the last time she and Delilah had been out this way and shuddered at the memory of their gruesome discovery at the side of the road.

"Are you cold?" Gordon asked.

"What? No. I'm fine. Am I going the right way?"

"I don't know. It doesn't look familiar."

"Concentrate, Gordon."

"I *am* concentrating." He trained his deeply crossed eyes on her right profile. "You're a very beautiful woman, you know that?"

"I turn left, right?"

"Left. Right. What?"

"Oh, God. Gordon, you have to pay attention. I'm supposed to turn left now. Is that correct?"

"Yes."

"Okay. Good."

"Although it's faster if you turn right."

"What?"

"It's a shortcut."

"It is? You're sure?"

"Of course I'm sure."

Sandy marveled that he'd actually managed to sound insulted. "Okay. So you'll be able to direct me?"

"Yes, dear," he said with that stupid grin. "It's what I do. I direct." For the third time that night, he laughed his high-pitched cackle. "Actually, I was thinking of directing *Rent* next year. What do you think?"

"Sounds very ambitious," Sandy said distractedly. She was trying to focus all her concentration on the unfamiliar road ahead.

"Nothing wrong with a little ambition." Gordon's voice was ice-cold.

"No, of course not." Where were they going? She should have stuck to the route she remembered. What would happen if he'd taken her in the wrong direction, if they ended up driving around in circles half the night? Why had she volunteered to drive him home in the first place? Why hadn't she suggested he simply sleep it off in his car until morning? Why weren't there any taxis in Torrance? Why weren't there more lights along this stretch of road? What would happen if her car were to break down, her tire go flat? Why didn't she have a cell phone so that she could call for help in case of an emergency? What was the matter with her?

"Did you see it?"

"See what?" Had she missed the turnoff onto Admiral Road?

"*Rent.*"

"Oh. Yes, yes, I did."

"On Broadway?"

"Yes."

"With the original cast?"

"I think so. Yes."

"I have the original-cast album."

"That's good."

"Not exactly the same thing as actually seeing the play."

"I guess not."

"I *wanted* to see it," Gordon said mournfully. "But my mother refused to travel all that way to see a bastardized version of *La Bohème*. That's what she called it. A *bastardized* version." He shook his head. "Oh, dear. Probably shouldn't have done that."

"Take deep breaths," Sandy reminded him.

"Yes, Mother."

"Do I just keep going straight?"

"The straight and narrow."

"Gordon . . ."

"Besides, we couldn't leave the cats."

"What?"

"It was hard to go away and leave the cats."

"You could have gone without her," Sandy ventured, then immediately wished she hadn't. Did she really want to be having this conversation?

"Oh, no. I could never have done that."

"You were a good son."

"Well, what could I do? She had no one else to look after her."

"No other family?" Sandy remembered the photographs she'd seen in Gordon's house, the two pretty, young girls luxuriating in each other's company.

"She had a sister, but she died a long time ago. Car accident. How fast are you going, by the way?"

Sandy realized she was speeding and quickly brought the car back to below the thirty-mile-an-hour limit. "What about you?" she asked him. "No siblings?"

"No. I'm an only child. One of a kind," he said with another of his creepy little half-smiles.

"That you are."

"And you?"

"I have a brother in California."

"Is he in the movie business?"

Sandy laughed in spite of herself. "No. He works for some big dot-com organization."

"Really? And yet he has a sister who doesn't even own a cell phone. How curious."

Sandy felt a vague stirring of unease. "How do you know I don't have a cell phone?"

"Oh, I know a great deal about you, Mrs. Crosbie."

"Such as?"

"I know you're very beautiful."

Sandy groaned audibly. "How do you know I don't have a cell phone?"

"I know your husband left you for Delilah's mother."

"How do you know I don't have a cell phone?"

"I know you still haven't filed for a divorce. Turn right at the next intersection," he advised, before continuing on in the same breath, "I know you're lonely."

"How do you know I don't have a cell phone?"

He laughed. "I'm sorry. Could you repeat the question?"

"Gordon . . ."

"Yes, yes, yes. How do I know you don't have a cell phone?" He paused dramatically. "I believe Delilah mentioned it in passing whilst regaling the cast with the details of how you two stumbled upon Mrs. Hamilton's body the afternoon I sent her to fetch my sheet music. Which the clumsy girl totally ruined, by the way. Turn right here."

"You're sure?"

"Quite sure," he told her, sounding suddenly very sober and very much in control.

Whilst regaling, Sandy repeated silently as she turned right and continued down the road. Could he be any more pretentious? And was it possible this road could be even less interesting than the one they'd just turned off? Her eyes strained through the darkness toward the empty field on her right. Not even any orange trees, she was thinking, as an old, abandoned farmhouse popped into view at the far end of the field. She couldn't recall having seen it before and would probably have missed spotting it this time had it not been for the circle of bright stars that were gathered like a halo over its collapsing roof. "What's this place?" she asked, glancing just past Gordon's head.

It happened so fast, she didn't have time to see it coming. One second she was peering out the side window, and the next instant she was staring into the leering face, the crossed eyes, the bulbous nose of Gordon Lipsman, as his too soft lips squished against her own. The back of her head crashed against the glass of the side window as her hands lost control of the wheel and the car veered sharply to the left. Instinctively, Sandy's foot slammed on the brake, and the car careened to the side of the road, spinning around in a free-form half-circle before finally coming to a stop. "What the hell do you think you're doing?" she yelled, slapping at Gordon's arms and trying to get out from under those massive lips.

"Ouch!" he yelped, pushing her hands away even as his lips remained fastened to hers, as if they were stuck there with Krazy Glue.

"For God's sake, Gordon, get off me."

"It's okay."

"It's not okay. Are you crazy?" She finally managed to push him an arm's length away. He fell back against the passenger window, his breathing labored and loud. He took several deep breaths in rapid succession, and for one awful moment Sandy thought he was about to throw up all over her.

Instead, he shouted, "Kiss me, Kate!" and lunged again.

It might have been funny had it not been so nausea-inducing. "Oh, for heaven's sake," Sandy sputtered, narrowly avoiding being pinned again by that leechlike mouth. "Stop it. Stop it this instant." When he persisted in his attempts to kiss her, she slapped him hard across the face. That stopped him.

"What happened?" he asked, his eyes trying to focus.

"You tell me."

"How am I supposed to know?" he demanded angrily. "One minute, you're telling me how lonely you are—"

"I never said I was lonely. *You* said I was lonely."

"You're confiding in me about your divorce, your family—"

"I did no such thing."

"You didn't tell me about your brother in California?"

"I was making small talk, for God's sake."

"You offered to drive me home."

"Because I was being nice."

"Because you're interested."

"I'm not interested, you idiot!"

"I've seen the way you look at me."

"What?" Was she losing her mind? "What are you talking about?"

"You send mixed messages."

"I send mixed messages?"

"You don't make yourself clear."

Sandy tried to make sense out of what he was saying. Was it possible she'd misled him in any way, that her actions tonight could have been so badly misconstrued? Was she really trying to talk sense to a man who only minutes earlier had been lying on his back in a hibiscus bush? "Okay, listen. If what you're saying is true—"

"It's true."

"If I've given you the wrong impression in any way, then I'm sorry." Was she really apologizing, just as she'd apologized to Will Baker a month ago? And while Will Baker could at least make a case for his egregious behavior, could Gordon Lipsman? Did she really not make herself clear?

"Can we go now?" Gordon asked.

Wordlessly, Sandy restarted the car and steered it back on the road.

"Turn left at the next intersection," Gordon directed icily.

Sandy signaled her intention to make the turn, even though no other cars were on the road. She glanced into her rearview mirror, watched the old farmhouse with the collapsing roof vanish into the night.

chapter thirty

"Hey, everybody, Joey's here," Joey Balfour shouted over the loud music blasting from the new surround-sound system. Brandishing a case of beer over his head, he strutted through the front door. "The party can now officially begin."

Megan listened to the prolonged applause, accompanied by a series of admiring hoots and whistles, that greeted Joey's entrance, along with a few dissenting groans and a smattering of boos. Someone yelled, "There goes the neighborhood!" Someone else muttered, "Asshole."

The party was being held at the home of Lonny Reynolds. And even though Lonny had only had a small part in *Kiss Me, Kate*, he had a large house, and best of all, his parents were away for the weekend. The living room had been emptied of furniture for the event, and Lonny had been assured that the entire cast of *Kiss Me, Kate* would be back on Sunday to return everything to its previous position, so that his parents would never be the wiser.

"Out of my way, faggots," Joey ordered, laughing as he roughly navigated his way through a group of revelers dancing in the middle of the crowded living room. He pushed past a small circle of boys talking animatedly about a basketball game they'd missed on TV earlier in the evening and winked knowingly at Greg en route to the kitchen at the back of the house.

The wink made Megan uncomfortable. It spoke of secrets and hidden agendas. She glanced up at Greg, who was standing beside her, one hand draped casually over her shoulder, the other clutching an almost empty bottle of Miller by the neck. It was his fourth beer of the night, and they'd been here less than an hour. She knew he was already more than a little drunk by the steadily increasing weight of his arm on her shoulders. "What was that about?"

"What was what about?"

"The wink."

Greg laughed. "What wink?"

"The one Joey just gave you."

Greg shook his head, took a sip of his beer. "Didn't notice any wink."

Megan almost said, How could you not notice? He winked right at you. But she didn't because it sounded like something her mother would have said to her father. Instead she said, "I wish he wouldn't say things like that."

"You wish who wouldn't say things like what?"

"Joey. He calls everyone a faggot."

Greg dismissed Megan's concerns with a wave of the hand holding the bottle. A thin arc of beer sprayed into the air, depositing several coin-shaped drops dangerously close to Megan's new tan suede boots. "He's just kidding around. He doesn't mean anything by it."

"Then why does he say it?"

Greg's response was to lean over and kiss her. Megan's annoyance disappeared as soon as his lips touched hers. She tasted the beer on his tongue and wondered if it was possible to get intoxicated by proxy, like secondhand smoke. Which could kill you, she remembered, as he kissed her again, the second kiss even longer and deeper than the first.

"Bedrooms are upstairs," Victor Drummond said as he brushed past, the scent of marijuana snaking after him.

Megan quickly pulled out of the embrace and lowered her head to stare at the beige marble floor.

Greg laughed. "What's the matter now?"

The *now* lingered, a subtle rebuke. "Nothing."

"Anybody ever tell you you worry way too much about what other people say?"

The question poked at her psyche, like a sharp jab to the ribs. "I don't worry about what other people say," she protested, sneaking a glance around her to ascertain whether anyone was listening to their conversation.

"You don't?"

"No."

"Really? Then come upstairs with me." He backed away, depositing his empty beer bottle on a nearby table and extending one arm toward her. Joey Balfour immediately thrust a fresh bottle of beer into his open palm.

"Trust me. A cold one is even better than sex," Joey said.

"Only if you keep doing it by yourself, faggot." Greg laughed. "Oh, come on," he said, as Megan's face grew dark. He took a long swig of his new beer, then held the bottle out toward her. "Come on. Have a sip. It might loosen you up a bit."

"No, thanks. I don't like beer."

"Is there anything she *does* like?" Joey asked pointedly.

Megan felt her cheeks grow warm and the air grow heavy. A wary silence suddenly replaced the blaring rock music. Gyrating bodies swiveled toward her expectantly. Curious eyes waited to see what she would do.

At least that's what it felt like to Megan, although in truth the music continued, the dancers kept moving, and only a few people were watching. It seemed as if everyone was letting go but her, that she was the only one holding back, stubbornly refusing to cut loose, to have a good time. It was a party, for God's sake. The cast party. And she was the star of the show. The envy of every girl here. Because not only had she landed the part of Kate—a role she'd performed spectacularly, at least that's what everyone said—she'd also landed her sexy costar, the boy every girl wanted.

And he wanted her.

Except he was getting restless. She could feel it. The play was over. The game they'd been playing for over a month was getting old. Kate and Petruchio had left the building. Only Greg and Megan remained. And how long could Megan keep Greg waiting? *Why* was she keeping him waiting? the music asked, the relentless beat pounding the question into her brain. Because her *mother* wasn't ready?

It's just that it's easy to get lost in the moment, Sandy had warned.

I won't get lost.

Promise?

Megan suddenly snatched the bottle of beer from Greg's hand and downed half its contents in one prolonged gulp. She hadn't promised her mother anything.

"Wow. Would you get a load of that!" Joey exclaimed. "The girl's a pro."

Stop worrying. I'm a big girl. I can take care of myself.

Megan fought the urge to gag as a spontaneous burst of applause broke out around her. Soon bodies began swaying away from her, curious eyes retreated, then glazed over, lost in the insistent thud of the bass guitar. She turned to see her brother watching her from a nearby corner, caught the worry in the tilt of his head, and she purposefully took another swig. The beer spilled from the bottle and dripped down her chin. Greg's tongue was immediately at her throat, licking it up.

"Hey, Meg," Tim cautioned, approaching, Amber right behind him, her fingers tucked into the back pocket of his jeans, "go easy with that stuff. Okay?"

"What if she doesn't like it easy, faggot?" Joey asked.

"Fuck off," Tim said.

Megan's eyes widened in alarm. Had her brother really just told Joey Balfour to fuck off?

Joey stumbled backward, clutching his heart, as if he'd been shot. "Excuse me? What did you say to me, faggot?"

"He said, everybody dance!" Amber interceded, pulling Tim into the middle of the room, where they were quickly surrounded and absorbed by the other dancers.

"That's the sheriff's daughter, buddy," Greg reminded Joey, who looked poised to take the room apart. "Wouldn't want her calling her daddy, now would we?"

Greg's warning sunk slowly into Joey's dull eyes. "Your little brother's got a big mouth," he told Megan.

"He's just kidding around," Megan said, purposely using Greg's earlier words. "He doesn't mean anything by it."

Greg smiled.

"What the hell are you smiling about?" Joey demanded, clearly itching for a fight.

"Take it easy, man," Greg said. "You're getting paranoid."

"Yeah? Well, you're starting to get on my nerves. You and the little princess here."

The front door opened and in walked Delilah Franklin.

"Good God. What's that horrible smell?" Joey asked, sauntering toward her. "Hey, Deli. Forget to use toilet paper?"

Delilah ignored Joey in much the same way the other kids were ignoring her. "Hi, guys," she said, although only Brian Hensen and Perry Falco smiled in response, and those smiles were tentative at best. "Hey, Megan," Delilah said when she spotted her.

Megan felt her heart sink as Delilah made her way across the room. What was the matter with her, for God's sake? Was Delilah purposely trying to make her life miserable? Why had she come here? Couldn't she sense she wasn't welcome? It was bad enough Megan had had to put up with her every day at rehearsals. Did she have to endure her presence now as well? *Be nice,* she heard her mother say, so since she was already feeling guilty, Megan said, "I thought you had to take your grandmother home."

"I did. She even made me wait until she fell asleep before I could leave. Every time I tried to sneak out, she'd open one eye and tell me to stay put."

"Grandmother, Grandmother, what big ears you have!" Joey sang out, swooping back toward them.

"Joey . . ." Megan warned.

"It's all right. She does have big ears," Delilah agreed with a wobbly laugh.

"What's her problem anyway?" Greg asked.

"Congestive heart failure," Delilah said.

"What's that?"

"Her heart is failing—congestively," Delilah said with a smile, and both Megan and Greg laughed.

"Hey," Joey said. "The Deli made a funny."

"Thanks for asking," Delilah said to Greg, who turned away self-consciously.

"Smells like that's not all she made," Joey continued, waving his hand back and forth in front of his nose, as if to banish an unpleasant odor. "Granddaughter, Granddaughter, what a big ass you have!" Joey slapped Delilah's backside.

"Ouch," Delilah yelped, trying to elude a second slap, even as Joey's hand made sharp contact with the denim of her jeans.

Megan felt the sting of Joey's fingers without being touched. She flinched.

"Better wash your hands," Ginger warned, laughing as she and Tanya walked by.

"I think I broke my wrist," Joey joked, doubling over and grabbing his hand.

Tears filled Delilah's eyes. She looked toward the ceiling, as if trying to prevent them from falling.

"Okay, that's enough," Greg said.

"What's your problem tonight?" Joey shot back. "The princess got you pussy-whipped already?"

"You're being an asshole."

"Yeah? Better than a pussy."

"Come on, guys. Chill," someone said. "It's a party, remember?"

"People should remember who their friends are" came Joey's instant retort.

"I'm out of here," Greg said. He took Megan's hand, began leading her from the room.

"Catch you later, faggot," Joey called after them.

"Where are we going?" Megan asked.

"You'll see."

Megan said nothing as they reached the front door. She was trying to decide what to do. On the one hand, this was her big chance to be alone with Greg. On the other hand, this was Greg's big chance to be alone with her. And as much as she relished the former, she wasn't sure she was ready for the latter. Greg could be a real sweetheart. He could also be a real . . . a real jerk. He'd been both in the last ten minutes alone.

She felt Greg's tug on her arm and looked back toward the living room, trying to locate her brother in the middle of the dance floor. At the very least she should tell him she was leaving, she thought, remembering the fallout from Liana's wake. But she knew he'd look at her with their mother's eyes and urge her not to go, which would ruin not only her evening but his, and what a night this was turning out to be for both of them. She'd call him later on his cell to assure him of her safety, she decided, making up her mind to go with Greg.

But instead of whisking her out the front door, Greg was heading up the staircase that led to the second floor. Holding her breath, Megan allowed herself to be led up those stairs, past a wood-paneled den, a blue marble bathroom, and another room on the right, from which the pungent smell of marijuana was leaking from underneath its closed door. "Maybe we shouldn't be up here," Megan whispered, the words painful against her throat.

"Ssh."

They continued down the hall to a large room, the center of which was occupied by a canopied, four-poster, king-size bed. "Greg, I don't think—"

"That's right. Don't think." He pulled her inside the room, closing the door behind them.

"What arc you doing?"

"This." He took her in his arms and kissed her. Megan felt herself go weak in the knees. Then she heard a click behind her and realized he'd locked the door. "Greg, don't . . ."

"Don't what?" He pulled her toward the bed.

"I don't think we should be in here."

"Why not?"

"Because it isn't our house." Megan glanced around the room, casually absorbing its details: the cream-colored walls covered with family photographs, the golfing and fishing trophies that sat across the top of the ornate, hand-painted dresser, the dozen beige-and-gold-striped pillows that rested on the thick, cream-colored bedspread, the lush satin drapes that hung on the four-poster, the two beige chairs hugging a small, round table in front of the large bedroom window overlooking the backyard.

"You never heard the old saying, make yourself at home?"

"I don't think this is quite what they had in mind," Megan said as Greg pulled her down beside him. She heard the hard mattress squeak, like crickets, beneath the soft bedspread.

"Who's they?" Greg asked, kissing the side of her neck.

Her arm brushed against one of the satin pillows, dislodging it. Were they in any special order? she wondered, trying not to panic. Would anyone notice if their arrangement was disturbed? "Maybe we should sit over there." With her chin, she indicated the two chairs by the window.

Greg took the opportunity to plant a series of soft kisses along the strong line of her jaw. "Maybe you should stop talking," he suggested gently.

And then he was kissing her on the side of her mouth, then directly on her lips, just as he'd said he was going to do that afternoon under the tree in the school yard when he was telling her how he would go about seducing her, and now that's exactly what he was doing, he was seducing her, and if she wasn't careful, if she wasn't *very* careful, he'd succeed, and as much as part of her wanted him to succeed, as much as a *big* part of her was, in fact, rooting for him, another part of her, a teeny part, albeit an important part nonetheless, because it was the part that had promised her mother she wouldn't lose herself in the moment—well, no, she hadn't exactly promised—the part that her mother still held claim to and was apparently refusing to let go of without a knockdown, drag-out fight, *that* part was telling her not to do this, that it wasn't the right time, that there must be better places than Lonny Reynolds's parents' bedroom to make love for the first time, with its cream-colored bedspread that was undoubtedly a major stain magnet, and a bunch of smiling strangers watching her from framed photographs on the walls. Not to mention the looks that would greet her when she and Greg finally returned to the party. Enough people had seen them going up the stairs. Surely everyone would know what they'd been doing. Were they even now gathering outside the door, listening at the keyhole?

It's just that it's easy to get lost in the moment.

I won't get lost.

Promise?

She tried to block out her mother's voice, to block out her *own* voice, but it was no use. She couldn't do it.

Greg's hand slipped inside her blouse.

Oh, God. Had anything ever felt so good? She had to stop this. She had to distract him. She had to distract herself. She had to think of something unpleasant, something to counteract the sublime feel of his fingers as they danced across the lace of her bra. "Do you think they have termites?" she asked, the first thing that popped into her head.

His hand froze on her right breast. "What?"

"I was just wondering if they have termites."

"What are you talking about?"

"I only wonder because my uncle and aunt had a house that looked a lot like this one—this was back when they lived in Rochester—and they had termites. It was really awful. They had to fumigate the whole house. Everybody had to move out. I remember because they moved in with us for about a week, and I had to share my room with my cousin, Sasha, who's a real slob, and I didn't like that at all."

"Megan . . ."

"They moved to California about ten years ago when the whole dot-com business exploded. My uncle's a whiz at that sort of thing. He's my mother's brother."

"Megan . . ." Greg's hand found the clasp at the front of her bra, and in the next second, his fingers were pushing the delicate lace aside to caress her bare flesh.

"Anyway, they covered the house with this big, blue tent. Well, not a tent exactly. It was more like a huge piece of blue cellophane— well, no, not really cellophane, it was more like heavy plastic wrap, like the covers they put on swimming pools, at least up north. You don't have to cover your pools down here because it never gets very cold. Oh, God," she said as his fingers began circling the nipple of her right breast. God, that felt amazing. "Anyway," she tried to continue between kisses that grew ever more urgent, "they got rid of the termites, but my aunt never felt the same way about the house after that. She said that even though she knew they were gone, she still imagined them chewing away at night, and it freaked her out, so they moved. Not to California. At least not right away."

"Ssh," Greg said as his hand left her breast.

No, she thought. Don't go. Come back. Come back.

Except it didn't come back. It moved to her thigh. Then up her thigh and between her legs. The jolt of electricity she experienced almost knocked her on her back, and she struggled to remain upright. "Greg, I really don't think—"

"Ssh." His fingers began tugging at the zipper of her jeans.

"No. Stop. I don't want—"

"Ssh."

It was the last "Ssh" that did it. It was one thing for *her* to ignore the voice in her head; it was quite another for *him* to ignore it, especially when it was telling him, loudly and clearly, to stop. She pushed his hand away, jumped to her feet, began zipping up her jeans. "Stop telling me to ssh! I don't want to ssh!"

"What the hell *do* you want?" He grabbed a pillow from the bed, threw it angrily in her direction.

Megan watched the pillow fly by her head, then plummet to the ivory-carpeted floor. "I want to go back downstairs. I want to dance. I want to have fun."

"I thought we were *having* fun. I thought you liked me."

"I do like you, Greg. I like you a lot. I'm just not ready to—"

"—be more than a cock-teaser."

The word slapped at her cheek. She felt it grow red. "I'm not a . . . That's not what I am."

"Then you're an even better actress than I thought."

Megan took a deep breath, straightened her hair, tucked in her sweater, and checked the zipper of her jeans. He didn't mean the things he was saying, she told herself. He was just angry and upset and more than a little drunk. He'd apologize later. She'd accept. They'd spend the summer getting to know each other better. They'd take things nice and slow. "I'm going downstairs."

"So, go. What are you waiting for?"

"Aren't you coming?"

Greg remained seated on the bed, refusing to look at her. "Just send in whoever's next in line."

Megan's heart did a somersault inside her chest. She felt sick to her stomach. Her whole body ached. This is how Delilah must feel every day of her life, she thought, swallowing whatever protest was forming in her mouth, and walking to the bedroom door. She unlocked it, the loud click sounding like the cocking of a gun at the side of her head. Then she ran from the room.

She raced down the stairs and out the front door without a backward glance. She thought she heard someone say, "Megan? Is something wrong? Wait up!" But she didn't wait. Instead she ran. She ran out into the empty street, the noise of the party spilling out after her, chasing her down one block and then the next until, finally, she didn't hear it anymore.

It wasn't until she stopped to catch her breath and wipe the tears from her eyes that she realized someone was behind her. "Megan," a voice said, and then she heard nothing.

chapter thirty-one

Sandy! Over here."

Sandy peered through the dim light of Chester's, trying to ascertain the direction of Rita's voice. She finally located her at a large, round table around the far side of the bar, sitting between a morose-looking John Weber and his obviously intoxicated wife, Pauline.

"I didn't think you were coming," Rita said, her forced smile a sign of just how grateful she was to see her.

Sandy sank into one of the three empty chairs around the table, making a conscious effort to ignore the obvious tension between the sheriff and his wife. She counted at least a dozen glasses, most of them in front of Pauline.

"These aren't all mine," Pauline said defensively, noting the direction of Sandy's gaze. One hand fluttered nervously over the top of the table; the other clung tightly to her gin and tonic.

"Avery and Lenny were here. Avery left about half an hour ago," Rita explained. "You just missed Lenny by not more than five minutes."

"Good." Sandy decided she'd had quite enough of the staff of Torrance High for one night. She signaled for the waitress. "A green-apple martini," she told her. "Please."

"You sure?" Rita asked. "Remember what happened the last time you had a green-apple martini."

"Trust me. That was nothing compared to what happened tonight."

"What happened tonight?" Rita leaned forward on her elbows. Pauline began tracing the rim of her glass with her right index finger.

"Do I want to hear this?" John asked. The look on his face said that three women in varying degrees of distress were simply too much for one not-quite-sober-but-not-nearly-drunk-enough man to bear. Especially when he was off-duty.

"Probably not," Sandy told him.

John pushed himself to his feet. He walked quickly to the pool-room, struck up an easy conversation with several of the guys gathered around the closest table.

Sandy heard one of the men mutter something about the disappointing score of tonight's baseball game. Man talk, she decided, uncomplicated and impersonal. She looked back at the two women at her table. Their eyes told her they were hoping for the exact opposite. Girl talk—as complicated and personal as it gets. Sandy obligingly filled them in on the events of the evening.

"You've got to be kidding," Rita exclaimed at the conclusion of Sandy's story. "Gordon?"

"Mr. Lipsman?" Pauline echoed. "Amber's drama teacher?"

"He actually attacked you?"

"Well, he tried. He was all over me." She dusted invisible cat hairs off her beige sweater.

"That's what they always say in the tabloids," Pauline said with a laugh. *"He was all over her. She was all over him. They were all over each other."*

Sandy stared at the sheriff's wife. What was she talking about?

"That, and the word *canoodling*," Pauline continued. "Celebrities always canoodle. Have you noticed? You're an English teacher. What does that mean exactly?"

"Where did this happen?" Rita asked, ignoring Pauline, her eyes urging Sandy to do the same.

"I don't know where exactly. Somewhere between Citrus Grove and Admiral Road. Right by this abandoned, old farmhouse at the end of a big field. It was really creepy."

Pauline's eyes narrowed in concentration. "You must mean the old Kimble house. What were you doing all the way out there, for God's sake?"

"Being a Good Samaritan."

"Good and stupid," Rita corrected. "When are you going to learn?"

"Do I send out mixed messages?" Sandy asked suddenly.

"What do you mean?"

"Do I not make myself clear?"

"What's she talking about?" Pauline asked.

Sandy couldn't help but laugh. "Guess that answers that question." What a night, she was thinking, as their waitress deposited her green-apple martini on the table and Pauline requested another gin and tonic.

"Nothing more for her," John called from the back room, obviously keeping an eye on things.

"Don't listen to him," Pauline told the waitress, managing not to move her mouth, so that the words slid off her bottom lip into the surrounding air. "The Kimble house was quite the place in its time," she continued, as if the two sentences were connected. "Very modern. Had a basement and everything. Now it's just spooky. Kind of like the Bates Motel. You know, from *Psycho*. Now, *that* was a great movie. I can't believe Mr. Lipsman would do such a thing," she continued in the same breath. "What was he thinking?"

Sandy was having a hard time keeping up with the various detours in Pauline's conversation. "He was pretty drunk," Sandy said pointedly. "We don't always think too clearly when we drink too much."

"I can't believe you actually drove that moron home," Rita marveled.

"Well, I couldn't very well leave him standing in front of the Bates Motel, now could I?"

"Why the hell not?"

"I don't know. I just couldn't."

"Oh, God," Rita said, her eyes widening in alarm.

"Do you think that was sending him a mixed message?" Sandy asked, unnerved by the disapproving look on Rita's face. "What's the matter?" she asked, her eyes following the direction of Rita's gaze.

"Don't look," Rita warned.

Sandy spun around in her seat, looked toward the entrance. Her husband was standing just inside the front door. Beside him was Kerri Franklin.

"Oh, God. Please tell me I'm hallucinating."

"I told you not to look."

Pauline swiveled around in her chair. "Well, well. Look who's here."

"Have they seen us?" Sandy sank down low in her seat, pushing her shoulders up around her neck, like a turtle retreating into its shell.

"Not yet," Rita said.

"What are they doing?"

"They're sitting down in one of the booths at the front."

"'Of all the gin joints in all the world,'" Pauline said in her best Humphrey Bogart imitation, "'they have to walk into this one.'"

"I don't believe this," Sandy said. "What are they doing now?"

"Just sitting there."

Sandy snuck her head out of her protective shell to peek in their direction. Ian and Kerri were sitting across from one another, their hands clasped together in the middle of the table. She turned quickly away. "You didn't tell me they were holding hands."

"I didn't think that detail was necessary."

"You ever notice that nobody names their kids Humphrey anymore?" Pauline asked, as if she were in the middle of an entirely different conversation. "It's gone the way of Gertrude and Ethel and Homer. Now we have names like Tiffany and Ashleigh and Tyler. Although Richard Gere named his kid Homer. But that's celebrities for you. When they aren't canoodling, they're naming their kids Homer."

Again Sandy found herself staring at the sheriff's wife. Where did she get these thoughts?

"Has John seen her yet?" Pauline asked.

"Seen who?"

"Suzy Slut," Pauline answered, the words blasting from her mouth as if shot from a cannon, short explosions of sound that were loud enough to pierce the eardrums of everyone in the vicinity. "She was sleeping with *my* husband, you know," she continued, her voice gaining strength with each syllable, "before she started sleeping with yours."

What?! thought Sandy.

"Speaking of husbands," Rita began, eyes moving warily from side to side, "I think we may have caught the attention of a few."

"It's been going on for years. On-again, off-again, on-again, off-again," Pauline continued as John advanced toward her. "Of course the idiot doesn't think I know anything about it. Isn't that right, sweetheart?"

"Okay, Pauline," John told her firmly. "That's enough mischief for one night. Time to go home."

"You want to go home? Now? When things are finally getting interesting?"

John glanced toward the front of the crowded restaurant, flinching visibly when his eyes connected with Kerri Franklin's. "It's okay, everybody," he said, eyes retreating. "Go on about your business. The lady's just had a few too many gin and tonics." He made a grab for his wife's elbow.

"The lady's just had a little too much bullshit," Pauline countered, pulling her arm out of his reach. "Too many years of too much bullshit."

"Pauline . . ."

"John," Pauline parried, stretching out the word as if it were an elastic band.

"You're embarrassing yourself."

"You mean I'm embarrassing *you,* is what you mean."

"Let's get out of here before you say something you'll regret."

"Au contraire," Pauline said, pulling her shoulders back and smoothing out the front of her ivory silk blouse with unsteady fingers. "The only things I ever regret saying are the things I *haven't* said." She struggled gamely to her feet, having to balance herself against the table to keep from falling over. "For instance." She stopped, looked around the room, as if searching for an example. "I very much regret not having said anything about you and that bloated, blond bimbo you've been boinking all these years."

Sandy almost smiled. Bloated, boinking, blond bimbo, she repeated silently. A perfect example of alliteration. She took a sip of her martini and found herself wondering which came first, Pauline's drinking or her husband's infidelity.

"Is there something you'd like to say to me, Pauline?" Kerri asked, suddenly appearing at the side of their table. Sandy took another quick sip of her drink.

"Boobs and baubles," Rita whispered under her breath.

Boobs, baubles, and bloated, boinking, blond bimbos, Sandy recited in her head, almost starting to enjoy herself. Then Ian entered her line of vision.

"What's going on here?" he asked the sheriff.

"Nothing to get all exercised about," John said, finally succeeding in pulling Pauline away from the table.

"You don't get a body like that from exercising," Pauline huffed in Kerri's direction, obviously having misunderstood the word. "You get it courtesy of MasterCard."

"Priceless," Rita whispered under her breath, and Sandy smiled in spite of herself.

"Something funny?" Ian asked.

Sandy's eyes dropped to her feet. What we could use right now is an earthquake, she was thinking, something that would split open the hardwood floor and swallow everybody up.

"I take it you know all about your girlfriend's affair with my husband," Pauline said to Ian.

"I never concern myself with things that happened before my time."

"What time *is* it?" Pauline asked.

"Crazy bitch," Kerri muttered.

"I may be a bitch," Pauline said. "But I'm definitely not crazy."

"Okay, Pauline," John said. "Now you *are* embarrassing me."

"Oh, poor baby."

"We're going home."

"Go to hell."

"First I'm taking you home."

Again Pauline managed to elude his grasp. "Would you just

look at him," she scoffed. "The town hero. I know what you're thinking. You're thinking, Poor guy, he puts killers like Cal Hamilton behind bars but he can't control his own wife. Did you know about his affair with Kerri Franklin?" she asked one of the men leaning against the closest pool table. "Or did you sleep with her too?"

"Pauline, why don't you let me drive you home?" Sandy interjected, jumping to her feet.

"Why are you being so nice about this?" Pauline demanded, suddenly turning on her. "At least *my* husband *tried* to be reasonably discreet."

"Sheriff," Ian pleaded.

"Why haven't you filed for divorce?" Pauline continued. "What are you waiting for?"

"The woman has a point," Rita said out of the side of her mouth.

"Okay, that's it." John Weber grabbed Pauline's arm and guided her roughly toward the front of the restaurant.

When they reached the door, Pauline dug in her heels, spun back around. "You are so much better off without him," she shouted at Sandy before John managed to usher her out the door.

For several seconds, nobody moved. Then Rita reached down, grabbed her purse from the floor. "Well, I don't know about you, but I think I've had just about enough excitement for one night."

Kerri nodded agreement. "I should probably go check on my mother," she said to no one in particular.

Ian reached into the pocket of his black pants, handed Kerri the keys to his Jaguar. "If you don't mind, I think I'll stay and finish my beer," he said, looking directly at Sandy. "Why don't you check on your mother and then pick me up in say"—he glanced at his watch—"half an hour."

Kerri hesitated.

"Half an hour," he repeated.

Kerri nodded, balancing on the tips of her toes, the narrow heels of her sling-back stilettos lifting right off the floor, to plant a proprietary kiss on the side of Ian's lips. "Nice seeing you again, Sandy," she said.

"Twice in one night," Sandy acknowledged. "How lucky can I get?"

"You coming?" Rita asked Sandy as Kerri sashayed her way past the bar, all eyes on her backside.

Ian's shoulder brushed against Sandy's. "Stay," he said.

Sandy's eyes shot to his. Dear God, what was going on? "What's going on?" she asked.

"You coming?" Rita said again.

"I might as well stay and finish my martini."

Rita glanced from Sandy to Ian and back again. "You sure?"

"She's sure," Ian answered for her.

"I'll call you tomorrow," Sandy said, bending over to kiss her friend's cheek.

"No mixed messages," Rita whispered in her ear.

And then she was gone, and Ian was signaling for the waitress. "Could you bring my beer from the booth at the front?" he was asking, as Sandy grabbed her martini from the table and followed him to a small table in a relatively quiet corner of the restaurant. "You want anything to eat?" he asked, settling into his chair and ignoring the curious glances of the couples sitting nearby. Tomorrow, Pauline's little outburst would be all over town, as would the fact Sandy was enjoying a drink with her estranged husband.

Was *enjoying* the right word? Sandy wondered, not sure what she was feeling. "No, thanks. I'm not hungry."

"Thought you always liked a little late-night snack."

Sandy felt an unwanted twinge at the reference to their shared past, and she struggled to keep it from registering on her face. "Not so much anymore. They say it isn't a very good idea to eat anything after ten o'clock." Did they? she wondered.

"Anything?" he asked provocatively.

Sandy tried not to read anything sexual in the inference—was he really flirting with her?—and kept her eyes on the table.

"Don't tell me you're worried about gaining weight."

Why were they talking about her weight? Why the suggestive banter? Was he hinting at a possible reconciliation? Was he testing the waters before breaking the news to Kerri?

"You look terrific," he told her, as he'd said earlier.

"Thank you." She leaned back in her chair and looked him right in the eye. He was staring at her as if he expected her to return the compliment. "So do you," she complied, then bit her tongue to keep from saying more. The truth was he looked better than terrific. The truth was he'd never looked better.

"I saw your car in the parking lot," he told her. "I knew you were here." The waitress brought over his beer. Ian lifted the tall glass into the air, clicked it against hers. "What are we toasting?" he asked, as if the toast had been her idea.

Sandy wasn't sure what to make of his latest confession. "To Megan," she said, deciding her husband would make himself clear when he was ready. He always did.

"She was pretty amazing tonight, wasn't she?"

"She certainly was."

"I had no idea she could sing and dance."

"She's full of surprises lately."

"Such as?"

Sandy shrugged. She had no idea how much Megan confided in her father these days, and she didn't want to betray her trust by speaking out of turn. If Megan wanted her father to know anything about Gregg Watt, she'd have to tell him herself. Still, it felt strange not to be able to talk to her husband openly about their children, even stranger to be talking to him at all.

"She's turning into a very beautiful young woman," Ian said.

"Yes, she is."

"Looking more like her mother every day."

Okay, so what's going on? Sandy wondered again. That was two compliments in as many minutes. Two more than he'd given her in the past two months, possibly even the last two years. She should ask, she decided, opening her mouth to speak. Instead she clicked her glass against his a second time and said, "To our son."

"To Tim," Ian echoed. "Looks as if the sheriff's daughter has a crush on him."

"She has good taste."

Again Ian clicked his glass against hers. "To new beginnings."

"New beginnings," she agreed. What kind of new beginnings?

Suddenly he leaned across the table and kissed her.

She drew back. "What are you doing?"

"I've been wanting to do that all night. Ever since I saw you in the auditorium." He leaned forward, kissed her again.

This time she felt her lips open, her mouth responding to the gentle ministrations of his tongue. Was she really kissing him back? She pulled away slowly, reluctantly. He looked at her and smiled.

"We should talk about our divorce," he said.

Sandy almost laughed. Instead she waited for him to finish the thought. *I don't want one,* she waited for him to say. *I've changed my mind. I want to come home.* But he said nothing, only sat there smiling at her from across the table. "What?" she finally managed to spit out.

"We should talk about our divorce," he repeated, as if she hadn't heard him the first time.

"What about it?"

"I know you still haven't consulted a lawyer, so I thought that if you were amenable, you could just use mine. He's already drawn up a settlement agreement that I think is more than fair. All you have to do is sign it."

Sandy sank back in her chair. "How very thoughtful of you."

"I thought it would make things easier on everyone," he said, completely missing the sarcasm in her voice. "Not to mention, less expensive."

"Is this a joke?" Was someone taping their exchange? Was she being "punked"?

"You look surprised," he said, managing to look surprised himself.

"You just kissed me."

"And it was lovely. I hope to do it again soon."

"Before or after our divorce?"

"Before *and* after."

"What?"

"There's no reason our divorce can't be amicable, or that we can't continue to be friends. Friends with benefits," he added slyly, reaching across the table to stroke the back of her hand. "Isn't that the current expression?"

Pauline would probably know the answer to that one, Sandy thought, lowering her hand to her lap, and deciding never to drink another green-apple martini as long as she lived. Clearly they distorted her brain waves. "Just so we're clear," she said, "you're saying you want a divorce, but you'd still like the option of having sex with me every now and then. Is that what you're saying?"

"Why not? Divorced couples do it all the time."

"Oh. I didn't realize that."

"We're obviously still very attracted to each other. And we were always so good together," he reminded her.

"And Kerri?" Sandy reminded *him*. "How good together are the two of you?"

Ian lowered his chin, stole a sideward glance toward the front of the restaurant. "Truthfully"—he smiled—"being with Kerri is a bit like being on a trampoline."

Sandy stared at her husband in slack-jawed amazement. "How do you do that?" she asked when she finally found her voice.

"How do I do what?"

"How do you manage to make a mind-bogglingly stupid statement like that without any obvious shame or embarrassment?"

This time it was Ian who looked surprised. "What—now you're getting indignant on Kerri's behalf? Is that what's happening here?"

Was it? Sandy wondered. Or was she finally realizing just what a piece of work her husband really was? "You are such an asshole," she marveled, the word escaping her lips before she even realized it was on her tongue.

"There's no need for name-calling."

"*Au contraire*," Sandy countered, borrowing Pauline's earlier expression. "I don't want to be accused of sending out any mixed messages." She picked up her martini glass. "To new beginnings," she toasted again. She took a sip, then tossed the remaining liquid in Ian's face.

Ian shot to his feet, knocking over his chair. For an instant he looked as if he might retaliate, throw his beer, grab her by the hair, knock her to the floor. But he merely flailed about uselessly for several seconds, the liquid dripping from the tip of his nose to the front of his black shirt. "You're crazy," he said, before storming from the restaurant.

Sandy shrugged. "I just wanted to make myself clear."

chapter thirty-two

Megan was dreaming.

The dream came at her in fits and starts, a series of blurred, fluctuating images that refused to form a cohesive whole. One minute she was running along the side of a road; the next minute she was sliding headfirst into a large crater. The crater was the result of a recent storm, whose high winds had uprooted all the old banyan trees in the vicinity. One such tree lay on its side, its spindly roots exposed and trailing from its underbelly, like a bunch of severed arteries. Megan tried to grab on to them as she slipped through the giant hole, but her descent was too quick and the roots too fragile to sustain her, and she was rapidly swallowed up by the soft, moist earth, disappearing without a trace. Above her, she heard footsteps and laughter. "Where's Kate?" someone was asking, and Megan recognized the voice immediately as belonging to her mother.

"She's at Mr. Lipsman's," came the answer.

An orange-and-white tabby cat suddenly jumped into Megan's lap. "No, I'm not," she tried to call out as dirt filled her mouth, clinging to her teeth like bits of leftover fillings. "I'm here. Right under your feet."

And then suddenly she was walking through the perfume counters at Bloomingdale's, and salesgirls, some of whom wore clinical white smocks over their smart black suits, were indiscriminately spraying various scents in her direction. She felt her neck grow moist with aromatic mist, her eyes start to water. And then someone shoved a particularly foul-smelling sample right underneath her nose, and she shrank from its poisonous fumes. "I don't think so," she told the smiling woman, whose name tag identified her as Fiona Hamilton. "I don't like that smell at all."

And then Greg was at her side, lapping up the perfume at her neck, as if it were milk and he one of Mr. Lipsman's cats. And Ginger and Tanya were dancing around her, and Liana was sitting in a corner, chewing on a piece of candy and watching them.

"What are you doing here?" Megan asked her. "I thought you were dead."

"I'm not dead," Liana answered. "I just had a face-lift."

"You look great," Megan told her as Delilah Franklin and her mother strolled by arm in arm.

"What are you doing here?" Delilah asked her accusingly. "You should be home in bed."

The dream ended, yanked from view with the suddenness of a movie projector breaking down.

Slowly Megan opened her eyes and pushed herself up on one elbow, watching the details of the room slowly shift into position. It took a few seconds for the realization to sink in that she wasn't in her bed, in her room, in her home, that she was, in fact, lying on a narrow cot in dimly lit and unfamiliar surroundings, with no other furniture, no paintings on the four blank walls, and no carpeting on the concrete floor. A thin, blue blanket clung to her shoulders, and a single light fixture, possibly a lantern, sat on a high ledge, far out of her reach. The room smelled dank, the way the unfinished basement of her grandparents' house in Rochester used to smell before they sold their house and moved to the eighteenth floor of a new condominium, overlooking Lake Ontario.

Where was she?

Megan looked down at herself. She was wearing a black sweater and blue jeans, the same sweater and jeans, as well as the same tan suede boots, she remembered she'd worn to the cast party. How long ago was that? Tonight? Last night? The night before? Was it daytime or evening? How long had she been here, wherever here was?

Where was she?

She felt a glimmer of panic, like a heartbeat, against the inside of her breast. Relax, a little voice cautioned. Obviously you're still dreaming. Everything you're seeing—the room, the cot, the blanket, the lantern, even the dank smell—it's all part of another series of confusing symbols that don't add up to anything, and that you probably won't even remember when you wake up.

Please let that be sooner rather than later, Megan prayed, closing her eyes on her unpleasant quarters, although the dank smell lingered. "I don't like this dream," she said out loud, trying to force herself awake, hoping her voice would be powerful enough to jolt her into consciousness, then lying back down when it proved insufficient. She pulled the worn blue blanket up over her shoulders and curled her legs against her chest.

She lay that way for what felt like an eternity, although it was probably only a few minutes. Her watch was missing, Megan realized, feeling the empty space on her left wrist where her watch used to be. The watch had been a present from her parents on her sixteenth birthday. It was thin and gold and had a delicate, heart-shaped face. "Just like yours," her mother had said.

Where was her mother?

"It's okay," Megan tried reassuring herself in her mother's soothing voice, the one she used whenever Megan wasn't feeling well. "It's okay, sweetheart. Everything will be okay. I promise you'll feel better in the morning." Would she? Or was it already morning?

Where was she? What time was it?

Megan didn't remember having removed her watch, but then, she reminded herself again, this was a dream, and so memories couldn't be counted on. There were no memories in dreams. No conjunctives either. She'd read that somewhere. Dreams carried you from one strange place to the next without so much as an *and, if,* or *but,* replaying the day's events in a variety of seemingly nonsensical ways, combining voices and faces that didn't normally belong together, mixing the banal with the bizarre, the everyday with the never-was, the living with the dead, without apology or explanation. Sometimes dreams were soothing and pleasant. More often, at least in Megan's case, they were the opposite. She'd always had a lot of nightmares, and their numbers had increased since her father had moved out. This was just another bad dream, she told herself.

Although it didn't feel like any dream she'd ever had before.

Megan reopened her eyes and sat back up, the thin blanket slipping from her shoulders and sliding down her arm.

The room was exactly the same as it had been minutes ago. The same blank walls, the same uncarpeted, concrete floor, the same fusty smell. For the first time, Megan noticed a beige plastic pail at the foot of the cot, and a jumbo roll of toilet paper beside it. Gross, she thought, and laughed out loud, hoping again that the sharp sound would be enough to finally dislodge her from this tiresome ordeal. But the sound bounced off the bare walls and rolled toward her feet, like an abandoned rubber ball.

In the corner stood two plastic bottles of water. Had they always been there, or was this something new?

Megan considered getting up and walking over there—she was thirsty—but to do so meant taking an active role in this nightmare, and she had no desire to prolong it. So she remained where she was, her back pressed against the hard wall, trying to ignore the increasingly certain feeling that was circulating through her veins, the sinking sensation that was growing in her gut, the cruel, unthinkable understanding that this was not a dream, that she wasn't going to wake up. Because she was already up, she realized with an intake of breath so sharp it felt as if someone had stabbed her through the heart.

She wasn't asleep. This wasn't a dream. She was wide-awake, and she had no idea where she was, except she'd never been here before, of that she was certain. "Hello?" she called out. "Hello? Is somebody there?"

And then she saw the door.

"For God's sake," she muttered, propelling her body off the cot toward it. How stupid could she be! What a jerk she was, to get herself all worked up over nothing. The door was right there. How had she missed seeing it before? She was standing right in front of it, and all she had to do was open it.

Except it didn't open, didn't even budge, no matter how hard she twisted and pulled and ultimately banged and punched and kicked at it with her new boots, until the delicate suede was scratched and scuffed. "What the hell is going on here?" she cried out, beads of sweat breaking out across her forehead. For the first time she realized how warm it was, how still was the air in the windowless room. "Open the door," she screamed. "Somebody. Open the damn door this minute."

Where was she?

"Where am I?" she asked out loud, pacing from one side of the room to the other. Think, she thought. "Think," she shouted, banging her fists repeatedly against her sides. "What's the last thing you remember?"

She remembered being onstage. She remembered singing and dancing. She remembered basking in the applause. She remembered Greg's hand proudly clutching hers as they took their final bows.

Greg, she thought.

Of course.

"Greg?" she cried. "Greg, are you there? Greg, let me out of here. This isn't funny."

No answer.

"Greg! Listen to me. The joke's gone on long enough. You're not Petruchio. I'm not your stupid Kate. And I really don't appreciate being locked up like this. Let me out. *Now.*"

This had to be Joey's idea, Megan decided, finally giving in to her thirst and opening one of the bottles of water. Joey's idea of a joke. A damn sick one. *The Taming of the Shrew* indeed. She lifted the bottle to her lips, her head falling back across the top of her spine as she drank, her eyes slowly panning the ceiling. She felt the water trickle down her throat, felt it turn to a block of ice in her stomach. Was someone watching her?

"Is somebody there?" she whispered, then again, louder this time. "Is somebody there?" Her eyes scanned the walls, searching for holes or hidden cameras. But the light was too dim to make anything out, and the walls were too high for her to check every nook and cranny. She could turn the cot on its side, she realized, use it as a ladder, make a grab for the lantern, but what good would that do? She'd just expend a lot of energy she might need later.

Need for what?

"Greg! Joey! Open the door. Damn you! This is so not funny."

Megan spun around. What was that sound? Had she heard laughter, or was that just her imagination getting the better of her? She stood absolutely still, waiting to hear it again, but the only sound she heard was the ragged rhythm of her own breathing. Okay, she told herself. You have to calm down. You're giving them exactly what they want. It's just a bunch of stupid kids playing a stupid joke, trying to teach me some sort of lesson. Tanya and Ginger were probably involved, getting back at her for her stealing the part of Kate right out from under their stuck-up noses. And for sure, Joey had something to do with it. But Greg—could he really be involved?

This is our night, he'd told her as the curtain came down.

Ssh, he'd told her later.

When was that? When had he told her to be quiet?

At the cast party, Megan remembered, the scene suddenly taking shape around her: Lonny Reynolds's living room, the music, the dancing, the drinking. The angry exchange with Joey. Going upstairs with Greg. The master bedroom with its king-size bed and satin pillows. The feel of Greg's lips on hers, the taste of his beer on the tip of her tongue, his hands on her bare breasts. Her inane chatter. His telling her to *ssh*. Her walking to the door. The click of the lock as the door opened and she'd left him sitting there alone.

Just as she was now.

Was this his way of getting even?

Yes, he'd been angry. There was no doubt about that. He'd obviously had big plans for tonight, *our* night, he'd said—was it still tonight?—and she'd put a damper on them. More than a damper. She'd blown them away. She'd talked about her aunt's termites, for God's sake. No wonder he'd told her to *ssh*. She'd tried to tell him she just wasn't ready. But his response had been to call her a cock-teaser and tell her to send in the next girl in line.

She'd fled the room, the house, the block.

And then what?

What happened next?

One street had quickly become another. She'd run, all the while listening for the sound of Greg's footsteps behind her, the touch of his hand on her shoulder, his plaintive voice telling her to stop, wait, slow down. *I'm sorry,* she could hear him say. *I didn't mean any of it.*

And then someone *was* behind her, whispering her name, and she was turning around, so relieved because he was there and she didn't have to run anymore, and then . . .

And then, what?

What?

And then—nothing.

A faint memory—or was it her imagination?—of someone pushing something into her face, of noxious fumes filling her nostrils, of the world fading to black. Had that really happened?

How had she gotten here?

Where was she?

Megan returned to the cot, sank back down. She took another sip of water, then lowered the bottle to the floor. If she drank too much water, she'd have to go to the bathroom—her bladder was already pinching, making its presence known—but no matter what, no matter how insistent her bladder became or how painfully her stomach cramped, she would never use that stupid bucket. She would never give them—whoever they were, Joey and Tanya and Ginger and Greg—please don't let it be Greg—that kind of satisfaction. So it was better not to drink, and better not to cry out, because the more she used her voice in this dank, depressing, hot, little room, the thirstier she'd get, and the thirstier she got, the more she'd drink, and the more she'd drink . . . No, enough. She was going to make herself crazy. And for what? For the amusement of a bunch of perverted cretins?

Thank God Liana's killer had been found. Thank God Cal Hamilton had been arrested and was in jail awaiting trial. Or she'd really be making herself nuts. She'd be having all sorts of wild and crazy thoughts. Thoughts of sadistic serial killers. Of being raped and tortured and brutalized. Of having half her face blown away with a single shot. Of her lifeless body lying for days in some snake-infested marsh, of insects and alligators feasting on her remains. Of her mother being called to identify what was left of her body.

A stream of involuntary tears washed down Megan's cheeks when she pictured her mother's anguished face, and she wiped them away. They will not see me cry, she determined. Damn you, Joey. Damn you, Tanya and Ginger. Damn you, Greg. Damn you most of all.

It's just that it's easy to get lost in the moment, she heard her mother say.

I won't get lost.

Promise?

Except that's exactly what had happened. She was lost. And one moment was pretty much the same as the next when you didn't know what time it was. And maybe if she hadn't said no, if she *had* gotten lost in the moment, then she wouldn't be here now. So in a roundabout way, this was all her mother's fault.

So damn you too, Mommy. Damn you.

Where are you?

What was her mother doing now? Megan wondered. Was she asleep? Did she even know her daughter was missing? Was she anxiously waiting for her to come home, trying to decide on the proper consequence for staying out past her curfew? *Was* it past her curfew? Was her mother out looking for her? Was she even now combing the streets, waking up the neighbors, rousting the sheriff from his bed? Would they find her before it was too late?

Too late for what?

Cal Hamilton was in jail. She had nothing to worry about.

Unless.

Was there any chance he'd gotten out?

The horrifying thought pushed Megan off the cot and into the middle of the room. Was it possible Cal Hamilton had escaped or that someone had posted his bail? He had a reputation as a ladies' man. Had one of those silly women actually believed his stupid story about being framed and come up with the money for his release?

Or maybe it was a copycat. Another sicko who'd heard about what Cal had done to his wife and Liana and that other poor girl, Candy whatever-her-name-was, and he'd seen Megan fleeing the party and seized the opportunity. Somehow he'd managed to spirit her away without anyone seeing him.

Had anyone seen him?

"No one saw him," Megan said out loud, "because he doesn't exist." She hoped the sternness in her voice would succeed in dispelling such ridiculous thoughts from her brain. The idea of another killer targeting the tiny town of Torrance in so short a time was too ludicrous and far-fetched to be taken seriously.

Reality was much more ordinary. And the reality was that Joey Balfour had come up with this stupid idea, and that he'd somehow managed to convince Greg to go along with him, and even now, the whole cast of *Kiss Me, Kate* were probably sitting somewhere watching her rant and rave and carry on, and were all having a good laugh at her expense. Hell, she was probably in the basement of Lonny Reynolds's house. Of course. That's where she was. Although she didn't remember his house having a basement. Most homes in Florida didn't.

Was she still in Florida?

"Okay, this is silly. You're being really silly now." Of course she was still in Florida. Where else would she be? Did she think she'd been driven out of state? That she was in some kind of holding cell, about to be sold into white slavery? She'd seen this show on television about girls being kidnapped and sold into prostitution, having to work for years before being released or, more likely, killed by their pimp. But those women were usually poor girls from destitute countries, not pampered American teenagers. As for the sex trade in America, wasn't that restricted mainly to children? Surely she was too old for the child porn industry. Although there were those disgusting websites she'd stumbled across before her parents had put a block on her computer, sites filled with photographs of young women just like herself, some of them bound and gagged, others being whipped, still others being probed with cattle prods. It seemed there were sites for every conceivable depravity, including films where they actually killed people. Had she just landed another starring role?

"Oh, God. Oh, God."

No, don't be silly. Calm down. You see what you're doing? You're getting yourself all worked up. This isn't about porn. This isn't about being sold into slavery. This is about a bunch of stupid kids being even more stupid than usual. This is about knocking you down a peg or two. It's about being jealous and small-minded and angry because you wouldn't come across. It's about seeing what you're made of, a rite of passage, a hazing you have to go through to get accepted into the club.

Not that she wanted anything to do with any of them anymore. As soon as she got out of here, as soon as she got home, she was going to tell her mother she was ready to move back to Rochester. In fact, if this was a dream—and she still had hopes that's what it was—then obviously this was exactly the message it was trying to impart: that it was time to leave Torrance, that they'd overstayed their welcome, that it was time to cut their losses and run.

"Please let me wake up," she whispered under her breath.

She returned to the cot. Once more she closed her eyes, although she didn't lie down. Think pleasant thoughts, she told herself. Think about that bikini you saw in that little shop in South Beach, the black one with the tiny blue bows, the one your mother said was too expensive, except that you heard her telling the salesgirl to put it aside, that she'd come back for it later. So she was probably saving it as a surprise for her birthday, which was on July the first, July the first being a big deal in Canada, sort of like the Fourth of July in America.

She liked Canada, Megan decided, going with the random flow of her thoughts. Not that she'd seen very much of it. Only Toronto, which she loved because it was so beautiful and there was so much to do there—the CN Tower and the Science Centre and the theater district—and all of it right across the lake from Rochester. Just last year, they'd taken the ferry there one Saturday morning, toured the dinosaur exhibit at the Royal Ontario Museum that afternoon, had a wonderful meal at a celebrity-frequented restaurant called Sotto Sotto, where they'd actually seen Kiefer Sutherland dining with Ethan Hawke—Kiefer was much cuter than Ethan, who was way too thin and looked like he could use a good bath—then taken in the latest touring production of *Les Misérables,* before returning by ferry to Rochester the following day. They'd had such a good time, she remembered. Of course that was before her father met Kerri Franklin in an Internet chat room, before he'd talked Sandy into moving the family down to Florida. If only she could hop on that ferry now, Megan thought. If only she could get the hell away from here.

Where was she?

Her stomach rumbled, and she wondered how long it had been since she'd last eaten. "I'm getting hungry, guys," she called out. "I think the joke's gone on long enough, don't you?"

But nobody answered.

Despite her best intentions and stubborn resolve, Megan lowered her head to the cot and cried.

chapter thirty-three

For God's sake, stop crying," John pleaded angrily, trying to keep what remained of his temper in check. After all, *he* was the aggrieved party, not his wife. *He* wasn't the one who'd drunk herself into a— he wished he could say stupor—state of hysteria. He wasn't the one who'd embarrassed them both publicly, airing their dirty little secret—all right, *his* dirty little secret, and was it really a secret if everybody already knew it?—in the middle of the most popular restaurant/bar in town. He wasn't the one who'd been sick in the car on the way home, then sick again as soon as she'd walked through the door. Hadn't he cleaned it up, for God's sake? Hadn't he bitten his tongue and refused to take the bait when she'd called him a bastard, an adulterer, a fat pig? Hadn't he refrained from putting his foot through the television when she'd stumbled into the bedroom and turned it on full blast? He was the very *model* of restraint, for God's sake, he thought, pacing back and forth in front of the bed. "What the hell are you crying about?" he shouted over the noise of the TV.

"I'm crying because of the way you treat me," she shouted back. She was sitting on the bed, her back against the headboard, one leg stretched across the bedspread, the other foot reaching for the floor, the front of her blouse open and disheveled, her normally lush auburn hair hanging limply, her mascara outlining the flow of her tears in black.

"The way *I* treat *you*?"

"Everybody knows about your affair with Kerri Franklin."

"Well, if they didn't, they certainly do now." John unbuttoned his navy sports jacket, the jacket he kept for special occasions. And tonight had started out very special indeed. The spontaneous burst of applause that had greeted him at the school auditorium, his daughter's terrific performance in the play, the impromptu celebration at Chester's that followed. Everything had been going along great, until Pauline had ordered one drink too many, and the little barbs she'd been tossing his way all evening became more pointed, the veiled references less hidden. Both Avery Peterson and Lenny Fromm had sensed disaster lurking and exited the premises as quickly and graciously as they could. Rita had tried to deflect the escalating animosity with a barrage of inane banter. Eventually Pauline had settled into a morose stillness. And then Sandy Crosbie had wandered in and given him the excuse he'd been looking for to leave the table. He'd even picked up a game of pool and was busy congratulating himself on his self-control, when whammo! *The pièce de résistance,* as Pauline would say: the entrance of Kerri and the good doctor, and the eruption that followed. Would he ever live it down? "Look. I don't know why we're talking about this now. It's old news. The affair with Kerri happened a long time ago."

"It shouldn't have happened at all," Pauline snapped.

John nodded. What else could he do?

"And don't insult my intelligence by telling me it won't happen again. As soon as the doctor dumps her, she'll come crying on your shoulder—"

"He's not going to dump her. She's not going to come crying."

"—and you'll go running."

"In case you haven't noticed, I don't run so fast these days." John was exhausted. All he wanted was to climb into bed and fall into unconsciousness.

"What? Is that a joke? Is that supposed to be funny? You're a pig, you know that?"

"I believe you may have mentioned it earlier."

"Yeah? Well, guess what? I'm mentioning it again." Pauline began pulling at the sheets beneath the bedspread, trying to gather them around her shoulders.

"What the hell are you doing?"

"I'm cold."

"You need to take a shower."

"You need to take a hike."

John threw his hands up in disgust. "Is this how you want your daughter to see you?"

Pauline waved away his concern with a flick of her wrist. "Amber's not home. She's at the cast party. In case you've forgotten."

John checked his watch. He hadn't forgotten. It was after midnight. "She'll be home in less than an hour."

"I think she likes that boy," Pauline observed, as if they hadn't been screaming at each other only seconds ago.

"What boy?"

"Sandy's son. What's his name? Tom? Tim? Timber?"

"You're imagining things. As usual."

"And you're oblivious. As usual." She laughed. "It's really quite ironic, when you think about it. I think *ironic* is the right word. Have to ask Sandy next time I see her."

"What are you nattering about?"

"Our daughter and Sandy's son. It's kind of poetic, don't you think? Almost like it's meant to be. I mean, here we have Sandy, wife of Ian, and Ian, lover of Kerri, and Kerri, former paramour of John, and John, cheating, no-good husband of Pauline. What did you say? Did you say I was nattering?"

"I said I think you need to clean up and pull yourself together before Amber gets home."

"She won't come in here. She never does."

"You're drunk."

"I am? No! Why didn't somebody tell me?"

"Get in the shower."

"Get lost."

"Look," John began. "You're going to take a shower whether you like it or not."

"Really? Who's going to make me? You?"

"If I have to."

"And how are you going to do that exactly?" Pauline goaded. "Are you going to pick me up and throw me over your shoulder à la *Kiss Me, Kate*?"

"I think I'd rather drag you by the hair." John lunged toward her.

He had no intention of resorting to violence, although the *à la* almost did it. But he'd seen enough of innocuous family squabbles gone bad, and he had no desire to join the ranks of men who physically abused their wives. Wasn't cheating on her abuse enough? "Come on, Pauline. Don't give me a hard time." He grabbed at her hand, and she slapped his arm, but ultimately he got a grip on her elbow and pulled her from the bed.

"I was watching that show," she yelled as he dragged her down the hall to the bathroom.

"You can finish watching it after your shower."

"I'll miss the best part."

"You won't miss anything." John stopped. Were they really arguing about some dumb late-night TV show she'd probably seen a hundred times already? "Just get in the damn shower." Holding tightly to her arm, he managed to open the shower door and turn on both taps full blast. "Get undressed."

"Get stuffed."

"Fine. Don't get undressed." He picked his wife up by the waist and deposited her in the middle of the stall, the torrent of tepid water soaking her hair and tumbling from her forehead into her open mouth. It quickly saturated her silk shirt and linen pants.

"My shoes!" she shrieked, tearing the beige leather pumps from her feet and hurling them at John's head.

He ducked the shoes, but was unable to avoid her fingers, which somehow managed to latch onto the silver buckle of his gray pants. She yanked, and he tumbled forward into the shower, his knees slamming into the butterscotch-colored tiles, as he wrestled with Pauline under the water's steady downpour. He grabbed for the wall, found Pauline's breast instead, and pulled his hand away, as if he'd been burned. The last thing he needed was for her to accuse him of assaulting her.

"What's the matter?" she chided. "Did I scare you? Did you forget what a real breast feels like? God knows it's been a long time since you've been interested in mine." She began pulling at her blouse and eventually succeeded in peeling the clinging, wet fabric from her arms, although it took slightly longer to undo the buttons

at her wrists. In the next seconds, she managed to remove the rest of her clothes—her bra, her slacks, her panties—until she was standing in front of him fully naked. "Look at me!" she cried. "This is what a real woman's body looks like."

John's eyes traveled reluctantly across his wife's naked torso. He saw the large, pendulous breasts, the slight rounding of her stomach, the dimpled thighs, the thatch of dark brown pubic hair, the still shapely legs. And he realized, with no small measure of alarm, that he was aroused. Jesus, what was wrong with him?

Pauline saw it too, and in the next minute she was pulling his pants down around his ankles and taking him in her mouth, the water from the shower cascading over them both. And then he was lifting her up, using his left hand for balance as his right hand guided his penis inside her, and soon they were crashing against the spigots and bouncing between the tile and the glass, and the water was pouring into his eyes and nose and mouth, so that he couldn't see, he couldn't hear, he could barely breathe. The rest of the night fell away—the accusations, the embarrassment, the fatigue. All he could feel was his body slamming into hers, and it felt good. God, he'd forgotten how good it felt. Hell, it felt great. Until his hand lost contact with the wall, and his feet got tangled in the puddle of his pants around his ankles, and he lost his balance, and they both crashed to the floor. Even then they kept at it, and he was reminded of the story of the two copulating dogs whose owners finally threw a bucket of water over them to pry them apart, and he laughed because not even a shower full of water was enough to stop him and Pauline.

"Come here often?" she asked after the water had finally been turned off, and the two of them sat gasping on the shower floor.

He took her in his arms and kissed her, and she looked surprised, but pleased.

John thought of saying, I'm sorry, but he wasn't sure what he'd be apologizing for. For being a lousy husband? For his multiple affairs with Kerri Franklin? For not loving his wife the way she needed to be loved? And would saying he was sorry change any of those things?

"I'm sorry," he heard Pauline say at that moment. "I haven't been a very good wife to you, have I?"

"I haven't given you much of a chance."

A slight pause, a shake of the head, a sigh.

"So what now?" Pauline asked.

"We get dry, get into bed, get some sleep."

"There are things we still need to talk about."

"Agreed. But not tonight."

"Maybe we could go on *Dr. Phil*," she said.

"Who the hell is Dr. Phil?"

In the distance a door slammed. "Mom? Dad? Are you up?"

John checked his watch, the only thing he still had on. Thank God it was waterproof, he thought as he pushed himself to his feet, stepped out of the shower stall, and wrapped a towel around his hips just before Amber came bursting through the bathroom door.

"Dad, are you—" Amber's eyes shot from her father to her mother and back again. "Whoops."

"Hi, sweetheart," Pauline said, as if she weren't sitting naked on the shower floor, surrounded by two sets of sopping-wet clothes. "Did you have a nice time tonight?"

Amber's mouth opened, but no words emerged.

"Is something wrong?" John asked. Could this night get any stranger?

Amber's eyes traveled between the ceiling and the floor, afraid to touch down. "We can't find Megan."

"Megan Crosbie?" Pauline stepped from the shower and wrapped herself in a white terry-cloth robe.

"Yes. Tim's sister."

"What do you mean, you can't find her?" John asked.

"She disappeared from the party a couple of hours ago. Nobody's seen her since."

"She probably went home. Have you checked with her mother?"

"Tim called her half an hour ago. He didn't want to worry her so he just asked if he and Megan could stay out a little later, and she said okay. So obviously, Megan's not at home."

"Is there any chance she's with a boy?" Pauline broached.

"That's what everybody thought at first," Amber agreed. "She and Greg have been pretty tight lately."

"Greg Watt?" John asked, and Amber nodded.

"My, my," said Pauline.

"But apparently they had a fight, and that's when she left."

"Anybody see her leave?"

"Delilah said Megan ran right past her, and she yelled after her, but Megan just ignored her. And then Greg took off a few minutes after that."

"Well, there you go. He probably caught up with her, and they're somewhere making up as we speak." Case closed, John thought, every muscle in his body aching to climb into bed. Which is where he was sure Greg and Megan were right now—if not in bed, then in the closest thing to a bed they could find, most likely the backseat of Greg's van.

Amber was shaking her head furiously back and forth. "No. We just came from Greg's house. He was there, and Megan definitely wasn't with him. He got real upset when we told him we didn't know where she was. He said he was gonna go out looking for her."

Just what I need, John thought. "Okay, okay. Just because she wasn't with Greg doesn't mean anything's happened to her." Alarm bells were beginning to ring in the back of John's head. He pretended he didn't hear them. "Did anybody else leave the party early?"

"Victor Drummond's the only one I can think of. It was so crowded, and people were going in and out all night. I only know about Victor because I saw him sneak out just before the fight started."

"What fight?" John asked.

"There was a fight?" Pauline echoed. "Are you all right? You're not hurt, are you?"

"I'm fine. Everybody's fine. Except Joey."

"Joey Balfour?"

"Yeah. Brian clocked him pretty good."

"Brian?" Pauline asked. "You don't mean Brian Hensen, do you?"

"You should have seen him. He was like a madman. It was amazing." Amber's eyes grew wide with admiration.

"Okay. You're losing me," John interrupted. "Let's start again. You're at the cast party . . ."

"At Lonny Reynolds's house," Amber elaborated.

"Aren't his parents out of town?" Pauline asked.

John gave his wife a look that said, Please, let me handle this, and she fell silent. "Okay, so you're at the party and a fight breaks out . . ."

"Not right away," Amber qualified. "At first everything was fine. Everybody was dancing, having a good time. Everything was great."

"Anybody there you didn't know?"

"Maybe a few kids. It was very crowded. People were all over the place—the living room, the kitchen, the bed—" Amber stopped. "You couldn't keep track. That's why nobody realized Megan was missing until later."

"Okay, so you're dancing and having a good time . . ."

"Yeah. And Joey's being his regular, obnoxious self, calling everyone 'faggots' and stuff like that, and suddenly Brian just took off on him. And then Perry Falco took a swing at him, and before you knew it, everybody was getting in on the act. Turns out Joey's not nearly as popular as he thought."

"Is he all right?" Pauline asked.

"Yeah. I think his pride's more hurt than anything else."

"Where is he now?"

"Don't know. He took off. The rest of us stayed to straighten up a bit 'cause Lonny was freaking out about the mess and his parents finding out, and that's when Tim realized his sister wasn't there."

"And Delilah was the only person to see her leave?"

"She was all upset, kept saying she should have gone after her. She's the one who drove Tim and me to Greg's house."

"Where is she now?"

"She was gonna drive Tim home, and then she said she was gonna check on her grandmother before seeing if she could find Megan."

John shook his head. God save me from these amateur detectives, he thought. Although he was grateful Delilah had been around to drive his daughter home.

"She's actually a pretty nice girl," Amber said, as if reading his mind.

John marched from the bathroom to his closet, began rifling through his drawers for a fresh pair of boxers.

Pauline was right behind him. "What are you doing?"

"I can't have a bunch of kids out there doing my job." He stepped into a pair of jeans, pulled a white sweatshirt over his head.

"Can I come with you?" Amber asked, following him to the front door.

"You certainly can't."

The phone rang. John waited while his wife answered it.

"It's Sandy Crosbie." Pauline approached, handed John the portable phone.

"Has Amber talked to you?" Sandy was crying, even before John got the phone to his ear. "Has she told you that Megan's missing?"

"We don't know that she's missing," John tried to reassure her. How many times had he had this conversation in the last few months? First with Candy Abbot's mother, then with the Martins, and finally with Cal Hamilton? He shuddered. Three different discussions. Two dead bodies. Cal Hamilton had been arrested and was safely locked up, awaiting his trial. So there was nothing to worry about. Megan had had a fight with her boyfriend and probably hooked up with another guy as a way of getting back at him. She'd turn up in the morning, sheepish and apologetic, like that Vinton girl over in Collier County. "Is there any chance she's with her father?"

"I just called him. He hung up on me before I could get a word out."

"All right. What's his number? I'll talk to him." John repeated the number she gave him as Pauline ran for a pencil and piece of paper.

"I'm going out to look for her," Sandy said.

"Please don't do that," John urged, knowing his plea was falling on deaf ears. "Look, at least let me talk to Dr. Crosbie first."

"You'll call me right back?"

"As soon as I speak to him." John pressed the button to disconnect. "Shit," he yelled. "Women! Why can't you just stay home and"—he looked at his daughter—"eat!" he bellowed.

Amber stared at him defiantly. "Aren't you going to call Dr. Crosbie?"

John took a deep breath to calm himself down as Pauline placed the call to Ian Crosbie's cell phone.

"What is it, Sheriff?" Ian said instead of hello. Clearly a subscriber to caller ID. "I'm kind of busy here."

John didn't have to ask where Ian was. He could hear Kerri in the background.

"Is that the ambulance?" she was saying.

"Is there a problem?" John asked.

"Kerri's mother had a heart attack," Ian said, before lowering his voice to a whisper. "She's dead."

John tried to absorb this latest piece of information. What else could possibly happen tonight? "Please give Kerri my condolences," he said as Pauline stiffened beside him. "Is Megan there, by any chance?"

"Megan? No. She's at the party. Look, you'll have to excuse me."

The phone went dead. John immediately called Sandy back. "She's not with him," he told her. "I'll pick you up in five minutes. We'll look for her together. And, Sandy," he added with quiet conviction, "we'll find her. I promise."

chapter thirty-four

Megan awoke to the sound of distant moaning.

The eerie sounds wafted toward her as part of a dream. *Can you save me in the morning?* Liana Martin was singing beside a glowing campfire, her girlfriends gathered around her, mouthing the words to the song along with her.

I've got another void to fill
I've got another urge to kill.

And then Joey Balfour arrived with a case of beer, and everyone was drinking and talking loudly, and the beautiful words to the song—

Give me a chance to be somebody else, 'cause it's so easy

—were being drowned out.

I've got another bone to pick
I've got another wound to lick.

And the delicate trill of Liana's voice was wavering, deepening, veering from soprano to alto—

Can you save me in the morning? Can you save me in the morning?

—until it became distorted, the words catching on one another, the chords skipping and disconsonant. The song became a lament, the lament a long and mournful cry.

Come on, sugar. Let's be brave.
Don't have to participate
In anything that makes you feel
You're anywhere except for here. . . .

Megan opened her eyes and sat up. This time there was no unpleasant jolt of surprise, just a sad acknowledgment of her now-familiar surroundings. She was nowhere *except for here*. Nothing had changed since the last time she'd dozed off. She was in the same awful, little room, with the same empty plastic bucket beside the same uncomfortable, narrow cot, under the same flickering, dim light. She had no idea how long she'd been asleep, whether it had been minutes or hours, whether it had been longer or shorter than the last time she'd drifted off, whether it was night or day.

Can you save me in the morning?

"Can you save me?" Megan repeated, listening to the music in her head.

Except it wasn't music, and it wasn't in her head.

What was it?

Megan pushed herself to her feet, her legs weak and unsteady. Someone was moaning, she realized, a rush of adrenaline propelling her forward. Someone just beyond the door. Her heart began pounding wildly in her chest, so fast that Megan could barely breathe, the blood rushing so loudly against her ears she could barely hear herself think.

And think was exactly what she had to do, she knew, because this was no time to go running off half-cocked, to act impulsively and recklessly, to put herself in more danger than she already was. Because the one thing that had become clear to her in the minutes or hours or days she'd been locked inside this awful little prison was that this was no silly prank, and that whoever had brought her here had more in mind than mere comeuppance. Someone meant to do her serious harm. Possibly the same person who'd murdered Liana and Candy and Fiona. And it didn't matter if that person was Cal Hamilton, a copycat, or someone else entirely. What mattered was that Megan keep her wits about her, if she didn't want to meet the same fate as the others.

The moaning grew louder. Someone was definitely out there.

Megan's hand reached for the door, her fingers trembling as they gripped the handle and pulled, painfully aware that each time she'd tried the door before, it had been locked.

This time was different.

The door opened.

"Oh, God," Megan muttered, holding her breath and closing her eyes, afraid of what she might see.

"Megan?" a frightened voice asked.

Megan opened her eyes.

The girl was on the floor, her legs curled up under her torso, one hand in her disheveled hair, the other by her open mouth. Her face reflected equal parts confusion and fear.

"Delilah!"

Delilah struggled to her feet, her eyes flitting about the small, empty space. "What's happening? Where are we?"

Megan rushed into Delilah's arms. "Oh, God. I'm so glad to see you. You have no idea."

"Where are we?" Delilah repeated.

Both girls took a second to scan the room, which, Megan noted, was essentially the same as the room in which she'd been kept, except this one lacked even that room's basic amenities. There was no cot, no bucket, no bottles of water. Megan approached the door behind Delilah, pulled frantically on its handle.

"Is it locked?"

Megan nodded.

"But why? Where the hell are we?" Delilah asked a third time.

"I don't know. I don't know where we are, or how long I've been here, or how I got here. I don't know anything." The tears Megan had been trying to suppress began washing across her face in waves.

Delilah wrapped her arms around Megan's trembling shoulders. "It's okay. It's okay. We'll figure it out."

"Do you remember anything?" Megan asked.

Delilah shook her head, as if trying to clear it. She looked as if she were about to speak, then she stopped, as if searching for the right image. "I'm not sure. Everything's kind of blurry around the edges."

"I know."

"We were at the party . . ."

"Yes. I remember that too."

"You ran out!" Delilah exclaimed. "I called after you, but you didn't stop."

"I was upset. I'd had a fight with Greg."

"There was a fight," Delilah said, pouncing on the word. "Joey got beat up pretty bad."

"Joey?"

"And then your brother started asking, 'Where's Megan?' "

"Oh, God. They must be so worried."

"We figured you must be with Greg. He'd left early too. So we went over to his place."

"He left early?"

"He said you weren't with him, so I drove Amber and Tim home. And then I was gonna go check on my grandmother, but when I got there, your father's car was in the driveway, and I didn't want to interrupt anything, so I decided to drive around for a while, and see if I could find you." She stopped, as if trying to locate the next piece of the puzzle. "I remember driving out to Citrus Grove, past where Mr. Lipsman lives, past the spot where we found Fiona Hamilton's body, and I must have taken another wrong turn because somehow I ended up around the old Kimble house. Do you know it?"

Megan shook her head.

"No. You wouldn't. It's way out in the middle of nowhere, at the end of this big, empty field. Anyway, I thought I saw a light flickering in one of the windows, which was pretty strange because nobody's lived there for years. So I got out of the car, and I was cutting across the field on foot, which I remember thinking was a pretty stupid thing to be doing. And I was just gonna turn back when I heard someone say my name." Delilah stopped. "At least I *think* someone said my name." She paused, her eyes narrowing in concentration. "That's it. I don't remember anything else."

Megan tried to make sense of what Delilah was saying. "So you think we might be in this Kimble place?"

"Maybe," Delilah agreed. "They say it has a basement. Why? What are you getting at?"

"I don't know," Megan said truthfully. "I don't know what I'm getting at." She felt her earlier panic returning. "All I know is I'm tired and I'm hungry and I'm scared."

"You think this is some sort of sick joke?" Delilah wondered out loud, as Megan had initially wondered. "You think Joey or Greg might be behind it?"

"I hope so," Megan said, although she didn't really want to believe Greg could be involved in anything so cruel.

"Who else do you know who would do something like this?" Delilah asked pointedly.

"Maybe it isn't anybody we know."

"What do you mean?"

"Maybe it's the same person who killed Liana."

"What? What are you talking about?" Delilah began circling the small room, like a caged tiger in a zoo. "Cal Hamilton killed Liana, just like he killed his wife and probably that other girl."

"What if he didn't kill them?"

"Of course he killed them. They found Liana's necklace in his house," Delilah reminded her. "They found that other girl's bracelet."

"Somebody could have planted them there."

Delilah's face went ashen with alarm. "But that doesn't make any sense."

"Why doesn't it?"

"Because it just doesn't."

"If Cal didn't kill them, that means whoever did is still out there," Megan persisted. "And maybe he's just been biding his time, waiting until everybody's guard was down to strike again. Maybe he's been out there waiting and watching, and when he saw me walking alone, he took advantage of the moment. And he somehow managed to knock me out and bring me here. And then you started snooping around, so he had no choice but to bring you here too."

Delilah looked unconvinced. "I'm not exactly someone you toss over your shoulder. Whoever it was would have to be pretty strong. And pretty determined."

"It has to be someone we know," Megan said. "Because he knew our names."

"It's got to be Joey," Delilah insisted, although she sounded far from sure. "And probably Greg too. The two of them together would be strong enough to carry me."

"I just can't believe Greg would do something like this."

"You'd rather believe we're in the clutches of some cold-blooded serial killer?"

"Oh, God. Oh, God."

"Okay, take it easy," Delilah said. "There's two of us now, remember. And if it *is* some crazy psychopath, it'll be two against one."

"But why give us that opportunity?" Megan asked quietly, as if the words themselves were afraid to register.

"What do you mean?"

"It doesn't make sense. Why unlock the door between our rooms? Why let us get together?"

Delilah's head shot from side to side, her eyes scanning the walls. "He's watching us, isn't he?" She ran to one wall, began running her fingers along its hard surface. "He's listening. He's getting some perverted thrill out of seeing us together. Why? What does he want? You think he wants to, you know, see us *together*?"

Megan shuddered at the thought, then remembered the horrific descriptions she'd read of Liana's shattered face and burst into tears.

Delilah quickly returned to Megan's side, wrapped her in a suffocating embrace. "Listen to me," she whispered into Megan's ear. "Just keep crying and don't react." A slight pause, then: "I have a gun."

Megan instinctively tried to pull back, but Delilah held firm.

"It's under my shirt, tucked into the back of my jeans. Whoever brought me here obviously didn't see it." She kissed the side of Megan's cheek. "There, there. It'll be all right," she said loudly, as a salve to whomever might be listening.

"But—"

"It's my grandmother's," Delilah said in a single breath that warmed the side of Megan's face. "Let's not talk about it now." She pushed Megan an arm's length away. "You okay?"

Megan nodded, too numb to say anything. Delilah had a gun. There was a chance they might get out of here alive after all.

"We might as well sit down. *Make ourselves comfortable,*" Delilah shouted sarcastically at the walls. She put her arm around Megan, and together they lowered themselves to the floor, facing the locked door.

Megan's stomach rumbled loudly. "I can't believe I'm hungry."

"I can't believe I'm not," Delilah countered.

Megan heard herself laugh. "I can't believe you made me laugh."

"I'm actually pretty funny when you get to know me."

Megan lowered her head in shame. "I'm sorry I haven't done that."

"Are you kidding? You're my best friend."

"Don't say that."

"It's true."

"I haven't been very nice to you."

"Sure you have. Well, nicer than most," Delilah amended.

"You make me feel awful."

"I don't mean to. Look, what is it they say? Water under the bridge? Let bygones be bygones? I think we should do that. Start fresh."

"Sounds good," Megan agreed, as her stomach rumbled again. She pounded her fist against it. "Stupid stomach won't shut up."

"What would you eat right now, if you had the choice?" Delilah asked. "Come on. What's your favorite food?"

Megan didn't have to think long. "Hot turkey sandwiches."

"You're kidding. Those open-faced things smothered in gravy?"

"Don't forget the french fries."

"How do you eat those things and stay so skinny? All I have to do is look at them and I gain ten pounds."

"I'm just one of those people who can eat everything. I'm sure one day it's all going to catch up with me, and I'll wake up as fat as . . ."

"Me?" Delilah asked, although it was less a question than a statement of fact.

"No, of course not. You're not—"

"Yes, I am. It's okay. I mean, it's not okay. I know I have to lose weight."

"Well, maybe five or ten pounds," Megan conceded. It wouldn't be nice to insult Delilah's intelligence by saying otherwise.

"Maybe twenty or thirty."

"Not everybody has to look like Jennifer Aniston."

"Sure they do."

"What food do *you* like?" Megan asked.

"Me?" Delilah sounded almost surprised Megan had asked. "I like just about anything, but I especially like prime rib, medium rare, a baked potato with lots of sour cream, and a Caesar salad on the side. Oh, and a hot fudge sundae for dessert."

"I'm a big fan of hot fudge sundaes."

"You are? Then I have an idea," Delilah said almost giddily. "We should go to Chester's as soon as we get out of here and share one."

"As soon as we get out of here," Megan agreed. "Keep talking," she urged, trying to keep her panic at bay. "Who's your favorite movie star?"

"Brad Pitt," Delilah said with a shrug. "Same as everybody."

"I kind of like Matt Damon."

"Yeah. He's cute too. He looks a bit like Greg."

"You think?"

"Don't you?"

Megan pictured Greg's strong jaw, his brown eyes, and closely cropped hair. "I guess."

"You really like him, don't you?"

"I did."

"Why were you guys fighting? I mean, if you don't mind my asking."

Megan pulled anxiously on her hair. "The usual."

"You mean, sex?"

Megan stole a look around the room, wondering if anyone was actually eavesdropping on their conversation, and if so, could it be Greg? "Yeah," she acknowledged.

"He tried to force you?"

"No. No. He just wanted . . . I wasn't . . ."

"You weren't ready," Delilah said, finishing the sentence for her.

"Yeah."

"Have you ever gone all the way? I know it's none of my business . . ."

"I'm still a virgin," Megan admitted. What the hell? she was thinking. Why hold anything back now?

"Me too. Not that anyone has ever even tried . . ."

"They will."

"Maybe once I lose the weight."

"Boys are so stupid," Megan said.

"Your brother's nice."

"Yeah. He's sweet."

"What do you think of him and Amber?"

"They're kind of cute together."

"Yeah, I think so too." There was a moment of silence. "Can I ask you something else?" Delilah asked.

"Might as well."

"I don't want to upset you."

Megan almost laughed. "You think I could be any more upset than I already am?"

"It's about my mom and your dad."

"What about them?"

"How do you feel about them being together?"

"Not great. Nothing personal," Megan added quickly.

"I understand. I really like your mom."

"Me too." Megan crossed her fingers in her lap. Please, God, she was thinking. Please let me see my mother again. I promise I'll be the best daughter a mother could have.

"She's like, you know, a *real* mom. Kerri tries but—"

"How come you call your mother by her first name?"

"She prefers it that way. I guess it makes her feel—" Delilah stopped suddenly, looked up at the ceiling. "What was that?"

"What was what?"

Delilah clambered to her feet, Megan instantly beside her. "I thought I heard something."

Both girls waited. At first there was nothing. And then, there it was again, the sound of footsteps. It was unmistakable. Someone was moving around above their heads.

"Oh, God," Megan wailed as Delilah reached behind her back to withdraw her gun. "Help!" Megan started screaming. "Somebody help us!" Seconds later, they heard footsteps descending a flight of stairs outside their room.

Delilah pointed the gun at the door.

The footsteps drew closer, stopped on the other side. Megan gasped as the handle began to twist. There was a pounding on the door, followed by the sound of a boot connecting with the wood. The door exploded off its hinges and fell into the small room.

The man who stood on the other side was tall and muscle-bound, with closely cropped blond hair and brown eyes full of confusion and disbelief.

"Greg!" Megan cried.

Beside her, shots rang out.

In the next second, Greg was on the floor.

"Greg!" Megan shouted again, running to his side and gathering him into her arms, cradling his head in her lap. Blood was gushing from his stomach. His skin was turning the color of the concrete, his eyes receding into the top of his head.

"I found you," he said before losing consciousness.

"Oh, God. Oh, God. What have you done?" Megan looked from her lap to the girl standing on the other side of the room. "He was coming to rescue us."

"I know that," Delilah said evenly, pointing the gun directly at Megan's head. "And we couldn't have that, now could we? Not when I've worked so hard for so long."

The words froze the air in Megan's lungs, so that she could barely breathe. "What? What are you saying?"

"He must have seen my car. I guess I didn't do a very good job of hiding it. I was so anxious to get back to you."

"I don't understand."

"Yes, you always were a little slow. What is it exactly you're having trouble understanding, Megan?"

"*You* did this?"

"I did. Little me," Delilah acknowledged with a smile. "Well, maybe not so little. That's the sort of comment you'd make behind my back, isn't it, Megan? By the way, did you know that *Little Me* is the name of an old Neil Simon musical? I know stuff like that. My grandmother has this huge collection of old LPs. That stands for 'long-playing' records, in case you didn't know. Which I suspect, you didn't. So I know a lot about music, which you might have found out had you expressed any interest in me whatsoever. Water under the bridge. Isn't that what we decided? Anyway, I think Mr. Lipsman should really consider doing it next year. You'd be perfect for the part of Belle. It's the lead, of course. Not that you'll be available to audition."

"But why?"

"Why what? Why did I kidnap you? Or why did I kidnap the others?"

"Oh, God." Megan felt dizzy and light-headed, as if she might faint.

"Well, I don't really see that I owe you any explanations, but what the hell? We're practically family, so I'll tell you. Candy was my test case. And Fiona was more of a red herring. But Liana, well, she was just a pleasure. Like you'll be. And Greg, well, he was, what do they call it? Collateral damage? Oh, and there's my grandmother, of course."

"Your grandmother?" Was Delilah completely insane?

"I have to tell you—she was the most fun of all. Partly because I've been planning her death for so long, and yet killing her happened kind of impromptu. If my mother hadn't insisted I drive her home, she might have had a few more days. It was a case of opportunity knocking, as they say. But you want to know the best part? The best part is that everybody's going to assume she died of congestive heart failure. The same way they thought my aunt Lorraine fell down a flight of stairs. They won't bother with an autopsy. They won't even check her pills, and even if they do, I've already put back the right ones. God, you should have seen her face when I wrapped that plastic bag around her head. She looked so surprised. Did my own heart good, I tell you. Oh, please. Don't look so shocked. She was a witch and you know it. Trust me, there aren't going to be a lot of tears wasted over her. Maybe a few more on you, though. I wonder if they'll hold another vigil."

"Please . . ."

"Please, what?"

"Don't do this."

"Sorry. I kind of have to. I mean, here I've been confiding in you and everything about all my nasty little secrets. You'd think we were really friends."

"We *are* friends."

"Ha! Yeah, sure. Until you get out of here and off you run to Ginger and Tanya. Who are next on my list, by the way. Although I may have to wait a little while. Don't want people to get too spooked."

"You know you'll never get away with this."

"Why does everybody always say that? Statistics show that people get away with murder all the time. And look at me. The proof is in the pudding, as they say."

"Please," Megan pleaded. "I don't want to die."

"No? I guess not. I mean, how often do people call you nasty nicknames and post filthy songs about you on the Internet? How often do they tease you about your weight and make fun of you in class? How many times have you been passed over for a good part in the school play because there's someone prettier and skinnier around, even if she can't sing worth a hill of beans? That's two expressions I've used regarding food," Delilah continued, as if one sentence naturally followed the other. "Interesting. Food metaphors—your mother would be so proud. I wonder where those expressions come from. Do you ever wonder about stuff like that?"

"Sometimes."

"Really? Do you mean that, or are you just humoring me, trying to get me to see you as a human being, so I'll have a hard time pulling the trigger? Which I won't, incidentally. I kind of enjoy pulling the trigger, although not nearly as much as I've enjoyed our little chat."

Megan shook her head. What was the point in saying anything more?

"Now, move away from Greg and go sit over there, like a good little girl." The gun in Delilah's hand motioned toward the wall.

And then they heard the sound of a door bursting open overhead, and voices, one on top of the other, racing down the stairs. "Greg? Are you here?" the sheriff was shouting. "Greg? Megan?"

"Megan?" her mother yelled.

"Mommy!" Megan screamed. "Sheriff! In here!"

And suddenly the sheriff was standing in the doorway, his massive bulk filling its entire frame. Megan thought she'd never seen a more beautiful-looking man in her entire life as he raised the gun in his right hand and pointed it directly at Delilah. "Drop the gun, Delilah," the sheriff instructed as he released the safety catch of his weapon. "Drop it now."

"Oh, my God," Megan heard her mother whimper behind him.

"Drop the gun," the sheriff said again, advancing cautiously into the room.

Megan watched Delilah's eyes travel back and forth between her and the sheriff, as if trying to decide what to do. She watched the confusion and indecision in those eyes quickly disappear, replaced with fresh resolve. She was still watching when, seconds later, Delilah turned the gun on herself and pulled the trigger.

35

KILLER'S JOURNAL

Okay, so obviously, I didn't die.

Turns out I wasn't a very good shot after all. Well, how could I be, with everything that was happening? Megan's mother was screaming and the sheriff was coming at me. Or maybe I just chickened out. Hard to say. In any event, the bullet only grazed the side of my temple, and while it resulted in a bucket-load of blood—head wounds are the worst when it comes to bleeding—I never actually lost consciousness. Much as I longed for it. If only to escape the outrageously melodramatic mother-daughter reunion that followed— "My sweet baby! My sweet angel!" Please. Megan was hardly an angel. Trust me. Although why would you? I haven't exactly proved to be the most trustworthy of persons, now have I?

It turns out it's not exactly fun to get shot, even if you survive. The fact is, it hurts like hell. It's been almost ten months since that night in the basement of the Kimble house, and I still get headaches and suffer from bouts of blurred vision. I've had two operations. They had to shave my head for the first one, and my hair's just now starting to grow back. It's coming in curlier than it was before, which is a drag. No matter what the fashion magazines keep telling us about curly hair being "in," the truth is that it's the girls with the long, straight hair—sometimes parted down the middle, sometimes combed to one side—who always wind up on the covers of those same mags. Straight hair is sophisticated. It gives off an aura of order and calm. Curly hair suggests a frazzled mind, as if its possessor is in a permanent state of electric shock. Plus it's just harder to manage, no matter how much "product" you apply.

Aside from the headaches and the bouts of blurred vision, I also suffer from occasional—some might say convenient—lapses in memory, which is why I think it's so neat they've given me back my journal. It helps me remember things, provides me with context, allows me to manage my thoughts, give vent to my frustrations. It's also part of my therapy. Dr. Mandy Biehn, age forty, tall, slender, shoulder-length, straight, black hair parted to the left, is my principal psychiatrist here at Maple Downs Mental Health Center—I generously spared the state the expense, and my victims and their families the pain, of a lengthy trial by pleading guilty to all charges and agreeing to serve out my sentence here—and she thinks the journals are a great idea. I told her it was Sandy Crosbie's idea originally, that I resisted the whole thing at first, but that she insisted everyone in her English classes keep one. Although she never once called on me to read my journal out loud in class. I wonder what would have happened if she had.

Kerri didn't want me to plead guilty, of course. She said a strong argument could be made in favor of a chemical imbalance, that something is obviously missing from my genetic code, courtesy of my father. She claims a difficult childhood and the hostile environment at Torrance High only exacerbated the situation and blames my fellow students for ultimately pushing me over the edge into madness. If you ask me, such speculation is pointless and self-defeating, rather like trying to solve that age-old riddle about the chicken and the egg. Does it really matter which came first?

No. What ultimately matters is who's left standing at the end.

Kerri wanted me to plead not guilty by reason of insanity. But I would never agree to that. How could I? I knew what I was doing, and I knew it was wrong, which is the legal definition of sanity, as my lawyer, Mitchell Young, Senior—HAPPY TO SERVE, WILLING TO SUE, HOPING TO SETTLE—pointed out. That didn't hold too much weight with Kerri, who was somehow more comfortable with the idea of her only child being crazy than she was with having given birth to a cold-blooded killer.

Oh, well. Can't please everyone.

Besides, that's not how I see myself. My blood is as warm as the next girl's.

The good news is I've lost weight.

Almost twenty pounds, despite that the food they give you in this place consists primarily of starches and carbs. Still, I don't have the appetite I used to have. Maybe that's the part of my brain the bullet ripped away. Or maybe it's all the drugs they give you here. Whatever the cause, I'm just not hungry the way I used to be, so as a consequence—they're big on consequences here—I eat less, not to mention less often. They don't serve snacks at the Maple Downs Mental Health Center, unless you count raisins and fresh fruit, which I most decidedly do not. I mean, if you're going to snack, they should be serving chips and licorice sticks. Sugar and salt. Stuff like that. At least that's what I think.

They also don't have an exercise room here, which is unfortunate. Especially for someone like me, who's used to physical activity. Remember all those walks my grandmother used to make me take? Not to mention lugging around all those bodies. That'll build the muscles. Those girls might not have weighed more than 120 pounds each, but that's still pretty heavy when you consider it was all dead weight . . . literally.

So I've actually started an exercise program of my own. It consists mostly of stretches, a few push-ups, maybe a dozen squats, some tummy crunches, all of which I perform religiously for half an hour every day. I do them in my room, although there's not a lot of space. The room is very small. About half the size of the basement rooms at the old Kimble house. Big enough for a twin-size bed and a white, plastic dresser. No sharp edges, of course. Nothing I could use to hurt myself with.

Not that I have any intention of hurting myself. Not when I'm actually starting to like what I see in the mirror. Except for the already noted curly hair, which I'm hoping will straighten out as it gets longer. I'm looking pretty damn good these days, if I do say so myself. Who knows—I may yet earn the sobriquet *People* magazine bestowed on me at the time of my incarceration—Heartstopper.

Actually the reporter stole that from my journal. Somebody in the sheriff's office leaked them some of the juicier excerpts, and they printed them. I didn't mind, although I found the story a bit one-sided. And I thought they devoted too much space to pictures of Liana Martin and Megan Crosbie. "Budding actress and singer," they actually called her. Can you believe it? I couldn't. Truth is, she sings like a frog, and her range is—what is it someone once said about Katharine Hepburn? *She ran the gamut of emotions from A to B?*

Something else that's true: I rather like it here. It's clean and comfortable. The view from my room is nice. It's quiet. Some of the less stable residents have an unfortunate tendency toward screaming and acting out. But in general, the residents, a term I prefer to *inmates,* are really quite nice, which is more than I can say for the general population of Torrance High. And the doctors are kind and encouraging. Nobody is on my back to do things. Everybody just wants to help me get well. They want to understand what drove me to do the things I did. They really want to hear what I have to say. And the best part is, they actually listen.

They take me very seriously here at Maple Downs Mental Health Center.

I like that.

So, as a result, I try to be obliging, and I go along with virtually all their requests. I told them where they could find Candy Abbot's body, and I talk to whomever they ask me to see. I explain as best I can what led me to commit such heinous acts. I tell them about my dysfunctional childhood: the cruel father who deserted me when I was a toddler, my mother's subsequent, ill-fated marriages to similarly abusive men, the plastic surgeries that transformed her into a virtual stranger, her string of affairs with married men, including John Weber and Ian Crosbie, the constant verbal and emotional abuse I suffered at the hands—mouths?—of my dear departed aunt and grandmother, two proverbial peas in a poison pod. (Sorry—I couldn't resist the alliteration. Mrs. Crosbie would be proud.) I tell them about the daily harassment I endured at school, the taunts and indignities from students and teachers alike. After all, everybody knew what was going on, and nobody did anything to stop it.

In some ways, Mrs. Crosbie was the worst, because she was such a hypocrite. Oh, she said and did all the right things—she even drove me all the way over to Mr. Lipsman's house that afternoon we discovered Fiona's body by the side of the road. (By the way, that was hardly an accident. I led her right to the spot I'd dumped poor, dead Fiona. I knew it was risky, that I was being almost recklessly bold. My original plan was just to dump the body in plain sight and wait until somebody—anybody—stumbled across it. But it was just too good an opportunity to pass up.) Anyway, Mrs. Crosbie tried to hide her true feelings, but you couldn't miss the look of revulsion on her face every time she had to call on me in class, and she physically cringed every time I came near her.

That wasn't entirely her fault. Or mine. I don't think Mrs. Crosbie was reacting that way because she found me physically repulsive per se, although she might have. We've all witnessed the casual, almost automatic way the more attractive shrink from those they consider less fortunate. No, I think her negative attitude toward me had more to do with my being Kerri Franklin's daughter, that my mother was responsible for the breakup of her marriage, and that every time she looked at me, she was reminded of that, as well as of her own failure as a wife. It was she who was responsible, however inadvertently, for the worst humiliation I suffered in recent years. "Dee," she called me one day in class, stripping me of even my name. And of course, *Dee* begat *Deli,* and worse, *Big D,* with that gleefully obscene song plastered all over the Internet.

But why target her daughter? I'm repeatedly asked. Hadn't she stuck up for me on more than one occasion and tried to be supportive, even at the cost of her own burgeoning popularity? I've wrestled with that one. Did I choose Megan because of her natural heart-stopper qualities—her fresh-faced good looks, her perky breasts and tiny waist, her easy grace, her effortless command of center stage? Or did I select her because she was the daughter (the granddaughter, the niece) my mother (and grandmother, and aunt) had always secretly coveted? They wouldn't be embarrassed to introduce her to their friends or to pass her picture around. She was perfect, after all. Everything I wasn't. And if Ian Crosbie had married my mother—and at the time, this seemed highly likely—not only would my mother have a new husband, I'd have a new stepsister. We'd be family. The comparisons would be endless, my flaws on constant display, my every shortcoming exaggerated and remarked upon. Kerri would grow increasingly distant as she basked in the glow of her more socially acceptable new daughter. Wasn't her whole life about replacing the old with the new? I'd lose whatever remained of the mother I'd loved—and disappointed—my entire life. And the thought of playing second fiddle to that talentless twit for the rest of my days was just too much to bear.

One thing I admit I underestimated was Kerri's reaction to her mother's death. I'd often fantasized about posting the news of Rose's demise on the Internet, in a combined birth/death notice: *Kerri and Delilah Franklin are thrilled to announce the death of their mother and grandmother.* But such was not to be. Even when Kerri thought her mother had died of a mere heart attack, she was surprisingly distraught. Maybe it had something to do with her now being officially an orphan, and the unstated acknowledgment that not even a thousand plastic surgeries could keep the so-called grim reaper at bay forever. Or maybe she'd actually loved that miserable old bat. Whatever it was, she took Rose's death hard. And when she found out my part in what had happened, and then the truth about my aunt's "accidental" drunken fall—because, of course, Megan couldn't wait to tell everyone—well, she was almost apoplectic.

Apoplectic—don't you just love that word? It sounds just like what it means. I think there's a literary term for that, but I don't know what it is. I guess I could write to Mrs. Crosbie and ask, but somehow, I don't think she'd be too glad to hear from me, and I doubt she'd respond. But who knows? She might surprise me. God knows she's done so in the past. Anyway, *apoplectic* means a sudden, marked loss of bodily functions due to a rupture of blood vessels. I looked it up.

I was almost apoplectic myself, by the way, when I heard Greg's footsteps moving around upstairs that night almost ten months ago. And then the arrival of Torrance's own Dynamic Duo, the sheriff and Mrs. Crosbie. Talk about surprises! It was just too much. I panicked. That's why I put the gun to my head and pulled the trigger. I didn't know what else to do.

Actually I'm glad Greg survived, even though it was touch and go at first. He was listed in critical condition for more than a week. He was in the hospital for a month after that, and then he convalesced at home until he was strong enough to stand up to his father and tell him he'd been accepted, with a full scholarship no less, into some big-shot art college in Chicago. Mrs. Crosbie helped him fill out his application and was apparently instrumental in his getting accepted. What did I tell you? That woman is just full of surprises.

Greg left for Chicago in January. Happy New Year indeed.

Not that I begrudge him his success. To be honest, I've always had a soft spot for Greg, maybe even a bit of a crush, and I was sorry he was the one who'd come bursting through the door that night. I'd hoped it would be Joey. But it wasn't, and unfortunately, I had no choice but to shoot him. (Not that I didn't *enjoy* shooting him— it made me wonder why I hadn't gone after more of my male tormentors.)

My mother filled me in on the details: apparently he'd run into the sheriff and Mrs. Crosbie earlier that evening, and the three of them had frantically been searching for Megan for the better part of an hour. I was right, incidentally. He *had* seen my car off the side of the road and decided to investigate. The Dynamic Duo then saw *his* car, and suddenly, what do you know? Why, lookee here, we have a full house.

You'd have thought an alligator could have sunk his teeth into at least one of them. I mean, it *is* called Alligator Alley, even on maps of Florida.

Poor Kerri. When she found out what I'd done, she was beside herself. Another good expression, I think, because it perfectly describes the way you sometimes feel when you're upset. I love the image of someone actually standing next to their own body. I think it's neat. Like looking in the mirror, except this time it's your reflection that's real, not you.

At first, my mother didn't want to see me or talk to me or have anything to do with me. But after a few weeks she had a change of heart. Maybe because Rose's death had made her a rich woman, or maybe because I was still her flesh and blood after all, no matter what I'd done, or maybe because Ian had dumped her within days of my arrest, and she didn't really have anybody else to turn to. Kerri's never been very good at being alone.

I feel bad about Ian dumping her. I hadn't intended for that to happen. Not that I'm surprised. Any man who leaves one woman for another one isn't to be trusted, and chances are he'd have left my mother sooner or later anyway. I'm not even sure Kerri was all that unhappy, despite claims of being brokenhearted. I think she's more upset that her sister Ruthie, who's been living in California for the past decade, has suddenly reemerged to assert her claim to half of Rose's estate. I think a little part of her even wishes I were home, so I could take care of things, the way I did with her other sister, Lorraine.

Anyway, Kerri visits twice a week, which is a bit hard on her, because Maple Downs is in Fort Lauderdale. She combines seeing me with shopping excursions—I can actually fit into that pretty blue sweater she bought me last year, hooray!—and visits to her cosmetic surgeon. When I saw her last week, she said she probably wouldn't be able to see me for a few weeks, which I assume means more plastic surgery. She's been complaining about her nose a lot lately, and she's still not satisfied with her lips. I've given up trying to change her mind. People do what they have to do.

I asked her if the good folks of Torrance were giving her a hard time, and she said no, most of them had been amazingly kind, probably because they considered her a victim as well. After all, I murdered half her family. And then her boyfriend left her, relocating to Palm Beach within weeks of Sandy's filing for divorce. Word is he's since gone into practice with a former classmate from medical school, and that he already has a new girlfriend. As for Sandy, she packed up Megan and Tim and returned to Rochester as soon as she knew Greg was out of the woods.

I sometimes wonder if Greg and Megan will keep in touch, if there will be the same happy ending for them that there was for Petruchio and Kate. Ironic how they almost ended up like Romeo and Juliet.

As for everybody else, my mother does her best to keep me abreast of all the latest news. Apparently Brian Hensen came home from college for Thanksgiving—along with his new boyfriend, a fellow psychology major at the University of Miami—and announced to all and sundry he was gay. So, it turns out Joey was right about him after all. But then, when you call everyone a faggot, you're bound to hit pay dirt occasionally.

Surprisingly for a conservative town like Torrance, everyone's been supportive of Brian, including his mother and *her* new boyfriend, a lawyer named Bob, whom she met through an Internet dating service last year. More irony—he wasn't even her date. He was Mrs. Crosbie's!

Kerri's been talking about possibly signing up with the same service as soon as she's feeling "more herself," as she puts it. I doubt she has any idea who "herself" is anymore, although sometimes I catch a glimpse of her in the frightened irises of her eyes. It's almost as if she's the prisoner, and not me. Her body has become a jail. Maybe one day she'll find a way out, though I doubt it. Society's expectations will never grant her parole.

As for Joey, after flunking out of school again, he got some girl in Fort Myers pregnant and they're getting married this summer. Don't think I'll be invited. Joey's already in Fort Myers, working for his girlfriend's father. Apparently the family owns a couple of resort hotels. I can already picture Joey hitting on the chambermaids and beating up the waiters.

Victor Drummond got into the Yale School of Drama, where presumably he fits right in. Next thing we know, he'll be starring in some Broadway play, or maybe in his very own Hollywood sitcom. He'll supply his own makeup. I'll be able to say, I knew him when.

As for the other kids, not much has changed. Ginger and Tanya are as popular and obnoxious as ever. They're both working over at the mall. Peter Arlington has a new girlfriend. Her name is Rebecca, and she looks a lot like Liana. As for Liana's little sister, Meredith, she won some major beauty competition in Atlanta. Following in her mother's footsteps.

Definitely *not* following in her mother's footsteps, Amber Weber missed about a month of school because she was being treated for anorexia in some clinic in Tampa. Apparently, she put on about ten pounds during her stay there, but lost it all within months of her return home.

As for the staff of Torrance High, everything's pretty much the same as it was a year ago. Avery Peterson continues to teach science and favor women a generation his junior; Gordon Lipsman continues to miss his mother and look after her cats. Kerri says she has no idea which musical he's planning to put on this year, especially with most of his star players gone. And our esteemed principal, Lenny Fromm, remains at the helm, guiding the good surfers of Torrance High through the treacherous waters of adolescence.

Then there's Cal Hamilton, who's still in Torrance, still running Chester's, still a "babe magnet," as they say. Probably still carrying out his "inspections." No shortage of women hoping to pass, willing to be the *Property of . . .* Lots of stupid people in this world. Including, it turned out, Cal Hamilton himself, the biggest patsy of all.

Setting him up was almost too easy. Not that it was part of my original plan, any more than killing Fiona was. But she was just so pathetic, and he was such a jerk, it was too tempting to pass up. It was simple to plant those trophies—although I hated to part with Liana's necklace. It was real gold, unlike Candy's cheap charm bracelet. And knocking on Mrs. Crosbie's door after I'd already taken Fiona to the Kimble house, asking if anyone had seen her? That was inspired, if I do say so myself.

As was the ingenious way I coaxed each girl into my confidence, pretending to be a victim, as frightened and confused as they were, the way I got them to share the most intimate details of their lives, things they'd never have told me in other circumstances. And then the moment when they realized it was all an act, that they'd been duped, that far from being a hapless victim, I was the instigator, indeed the perpetrator of this giant fraud, the one responsible for their terrible plight, that their fate was in my hands, and that those hands were around the handle of a gun, a gun that was pointing at their head. I can't begin to describe the pure joy I felt in those moments.

I also have Cal to thank for some of the most satisfying moments of the past year. I mean, who will ever forget that scene of his breaking into our house and tearing up the place? Of my mother ordering us upstairs? Of me locking my grandmother and myself in her room and pretending to stumble across her gun, a gun I'd discovered not long after she'd first moved in with us, while I was snooping through her things?

I bought the bullets myself at Wal-Mart.

Of course the best moment of all was when I stood there trembling, threatening to shoot Cal, and then collapsed in tears when I couldn't pull the trigger. Wow! What a performance. I should win an Oscar for that one.

How did you prepare for the role? I can hear the paparazzi ask.

Oh, I tell them, modestly dismissing their adoration with a toss of my long, straight hair. *I've been preparing for it all my life.*

Turns out I was a better actress than anyone ever suspected. I fooled everyone: my mother, my grandmother, my aunt, my teachers, my neighbors, my friends. Oops. I forgot. I didn't have any friends.

I even fooled the sheriff, although he proved to be far more capable at his job than I'd initially suspected. Yes, sir, I'm the first to admit I seriously underestimated that man. Not that I was the only one to do so. I think the whole town felt he was decidedly past his prime. Maybe even Sheriff Weber felt that way. At any rate, it was interesting to watch him grow in stature as his investigation proceeded, the natural way he assumed control, the dramatic way he came through in the end. My mother claims he's a shoo-in for reelection, unlike our tiny, perfect mayor, who she says the town now regards as a tiny, perfect ass. No, if there's room in this story for a hero, I think John Weber, with all his flaws, is it. And I like to think I can take at least part of the credit for that.

Which brings us back to me.

Things didn't turn out quite the way I'd planned. I certainly didn't anticipate getting caught. And I sure didn't envision being locked away for the rest of my life. Not that that's likely to happen. As it turns out, that's not the way things work in our criminal justice system.

When I was sent to the Maple Downs Mental Health Center, it was my assumption, as well as, I'm sure, the assumption of most of the good people of Torrance, that I'd be here for the rest of my days. I'd received a life sentence after all. But as luck would have it, a life sentence doesn't necessarily mean they put you away for life. My situation will be reviewed every couple of years. If I keep going to therapy, and taking my meds, and cooperating with the doctors, and behaving myself, well, I could be out a lot sooner than anyone realizes.

I'm only eighteen after all.

What's that old song? *I've got a lot of living to do?*

Stay tuned.